Praise for The Storyteller

'A literary debut of astounding maturity, refinement, and narrative power'
Abendzeitung

'Jarawan's narrative is captivating, fast-paced, and true to life—a fascinating exploration of the question of what it means to be influenced by several cultures at the same time'
Frankfurter Neue Presse

'His masterful debut successfully interweaves historical events and a suspense-filled investigation of one family's fate into a novel that deeply moves its readers'
New Books in German

'In a sweeping style reminiscent of oriental storytelling, Jarawan tells of escape, migration, and a family torn between two cultures. His debut succeeds in bringing a foreign culture into focus and awakens in the reader a fascination with the Land of the Cedars'
Kulturtipp

'The story of an escape, of a family, and of the Middle East: how the fate of one family is inevitably linked with Lebanon's history. An enthralling novel which couldn't be more timely'
Rhein-Zeitung

'Pierre Jarawan has brilliantly worked Lebanon's complicated history into his debut novel'
TAZ

'This book is a masterwork—a debut of great class'
Booklover & Dreamcatcher

'There are many good reasons to read this book immediately. Above all, it's a wonderful, terrifically narrated story that will enchant you timelessly!'
MIKE LITT, *WDR 1Live Klubbing*

'This new literary voice is particularly melodious and memorable. *The Storyteller* is an elegantly and unobtrusively narrated novel that shows us what is behind and beyond the narrow stuffy rooms that we call "our world," our Europe, our West. With this novel, the doors open to a thousand other beautiful, incomprehensible worlds'
ALEXANDER SOLLOCH, *NDR Culture New Books*

'A moving and wonderfully constructed story, full of beautiful images—Jarawan teaches us about history and the future, without ever becoming didactic'
Tzum

'An exciting family mystery, focusing on both historical and current political situations; a testimony to the way migrants are torn between their old homeland and their new'
Ruhr Nachrichten

'A beautiful book full of fascinating storytelling and poetic language that you devour without stopping for breath.
If you start reading this book, you'll want to keep reading it, rereading it'
Leeskost

PIERRE JARAWAN was born in 1985 to a Lebanese father and a German mother and moved to Germany with his family at the age of three. Inspired by his father's imaginative bedtime stories, he started writing at the age of thirteen. He has won international prizes as a slam poet, and in 2016 was named Literature Star of the Year by the daily newspaper *Abendzeitung*. Jarawan received a literary scholarship from the City of Munich (the Bayerischer Kunstförderpreis) for *The Storyteller*, which went on to become a bestseller and booksellers' favorite in Germany and the Netherlands.

SINÉAD CROWE is a native of Dublin, Ireland, and currently works as a freelance translator in Hamburg, Germany. Her short-story translations have appeared in *The Short Story Project*, and her translation of Ronen Steinke's *Fritz Bauer: Auschwitz vor Gericht* is forthcoming from Indiana University Press.

RACHEL MCNICHOLL is a freelance translator and editor based in Dublin, Ireland. Her translations have appeared in journals and anthologies including *The Stinging Fly*, *Manoa*, *No Man's Land*, *Best European Fiction* and *The Short Story Project*. Her translation of Nadja Spiegel's short-story collection *sometimes i lie and sometimes i don't* was published by Dalkey Archive Press in 2015. PEN America awarded Rachel a PEN/Heim Translation Fund Grant in 2016. In 2018, she had a funded residency at the Europäisches Übersetzer-Kollegium in Straelen, Germany, during which she worked on the final stages of *The Storyteller*.

The Storyteller

Pierre Jarawan

The Storyteller

Translated from the German
by Sinéad Crowe and Rachel McNicholl

WORLD EDITIONS
New York, London, Amsterdam

Published in the USA in 2019 by World Editions LLC, New York
Published in the UK in 2019 by World Editions Ltd., London

World Editions
New York/London/Amsterdam

Printed by Sheridan, USA

Library of Congress Cataloging in Publication Data is available

ISBN 978-1-64286-011-5

First published as *Am Ende bleiben die Zedern* in Germany in 2016 by Piper Verlag GmbH

Twitter: @WorldEdBooks
Facebook: WorldEditionsInternationalPublishing
www.worldeditions.org

Book Club Discussion Guides are available on our website.

For Kathleen

If you think you understand Lebanon, it's because someone has not explained it to you properly.
Lebanese saying

I

How was I to know I'd be haunted
by that photo forever?

Prologue

Bright lights, throbbing sounds. Beirut by night, a sparkling beauty, a twinkling tiara, a breathless trail of flickering lights. As a child, I loved to imagine myself here someday. Now there's a knife stuck in my ribs, and the pain shooting through my chest is so intense I can't even scream. *But we're brothers*, I want to shout, as they tear the rucksack off my back and kick me till I sink to my knees. The pavement is warm. The wind is coming in from the Corniche; I can hear the sea lapping at the shore and music drifting out of the restaurants along the street. I can smell the salt in the air, and the dust and the heat. I can taste blood, a metallic trickle on my lips. Fear wells up inside me, and rage. *I'm no stranger here*, I want to shout after them. Their echoing footsteps taunt me. *I have roots here*, I want to cry out, but all I manage is a gurgle.

I see my father's face. His silhouette framed in the bedroom door, that last shared moment before my sleepy young eyes closed. I wonder whether time and regret have haunted him.

I remember the verse the old man with the beard had muttered: *... then no one responding to a cry would be there for them, nor would they be saved.*

Then I remember the rucksack. But it's not the money or my passport I'm thinking of—they're gone. It's the photo in the inside pocket. And his diary. All gone. The pain is so bad I almost pass out.

I am responsible for a man's death, I think.

Then, as the blood seeps out of my chest: Pull yourself together. It must mean something. A sign.

The men's footsteps fade and I am alone; all I can hear now is my own heartbeat.

A strange sense of calm comes over me. If I survive this, I think, it will be for a reason. My journey won't be over yet. I'll make one last attempt to find him.

1

1992.
Father was standing on the roof—balancing, rather. I was standing below, shielding my eyes with one hand and squinting up at him, silhouetted like a tightrope walker against the summer sky. My sister sat on the grass, waving a dandelion head and watching the tiny seed parachutes twirl. Her legs were bent at the kind of unnatural angles only little children can achieve.

"Just another little bit," our father shouted down cheerfully as he was adjusting the satellite dish, his legs spread wide to retain his balance. "How about now?"

On the first floor, Hakim stuck his head out the window and shouted: "No, now there's Koreans on the TV."

"Koreans?"

"Yeah, and ping-pong."

"Ping-pong. How about the commentary? Is that Korean too?"

"No. Russian. Koreans playing ping-pong, and a Russian commentator."

"We don't want ping-pong, do we?"

"You might be too far to the right."

By now my head was also caught up in a game of ping-pong, looking back and forth to follow their conversation. Father pulled a spanner out of his pocket and loosened the nuts on the mounting. Then he produced a compass and skewed the satellite dish a bit more to the left.

"Don't forget—26 degrees east," shouted Hakim, before his grey head vanished back into the living room.

Before going up on the roof, Father had given me a detailed explanation. We had been standing on the small strip of grass in front of our building. The ladder was already up against the wall. Sunlight shimmered through the crown of the cherry tree and cast magical shadows on the pavement.

"Space is full of satellites," he said, "ten thousand of them and more, orbiting the earth. They tell us what the weather will be like, they survey earth as well as other stars and planets, and they relay TV to us. Most of them offer pretty awful TV, but some of them have good programmes. We want the satellite with the best TV, which is just about there." He looked at the compass in his hand and kept rotating it until the needle lined up with the 26-degree mark on the right-hand side. He pointed at the sky, and my eyes followed his finger.

"Is it always there?"

"Always," he said, and bent down, stroking my sister's head before picking up two cherries that lay in the grass. He put one of them in his mouth. He held the other out at our eye level, and, holding the stone of the eaten cherry in the fingertips of his other hand, revolved the stone around the whole cherry. "It travels around the earth at the same speed as the earth spins on its axis." He drew a slow semi-circle in the sky with the stone. "That's why it's always in the same position".

The idea of extra-terrestrial TV appealed to me. I was even more taken with the idea that somewhere up there a satellite was in orbit, always in the same position, always following the same course, constant and reliable. Especially now that we too had found our fixed position here.

"Is that it now?" Father shouted again from the roof.

I shifted my gaze to the living-room window, where Hakim's head appeared instantly.

"Not exactly."

"Ping-pong?"

"Ice hockey," shouted Hakim, "Italian commentator. You must be too far to the left."

"I must be mad," answered Father.

In the meantime several men had gathered on the street in front of our building, offering pistachios around. On the balconies opposite, women had stopped hanging out their washing and were watching the action with amusement, their hands on their hips.

"Arabsat?" shouted up one of the men.

"Yes."

"Great TV," shouted another.

"I know," replied Father, as he loosened the nuts again and adjusted the dish a bit to the right.

"Twenty-six degrees east," called up one of the men.

"Too far to the left and you'll get Italian TV," said another.

"Yeah, and the Russians are just a bit to the right of it, so you need to watch out."

"They're all playing sports, the whole world—I should play a bit more myself," said Hakim with a hint of desperation. Then his head disappeared back into the living room.

"My father-in-law fell off the roof once, trying to rescue a cat," said a man who had just joined the others. "The cat is fine."

"Want me to come up and hold the compass?" said a younger man.

"Go on, Khalil, give him a hand," said an older man, presumably his father. "Russian TV is a disaster—have you ever watched the news in Russian? It's all Yeltsin and tanks and an accent like crushed metal!" He popped another pistachio in his mouth, then shouted up, half-joking: "Should I get out the barbecue? Looks like you might be up there a while yet." The men around me laughed. My father didn't laugh. He paused for a moment and smiled the mischievous smile that always played around his lips when he felt a plan coming on:

"Yes, my friend, go and get the barbecue. When I'm finished here, we'll have a party." Then he looked down to me: "Samir, *habibi*, go and tell your mother to make some salad. The neighbours are coming to dinner."

This was typical of him, the spontaneous ability to recognise a situation that ought to be savoured. If there was any opportunity to turn an ordinary moment into a special one he didn't need to be asked twice. My father was always cloaked in an air of assurance. His infectious cheer enveloped everyone near him, like a cloud of perfume. You could see it in his eyes (which were usually dark brown but occasionally tinged with green) when he was brewing mischief. It made him look like a picaresque rogue. He always had an easy smile on his face. If the laws of nature dictated that a plus and a minus make a minus, he simply deleted the minus so that only the plus remained. Such rules did not apply to him. Except for the last few weeks we spent together, I always knew him to be a cheerful soul, tipping along with the good news in life while the bad news never found its way into his ears, as if a special happiness filter blocked it from entering his thoughts.

There were other sides to him too, times when he was stock still like a living statue, set in stone, imperturbable. He was buried in thought then, his breathing slow and steady, his eyes deeper than a thousand wells. He was also affectionate. His warm hands were always stroking my head or my cheeks, and when he was explaining something, the tone of his voice was encouraging and infinitely patient. Like when he told me to go in to my mother because he'd just decided to have a party with people he'd barely met.

I went in and helped my mother chop vegetables and prepare salad. The apartment building we had just moved into seemed very old. There were fist-sized hollows in the treads of the stairs, which creaked at every step. It smelled of damp timber and mould. The wallpaper in the stairwell was bulging. Dark, cloud-shaped stains had spread over the once-white walls, and a naked bulb that didn't work dangled out of the light fitting.

To me, it all smelled new. The boxes we'd moved our stuff in were still piled in the corners of the apartment, and the smell of fresh paint drifted like a cheerful tune through the rooms. Everything was clean. Most of the wardrobes and cupboards had already been assembled; odd screws and tools still lay around—an electric drill, a hammer, screwdrivers, extension leads, a scattering of wall plugs. In the kitchen, the pots, pans, and cutlery had already been stowed. We had even polished them before putting them away, and the rings on the stove were gleaming too. We'd never had such a big and beautiful home before. It was like an enchanted castle, crumbling a little with age but steeped in the splendour of bygone days. All that was missing was some bright curtains, a few plants, and some photos of my parents, my sister, and me. I could already see them hanging beside the TV wall unit. There'd be a blown-up family photo by the living-room door too. You'd see it every time you went out into the hall, which is where I was standing now.

I stuck my head into the living room. Hakim was sitting in front of the TV, which was showing nothing but snow and static noise. He saw me, smiled, and raised a hand in greeting. Hakim was my father's best friend. I had known him my whole life and I loved his idiosyncrasies. His shirts were always crumpled, and his hair stuck out every which way, lending him the appearance of a scruffy genius you'd love to take a comb to. His inquisitive eyes darted around in their sockets, which gave him the slightly startled look of a meerkat, only more rotund. Hakim is one of the kindest people I've ever met, always willing to listen and never short of a joke or some friendly advice. These aspects of his personality are foremost in my memory, despite the things he kept from me for so many years. He and his daughter, Yasmin, had been daily visitors in our old apartment, and when we moved to this address they took the apartment below us. To all intents and purposes they were part of the family.

When Mother and I went out with the salad and flatbreads, the smell of grilled meat was in the air. Some moustachioed men were sitting around a shisha pipe on the small patch of grass. The smell of the tobacco—apple or fig, I don't really remember—was pleasant, though it made me slightly dizzy. Two men were playing backgammon. Someone had found three sets of folding tables and chairs and set them up in our courtyard, and some of the women were setting them with paper plates and plastic cutlery. Kids were playing in front of the shed amid repeated warnings not to go out on the road. There were at least two dozen friendly strangers milling around in front of our building. Gradually, more people from our street came along. Some of the men had children in their arms. Women in ankle-length dresses arrived bearing huge pots of food.

There's one thing you should know about my father, a rule I saw proved many times—no one ever refused an invitation from him. Everyone accepted, even if they'd never met him.

It was a warm summer afternoon in 1992 when we moved in. I remember it well. We'd left behind the tiny social-housing apartment on the outskirts, where we'd never really felt at home. We had arrived at last, bang in the middle of the town. Now we had a lovely spacious home, and Father was up on the roof tightening the nuts on a dish that was pointing at a satellite orbiting the earth at a fixed position in relation to us. All was well.

"Are you ever coming down from that roof?" Mother called up to him.

"Not till we get it working," he called back, taking the spanner Khalil handed him. The men around me nodded politely at Mother.

"Ahlan wa sahlan," they said. *Welcome.*

A man tapped me on the shoulder.

"What's your name, young man?"

"Samir."

"Let me carry that for you, Samir," he said, smiling and taking the salad bowl from me.

All of a sudden we heard Arabic music coming from our living-room window. A few seconds later, Hakim's face appeared, bright red.

"It's working!"

"Are you sure it's not tennis?" Father shouted from the roof.

"It's music!" shouted Hakim. "Rotana TV!"

"Music!" shouted another man, jumping up. And before I knew it, this stranger grabbed me by the hands and had me dancing in circles, hopping from one leg to the other and twirling like a merry-go-round.

"Louder, Hakim!" Father called down. Hakim disappeared from the window. Moments later, Arabic music was reverberating from our living-room window out onto the street. Drums, tambourines, zithers, fiddles, and flutes blended into a thousand and one notes, followed by a woman's voice. People began to dance, clapping to the rhythm. The children twirled in unsteady circles. The men picked them up and spun them around while the women cheered and trilled with excitement. Then everyone lined up, arms across each other's shoulders, to dance and stomp the *dabke*. It was crazy. It was magical! At this moment, there was nothing that would have indicated we were living in Germany. This could have been a side street in Zahle, the city where Father was born at the foot of the Lebanon Mountains. Zahle, city of wine and poetry, city of writers and poets. Around us, nothing but Lebanese people, talking and eating and partying in Lebanese fashion.

Then Father came out of the house. He was limping a little, as he always did if he'd been exerting himself. But he was smiling and dancing in quick little steps, whistling to the music, with Hakim and young Khalil in tow. The other dancers created a path for him, slapped him on the back, hugged him, and welcomed him too with an "Ahlan wa sahlan".

I looked over at my sister, who was clinging in wonder to our mother's leg, her big round eyes taking in all these people who greeted us like old friends, like a family they knew well, a family that had been living here for ages.

I lay in bed some time later, satiated, sleepy, and exhausted. The music and the babble of voices still rang in my ears. Snapshots of the day kept flashing through my mind—the dishes of vine leaves, olives, hummus, and fattoush; the barbecued meat, olives, pies, and flatbread; star anise, sesame, saffron. I saw all the different families. The women wiping the mouths of children wriggling on their laps. The men stroking their moustaches while they smoked shisha, laughing and chatting as if this street was a world of its own, a world that belonged only to them. Hakim telling them his jokes. Yasmin, two years older than me, sitting to one side with pencil and paper, her unruly black locks falling into her face as she drew. Every now and again she would brush them across her forehead with the back of her hand, or blow the strands of hair out of her eyes, giving me a wave whenever I looked over at her. And Mother, smiling that private smile of hers. The happy feeling of having arrived. This was our place, our home. Here people helped each other. Here no one needed a compass. All the satellite dishes on our street pointed 26 degrees east.

And in the thick of it all, Father, who loved a party and limped in circles around all his new friends, like a satellite in orbit.

2

A few days later, the two of us were relaxing by the lake. The mountain range on the other side etched a restless cardiogram on the sky, spiking into the clouds. We were at rest, though. Father-and-son time. A day to ourselves. At the water's edge, the densely cloaked fir trees seemed so firmly rooted that nothing could topple them. The two of us on the grass, each holding a sharp stone, with a couple of dozen walnuts on the grass in front of us.

"Careful—try not to damage the shell too much," Father had said. "Ideally, we want both halves to stay intact."

I didn't know what he was planning to do, but it didn't matter. I was just happy to be here, with him. The days had flown; now the packing boxes were all folded up in the basement, everything had been put away in the cupboards, and the smell of fresh paint had faded. Now the living room smelled of fresh laundry. And if there was no laundry on the line, the living room smelled of my parents, since they spent a lot of time in it. The kitchen smelled of washing-up, or of spices, or of the flour Mother sprinkled on the rolled-out dough when she was making flatbread. The bathroom smelled of soap, lemon-scented cleaner, or shampoo, often with the smell of damp towels mixed in. It all smelled of home. The halls smelled of shoes, but that didn't matter; it showed that someone lived here, someone who was always going in and out, who came back here, took off their shoes, and walked around the apartment, absorbing the smells of this family. And all around us: more families. Whenever I left the house, someone would nod or give a friendly wave; moustachioed men in berets would be sitting at folding tables near the edge of the pavement, playing backgammon or cards, eating pistachios and blowing rings of shisha smoke around our neighbourhood. I felt at home.

We cracked the walnuts open with our sharp stones, doing our best not to damage the shells. It was a warm afternoon in late summer. Scattered clouds created strange, fanciful shapes in the sky; a gentle breeze whispered secrets across the water. Two dragon flies circled above us. Father noticed that I kept looking over at the fir trees on the water's edge.

"Shame they're not cedars."

Cedars. Even the sound of the word set me dreaming.

"But you like them all the same?"

"Mhmm."

"Then you would love cedars. They're the most beautiful trees of all."

"I know," I whispered. Not that I'd ever seen any—a fact that bothered me. I desperately wanted to be able to join in the conversation when the men sat around together, wallowing in memories.

"Do you know why the cedar is on our flag?"

"Because it's the most beautiful tree of all?"

Father laughed.

"Because it is the *strongest* tree of all. The cedar is the queen of all plants."

"Why?"

"That's what the Phoenicians called it." As always when he spoke of Lebanon, his voice was charged with secret longing and imbued with the undertones of someone speaking about a lover they missed very deeply. "They built ships out of cedar. It made them very powerful traders. The Egyptians used our cedar to embalm their dead, and King Solomon built his temple in Jerusalem out of it. Imagine—our cedars on Mount Zion, and in the pyramids of the Valley of the Kings ..."

I conjured up images of everything Father described, as vividly and colourfully as any seven-year-old does when their father tells a story with passion and conviction.

Father often spoke of Lebanon's magnificent cedar groves. In his childhood and youth he must have spent a lot of time in the Chouf Mountains. He would sit in the shade of the giant, centuries-old trees and inhale the reassuring, resiny smell of a secure future. In the shelter of the conifers, beneath a dense needle canopy, he would sit with his back against a cedar trunk, his gaze wandering across sparsely populated mountain valleys towards the coast, where the Mediterranean lay silver and glittering and Beirut shimmered in the curve of its bay. As I grew older, I often imagined him like this. And again and again, I mistook this image of him for the image of a happy childhood.

From his shirt pocket, Father produced a few toothpicks. From a cloth bag, some red crepe paper. He tore off some and handed it to me.

"For the flags," he said, and began to tear the paper into small, narrow strips.

We patiently attached the paper strips to the toothpicks, which we then stuck into the nutshells that were still intact. At some point we stopped and looked at the grass, where lots of little nutshell ships lay between our feet. A whole fleet, complete with red flags, ready to set sail.

"Come on." He stood up, and we went down to the water, which was lapping at the shore. The sun and the mountain chain were mirrored in the malachite-green lake. For a while we just stood there, holding the little ships in our hands, breathing together. "A cedar can grow to be several thousand years old," he said. "If a cedar could speak, it would tell us stories we would never forget."

"What kind of stories?"

"Lots of funny ones, I expect. But lots of sad ones too. Stories about its own life. Stories about people who passed by or who sat in its shade."

"Like you?"

"Like me. Give it a go. Try it with the fir trees."

As we stood by the water, I thought about the wind swishing through the needles. The sound it made was the fir trees whispering, telling each other about their lives. I hoped that one day they'd remember how we stood here by the water and I tried to imagine what they were saying about us.

As a boy, I felt an insatiable longing to see Lebanon. It was like the enormous curiosity inspired by a legendary beauty no one has ever seen. The passion and fervour in the way Father spoke about his native land spread to me like a fever. The Lebanon I grew up with was an idea. The idea of the most beautiful country in the world, its rocky coastline dotted with ancient and mysterious cities whose colourful harbours opened out to the sea. Behind them, countless winding mountain roads flanked by river valleys whose fertile banks provided the perfect soil for world-famous wine. And then the dense cedar forests at the higher, cooler altitudes, surrounded by the Lebanon Mountains, whose peaks are snow-capped even in summer and can be seen even from an inflatable mattress on the sea far below.

We stood on this lakeshore, breathing the same air and sharing the same longing. In my opinion, after love for one another, there is no stronger bond between two people than a shared longing.

"What would the cedar on our flags say?" I wanted to know.

Father smiled briefly. I could almost sense the words on his tongue as he struggled to find an answer. But he just pressed his lips together.

We launched our little ships. Only a small number lost their flags a few metres along the way; most flew them proudly in the breeze. Father and I stood and watched. He had put his arm around my shoulders.

"Like the Phoenicians," he said.

I liked that. Me, Samir, captain of a Phoenician walnut-shell ship.

"May they sail for a thousand years!"

"May they return with heroic tales!"

Father laughed.

I have often thought back to that day in the late summer of 1992. I know that he wanted to do something to make me happy, and it did indeed make me very happy. Hardly any of our ships sank. Some of them rocked dangerously, but none capsized. We stood there watching until the very last nutshell was no more than a tiny dot, and I remember how proud I was.

But I also remember how his arm felt heavier and heavier on my shoulders. His breathing became deeper and deeper, his gaze more and more trance-like, as if he were no longer looking at the ships but at some point in the distance. The reason I remember it so clearly is that it was one of the last days we spent together.

3

Meanwhile, history was being made in Lebanon. Beirut, once a dazzling beauty, rubbed its disfigured face and staggered out of the ruins. A city felt for its pulse. In the neighbourhoods, people thumped the dust out of their clothes and wearily raised their heads. The war was over. Militiamen became citizens again, laying down their guns and taking up shovels instead. Bullet holes were filled in, facades painted, burned-out cars removed from the pavements. Rubble was cleared away, the smoke dispersed. The huge sheets hanging in the streets were taken down, as there were no longer any snipers whose view needed to be blocked. Women and children swept debris off balconies and removed boards from windows, while fathers carried mattresses back up to bedrooms from the cellars that had served as bunkers. In short, the Lebanese did what they've always done: they carried on.

At night, though, when the moon illuminated the freshly made-up facades and the sea reflected the city's lights, the clicking of boots reverberated through the streets and alleys. But not just there. In the slums at the city's edges, in the surrounding villages, in coastal towns, and in the mountains—from Tripoli in the north to Tyre in the south—the sound of clicking could be heard. Lebanon was hosting a ball, and Beirut wanted to be the prettiest one there. But the makeup artists were Syrian soldiers.

And when daylight returned, revealing how shoddily makeup and darkness had concealed the wounds, the handiwork of the men in clicking heels was displayed on the sides of every building. In the early hours of the morning, people in the streets stopped to stare up at walls now covered in posters of the Syrian president, Hafez al-Assad, who looked back down at them from beneath his neatly parted hair. So there could no longer be any doubt about it. It was undeniable, plain for everyone to see: the Syrians were in charge. And they were going to make sure that people danced to their tune. Parliamentary elections were to be held. The first since the war had ended. The first in twenty years.

Lebanon's principle of confessional balance means that each religious community has an allotted number of representatives in parliament. It's a unique system. The country's many religious groups, who had spent the past fifteen years slaughtering each other, were now expected to fight with words rather than weapons. And the same religious groups who had battled each other in the city's trenches were now supposed to sit opposite each other in parliament as if nothing had happened. A general amnesty. Time to close the history book and look to the future. But to anyone walking through the streets of Beirut in the feverish weeks leading up to the election, it was clear that chaos still reigned, except that its soundtrack was no longer gunshots and explosions, but the wild shouting and roaring of election campaigners distributing flyers. Armed with paintbrushes and glue, these commandos covered the neighbourhood walls with posters. They stopped cars in heavy traffic and thrust leaflets into the drivers' hands. From "I'm your man—in good times and in bad" to "This is my son—vote for him," the leaflets communicated everything but concrete promises. People took the leaflets home. Many threw them in the bin, embittered by the absurd show going on around them. Others put on their finest clothes and solemnly made their way to the ballot boxes, hoping to take a step into the future. During the election campaign, not one candidate presented persuasive arguments or plans for rebuilding the country. What was the point? Damascus had tailored the constituencies to fit certain candidates. The Syrians, who had first entered Lebanon in 1976 as a peacekeeping force and then never left, orchestrated an election in a country where they still kept forty thousand soldiers, a country where over half the population had only ever known the sounds of bomb blasts and gunshots. Hardly anyone believed the Syrians would actually leave Lebanon by the end of the year as promised. The election resulted in a parliament too fond of the Syrians to let that happen.

Beirut put on its best dress and danced. Extravagant weddings were held in the hotels along the Corniche again. The makeup stayed in place. New concrete held the crumbling facades together, making them appear stable. The cameras of the Arab and Western media clicked their shutters and framed the action for their audiences. TV screens in Germany showed a country that was still limping a little but managing to get by without crutches. A country that was perhaps even ready to blossom again, to recover its former beauty. And after the election: lots of hand-shaking and jubilant winners.

But nobody removed the posters from the walls. Hafez al-Assad continued to smile down on Beirut.

"They're thick as pig shit. Can't even be subtle about screwing us over," Hakim grumbled, throwing a peanut at our TV, which for days had been showing the same images of Beirut presented by different newsreaders. He saw my mother glare at him and gesture towards me. Hakim muttered an apology, leaned forward, picked up the peanut, and glumly put it in his mouth. His unkempt hair was standing on end as usual. And he still resembled a meerkat, even when he was getting worked up about politics.

"Some ballot boxes took nine hours to travel a ten-minute distance, and nobody thinks it's strange? People who never even bothered voting have handed the country to the Syrians on a silver platter. All the Lebanese who packed up and fled the country should have been allowed to vote. We would've given those asses their marching orders!"

"Hakim," Mother warned.

"Sorry."

"It will work," Father murmured. He was sitting on the right-hand side of the couch, where he always sat. My sister had fallen asleep on his lap.

"What Lebanon needs right now is a project," Hakim said. "If these people aren't given something to do, they'll start to miss their guns. We need to become a financial centre again so that the sheikhs invest their money with us—in companies, international schools, universities, infrastructure, hotels—rather than keeping it in the Gulf States. Then we'll be a country the world wants to visit again, a meeting place, a land of conferences and trade fairs ..."

"It will work," Father repeated. "It's good that Hariri won."

"He has money, his companies will rebuild the country, and everything will sparkle—the streets, the buildings, the squares. But then the other idiots who also got into parliament will come along and piss all over the beautiful buildings."

"Hakim," Mother snapped.

"Sorry," he said again and turned to me. "Samir, do you want to hear a joke?"

I did.

"A Syrian goes into an electronics shop and asks the salesman, 'Excuse me, have you got colour televisions?' And the salesman replies, 'Yes, we've a wide range of colour TVs.' And the Syrian says, 'Great! I'll take a green one.'"

I laughed. Hakim had lots of jokes about Syrians. He liked to tell them again and again, and he was usually the one who laughed hardest. I'd heard this joke at least three times before, though Hakim would always vary the colour in the punchline. I never asked myself why the jokes were always at the Syrians' expense. The Germans told East Frisian jokes, and the Lebanese told Syrian jokes. It seemed logical to me.

Father didn't join in the laughter. I wasn't even sure he'd heard the joke. He just kept staring at the TV, his eyebrows raised as if he were watching a storm approaching. He'd been behaving strangely over the past few days. I didn't know why and wondered if I'd done something wrong. His mood swings were extreme; it was like waking up on an April morning, looking out the window and seeing sunshine one minute, downpours and lightning the next. And he often seemed completely absent, failing to respond when I spoke to him. Something wasn't right. His behaviour unsettled me because I'd never seen this side of him before. Sure, he could be grumpy on occasion, and if I got up to mischief, he might get cross and tell me off, but such moods were fleeting shadows compared to his current state of mind. His behaviour now was uncharacteristic, both of the rogue who was always thinking of new ways to enjoy life and of the calm, measured father I'd seen in quiet moments. Mother, who had known him for much longer than me, was bewildered too, which unnerved me even more, as she had obviously never encountered this side of him either. He ignored her, barely replied to her questions, retreated into himself. It was as if the quiet, pensive part of him had mutated into something darker. The events in Lebanon that found their way onto our TV had put him under a spell, like black magic. All I could do was tell myself it was a passing phase, a reaction to the stress of moving, and so, like a dog that's not sure if it's done something wrong, I skulked around his legs every now and then, or quietly observed him from a corner. I just hoped his mood didn't have anything to do with our new home; I was afraid we'd have to move again if he didn't like our new flat. Being afraid of anything in relation to my father was new. Since my little sister had arrived, we were one big family living in a big flat. But now Father seemed sad.

I'd never seen him really sad before. Usually he was like a captain in whose wake everyone wanted to follow, someone who never had any difficulty striking up a conversation with strangers. He won people over with ease. The fact that he never once forgot a name certainly helped. If we were walking through town and he spotted someone on the other side of the street, even someone he'd met only briefly several weeks earlier, he would smile, raise his hand in greeting, and call the person's name. How many times did we stop to chat to a Mr al-Qasimi, a Mrs Fedorov, the el-Tayeb or Schmid family, a Bilaal, an Ivana, or an Inge? I never once got the impression these people weren't just as happy to stop and chat. Small talk was Father's trump card, because he remembered not just people's names, but also every other detail about them. He would casually ask, "How are the kids doing?" or "How is the treatment going? Is your back any better?" or "Did you sort out those squeaky brakes?" He would often offer to help: "If your shoulder is still bothering you, we'll get your groceries for you—just give us a list and Samir will bring you back whatever you need." Or: "How are you getting on with the house? Is your attic finished? If you need someone to help put in the insulation, give me a ring." Everyone who spoke to Father soon felt as if they'd known him for years, as if they were friends, even. I was often struck by the warmth with which he greeted people. He'd never shake a stranger's hand without resting his left hand on their shoulder for a moment. Or else he'd shake the person's hand with both of his. A cordial gesture, as if they were closing a deal, and indeed I often felt that was how he saw it too: Welcome! You're part of my world now.

Although he wasn't particularly tall, to me he seemed like a lighthouse, someone who oriented you, someone you could see from a distance. I'm certain many others saw him that way too. At the market, he would greet the traders, skilfully ask how they were doing, and get such an easy conversation going that they barely noticed when he got down to business. He loved haggling. He was a true Arab in that regard. He was always trying his luck, and not just when he took me to the market. Even in the supermarket, in the aisle where the porridge oats and ready meals were, he might take a bemused shop assistant aside, and, with a conspiratorial expression on his face, whisper, "The cheese ... can you do any better on the price?"

And he sang. He was a real Arab in that way too. He would sing on the street, unperturbed by the looks people gave him. "Germans don't burst into song on the street," he once said to me as we strolled back from the market hand-in-hand, laden with bags of fresh fruit and vegetables. It was a day made for singing, a day like a summer's tune: sunshine, awnings, children with chocolate ice cream smeared around their mouths, couples holding hands, a dreadlocked boy in cut-off jeans rattling over the kerb on his skateboard.

"Why not?" I asked.

"Because they care too much what other people think. They're worried people will think they're crazy if they start singing on the street."

"Maybe you're the one who's crazy?"

"Maybe I am." He winked at me, reached into a bag for an apple and took a bite out of it before handing it to me. "Or maybe deep down they'd like to sing in public too, but they don't dare because they think you need a permit."

He liked to joke about how you need a permit for everything in Germany. I overheard him laughing about it with Mother a few times, so I knew he wasn't being serious.

And then he sang: "B-hibbak ya lubnan, ya watani b-hibbak, bi-shmalak bi-jnubak bi-sahlak b-hibbak ..."

I love you, Lebanon, my country, I love you. Your north, your south, your plains, I love you.

I squeezed his hand tight. I knew the song. I knew the singer. I'd heard her voice many times before; steeped in sadness, longing, and poetry, it was a voice that gently eased over the melody and slipped into the foreground of almost every song. Fairuz, that was her name. I'd seen her on TV once, standing like a sphinx in front of the temple ruins of Baalbek as she sang this same song. In front of thousands of cheering people. A beautiful woman with striking, severe features, aloof, her hair as red as autumn leaves, a gold dress draped over her shoulders. In the spotlight, she looked slightly surreal, like a noblewoman's portrait come to life, striding across the stage to the microphone. Mother loved her songs too. Everyone loved Fairuz. She was the harp of the Orient, the nightingale of the Middle East, singing about her love of her homeland. Someone—I think it was Hakim—once called her "the mother of all Lebanese people."

This is how we walked home, with Father singing. I

joined in at some point. We weren't bothered by the funny looks we got. In fact, the more people crossed our path, the louder we sang, and we didn't care if we barely hit a note. Holding hands, our shopping bags rustling in the wind, we sang in Arabic, because we wouldn't have been able to express in German how we felt right then.

4

Father was quick to realise how important it was to learn German. After fleeing burning Beirut in spring of 1983, the first refuge my parents found in Germany was the secondary school's sports hall in our town. The school had been shut down the previous year when routine inspections during the summer holidays had revealed excessive levels of asbestos in the air. But there were no other options, so the sports hall ended up as a refugee reception centre. Father soon managed to get hold of books so that he could teach himself this foreign language. At night, while others around him slept wrapped in blankets on the floor, he clicked on a pocket torch and studied German. By day, he could sometimes be seen standing in a corner, eyes closed, repeating vocabulary to himself. He learned fast. Soon he was the one the aid workers sought out be their interpreter. Then he'd stand, a circle of others around him, and explain to the aid workers in broken German which medicine people needed or what it said on the certificates and documents they held out to him. My father was no intellectual. He'd never been to university. I don't even know whether he was smarter than average. But he was a master of the art of survival and he knew that it would be to his advantage if he could make himself indispensable.

The atmosphere in the sports hall was often strained. People who had arrived here with no possessions, nothing but hope for a new life, were now condemned to wait for their fate to unfold. The air was stuffy, the space cramped. A constant hum of voices hovered beneath the ceiling; there was never complete silence. At night, you'd hear children crying or mothers weeping, and the snoring, scratching, and coughing of the refugees. If one got a cold, many were sick a few days later. The aid workers did their best, but there were shortages of everything: medicine, toiletries, food, not to mention toys for the kids, or ways for the grown-ups to keep themselves busy.

Losing their homeland was a fate everyone shared; they were all refugees. But a residence permit was also at stake, and not everyone would be allowed to stay; they knew this too. Everyone had witnessed scenes in which screaming mothers clung to the poles holding up the basket-ball hoops as they resisted being carried out of the hall along with their children. Here, one person could be the reason why another didn't get to stay. That made fighting a serious problem. But settling fights was another thing Father was good at. He'd talk calmly and persuasively to the irate parties, stressing how important it was not to cause trouble, how it helped to make a good impression, because news of what went on in the hall would inevitably find its way to the outside world. Sometimes there were indeed people outside the hall, holding placards that said there wasn't enough room in this town for so many people.

There were others too, people who brought bags of clothes—even if they were in the minority. And many of the refugees began to see my father as an authority, someone they could go to with their worries. "We're people too," they'd complain, "not animals, and yet we're locked up in here." Or, "In Jounieh, I was a lawyer. I had a practice that got destroyed. Where am I meant to go if I they won't let me stay here? Go back? There is no going back. I have no house, no family ..." And Father agreed with them, though never absolutely. He always stressed how important it was to understand the people outside the hall, that they were probably afraid, the way lots of people fear the unknown. The more crowded the hall became, the trickier the situation became. People would suddenly overreact, but it wasn't only due to stress and uncertainty. Religious differences could also trigger insults and fist-fights. Many of the Lebanese refugees divided their camps up along religious lines. And so our sports hall mirrored the streets of divided Beirut: Muslims on the left, Maronite Christians on the right. Each blamed the other for their misfortune— for having lost everything, for being refugees, for having to live in a sports hall.

My father's friendship with Hakim was another thing that lent him authority. Hakim and Yasmin, who was barely two at the time, were Muslims. My parents were Christians. They had all fled Beirut together. Hakim and Yasmin were camped right beside my parents—in the Christian sector of the hall, so to speak. But Hakim encouraged his daughter to play with all of the kids, making no distinctions. My father and Hakim would say to the others, "We're not in Lebanon anymore. We all came here because we want peace, not war. It's not about Christians and Muslims here. It's about us. As Lebanese people."

But sometimes words were in vain. One night, Father was woken by a dull thumping, the sound of something hard rhythmically pounding something soft. Fumbling in the dark and aware of my mother breathing gently beside him, he sat up. All he could hear in the dark hall was that noise. He made his way towards its source, putting one foot carefully in front of the other to avoid stepping on sleeping bodies. In the dim shadows he could make out one figure bent over another. But he was too late. Father could see the battered face even as he leaned in to grab the shoulder of the man who was straddling his victim and punching him like a man possessed. The woman closest to them began to scream. Someone turned the lights on and people sat up suddenly, looking around in shock. More and more people started screaming. There was blood not just on the floor, but all over the hands and clothes of the man who had killed the other. Four men grabbed him and pinned him to the ground until the police arrived.

For a while, the dead man's place in the hall remained empty, and his death seemed to put an end to the fighting too. But more people were arriving in the sports hall every day, so it wasn't long before someone spread his blanket in the free space to lie down and sleep. After a few days, it was impossible to say where exactly the empty space had been.

Meanwhile, Father's German improved by the day. For him, the ability to master this language was inextricably linked with the fate that awaited him and his wife. Because he knew how important it was, he tried to teach Hakim what he learned too. In the evenings, he used to tell stories in the hall. In the beginning, he sat on the floor surrounded by children, their eyes wide, their mouths agape. He told them about a giant spaceship that brought everyone to the bountiful planet Amal. Different coloured lines on the floor of the spaceship led the way to the magnificent bathrooms or the splendid dining hall or the cockpit. In his head, Father had converted the sports hall into this spaceship. The dingy showers in the changing rooms became a hi-tech spa in which little robots scrubbed people's backs. The side-lines of the basketball court became energy-acceleration tracks, perfect for a kids' game in which all they had to do was take a running jump onto this line in order to whizz all around the spaceship at great speed. Its captain was a crazy camel who entertained the passengers with comical announcements. Father put on a funny voice for this purpose, making the children crack up. In Arabic, *amal* means hope. Soon everyone in the sports hall was familiar with the planet called Hope. Sometimes when even the grown-ups could no longer hide tears of despair and exhaustion from their children, the little ones could be seen stroking their cheeks, saying "It's not far to Amal now."

It wasn't long before parents began to join the circle around Father, and a few days later, some of the aid workers were also listening in. Soon this story time became a regular fixture, an evening ritual that brought people together. It was the only time when no one spoke but Father. His reassuring voice floated above the listeners' heads and filled them with a wealth of imagery.

These days, having learned so much more about him, I often wonder how he managed to keep his secret. And I always come to the same conclusion: his ability to escape reality must have helped him.

Hakim's asylum application was approved before my parents'.

As a single father, with passable German to boot, he and Yasmin could expect to get a permanent residence permit in the near future. My parents hugged and kissed them goodbye and waved them off when they left the sports hall. Their next stop was a little social housing flat on the edge of town. A few months later, Hakim also got a work permit and found a job in a joinery. He had played the lute all his life and had no trouble convincing the master joiner, who had a soft spot for refugees, that the calluses on his fingers were from years and years of working with tools. He enjoyed the work too. Being a lute-maker's son, he loved the smell of wood. Hakim had spent many childhood years in his father's workshop before heading to Beirut to become a successful musician.

My parents had to stay on in the hall for another while. When they eventually got the preliminary approval letter, many tears were shed. Mother cried tears of relief. Some of the grown-ups cried because they couldn't imagine the sports hall without my father. And the children cried because their storyteller was leaving. It was a Tuesday when the man arrived and started looking around the hall. An aid worker who had been leaning against a door pointed him in the right direction, and he made a bee line for my parents.

"Are you Brahim?"

"Yes," said Father.

"Brahim el-Hourani?"

"Yes, that's right."

"And you are Rana el-Hourani?" he asked my mother.

"Yes," she confirmed.

"A letter for you." And when he noticed how Mother shrank back a little, the man smiled and said, "Congratulations!"

And so Brahim the storyteller left the sports hall. Nearly everyone wanted to say goodbye. People came to wish my parents good luck, reassuring each other that they'd soon meet again, in town, as ordinary citizens, at the cinema, shops, or restaurants.

Brahim. That was my father's name. Brahim el-Hourani. Rana was my mother's first name. The el-Houranis—those were my parents. I didn't exist yet.

My parents got a flat in the same housing scheme as Hakim and Yasmin. Fate and a few case workers had been kind to them. They ended up living only a few hundred metres apart. And Father, whose German was pretty good by then, also got a work permit within a few months. Mother once told me how he went off to the Foreigners' Registration

Office with a bag of freshly baked baklava and put it on the baffled official's desk.

"My wife made that for you," he said.

"Oh," said the official, "I can't accept that."

"It's for the stamp," said Father.

"The stamp."

"On the work permit."

"Ah. The stamp," said the official, looking from Father to the plastic bag on his desk and back to Father again.

"We're very grateful to you."

"I'm afraid I can't accept it," the man repeated, clearly embarrassed.

"Please. I am a guest in your country. Regard it as a gift for the host."

"I can't."

"I won't tell anyone."

"The answer is still no."

"I saw what's on the menu in your canteen today," said Father. "Believe me, you do want this baklava."

"I'm sure it's perfectly delicious baklava," protested the man, "but I'm afraid I can't accept it."

"Maybe I should have a word with your boss?"

"No," cried the official. "No, Mr. ..."

"El-Hourani. You can call me Brahim."

"Mr. el-Hourani, please give my regards to your wife and tell her what a pleasant surprise this was. But my wife is baking a cake this evening, and if I eat your pastries beforehand, I'll be in trouble at home."

"In trouble? With your wife? You're not serious."

"I am serious."

"Well, we don't want that, do we," said my father.

"No, we don't."

"All right, then." Father took the bag off the desk. "Thank you very much for your help all the same. And if you ever do fancy some baklava, just give us a ring."

Then Mother recounted how Father came home and declared with a sigh, "In Beirut, if you need something stamped, you take baklava to the guy with the stamp beforehand. Here they won't even accept the baklava after they've given you the stamp."

The official didn't forget my father in a hurry. How could he? He saw him on three further occasions, when Father accompanied men he knew from the sports hall. Each time, he asked the official for a stamp. Each time, he got it.

The preliminary decision was soon followed by the final one. My parents were granted asylum and received permanent residence permits as well. Father got a job in a youth centre where many foreign kids spent the afternoons. He helped them with German after school, and they were happy to learn from him as he was such a good role model. He earned a lot of respect among the youngsters. One time he managed to invite a well-known graffiti artist to the centre. Between them they sprayed and decorated the grey exterior, transforming it into a colourful landscape full of Coca-Cola rivers, lollipop trees, and chocolate mountains with ice-cream peaks. A bit like the wonderful planet Amal.

Mother loved sewing. She would buy fabric at knockdown prices at the local flea market and make up dresses on a sewing machine that also came from the flea market. Father set up a corner for her in the living room, and she'd work in the pool of light cast by a desk lamp that wasn't quite tall enough, threading the needle and guiding the fabric with steady hands as the machine stitched and whirred. She sold the dresses through thrift shops, often earning ten times what the fabric had cost her. When she'd saved up enough money, she had business cards printed and designed a label to sew on to the dresses. "It doesn't matter which you choose: *Rana* or *el-Hourani*," Father said, "They both sound like designer labels." She went for *Rana*, and that became her brand name. One afternoon—I was six maybe—Mother got a phone call. It was Mrs. Demerici, whose surname, according to Mother, was actually Beck, except she'd married a Turk, the man who owned the thrift shop not far from the pedestrian shopping area. When Mother hung up, her face was glowing with pleasure. "A woman who bought one of my dresses wants to meet me," she exclaimed, grabbing my hands and dancing round the tiny living room. This was in our old flat, where I had been born in 1984. The woman's name was Agnes Jung, it transpired, and she really liked mother's sewing. Agnes Jung intended to change her name to Agnes Kramer in the near future, wanted Mother to make her four bridesmaids dresses, and was willing to pay so handsomely that Mother almost fainted before she managed to collapse into the living-room armchair. She spent the next few weeks sewing day and night. The bridesmaids eventually came for a fitting, and Mother kept making apologies for the neighbourhood and the size of our flat, and saying how much she hoped the ladies liked the dresses. They disappeared into my parents' bedroom for the fittings, and Mother put the key in the door from the inside so that the keyhole was no good to me.

When Yasmin and I were little, she spent a lot of time in our house. Hakim was in the workshop during the day. My mother sewed from home, and Yasmin was like a daughter to her. We got on well. What I liked about Yasmin was that she never made me feel like a little boy, even though she was two years older. Her eyes were dark brown and incredibly deep, and her long black curls always had a glossy shine. Her hair was usually falling into her face as if she'd just come through a storm. There was something untamed and boyish about her, but only when we were rambling around the flats on our own. She'd break branches off trees and drag them behind her, as if she was marking a boundary. She was better at climbing than me and never tore her clothes. There was an aura of effortlessness about her, yet you were sure to fail if you tried to compete. The results were obvious: I was always coming home with new holes in my trousers and pullovers, which would have to be patched and darned by Mother. Yasmin was quite the chameleon—in adult company, she was always perfectly behaved. She was polite, said thank-you for her dinner, and, unlike me, never put her elbows on the table during meals. She could also be patient and sit still for ages while Mother ran the brush through her hair over and over. I don't think any of the grown-ups would have believed me if I'd told them the other things Yasmin got up to.

That flat, in which I spent the first seven years of my life, was too small for three people, and describing it as dingy would be an understatement. Nearly all the walls were stained, and they were paper-thin too. Pots clattered constantly through the walls, TVs were too loud, heavy shoes clomped on bare floorboards. You didn't even need to strain your ears to hear what the neighbours were fighting about—if you could understand the language, that is. There were many different nationalities in this housing scheme: Russians, Italians, Poles, Romanians, Chinese, Turks, Lebanese, Syrians, and even a few Africans—Nigerians, I think. The satellite dishes on our balconies pointed in many different directions. Between the buildings, in the middle of a walled courtyard, there was a tiny playground. A bunch of older teenagers usually hung out there, smoking. It was full of broken glass, and if there was a lot of rain, the playground flooded and turned into a mucky lake. Yasmin and I never went there to play. In front of the buildings, the bicycles at the bike stands nearly always had their saddles or wheels stolen. And if you only locked your bike to the stand by the front wheel, you could be sure the frame would be gone the next day. Even buggies got stolen from halls and landings.

Sometimes Yasmin and I would try to sniff out where the different families hailed from—a "guess which country" game to keep ourselves amused. We'd walk along the dark passageways, their walls smeared in permanent marker, the neon lighting usually flickering, and the smell of disinfectant everywhere. When we were sure no one could see us, we'd go down on our knees or lie on our stomachs for a few seconds and put our noses to the crack of a door. Because there'd always be someone cooking somewhere, and we'd try to guess from the spices and other ingredients where the occupants came from. Mostly the smell was of cooking oil though, and very occasionally the door of the flat would open the minute we lay down in front of it. Then we'd jump up and scarper down the stuffy stairwells until we were completely out of breath. Once we'd reached safety, we'd laugh triumphantly, our lungs screaming for air, our hearts thumping wildly.

The many passageways, nooks, and crannies in our blocks of flats were a paradise for children who loved secrets and needed space away from the world of grown-ups. The grown-ups' world—in our flats, that meant the faces with downturned mouths. The parents with tired eyes who dragged themselves and their shopping bags up the stairs we hid under. Or the raised voices that filtered through the doors like the songs of sad ghosts.

One day when Yasmin and I were wandering aimlessly through the stairwells, not registering which turns we were taking, we ended up in the basement, in front of a door with peeling paintwork that we'd never seen before. Yasmin pushed the handle down gingerly. The door wasn't locked. Behind it was a small room and a pallet bed with a crumpled purple sleeping bag on it. The floor was littered with empty beer and schnapps bottles, and we found lots of syringes near the bed. There was no window, just an air vent with a thick layer of dust on the grating. The air was musty and a nasty smell assaulted your nose every time you inhaled. But there was also a shelf with tools on it—a hammer, pliers, wire, some rubber hose. And a large box full of artificial flowers. We had stumbled on what used to be the caretaker's cubbyhole. At one stage, our flats had a full-time caretaker, and this was presumably where he hung out. Now all the maintenance work was handled by the local authorities, and they only sent someone out as a last resort. This little room must have served as a hide-out for homeless people or junkies for quite some time. Yasmin took a flower from the box—there were a couple of hundred in it—and dusted the petals off on her sleeve. They were red.

"This is no place for a flower," she said, looking at the colourful object in her hand, which seemed as out of place among all the greys as a Pop Art print in a prison cell.

"I have an idea," she said, her brown eyes twinkling.

Adventure beckoned, I followed.

We sneaked back to the cubbyhole several times over the following days. Once we were sure everything stayed exactly the same between visits, we could safely assume that no one lived there anymore. We had found a secret place of our own, a magic room in an enchanted realm. It was Yasmin's idea to take the flowers to the world of grown-ups and brighten it a little. "Everyone loves flowers," she stated categorically, and there was no contradicting that. But there were more flats in our place than we had flowers, so we decided on a selection process: "Whenever we hear fighting or see someone sad going into their flat, we'll put a flower outside their door," she decided. "But they only get the flower once."

After that, whenever we heard someone shouting while we were on our rambles, we chalked a small cross on the bottom right of the door frame so that we'd find it again. Sometimes we hid round a corner so that we'd see people's reaction to the surprise splash of colour in the daily grey. We never actually saw anyone coming out, but when we went back to the scene later, the flowers were always gone. So we imagined the people finding them, picking them up, and smelling them. They'd peer furtively up and down the corridor before closing the door and putting the flower in a vase in the window, even though the flower wasn't a real one. We had great fun with this flower game; when we'd go back to the flat, Mother would ask what we'd been up to, but we never said a thing, just exchanged surreptitious smiles across the table.

There was often trouble with the police in our flats. Some of the kids hanging around the playground boasted that we lived in a place the cops were afraid to go after dark. They claimed to be kings of the streets once the sun went down. But it wasn't true. The police often came after dark. We'd see them and their torches through the window, entering one of the blocks and reappearing a short time later, hauling someone off to the station. The cops were definitely not afraid of our place, and I often saw them picking up one of the so-called kings.

If where we lived bothered my father, he didn't let it show, though I may have been too young to notice. He liked his job in the youth centre, and Mother managed to build up a regular customer base for her dresses. They were content, my parents, but money was always scarce. Father regularly had to send money home to his mother, my grandmother, who had refused to leave the country when they did. He explained this to me many times. The money was mainly for doctor's bills and medicine. One day when I asked why she hadn't left with them in the first place, or why she couldn't at least join us in Germany now, he just smiled and said, "It's Lebanon. No one wants to leave."

During our seventh year in that flat, Mother became pregnant for the second time. Now the place was definitely too small, and since we lived on the sixth floor, and the lift broke down almost every day, my parents decided it was time to move. Hakim agreed. Yasmin and I were thrilled. Besides, we had run out of flowers by then.

5

In that warm late summer of 1992 when we found our new home, I was seven, Yasmin nine. She and Hakim moved into the flat below us, which was similar in layout but a little smaller. On this street, nearly all the satellite dishes pointed 26 degrees east. We were happy. In the school-yard, we swapped Diddl Mouse characters and sealed friendships with colourful bracelets; Bill Clinton took the presidential oath; and Take That sang "Could It Be Magic." In Lebanon, the general election was held, and everything seemed to be heading in the right direction. Things were looking good. I felt like I was part of an animal pack calmly awaiting autumn and winter, safe in the knowl-edge that we had plentiful supplies and a warm and cosy den.

So there we were a few weeks after moving in, watching TV in the living room, the usual images of post-election Beirut. Hakim had told me the Syrian joke and I'd laughed. Father didn't laugh, though, which reminded me how dis-tracted he'd seemed of late and how rarely he was in good humour. Instead, he'd scratch the back of his neck abstract-edly, seeming to stare right through the walls, yet not see-ing anything. He spoke very little and withdrew into him-self. In the evenings he would sometimes disappear for hours at a time after dinner; out walking, he said. If I started putting on my shoes and jacket in the hall to go with him, he'd be gone before I was ready, the door closed behind him. Sometimes I imagined that his limp was worse when he got back. I didn't know my father without the limp. It was part of him, as normal as the colour of his eyes. If you didn't know he had a limp, you'd barely notice it, except when Father exerted himself. He still walked very straight, but his head was bowed and he rarely looked at me. Whenever I managed to catch his eye, he'd give me a smile, but he wouldn't say much, and he'd usually turn away quickly, as if he felt ill at ease or caught out. It sounded more like he was sighing than breathing then, a strained breath coming from somewhere very deep, as if he'd had to climb a thousand steps. Sometimes, in passing, he would stroke my head with his big hand. His eyes looked red occasionally, as if he'd been crying. But that's just a guess—I never did see Father cry.

Then there was the other extreme. Times I'd look over at him and find him staring at me, his eyes glued to me as if I had some weird marking on my forehead. Moments when I felt there was a tortured look in his eyes, just for a split second, before he'd catch me watching him and force a little smile. If he gave me a hug when he was in this kind of mood, he'd squeeze me far too tight, wouldn't want to let go. I'd stick it out, even if it nearly hurt. And if he spoke to me in moments like these, he'd talk really fast, without so much as a pause, as if he was trying to stop me getting up and leaving, to keep me sitting there listening. He'd gesticulate wildly and try to make it all sound very exciting, which worked every time. He did all this with my sister too, though I don't think she really got it. What worried me most of all about Father's behaviour was that he didn't talk to Mother. If she addressed him, he would just lift his head slowly and nod in awkward silence. For some reason, he couldn't bear to look her in the eye.

Only a few days earlier, we'd been at the lake with our nutshell ships. If I had to pinpoint a time when his behaviour changed, I'd say it was that day. Or rather, that night. After we'd come home from the lake, Father put on a slide show. That evening is burned into my memory. It is the reason why I remember that summer and the following autumn as if in sepia: every scene is tinged with a nostalgic glow and tightly cocooned by my memories.

I didn't even know it existed, the box Father placed on the living-room table in front of us. It never caught my attention when we were moving. Now Father had taken it from one of the shelves, turned to face us, and carried it over with great ceremony.

"What's that?" I asked.

"You'll see in a minute," he said, smiling mysteriously.

Mother smiled too. She still smiled a lot back then. I don't have many memories of my parents like that. Standing close together. So conspiratorial, so affectionate. I never saw them like that again after that evening. They had clearly planned it together and were looking forward to letting us in on the secret. I was very excited. I noticed that Mother was wearing her perfume, even though it was just us. I knew where she kept it in the bathroom, the little bottle with *Arzet Lebanon* written on it, and I imagined her standing at the mirror, dabbing a drop or two on her neck. She smelt divine.

"You smell nice," I said.

"Thank you, Samir," she replied, stroking my cheek.

At that very moment, there was a knock on the door.

"Shall I get it?" she asked.

"No, I'll go," Father said, planting a quick kiss on her forehead. Another thing I very rarely witnessed.

Hakim and Yasmin were at the door. She was wearing a blue dress with white dots and looked like an almost cloudless blue sky. Hakim had his arms clamped around a large object that I couldn't identify, as it was covered by a dark cloth. It seemed pretty heavy because Hakim practically staggered the last few metres into the living room, where he carefully deposited the object on the table.

"What's that?"

"You'll see in a minute," he said.

"That's what Baba said too."

"It must be true, then."

When I looked at Yasmin, asking with my eyes what her father had just lugged into our living room, she just shrugged.

Father told us to take a seat. The three grown-ups remained standing. I took my sister on my lap; she showed no interest but was happy to suck her soother. Yasmin sat beside us.

"Hakim," said Father, raising his index finger, "drumroll, please!"

Hakim started making drumroll noises and beating invisible drumsticks. Father approached the table, grabbed the cloth between thumb and index finger, and swept it off the object underneath, like a magician performing his favourite trick: "Ta-da!"

On the table was something grey that looked a bit like a snouted raccoon or coatimundi. Could it be a coati-robot? It had a rectangular metal base with an oval structure on top from which a longish tube projected like a snout. I hadn't a clue what it was.

"What is that?"

"A Leitz Prado," exclaimed Father.

"A what?" said Yasmin, her eyebrows raised.

"A Leitz Prado," he repeated, still in character, as if he was about to recite a magic spell. "The best slide projector money can buy."

I looked over at Mother, who lowered her head and smiled with embarrassment. If Father was convinced about something, it was the best thing in the world. End of story. He knew where you could buy the freshest lettuce, which second-hand car dealer had the safest winter tyres, and which kebab shop had the best doner in the world. The kebab shop might change, but the doner would always be the best in the world. And now, here in our living room, we were looking at the best slide projector in the world. A Leitz Prado.

"Why did you buy it?" I enquired.

"I didn't. Hakim borrowed it for us."

"Why?" asked Yasmin.

"We wanted to show you something." Father nodded to Hakim, who plugged the projector cable into the wall socket and turned off the overhead light. Then Father switched the machine on. It projected a large, bright rectangle onto our living-room wall. Dust motes danced in the beam of light.

"We wanted to show you photos," Mother said. "Pictures of Lebanon, of us. So that you can see where we come from."

"Where you come from, too," said Father.

I liked the sound of that. I, German-born Samir, was going to learn more about my family's homeland. Father had explained it to me once: "It's called nationality based on parentage. You were born in Germany but your mother and I are Lebanese, not German. That's why your passport says you're Lebanese." I had accepted this with a simple "OK" and hadn't given the document a second thought.

Now Father was putting the first slide in. The projector rattled. A colourful image of my mother appeared on our wall. She was sitting on a chair, wearing a magnificent wedding dress.

"Wow," said Yasmin. "That's beautiful."

Mother rarely wore make-up and hardly ever accentuated her eyes as much as on the photo. It looked like a very expensive portrait commissioned from an artist; there was something fragile about her, but also a special aura. I had never seen her in such finery. She really was very pretty.

The next slide showed Father standing beside a woman I didn't recognise. She had black, curly hair and very straight, dignified posture. Her air of gravitas was compelling, even in this old image. Father was noticeably taller than her. She had her arm linked with his and wore a thin-lipped smile.

"That's your Teta," he said, in response to my questioning look.

"That's Grandmother?" I took a closer look at the picture. "She doesn't look sick at all."

Father lowered his head but smiled.

"No. But she's sick these days, you know that."

I nodded.

"When was that picture taken?" Yasmin wanted to know.

"1982," said Mother. "It was our wedding day."

In the picture, Father had a smart suit on. Grandmother was wearing a blue dress and a lot of lipstick, which made it hard to tell her age. I reckoned early forties, maybe. I was struck by her enormous earrings, which were all the more eye-catching because she wore her curly hair short. Father's smile looked a bit strained, but then he'd never liked having his picture taken.

"Now, here it comes," said Hakim, all excited. The projector rattled.

Yasmin and I were amazed by the next slide. It showed my parents standing facing each other. And behind them was Hakim.

"You're playing the guitar!" I exclaimed.

"It's a lute," said Mother. "Hakim played beautifully for us."

In the photo, Hakim's eyes were fixed on some point in the distance, as if they were following the notes that soared out of his lute.

"How come you knew each other?"

"From another wedding," said Father. "Hakim played at lots of weddings."

"And where is Yasmin's mother?" I asked.

No one seemed to be expecting this question, and I realised that I'd never asked it before, of Hakim or of my parents. And in all the hours I'd spent playing and dreaming with Yasmin, all the times we'd gone in search of a secret to share, I'd never asked her this question either. Now it hung in the room like a heavy ball that could fall on top of us any minute. The three grown-ups looked at each other. Yasmin looked at me. I felt uncomfortable, partly because I didn't get any answer.

Several more slides followed, mainly of the wedding feast and of guests enjoying themselves, until Father said, "This is the last of the wedding photos," as he put another slide into the projector. There were so many people in the picture that it took me a minute to figure it out. It showed my parents in front of a tree, a magnificent fig tree. They were obviously dancing the wedding dance, with the guests gathered in a semi-circle around them, clapping. The women were all wearing lots of jewellery and make-up. It must have been a warm, sunny day. The sky was a glorious blue. The women were in colourful dresses, the men in suits. Some of them had their jackets slung over their shoulders, like film stars. Something struck me: there were other men too, men we hadn't seen in any of the other photos. They were standing in the background, in front of a brick and mud wall. Some had their arms folded, watching the dancing. They were wearing brown trousers and khaki-coloured T-shirts. They had a cedar embroidered on the left breast of the T-shirt. A cedar with a red circle round it. There was a gun propped against the tree.

"Who are those men?" I asked.

"Guests," said Father.

"Friends," said Mother.

Hakim said nothing.

A brief silence ensued.

"We've plenty more slides," Father announced, rubbing his hands. "Now I'm going to show you your country."

And he did. Whenever he got a chance to talk about Lebanon, he was in his element. We saw photos of the sea, of Beirut and its tall buildings, of the Pigeon Rocks, standing just off the coast like the city's sentinels. He showed us a photo of the six remaining columns of the Temple of Jupiter at Baalbek. It was after dark, but they were illuminated and very impressive. When he showed us a photo of a port, he said, "See that? That's Byblos. Where our ancestors, the Phoenicians, invented the alphabet. Not many people know that. They all say, 'Look at the Egyptians and the amazing pyramids they built—such a highly developed Arab culture!' But let me tell you, if we'd followed the Egyptians' example, we'd still be reading picture books today!"

I saw Mother and Hakim exchange glances. They knew there was no point in interrupting Father at this stage. But we kids were infected by his enthusiasm. He didn't just show the pictures, he told the stories behind them as well. At times he went into full lecture mode.

"Lebanon is the only Arab country with no desert," he informed us as he showed a slide of Lake Qaraoun in the Bekaa Valley. Its surface shimmered bright blue, reflecting the mountain chain behind it. "There is so much fertile land there, and so many vineyards."

"Especially in Zahle," cried Yasmin, her eyes sparkling.

"Exactly," grinned Father with pride. Then he reached for the next slide. The one that changed his behaviour.

Looking back, I think he just picked up the wrong slide in his excitement, because he wasn't watching what he was doing. My guess is he meant to pick the one next to it. The slide he actually showed us had been moved to the back of the bunch on purpose. He had filtered it out so that it wouldn't end up in the projector, so that we wouldn't get to see it.

The projector rattled.

My mother glanced at the photo, looked away, then back again suddenly, as if she had to convince herself it was really there.

At the right-hand edge of the image stood my father, beside a good-looking young man with thick black hair, dark brown eyes, and an engaging smile. They were posing beneath a chandelier in a large foyer, a wide carpeted staircase with a gilt banister behind them. Opposite them, at the left edge of the image, was a photographer. He had a camera held up to his eye and the others were looking at him. Curious onlookers had gathered around the photographer—more uniformed men, a young woman, people who looked like waiters. The man beside Father was wearing a uniform and had a gun tucked into his belt. There was a cedar stitched onto the left breast of his shirt. A cedar with a red circle round it. Next I studied Father. He was very young and seemed almost shy. The look in his eyes—today, I'd describe it as dreamy—didn't quite match the rest of the scene. Father was smiling a dreamy smile and saluting. He was wearing the same uniform as the other man, and he too had a gun tucked into his belt.

There are moments in life when you experience something that makes you wonder. Then more of those moments follow. But it's only much later, when you barely remember those moments, that they acquire new meaning, because in the meantime you've learned more about someone or something, more than you knew before. All the inexplicable gestures, looks, movements, and behaviour suddenly make sense. Like finding a piece of a jigsaw and fitting it into the unfinished puzzle you've kept for years in case you'd one day manage to complete it.

There are moments when you think about asking a question but decide not to. Your antennae sense a barrier. Your intuition tells you it's not the right time for that question. Adults can sense this. Children too. But years later, when you know more than you did then, you regret it. You regret not asking the question. The one question that might have explained everything. Why he was wearing a uniform, for example. Why he had a gun. Who the man was beside him. It would have made things so much easier.

Father stared at the picture as if he didn't recognise himself. There he was on our living-room wall, large as life, standing beside a man who looked as if his uniform was a second skin, as if he'd been wearing it his whole life. I can only speculate now what thoughts went through Father's mind in that moment. What feelings the slide must have triggered. What memories. What pain, even. We all stared at the picture. Nobody said a word for what seemed like an eternity. Then my sister began to squirm and cry on my lap. Mother snapped out of her stunned silence and took the wriggling bundle from me. She left the room, rocking the baby in her arms. Hakim signalled to Yasmin that they'd better go. She gave me an uncertain look, slid off the couch, took his hand, and they left. Father turned off the projector and slid out of the room with his head bowed. I stayed behind. A second earlier I'd wanted to ask him the story behind that picture. Now I'd decided not to.

6

Could I possibly have guessed how much that moment would change our lives? How the seeds of disintegration became slowly and imperceptibly embedded in our family from then on, like a malignant growth discovered too late. It's only a photo—that's what I thought back then. A picture of my father with a gun. How was I to know I'd be haunted by that photo forever?

What happened over the next few days is as I've described already. Father's behaviour changed. I sensed that it had something to do with the photo, and several times it was on the tip of my tongue to ask him about it. But I got the feeling that he didn't want to talk about it, so I held back. I was only seven. I found the world of grown-ups terribly confusing, and when it came to making decisions, I often felt like I was lost in a huge building with way too many doors and corridors, out of which I was supposed to pick the right one. Gut instinct told me it would be better not to ask Mother or Father about the photo. So I trusted my gut.

Now, some twenty years later, I frequently tell myself I should have listened to my head rather than my gut. People tell me it wasn't my fault. "You were only a child," they say awkwardly, because that's all they can think of. "A child can't read those kinds of signals." They say that he abused my trust when he made me promise not to tell anyone about the strange phone calls. And that I wasn't deceiving Mother when I kept quiet about it all. They say this because they don't know about all the times she shook me and begged me to tell her the truth. They say, "Even if you had done everything differently, what difference would it have made?" But the truth is, their words mean nothing, because I know better.

Even though Father's behaviour scared me, I still wanted to be close to him. One day I decided to collect him from work at the youth centre. When I set off, the sky was clouding over and the air was so humid that my skin felt clammy, but there was no sign yet of the storm that broke just minutes later. First, big fat raindrops hit the street and a wind gusted up, whipping the newspaper right out of a man's hands at the bus stop across the road. Waiters came scurrying out of cafés, holding trays over their heads, and glancing suspiciously at the sky or clearing away outdoor tables and chairs while the awnings flapped like startled pigeons. Then the intervals between the raindrops grew shorter and shorter, and seconds later everything turned grey. The rain came down in sheets of lead—and my clothes were far too thin. A cold wind whistled round my ears, and rainclouds trailed across the sky like giant turtles. There was no point in turning back; I was nearly there. I hurried along the pavement, shoulders hunched, hands stuffed into my pockets, trying to avoid the spumes of dirty water sprayed by passing cars. Near the entrance to the youth centre, a bunch of teenagers were sheltering under an overhanging roof, waiting for the storm to pass before going home. One of them—a guy with a striking horseshoe-shaped scar on his forehead—spotted me and held out a packet of cigarettes the way you'd offer a chimp a banana; the others burst their sides laughing. I entered the building. The empty hallway was quite a contrast to the noisy street. The air was stale, the oxygen all used up during the day. I walked past glass cabinets displaying photos of kids playing football or sawing big planks. Father was in some of the pictures, and I recognised the guys from outside too. My shoes left a wet trail on the lino floor. My father's office was behind one of the last doors on the corridor. Beside his name plate was a registration sheet for a night hike. I went in without knocking. I knew he had a desk with stacks of files on it and expected to find him half-hidden behind them. But he wasn't. He was standing in front of the desk. And when he saw me come through the door, he hung up the phone in shock.

"Samir! What are you doing here?" The way he said it sounded slightly cross—it wasn't *Samir, what a nice surprise*, or *Oh dear, you're all wet*.

"I wanted to pick you up from work." Suddenly I felt like a complete idiot, like someone who turns up at a friend's house for a surprise party but got the dates mixed up. I felt way too small for this big room I was in, soaked to the skin, and didn't know what to say.

He looked at me blankly for a minute, as if I'd addressed him in some rare language like Tofalar and was expecting him to decode it for himself. Then he muttered an "Oh," followed by, "Right. I'm finished here. Let's go."

We left his office together, but he didn't take my hand until we were outside.

"I'm parked over there," he said, pointing somewhere beyond the curtain of rain. He pulled me along; it was hard to keep up and I nearly tripped. Just before a mighty clap of thunder, I heard one of the gang from before say to the guy with the scar on his forehead, "Hey, guess what? You just offered Brahim's son a smoke!"

With Father in this kind of mood, it was hard to be positive. I'd never seen him like this. His dark moods were every bit as contagious as his cheerfulness could be. All of a sudden, the walls of our flat didn't seem so white and bright anymore. And I began to notice little stains and flaws on the wooden floor where we scuffed it pulling chairs in and out from the dinner table. The shiny oval keyhole plate in the living-room door had ugly scratches I had never registered before, and if the autumn sunlight fell at the wrong angle, I could see how dirty our windows were. I went traipsing around our neighbourhood breaking branches off trees and crawling through waist-high wet grass in the hope that my torn, sodden clothes would grab Father's attention.

I missed his stories, how he'd sit on my bed in the evenings and spin yarns, his eyes shining. It was a tradition and a ritual, this story time. Something that created a bond between us. The stories allowed this invisible bond to grow, and I had assumed that it was so strong no one would be able to break it. The worlds Father created in these stories were realms only the two of us could enter, through secret doors to which we alone had the keys. If he came to my room with a new story to tell, he'd hop from one foot to the other, rub his hands furtively and exude such an air of childish excitement that I knew he could hardly wait. Then we'd shut the door so that Mother wouldn't disturb us, dim the light, and dive into new worlds. The closed door was a signal to Mother to keep well away. She'd know that we were busy pursuing the adventures of the characters and creatures Father brought to life. I wanted my old father back, the one full of laughter, enthusiasm, and joie de vivre. My proud father, my patient father. Not the one who barely noticed me, no matter how hard I tried. Not the one who took my little sister in his arms and rocked her, but gave the impression that it was unbearably painful to look at her.

I missed Yasmin too. I missed her sticking her curly head round the door and coming in. Without knocking, naturally, because our flat was her second home. She too had sensed the change in Father, and she stopped coming up to us so often after that. His strange behaviour had unsettled her as well.

"What's wrong with him?" she asked me, after he'd once again passed her on the stairs without a word. All I could do was shrug.

The night after the slideshow, I lay in bed and heard my parents having a row, arguing the way parents do when they don't want children to hear—behind closed doors, in intense, hushed voices. I pressed one ear against my pillow and pulled the duvet over the other, but it didn't help much. I tried to focus instead on the blobs that seemed to float weightlessly in the lava lamp on my bedside table. They merged, separated, nudged against the glass, and formed new shapes all over again. But my parents' voices still slid under the bedroom door like toxic smoke. They were in the kitchen, and I could not block out their voices.

"But you promised," said Mother.

"I know."

"Do you realise what would have happened if they'd found it?"

Silence.

"Do you realise that we wouldn't be here today?"

Silence.

"We could be dead, Brahim. Tossed in a grave or thrown into the sea like the others."

Still no response.

"Why did you keep it?"

"I don't know."

"You don't know?"

"No. That was ten years ago."

"Ten years in which we've created a life for ourselves. A life together."

Silence.

"We came here so that our children might have a better chance. You were putting that at risk."

"We didn't have any kids then."

"But surely you expected us to have kids eventually."

"It's only a photo," my father yelled, in a voice that carried all the way to my room.

"It's more than that," my mother spat back. "I want you to throw it away. Even if it's ten years too late."

"Rana," he said, "that photo is of no interest to anyone in this place."

"I don't care what you say." Mother was furious. "Get rid of it once and for all!"

"That photo means something to me," he said.

"I know," she retorted angrily, "I know all too well what that photo means to you. That's why I want you to get rid of it! You're here now, with us. That should mean everything to you." She was sobbing now. Then I heard footsteps in the corridor. She walked past my room into their bedroom and shut the door.

I held my breath under the bedclothes. My teeth were clenched so tight that my jaw hurt. My ears were still pricked, but now all was quiet. Slowly, I pushed back the duvet, slid out of bed, and carefully opened the door. To my left, there was still light from the kitchen. Father was still in there. There was no sound from my parents' room. I hitched up my pyjama bottoms so that I wouldn't trip on the hems and tiptoed down the corridor to the living room.

I wasn't really thinking about what I did. The projector was still there on the table, in the dark. The slide was still in the slot. I withdrew it carefully. All I could make out in this light were vague shadows. I turned around and scurried silently back to my room.

Seconds later, I heard Father heave a sigh and leave the kitchen. He went into the living room; I held my breath. Then I heard a rustling and pictured him searching through the slides spread out on the table. The rustling didn't last long, though, because next thing he was coming towards my room. I closed my eyes, heard him open the door, and sensed him watching me from the doorway.

"Samir?" he whispered.

I didn't react. My heart was in my throat. I had the slide clasped in one hand, and the hand shoved under my pillow. Father entered the room slowly; I could hear his breath as he leaned over. Then it went dark behind my eyelids. He had switched off my bedside light. With heavy steps, he made his way back to the door.

"Goodnight, Samir," he said, as if I was still awake.

That's when I knew that he knew.

7

He never mentioned the subject, never took me to task. Not the next day, nor in the weeks that followed. It was as if it had never happened, that moment when he caught me but never said a word. As a result, I started to feel like we had a special bond again, a secret. But his mood changed very little. And the longer this strange behaviour continued, the more Mother suffered, despite her best efforts to hide it. If she caught me watching her while she was hanging up the washing, she'd try to whistle a cheerful tune. She never normally did that. One time I came into the kitchen when Father had just left the house.

"Are you crying?" I asked.

"No," she said and smiled. "I'm chopping onions, see?"

"Hakim says the trick is to hold your breath while you're chopping them. Then they won't make you cry."

"OK, but I can't hold my breath for ever, Samir."

It hurt to see my father the way he was, but it was almost more painful to see my mother trying to hide the wounds inflicted by his behaviour. Few things in this world seem sadder than a fake smile. Perhaps her perception of our flat changed too, like my own, because she started cleaning it from top to bottom every day, even the bits that couldn't possibly have got dirty again. She started cooking way more than we could eat too. Then she'd wrap the leftovers in tinfoil and have me take it round to friends and neighbours. If she was completely exhausted, I'd take my little sister from her, rock her in my arms, and sing her to sleep. Many's the time I found Mother asleep when I came back to the living room, curled up like a child on her side of the sofa, the left side. And if I went up close, I could make out traces of tears on her cheeks.

One day not long after the time Hakim told the Syrian joke while he and Father were watching TV and discussing the new beginnings in Lebanon, the phone rang in the hall. It was one of those old telephones with a rotary dial and a heavy handset. Ours was mint green. I was nearby, so I answered the phone.

"Hello. Samir el-Hourani speaking," I said.

Silence.

"Hello?" I said, shrugging at Father, who gave me a surprised look. It was a bad line, lots of crackling. I could hear someone breathing at the other end, as if they were taking a deep breath.

"Hello?" I said again.

The person at the other end exhaled. Someone was singing in the background. Next thing, Father was standing beside me, taking the handset.

"This is Brahim el-Hourani," he said.

I watched him and saw his eyes narrowing. Then he hung up.

"The line was cut off," he said brusquely. Then he turned on his heel, taking his jacket off the hook, fished a few coins from his pocket, and quickly worked out how much he had.

"Are you going out?" I asked.

"That was your grandmother," he said. "I have to ring her back."

"What do you need your jacket for?"

"I'm going to the phone box."

"But we have our own phone," I said, pointing out the obvious.

"I know, Samir. But it's very expensive to ring Lebanon. I've been saving coins especially so that I can ring your grandmother from the phone box."

He knelt down to tie his shoes.

"Can I go with you?"

"No," he said. "Wait here. Your mother will be back any minute with the shopping. I want you to help her carry it in."

With that, he left the flat.

A few days later, the phone rang again and I answered. Again, no reply. Just more breathing. No singing in the background this time, but I thought I could make out engine noises. "Grandmother?" I said into the silence. No reply. Maybe the line was even worse at the other end? I listened for a little longer this time. Then the line went dead. I told Father about the phone call, and off he went again to return the call from the phone box. But before he left, he went down on his knees, put both hands on my shoulders, and looked me straight in the eye.

"Samir," he said insistently, "promise me you won't tell your mother about the phone calls."

"Why not?"

"I don't want her to worry."

"But if Grandmother is sick, don't you think she'd want to know?"

His eyes narrowed.

"Of course. But you know your mother. She'd get upset, and that wouldn't be good."

I shrugged my shoulders.

"Do you promise?"

"Not to tell Mother?"

"Not to tell anyone."

I promised. And I kept my promise too.

Grandmother rang a third time, I think. Father answered the phone, said his name, hung up almost immediately and left the flat. This time, he didn't even put on his jacket.

Soon the weather turned colder. The leaves changed colour and cast our neighbourhood in a golden-red glow in the evening light. Then they turned brown and fell. A street in timelapse. The pretty autumn colours seemed to rub off on people too. I loved how the crisp air could bring a magic smile to rosy cheeks. Even the grown-ups were friendlier, out raking leaves on our street. Of course, I loved to kick up the piles of leaves again when no one was looking. For me, autumn was also full of things to look forward to. Winter—and the longed-for first snow of the season—was only round the corner. Then there were walnuts, which I loved not just because you could make little ships out of them, but because they tasted so good. And the dark evenings were great because it meant Mother would light candles and turn the heat up. Another reason I loved autumn was because it came with an image of my mother that has become one of my indelible memories of her. She's sitting on the sofa with a rug tucked round her legs, steam rising from a cup of tea in front of her. She's flicking through catalogues looking for inspiration for new dresses. Before turning the page, she briefly puts her left index finger to her lips to moisten it. I don't think she was even aware of doing this.

Eventually, the weather got so cold you could see your own breath outside. By then, the new Lebanese parliament was two months old, and it had quickly become clear that Rafiq Hariri, the prime minister, wasn't going to hang about. The reconstruction plans had already been drawn up. The Syrians were still in the country, of course, and they wouldn't be leaving in a hurry. But things were progressing that November. All that was missing was the first snow. Our snowsuits hadn't come out of the wardrobe yet. On 10 November 1992, I turned eight.

8

One day in the run-up to my birthday, Father drove out to our town's industrial estate. That's where the joinery was where Hakim worked. When he got back, he took a thick plank out of the boot. The timber was a pale but intense colour. I stood by the car and watched. He had gloves on and a warm jacket, and his breath came out in clouds as he wrestled with the board.

"Here, smell this," he said, holding the board under my nose.

"I can't smell anything."

"Exactly. This is dry cedar."

"What are you going to do with it?"

"That's a secret," he said, giving me a wink.

"Where did you get it?"

"I ordered it through Hakim's workshop. The boss there knows a wholesaler. It's not easy to get cedar in Germany."

"I thought cedar smelt different."

He carried the board past me and nodded in the direction of the shed.

"Come with me," he said.

I followed him, practically reeling with the euphoria of having some attention from him again after all these weeks. He leaned the plank up against the wall in the shed, took a small saw from his toolbox, and cut into the wood.

"Smell that."

A powerfully aromatic, woody smell hit my nose.

"That's the essential oils in the resin," he said. Then he put his own nose close to the fresh incision and inhaled the smell.

"What are we going to do with the wood?"

"*We* are not going to do anything. *I* am. And I might show it to you when it's finished."

"You might?"

"I might."

Then he straightened up, stroked my head, walked past me, and disappeared.

He spent the following weekend in the old wooden shed. I also spotted Hakim going in there at various stages, reemerging later and beating sawdust off his clothes. Yasmin and I, bundled in our winter jackets, sat on the steps of our building keeping a keen eye on the shed and watching the white clouds of vapour drifting from our mouths.

On my birthday, lots of neighbours came to my party. There were eight candles on the cake and everyone sang "Sana Helwa ya Gameel," the Arabic version of "Happy Birthday." I blew all the candles out in one go and everyone clapped. I got fabulous presents too. Khalil, the young man who had helped Father mount the satellite dish the day we moved in, gave me a diabolo. I'd often watched him on our street, spinning the double-cupped top on a string attached to two sticks. He could do amazing tricks with it, almost like at the circus. From Hakim I got a wooden sled he made himself, a really beautiful one with curved handles. It had a great smell of workshop and wax.

"Don't worry, the snow will come," he said. "The longer it keeps you waiting, the more you'll enjoy it."

Yasmin went as far as to give me a kiss on the cheek, which I brushed off rather sheepishly. All day long, my parents made obvious efforts not to let the strange atmosphere of recent weeks spoil my party. But there was an awkwardness to their attempts to play the perfect team; they kept bumping into each other, practically knocking each other down as they waited on the guests and put food on the table. And anyone who took a closer look couldn't fail to see how they tried to avoid each other, passed each other with their heads down, only spoke to guests separately, and never looked each other in the eye.

That evening, Yasmin and I tried out the diabolo. There wasn't a soul on the street outside our building. The cold made it hard to hold the sticks, but we were too captivated to go in for our gloves. Over and over, we spun the rubber top into the air and caught it with the string, competing with each other to see who could throw it highest, who could keep it spinning longest.

Soon the November evening fog descended, shrouding everything in grey until even the streetlights gave off no more than a dim glow. It crept over the nearby green and through the alleyways of our neighbourhood. Entire buildings vanished, their lit-up windows like ghostly eyes in the gloom. Eventually Hakim stuck his head out the window of their flat and called Yasmin in. It was late. She turned to me, her cheeks rosy, her eyes gleaming from the cold.

"I hope you had a nice birthday," she said, handing me the sticks.

I nodded. Yasmin turned and disappeared into the fog; the only sound was her footsteps, then the front door closing. I stood there for a moment. Nothing but silence around me, and a strange sense of impenetrable loneliness. I looked up and saw the light from our living-room window. I didn't really want to go back up.

On my bedside table I found a little present wrapped in

dark blue paper with a gold ribbon. It caught my eye the minute I entered the room. It was beside the lava lamp, which was on. I could hear Mother clattering in the kitchen as she washed the dishes. The TV was on in the living room. I'd seen the colours flickering on the hall floor when I came in, and judging by the theme tune, Father was watching the news on Al Jadeed. I'd taken off my jacket and shoes in the hall and put the diabolo in the corner.

I hadn't really felt like going into the living room. I was afraid Father would go back to ignoring me now that the guests were gone—or worse, stare at me as if I was about to go up in smoke and he had to imprint every detail of me in his memory. So I just sneaked into my room, where I found the present. It was surprisingly heavy for its size. When I tore off the paper, I held a little wooden box in my hand. The pale wood was streaked with darker shades of brown that ran down the sides of the box like veins or rivulets. I turned it in every direction and inspected it from all angles. The wood was finely polished, my fingers felt no unevenness. It wasn't big, but the smell of cedar was so powerful that I almost jumped back to catch my breath. I could picture Father in the shed, making this box for me. Sawing the board, hollowing and sanding the wood until he had the shape he wanted. Polishing it as he thought of me holding and feeling his work. Tears welled up but I held them back. I flipped open the lid of the box. There was nothing inside except a hollow about three fingers wide, roughly the length of my little finger, and not particularly deep. Mother had a similar box, lined on the inside, for her earrings. But I didn't have any earrings, and right now I couldn't think of anything else to keep in this box.

"Do you like it?" Father was watching me from the doorway. He had a dark blue jumper on with a high polo-neck. It looked cosy and warm. I was dying to run to him and bury my head in his woolly tummy, but I didn't dare.

"I wasn't sure ..." he said.

"It's beautiful."

"I'm glad you like it."

"I don't know what I'm going to put in it."

"I'm sure you'll think of something."

I nodded in silent agreement.

"May I come in?"

Still looking at the box, I nodded again. Father came into my room and looked around. His eyes took in my desk, the withered cyclamen sitting on it, and the little shelf that held my books and toys. He was studying the room as if seeing it for first time. I looked at him uncertainly. I didn't know what he wanted from me. The last few weeks had left their mark, and I no longer knew how to read him. So I just sat there and clung to the little box.

"When I was a little older than you," he said suddenly, pointing at my hands, "I had one of those too." He stroked his beard.

"Really? What did you put in your box?"

"Well, I used to write stories back then," he said, putting his hands in his pockets.

"What kind of stories?"

"Ones I made up."

"About what?"

"Anything and everything. They weren't particularly good, which is why I didn't show them to anyone."

"And you kept them in your box?"

"Yes. It was a bit bigger than yours, though." He smiled and looked at me. "It's always good to have somewhere to keep your secrets."

Now he was standing very close to me, so close I could inhale his smell. How I'd have loved to lean my head against him, but I didn't budge. "Will you tell me a story again some time?"

He seemed to hesitate. Then he said, "Yes, of course."

"One about Abu Youssef?" I looked at him out of the corner of my eyes, hoping desperately for a yes.

"A new adventure with Abu Youssef?"

"That would be nice," I said with massive understatement.

Abu Youssef was a character Father had invented for me. For years he'd regaled me with new episodes of his adventures. Abu Youssef was a bit of an oddball. He lived in humble circumstances in a Lebanese mountain village, but he was very popular because he loved to throw parties and gather his friends around him. He had a talking camel called Amir. Amir means "prince," which is why the camel always wanted to be addressed as Your Highness. Abu Youssef loved Amir. He groomed him every day at sundown, and Amir was even allowed to eat indoors with Abu Yousef, as he had very good table manners. Amir's favourite food was apple cake. They had many an adventure together, putting an end to evil scoundrels' games or coming to the aid of mighty kings whose councillors had run out of counsel. Abu Youssef was respected far and wide. But one thing even Amir did not know was that Abu Youssef had a secret. He was rich, very rich indeed, for he had a great treasure. The wind sometimes carried rumours of his wealth from mountain villages across the plateau and into the cities. On the main squares, they wound themselves around the columns, where they were picked up and spread through the markets or whispered behind closed doors. The gossip about Abu Youssef and his treasure spun from the humble carpet maker in the bazaar to the rich Saudi sheikh in his Beirut penthouse, though many people dismissed it as pure fantasy, for it was well known that Abu Youssef lived in humble circumstances in his village, where he liked to throw parties, if his latest adventure didn't get in the way. I pictured him as a cheerful old man with a long grey beard, imparting pearls of wisdom to the children who were always gathered around him. He would ride through the land on his talking camel, ready to tackle whatever new challenges came his way.

Father cocked his head and studied me.

"Aren't you getting a bit old for Abu Youssef and his adventures?

"I'll never be too old for your stories."

Father laughed out loud, taking himself by surprise, then cleared his throat.

"When?" I wanted to know.

"Soon."

"How soon?"

"Very soon. I have a story in mind already."

I had a lump in my throat.

"Really?"

"Of course. Would I lie to you?"

Soon I'd have him sitting on my bed again, telling me about Abu Youssef. The thought of it had me fighting back tears once more.

Then I felt his arm on my shoulder. It was only one brief moment of intimacy, but if I'd ever been granted a superpower, I'd have wished for the power to freeze time. The clusters of foggy droplets on my window would have stopped sliding down the pane. The shapes shifting in my lava lamp would have turned to stone. The dust motes dancing in the air would have come to a sudden halt. The withered leaf that just fell off the cyclamen on my desk would have been suspended in mid-air. And the astonished smile lifting the corners of my mouth would never have faded had his arm stayed on my shoulder. But I didn't have any superpowers.

Neither of us spoke. I just sat there feeling the weight of

his arm on my shoulder, feeling the gentle pressure as he drew me close. Then we both exhaled. We hadn't noticed Mother coming into the room. She had wet patches on her blouse, a strand of hair was falling into her face, and her smile was tired. I shoved the little box under the duvet because I didn't know whether Father wanted it to be our secret. I certainly did. If Mother had seen it, she didn't let on. Father slowly lifted his arm.

"Did you enjoy your birthday?" she asked.

"Yes, it was great."

"And what do you think of the diabolo? Is it fun?"

I grinned a little self-consciously.

"Yeah. I'm pretty good at it actually."

"I bet you are."

"It was nice that so many people came. I like our neighbours."

"And they like you too. They had a good time."

"I like Khalil. He's a nice guy and he gave me lots of tips."

"You can learn a lot from that young man," Father said.

I nodded uncertainly. I was remembering that afternoon—the party, our living room full of visitors speaking Arabic, the obligatory shisha pipe doing the rounds after coffee. I could even see the yellow packet of Chiclets that was shared around, the men chewing gum to conceal the smell of tobacco. And I remembered the sudden longing that I'd felt. I desperately wanted to be one of them. To be not just the German-born son of Lebanese parents, but to see Lebanon, to live there, surrounded by people who embellished every word with impulsive, sweeping gestures, who ate with their hands, who addressed everyone who spoke this wonderful language as *habibi* or *habibti*. There was a burning question on my lips, but I wasn't sure this was a good time to ask it.

"Is everything OK?" Mother asked.

I plucked up my courage.

"Will we ever move back to Lebanon?"

She clearly wasn't expecting this question and looked hesitantly from me to Father.

"No," she said.

"Maybe," he said.

They had both spoken at the same time.

Later on—my room was in darkness, the lava lamp switched off—I woke from a restless dream. I reached one arm to the floor and fumbled for my water bottle. I drank in big thirsty gulps. The dream was already fading like invisible ink, and I could no longer remember the details. Silence reigned in our flat, apart from the hum of the old water-heater above the kitchen sink. My fingers followed the flex of the lamp until they found the switch. I rubbed my sleepy eyes. Then I saw the little wooden box on my bedside table. It lay open; I could see the hollowed-out space that seemed so small. A key might just about fit in it, but the key to what? I picked up the box, turning it over and feeling it in my hands. Then, as I pictured my father carving this gift in what little light came through the shed window, it was as if I could hear his voice saying, *It's always good to have somewhere to keep your secrets.*

I flung back the duvet and slipped out of bed. The lava lamp only cast a faint glow around the room, but I'd have found my way in my sleep. I went over to the shelf and took down the fattest book, *Tales from 1,001 Nights.* These stories that Scheherazade told King Shahryar in order to delay her execution had always fascinated me. Of all the treasures on my shelf, this was the most precious. I shook the book gently until a small object fell out that I had secreted between the pages. I picked it up, returned the book to the shelf, and went back to bed.

The slide fit perfectly into the hollowed-out space, as if the box had been made for this very purpose.

9

My excitement grew by the day. I couldn't wait to be transported once more into the magical world of Abu Youssef and Amir, a world full of heroes and rascals, colourful costumes and glorious adventures. I recalled some of the earlier episodes, like the time Abu Youssef had to rescue Amir from Ishaq, a lizard-like animal dealer who had kidnapped Amir and was threatening to sell the talking camel to a circus in Paris. Ishaq was a formidable foe who had enslaved many animals because of their extraordinary talents. Among them was an extremely overweight rhinoceros who was unbeatable at cards. On full moon nights, Ishaq would turn into a green-eyed lizard with impenetrable black scaly armour. Abu Youssef used a clever ploy to rescue Amir. He knew that Ishaq's one weak spot was his fear of fire. So Abu Youssef followed the lizard man across the stormy sea to Paris, where the dealer intended to negotiate the sale of his extraordinary asset to the circus director. Then Abu Youssef challenged Ishaq to a duel. It took place at the Arc de Triomphe by the light of the full moon. Abu Youssef defeated his rival by forcing him into the eternal flame that burns in the Tomb of the Unknown Soldier.

All sons love their fathers, I believe, but I positively adored mine. He allowed me into his wild fantasies; he took me with him to worlds of wonder fabricated in his head; he intoxicated me with his words. He had made me promise something else early on—never to tell Mother what his stories were about. "If she finds out that I'm telling you stories about men who change into lizards every full moon, I'll get into trouble," he said with a wink. I nodded vigorously and promised to keep our secret.

Yasmin knew all about Abu Youssef too. She was green with envy when I told her Father was going to tell me a new episode soon. "Will you tell it to me later?" she asked. Her eyes gleamed like a sunlit lake. We had developed our own ritual. Father would tell me a story, and I'd then retell it to Yasmin. This made me proud to be a storyteller too, and I loved it when Yasmin listened as I repeated Father's words. She'd close her eyes tight and listen intently, and I could almost see the magic worlds opening up inside her head. It was as if we had created our own theatre, and Yasmin was the lighting, the stage, and the audience. I had no stories of my own yet, just my voice, my body. So a little boy would stand in front of a little girl and wave his arms about to represent the wind blowing in Abu Youssef's face, or dance on tiptoes to show how he crept up on an enemy. I whispered when Abu Youssef whispered, and I screamed when Abu Youssef screamed. Yasmin loved it, and nothing could beat her peals of laughter and applause at the end.

The first snow arrived a few days after my birthday, like cotton wool drifting down from the sky. It settled on the rooftops and the now bare branches of the trees, transforming everything into a glittering wonder. I woke up to the sound of a snow shovel on the pavement and sat up instantly. From my window I could see Hakim, his ears bright red, clearing the snow off the pavement. He waved up when he saw me. "Didn't I tell you the snow wouldn't be long in coming?" he shouted and laughed. I laughed too. Frost flowers had grown on the windowpane overnight. They were my favourite flowers, partly because you didn't have to water them.

That afternoon Hakim took Yasmin and me up the nearby hill to try out my sled. We sat one behind the other, with Hakim puffing and panting as he hauled us through the snow. Father didn't come. By now I'd almost grown used to his strange moods. The day after he'd promised to tell me another story, for example, there he was, pacing up and down again like a caged animal. The telephone had rung a little while earlier and Mother had answered it. She'd said "Hello?", repeating it in a loud voice several times, then hung up. Around half an hour later, Father slipped out of the flat. I knew he was going to ring Grandmother, but I resisted the urge to tell Mother she needn't worry.

Besides, the arrival of the snow meant there were far more important things on my mind. When I'd come down in my snowsuit, Yasmin was already out the front in her red hat and gloves, armed with a perfectly formed snowball. Now we were sitting on my new sled, urging Hakim to pull us faster, and roaring with laughter when he whinnied like a horse. We lost track of time as we whooshed down the slope over and over again. The air was cold and clear and full of shrieks of joy. Our cheeks were red, our eyelashes frosted over, our noses ran, but we barely noticed. Winter had come, the time for family fun. The air smelled of cinnamon and tangerines instead of damp cold and dead leaves, of log fires and cloves instead of chestnuts and musty earth. We left sled tracks in the snow. We were happy.

The hours flew by, and suddenly we realised it was dusk. "That's enough for today," shouted Hakim, his eyes gleaming with the cold. "There's plenty of winter yet. Next time we'll take the car and find a bigger hill." We protested, but only half-heartedly, as we could feel a pleasant tiredness taking hold. If Hakim was tired, he didn't show it. He just whinnied cheerfully and pawed the snow before pulling us home.

When we got home, the smell of hot punch already filled the whole stairwell. Yasmin and I pushed past each other into our flat, quickly discarded hats and gloves, and clambered out of our snowsuits. Mother was already waiting with two steaming mugs.

"You're frozen to the bone," she remarked, stroking our cheeks.

We were indeed, and all the more glad to wrap our hands round the warm mugs. Hakim closed the door behind us and knelt down to pick up the hats and gloves we had carelessly tossed on the floor.

"Give that pair a sled and a hill and they don't just forget the time, they forget their manners as well."

Mother smiled gratefully, relieved him of our things, and handed him a mug of punch. He closed his eyes and held it to his cold cheek. Then he followed us into the kitchen.

"Where is Brahim?" he asked, poking his head into the living room.

"He's not back yet," said Mother.

"When did he leave the house?"

"This morning."

Hakim raised his eyebrows and looked at the clock above the kitchen door. It was just after six. He'd been gone over seven hours.

"Do you know where he went?"

"No."

Mother sighed. Hakim frowned and took a seat. Outside, darkness had descended.

Mother turned to us. "Tell me all about the snow." She gently pushed a lock of Yasmin's hair out of the way before she bent over her cup.

We regaled her with our adventures on the slopes, each trying to outdo the other's descriptions of breakneck speeds and spectacular falls into the deep snow. Even Mother laughed out loud when we described our draught horse, Hakim. She really was so pretty when she laughed.

We sat in the kitchen for about an hour, drinking punch and eating our supper. Then we went into the living room. Yasmin and Hakim had gone downstairs briefly and reappeared in cosy sweaters. The four of us were wrapped up on the sofa now, the warmth of the heating behind us and a soft blanket tucked round our feet. Yasmin and I had found some notepaper and were making out our Christmas lists. I wanted a bike and Yasmin wanted a new schoolbag. Hakim was asking Mother about her sewing and her latest ideas. He had one of her sketchbooks on his lap and was running his flat fingertips over the drawings as if he could feel the fabrics' weft and weave. Mother was using the drawings to explain the different steps in her work and telling Hakim about a Christmas market where she was hoping to buy material at a keen price. Hakim already knew about the market. His boss had suggested that he carve nativity figurines to sell there and asked if that would be a problem for a Muslim. It was no problem for Hakim, of course.

We were so absorbed that we never even heard Father coming in. I've no idea how long he had been standing there before we noticed him. Mother startled as if she'd got an electric shock. Hakim looked up and the sketchbook fell from his hands. Yasmin dug her nails into my arm. Father stood there in the doorway, staring at us like we were ghosts. His clothes were all wet and crumpled, his face as grey as a November morning. Time seemed to stall for a moment. Water dripped from his hair and beard onto the wooden floor. A puddle had already formed around his feet. Then he closed his eyelids, raised his hands, and pressed the insides of his wrists to his temples, as if he'd felt a jolt of pain. It was as if he couldn't bear the sight of us and hoped we'd be gone when he opened his eyes again. But we still sat there, motionless, staring back at him. He lowered his hands, turned, and stumbled out of the room. A few seconds later we heard the click as he locked himself into the bathroom.

When I was younger still—three or four maybe—I almost drowned. It was summertime. A small river flowed through our town, and its grassy banks were very popular once the weather grew warmer. On a sunny day you'd see couples sprawled on rugs rubbing sun cream on each other's backs, popping luscious strawberries into each other's mouths, and gazing at each other with bedroom eyes. Youngsters with blaring boom boxes cooled their beers in the water; toddlers in nappies waddled across the grass, trailed by tail-wagging dogs; young guys playing football in their swimming trunks grinned cheeky apologies when they happened to hit the bikini-clad girls feigning disinterest at the edge of the pitch. Old folks summoned their dogs in vain when a refreshing dip proved irresistible; back on the riverbank, the dogs would shake rainbows of water off their fur. That's the kind of day it was. The sun shone so brightly that the water sparkled like a shop window full of diamonds.

We were a bit late getting there. The best spots along the riverbank—where the water was shallow and perfect for a quick dip—were already gone. We carried on upriver until we found a spot where the grass hadn't been flattened by too many towels. We spread out our rug. Father set up the barbecue and lit the coal. Mother sliced carrots and cucumbers. And I fell into the water. I'm hazy on the details now, but I remember the water being extremely cold and swallowing me up, and then the current sweeping me away. I have a memory of Mother's voice shouting Father's name, but that could also be my imagination. In any case, I saw Father jump fully clothed into the water and swim after me with powerful strokes. He made several attempts to grab hold of me before he eventually succeeded. He held me tight with one arm and slowly swam to the river bank with his free arm. Mother was in an awful state. She wrapped me up and rubbed me dry. As I sat there bundled in my towel, I looked up at Father, standing in the sun, soaking wet. I remember the water dripping from his clothes and beard, but the look in his eyes was very different that day. That day he was smiling.

It was a whole hour before Father came out of the bathroom. Hakim and Yasmin had left. I sat at the door, listening to the muffled sounds of the shower. Mother paced up and down the corridor. She had hastily knotted her woolly red cardigan round her waist. She kept running her hands through her hair. Eventually she told me to get up off the floor and go to my room. I pressed my ear to the bedroom wall but couldn't hear a thing. I was scared and confused. I'd never seen Father this way, so frightened, so vulnerable. As if he'd used his last reserves to escape from some dark torture chamber, or been chased through the snow by ghosts he had barely managed to shake off. I wondered what kind of terrible news he must have got in that phone call to come home in such a state. My vivid imagination conjured up the worst for Grandmother in Lebanon. Maybe she'd told him she was very ill; maybe she'd said that this might be their last phone call. I imagined how sad this made Father, how he'd dropped the receiver, slumped to his knees, then staggered out of the telephone box and spent hours wandering aimlessly in the cold dark night.

As I stood there with my ear pressed to the wall, I realised I was shivering, covered in goose pimples. I wished it would all stop, that he'd come out of the bathroom, hug me and Mother, kiss our foreheads, and tell us that that was the end of his strange behaviour. I wished he'd come out and say sorry for hurting us again and again.

The bathroom door opened moments later. I heard Mother say something but couldn't make it out. I resisted the urge to run out to them. I wanted him to come to my room. I wanted him to see how much he'd scared me, to sit down on my bed and talk to me, tell me what was wrong. I lay on my bed and stared at the door handle in the hope that he'd press it down and walk in. If he did, I'd quickly turn to face the wall so that he'd only see my back and would have to ask me how I was. But he never came. I heard two sets of footsteps heading for my parents' bedroom, and Mother speaking again. She sounded very upset. Soon after that, I heard their door opening and Father coming out. Mother stayed behind.

This time I couldn't resist. I darted out of my room and tugged him on the sleeve. He had changed into brown trousers and a check shirt, and smelled of shampoo and soap.

I whispered so that Mother wouldn't hear. "Is Grandmother sick?"

He shook me off.

"Not now, Samir. Not just now ..."

I wasn't giving up. I tugged at his sleeve again.

"What happened to you?"

"Nothing, Samir. I had a fall. It was nothing serious."

He took a few steps but I clung to his sleeve.

"But it looked serious."

"Listen, *habibi*. Go back to your room, please. Get into bed."

"But why?" I fought back tears of rage. I was sick of it, sick of trying to figure out what the point of his weird behaviour was. I wanted him to be himself again, immediately.

Father blinked nervously but his voice was calm and almost affectionate. "So that I can come to your room later and tell you the story."

He was standing in a semi-circle of light, silhouetted by the hall light behind him.

"Abu Youssef?"

"Yes. The next episode is ready."

He looked me in the eye, for the first time in ages. His gaze was unfathomable, alternating between sheer exhaustion and firm resolve.

"Can't you tell me the story right now?"

"Later, Samir. There's something I have to do first."

"What?"

"I need to see Hakim. To tell him he needn't worry and to apologise if I gave him a fright."

I nodded. Hakim and Yasmin had been very puzzled leaving our flat. She'd held his hand and kept looking back at me. Still, I held on to my father's sleeve and looked up at him.

"But you'll come back, won't you?"

He took a deep breath.

"Yes, Samir. I'll only be down with Hakim for a few minutes, then I'll come to your room."

I let go of his sleeve.

"Can I come with you?"

"No. I won't be long."

"Promise?"

"I promise. You get yourself ready to hear the story. It's about Abu Youssef's treasure."

"His big secret?"

"Yes, his big secret."

He swallowed.

"Go to your room and wait for me. I'll be back in no time."

I did what I was told, and I heard our front door open and close.

This time, though, I had no intention of letting him go alone. I wasn't going to let him out of my sight. I knew in my heart that he hadn't really been chased in the dark by sinister characters. It was just my imagination playing tricks. But what if it wasn't my imagination? Then they'd be out there waiting for him. They might have followed him all the way into our building and be lying in wait in a dim corner of the stairwell. And if they were hiding there, he'd need my help. I decided to follow him.

As soon as he was gone, I sneaked to the front door in my slippers. I opened it a crack and saw him disappear at the turn of the landing. I darted into the stairwell and stood with my back to the old wallpaper. I could still hear his footsteps and counted them as he descended. Too many steps—he had gone past Hakim and Yasmin's door. That meant he'd lied to me. My heart was thumping so loudly I feared it would give me away. But there was no time to lose. I had to catch him before he got away from me. This time, I wanted to be by his side if anything happened. I peered round the corner to see if the coast was clear. Then I tip-toed down the stairs, following the creaks of his footsteps. My heart was racing and I hardly dared to breathe. For a second I was sure I'd lost him because the sound of his footsteps suddenly died. I was at the front door of our building now, at the bottom of the stairs, but the door was shut. That only left the stairs to the basement, but there was no light coming from there. I don't think there even was a light down there. Suddenly I heard a sound, a bit like the squeal of wet brakes. I recognised it; I'd heard it a lot when we moved in. Father had opened the door to the basement.

It made me think of Yasmin, of the pair of us flitting around the haunted labyrinths in our old complex, following the strange smells that wafted through the walls. I wished she was by my side right now. She was far better at creeping up on people than I was. There was no way I could follow Father into the basement. The squealing door would give me away. He'd want to know why I followed him, why I didn't trust him. He might decide to punish me by not telling me the story. It wasn't worth the risk. Besides, I had no great desire to go down into the dark, dank basement where you could easily trip on the loose flagstones. Undecided, I looked around. Where should I go? Back upstairs until I heard him leaving the basement? But what if he slipped out the front door instead? I had no jacket; it would be crazy to follow him outside. Should I nip upstairs and get my jacket? But what if he left the basement in that space of time? What if Mother saw me and stopped me? What was he looking for anyway? As far as I knew, all we had in the basement were flattened-out removal boxes and a few smaller boxes storing stuff we didn't need all year round, like Christmas-tree baubles, straw angels, and old crockery. I decided to wait, trusting that I'd be quick enough to react according to the situation. The light in the stairwell timed out, and I was left waiting in the dark.

It didn't take too long. Ten minutes maybe. Ten minutes of sitting anxiously near the front door while my eyes got used to the dark. Then I heard the squeal again and Father closing the basement door behind him. This time I even heard the key turn and the lock click. I was already on my feet. The light came on again; he had pressed the switch. Once I heard him make his way upstairs again, I was certain that he wasn't going to leave the house, that he'd come back to our flat. So I withdrew quickly and silently. This time Father did stop outside Hakim's flat. I heard him knocking on the door. I peered cautiously round the corner. He was standing beneath the weak light bulb waiting for someone to open the door. In his two hands he clasped a rectangular object wrapped in black cloth. I couldn't see his face because he was looking down at what he had in his hands. I hadn't the faintest idea what was under that cloth. A gift to apologise to Hakim maybe? He knocked again. I heard steps and saw the door opening. Hakim was in his pyjamas, looking like a ragged seabird that's come through a storm. The two men exchanged a long look without saying a word. Then Hakim nodded silently and stepped aside.

If you sit in one spot for a long time, you see things you never noticed before. You wonder how this can possibly be, since you've passed this spot a thousand times. I noticed for the first time the fine structure of the wallpaper in our stairwell. It was made up of lots of little joined-up diamonds that looked like they'd been embroidered. I'd never noticed the big grey dust balls in the corner of the staircase either. I took in every detail of my surroundings. Then the light went out. I didn't dare turn it on again, so I started trying to identify animal shapes in the fine cracks in the wall—a squirrel, for example. But I grew bored once I realised I was only trying to distract myself. I stared at the outline of the door through which Father had disappeared. How I'd have loved to put my ear to it to hear what they were saying. Their muffled voices would have calmed me. But I couldn't risk it. If Father found me here, he definitely wouldn't tell me the story. And I had really earned it.

I felt entitled to it. So I stayed put on the stairs, even though I'd much rather have been inside with Yasmin, under her warm duvet. I'd love to have been able to tell her she needn't worry, that the whole thing with Father wasn't so bad after all, and that I'd tell her the Abu Youssef story the next day. It would be very special because it was going to be about Abu Youssef's secret treasure. I could already see her listening to me, throwing back her head and laughing at the funny bits. When she'd left our flat holding Hakim's hand, her eyes had looked frightened and kind of sad too. She was probably wide awake in bed now, wondering what I was doing. The urge to sneak in to her was almost irresistible. But the door was closed. Yasmin was on the other side, and so was my father. There was no way I could go in.

Who knows how long I sat there. The silence was like a vacuum, an eternity. Eventually my eyelids grew heavy. I nodded off several times, waking up whenever my chin lolled onto my chest. I was neither asleep nor awake but drifting in half-sleep, until the murmur of voices filtered through. I woke with a start and opened my eyes wide. I clenched my fists and tensed my muscles, ready to sprint upstairs. I recognised Father's voice, talking to Hakim. It was interrupted occasionally by what sounded like a short question; then Father's voice again, firm and insistent. Eventually, the door opened a crack, though no one came out. Instead, I thought I heard a sob.

"Promise me," I heard Father say, followed by louder sobs. The door opened a little wider. Now I could see the two of them. They held each other in a long embrace. Then Father took Hakim's face between his hands, and his old friend looked at him with tearful eyes.

"Promise," whispered Father.

Hakim nodded.

They looked at each other as if it was a staring contest.

Then Father turned away. Hakim, tears creeping down the creases on his cheeks, hesitated on the threshold before closing the door. I saw Father rub his eyes, straighten his shirt, and press the light switch. He must have left whatever he'd been holding in Hakim's flat. He looked up the stairs and took the first step, but by then I was well gone.

Back in my room, I stripped off my clothes and jumped into bed all out of breath. There was no sign of Mother. I could hear Father's heavy steps, then the sound of the front door closing. I forced myself to breathe slowly. Father took his shoes off in the hall, then opened the door of my room enough to stick his head in.

"Samir?"

"Yes?"

"You OK?"

"Yes, I'm fine. Are things OK with Hakim again?"

"Yes. All sorted. Are you still awake? Do you still want the story?"

"Of course I do."

Father smiled.

"OK. I'll be with you shortly."

He came back a few minutes later wearing pyjama bottoms and a soft sweater. I moved over so he could sit on the edge of my bed. I looked at him and tried to tell from his eyes whether he'd seen me out there, whether he knew that I'd followed him. There was no indication that he had.

"Why did it take so long?" I asked. When I saw him flinch, I added, "To finish the story?"

The light from my bedside lamp was reflected in his eyes.

"Good stories take time," he said, "I had to do a lot of thinking about Abu Youssef."

"So did I."

"But now the wait is over."

"About time too."

"Are you sure you want to hear the story?"

"How do you mean?"

"Well ..." He shrugged his shoulders and held out his hands, palms up. "I mean, maybe you'd rather keep it for another day?"

"Are you mad?"

"Once I've told it, the balance in the story account will be back to zero."

"I don't care."

"Is that how you treat your piggybank as well?"

"Piggybanks don't tell stories. Come on—please!"

Father pulled the duvet up around my shoulders and smiled.

"One day you'll put your own children to bed and tell them stories."

"You think?"

"Absolutely. It's a wonderful thing, you know. You'll spend lots of time thinking up stories, and your children will never forget them."

I liked that idea. Me, Samir, a discoverer of imaginary worlds, a storyteller like my father. I lay on my side and tucked my hands under my pillow. I was ready. Right now, it no longer mattered that his behaviour had been so strange. Whatever it was that had made him so cold and distant, it didn't matter anymore. He was here now. In my room, on my bed, with me. He had brought Abu Youssef along too. That was all that mattered.

10

Abu Youssef's return to Beirut was triumphant. News of his victory over the cruel Ishaq had spread like wildfire. When the assembled crowds caught sight of his ship approaching the harbour, they cheered with joy, waving bright banners and the Lebanese flag. Abu Youssef and Amir were on deck, delighted to hear the sound of cheering on the wind. The sails billowed in joyful anticipation and the coast grew closer by the minute.

"They love me!" cried the camel, baring his magnificent teeth in a shiny grin and waving one hoof at the crowd. Loud cheers erupted in response.

Abu Youssef stood silently on deck. Nothing was more beautiful than Beirut from the sea. The legendary Pigeon Rocks towering in front of the coastline, the skyscrapers glittering in the sunlight, the mountains rising up behind them, beyond the glass facades. He loved coming home, returning to his treasure.

Once they'd disembarked, Abu Youssef and Amir made their way through a forest of arms and hands. Everyone wanted to touch the heroes and clap them on the back. Amir was happy to give the odd autograph, but Abu Youssef was keen to get home without delay.

"Don't you want to celebrate with us, Abu Youssef?" the people said. "Don't you want to sing and dance with us all night? Don't you want to celebrate your good fortune?"

Abu Youssef replied, "Yes, I do, but not now and not here. If you want a real party, then gather on the street below my balcony at midnight. I'll show you the meaning of true happiness, and I'll dance and celebrate with you till long after dawn."

Amazed, the people wondered what this could possibly mean. Was Abu Youssef planning a party in the city? He had a small flat in Beirut, everyone knew that. And everyone knew his balcony because it was the only one on the street—and also because, in the right light, rumour had it, the balcony shone like it was made of pure gold. But Abu Youssef spent very little time in this flat. If he was going to throw a party, he preferred to do it in his village in the mountains, where he'd invite all his friends to join him.

The news travelled through the streets and alleys like a leaf on the wind. Children shouted it to their parents; the parents told their friends; and soon the whole city was bursting with excitement. "This evening," the people cried, "Abu Youssef is going to show us the meaning of true happiness."

Abu Youssef rode into the mountains on Amir's back. He had reached a decision. At first he'd thought it would niggle at him for a long time, but now that he knew what he had to do, he felt very calm. Back home in his village, he fed and watered his faithful friend Amir, then disappeared into his house.

He did not reappear until dark. And he was not alone. The stars shone down on his little homestead; the village lay deep in sleep. Under cover of darkness, two figures and the camel set off for the city. Even from a distance they could hear the murmur of voices as the side streets and alleys filled up. People streamed from the surrounding neighbourhoods into the centre, to the street where Abu Youssef's flat was, the building with the shimmering balcony. The camel and the two figures took shortcuts and secret paths so as to reach the house undetected. Clever Amir had tied cloths around his hoofs to muffle the sound. He reached his long neck round every corner and gave a discreet whistle when the coast was clear. They had a few near misses, but Abu Youssef and his companion were able to duck behind Amir's humps. In this way, they made their way through the streets and to the back entrance of the house.

The air in the flat was stale, like a big wardrobe that hasn't been aired for years. It was a long time since they'd been there. Through the closed shutters, they could hear eager voices calling Abu Youssef's name.

Abu Youssef signalled to the other person and gave a questioning look. His companion nodded. Slowly Abu Youssef opened the balcony door. The babble of voices died instantly. It was as if the whole city lay in silence. Not for long, though, because no sooner had Abu Youssef stepped out on the balcony than riotous cheers erupted. The sound of rejoicing swept through the streets again and shook the houses to their core. Fathers put toddlers on their shoulders so that they could see. Everyone was waving and calling out Abu Youssef's name, and he waved back.

Then he held up a hand. At this signal, the cheers dried up like a drop of water in the desert.

"My dear friends," he said, allowing his gaze to wander over the waiting crowd, "I'm so pleased that you've come." Everyone was staring up at him. No one dared to speak; no one wanted to miss what Abu Youssef had to say. He carried on, in the slow and deliberate manner he was known for. "There are two kinds of feelings associated with the word 'farewell'. A farewell can be sad because what you are leaving behind is so precious and important that you are loath to leave it. But a farewell can also be happy, because the power of what lies ahead does not stir sadness but joyful anticipation. Life is full of farewells, and our feelings change with each parting. But the word 'homecoming' is different. Why? Because we really only come home once. But where is home? They say home is where the heart is. You only come home once because you only have one heart, and it's your heart that decides." His eyes swept over his intent audience once more. "At least that is what I always thought," he said. "I thought you only have one heart, and therefore only one home. But I was wrong."

Abu Youssef turned from the crowd to face into the flat and held out his hand. Dainty fingers reached out to take his. Then a delicate figure in a veil joined him on the balcony. A loud murmur went through the crowd.

"I've had many adventures," said Abu Youssef, still holding the woman's hand. "And many of you have wondered about the wealth I'm supposed to have amassed, along with all the honour and glory. Many of you think I must live in the lap of luxury, in a palace with servants and date palms and a gold nameplate at the gate. But the truth is, I haven't got a bean. And yet I am the richest man on earth. Standing here, looking down at all of you, I see many wealthy men. Men who have more than one heart."

He turned to the petite figure who had been standing a little behind him and drew her closer. He took off her veil and revealed a woman as beautiful as any legend. Her hair was jet black and held by a golden clasp, her eyes were Mediterranean blue, and her skin as pure and white as marble. Everyone held their breath, afraid to exhale in case they might blow the delicate creature off the balcony. No one would have been the least bit surprised if she had suddenly flown away like a fairy.

"This is my second heart," said Abu Youssef. "My wife. And if you want to know what true happiness is, you must always remind yourself that you have more than one heart to which you can return." He smiled gently. "I have three of them. Three hearts."

With that he removed the woman's cape, and they saw a sleeping baby in her arms.

"My son!" said Abu Youssef.

The sky lit up all of a sudden. Fireworks transformed the street, the houses, the whole city into a dazzling spectacle. Blazing rockets whooshed into the sky, not just in the city centre but on the outskirts too, as if a crown of light was hovering over Beirut, turning night into day. Celebratory shots rang out in the sky, echoing off pavements and over walls to fill the air with thunderous noise. From the gardens to the rooftops and beyond, the night was full of shouts of joy. You could not fail to hear them. Red and yellow lights flared up and danced in the half-light. Suddenly, in this riot of colour, the balcony turned gold and shimmered as never before. It gleamed so bright that the people nearest had to shield their eyes. It lit up the street and bathed it in a deep gold that could be seen from a great distance, from as far away as the edge of the city. Its message was clear: Here stands Abu Youssef with his treasure beside him. He has come home to his three hearts.

11

"Am I your heart?" I mumbled, barely able to keep my eyes open.

"You are my greatest happiness," he whispered.

I was already half asleep, drifting in that pleasant land of shadowy darkness, transported there by his voice and the pictures he'd painted. It was a story of reconciliation, showing me how important we, his family, were to him. How important I, his son, was. And how he loved coming home to us, his hearts, no matter which adventures he'd just experienced within himself.

Father kissed my forehead. It was the last kiss I got from him. A feeling of utter contentment settled on me like a downy quilt tucking me in. Then he ran his fingers through my hair. It was the last time he'd do that. He smoothed my duvet one last time and turned out the bedside light.

"Sleep well, Samir," he whispered. He stood up and looked round at me one more time. "I love you."

Those were his last words.

Through a heavy veil, I could see him standing in the doorway. My eyelids grew heavier and heavier, as if a lead weight was pulling them down. If I'd known that these were the last few seconds I'd have with my father, I'd have made more of an effort. I'd have tried to look at him for longer, taking in the thick eyebrows above the friendly brown eyes set in a round face. I'd have tried to memorise how he looked so that in the weeks and months to come, when I'd wake from a dream he appeared in, I wouldn't panic and forget to breathe for fear he'd slip away. So that the teenage me wouldn't despair when I could no longer remember his face, just a blurry impression of it. So that I wouldn't keep cursing myself, years later even, when I couldn't remember how deep the creases at the corners of his mouth were when he laughed. How many lines his forehead had when he frowned. How far his Adam's apple protruded when he threw his head back to laugh. Whether he might have been greying at the temples. Or had a birthmark on the back of his neck. What direction the lifelines on his palms took when he waved his hands in the air. Which hand he used to stroke his beard. Exactly how his voice sounded when he was telling a story. I would have opened my eyes wide and looked at him and registered it all. So that I'd never forget. I would have forced myself to look at him. But I was too sleepy. And so the last I saw of my father was his silhouette in the doorway and him—so I believe—looking at me fondly.

II

There's something you should know: you're not the only one looking for your father.

1

I'm woken by someone knocking at the door. Quiet, discreet knocks. A moment ago, they were part of my dream, but now they've reached the surface of my consciousness. I jolt awake. Where am I? My skin is sticky with sweat, the sheet rumpled. White bedlinen. On the nightstand is a telephone next to a white lamp. White curtains too? They flutter in the breeze at the open window. On the other side of the room, a white desk next to a white wardrobe. The room feels clinical, like a conference room or a laboratory. The knocking starts again, louder than before. I start. There's a stabbing in my head, as if shards of glass are flying around inside, and my lips are dry and cracked.

"Not right now, please!" I shout.

No answer, but I hear footsteps retreating down the hall. I sit up and massage my temples.

Slowly, it all comes back to me.

The air smells unfamiliar. I'm rattled by how strange it feels to be here. I hear noises outside, the clamour of voices. I try to distinguish the sounds: revving engines, beeping horns, mopeds clattering, sirens wailing in the distance. Voices layered on top of each other, like at a market. A loudspeaker briefly clicks and crackles, and a second later a song floats into my room. It sounds like a slow lament.

Allahu akbar, ashadu an la ilaha ill-allah.

The muezzin calling for prayer. The words themselves have never meant anything to me, but I've always loved the way they sound.

I'm really here, then. The wind carries the call from the minarets of the Mohammed al-Amin Mosque down to me, mixing it with the noise of the city to create a sublime melody. I sink back into my pillow and close my eyes.

Ashadu ana muḥammadan rasulu-Ilah.

Memories pin me to the bed. I exhale and feel the tingle of goosebumps. It's as if for years I've only ever seen a cheap reproduction of a precious painting, but now I have the original in front of me, far more awe-inspiring and beautiful than I could ever have imagined.

When the call to prayer fades away, I throw the duvet aside and sit up. The rucksack beside the bed catches my eye. The airline tag is still attached to the strap. I go into the bathroom. Toiletries are arranged on the shelf above the sink: a nail file, soap, body lotion, and a folded hand towel. BEST WESTERN HOTEL. My swollen red eyes look back at me in the mirror.

Later, I scan the lobby for his face. Hotel staff push luggage trolleys through the foyer. A cleaner with a blue bucket wipes the windows. A man on a black leather armchair near the entrance reads a newspaper, two women with headscarves and red fingernails tap at their smartphones, and a child tries to reach the coin slot of a candy vending machine.

He's not here. I can't see him anywhere.

"Eight o'clock, no problem," he said when he dropped me off yesterday. It's almost 8:30 now. I'm late. I put my rucksack on the floor in front of the reception desk.

"I'd like to check out, please."

The young woman looks at me and gives a business-like smile. I can smell her perfume, which I suspect all the female staff here wear, as it pervades the entire hotel. Sweet and milky with a harsh edge, it's a typical hotel smell, designed to be registered briefly and immediately forgotten, yet strong enough to disguise the odour of carpets and cleaning agents.

"Did you have a pleasant stay, Mr. ..."—she looks at the computer screen—"Mr. el-Hourani?"

"Yes, thank you."

"Breakfast is served until ten. The breakfast room is on the first floor."

I'm not hungry; I can feel the tension in my stomach.

"Can I do anything else for you?"

I notice a little black dot on her eyelid and imagine her kohl pencil slipping as she was getting ready for work this morning.

"No, thanks."

From the reception desk I can see another part of the foyer. Men in suits sit on the leather armchairs, looking at laptops or holding mobile phones to their ears. He isn't among them. I turn back to the receptionist.

"Excuse me, was there a man looking for me earlier by any chance?"

"Someone looking for you? Not as far as I know. Just a minute. Hamid ..." She turns to a colleague who's pulling a suitcase out of the storage room. "Has anyone been asking for Mr. el-Hourani?"

"No," her colleague replies.

"Sorry," she says. "Have you got a number for him? I can call him if you like."

"No need, thanks."

He never gave me a card anyway.

The main door keeps opening and shutting, letting travellers and warm air in. Outside, the sun's shining. It's like walking into a hot, damp towel. The heat is so overwhelming that I barely hear the doorman's "Have a good day, sir." It's nearly nine o'clock. Above me, the hotel's logo emits a bluish-yellow gleam. Cars and mopeds speed by. Expensive pictures are on display in a window across the street; *Anaay Gallery*, an elegant font above the door announces. Next door, there's a McDonald's. Men with trendy beards wearing muscle shirts and sunglasses amble down the footpath. They look like surfers, like California beach bums. In fact, apart from the suited business people clutching briefcases as they frantically wave down taxis, the neighbourhood ahead of me looks more than modern; it actually seems pretty hip. A group of young women in blouses and miniskirts glides past me. They're followed by a man in a dirty white T-shirt pushing a cart full of oranges, sweat glistening on his forehead. I watch the girls nimbly skip out of the way as a man pours a cascade of water out onto the street. Through the shimmering air, amid the jumble of buildings, I make out the turquoise domes and two of the four towers of the Mohammed al-Amin Mosque. The street sign reads Bechara el-Khoury. It's surreal to be here at last. The city doesn't smell like I thought it would. I expected the aromas of falafel, thyme, and saffron, smells that had always filled our street. But it's hot and sticky here, and it smells of exhaust fumes and dust. It doesn't sound like I expected, either—not like animated chatter in cafés and music, not like the plucked string of a lute or qanun. It sounds like any other big city.

I shift indecisively from one leg to the other. If he's just late, it would be a mistake to set off on my own now. But it's already past nine. I've probably missed him.

Was he the person who'd knocked on my door earlier? Probably not, seeing as there was a laundry trolley and a vacuum cleaner in the corridor; chamber maids at work. Plus he would have had to ask for my room number at reception. We barely know each other. No, there's no point in waiting or looking for him any longer.

I'm here. In Beirut. For the first time in my life. Everything is foreign and new yet oddly familiar, like bumping into a once-close friend whom I haven't seen in a long time. *Home,* I think. *This is home.* Although my roots are here, it feels strange, unreal. Like in a long-distance relationship, when you spend the first hours of each reunion getting used to each other again, remembering familiar caresses. *So that's what it looks like when you smile.* Except this isn't a reunion.

"Hey … what are you doing here?" A dusty old Volvo is crawling along beside me. It seems out of place in this gentrified street. The cars behind it brake and beep. It's the same car, the same guy who brought me here from the airport yesterday. "It is you, isn't it?"

I slow down. The man leans across the passenger seat and shouts through the open window: "Didn't we arrange to meet in the hotel?"

Astonished that he's appeared here out of the blue, I feel like I've been caught red-handed.

"Yes, we did."

"At eight o'clock, right?"

"That's right."

"And look, here I am, as promised."

"Eight o'clock," I repeat.

"What time is it?"

"Almost half past nine."

He laughs.

"Welcome to Beirut! Get in."

The car jerks to a halt and the beeping around us becomes louder. The car is now blocking the street, and the other motorists have to cross into the other lane to get past. I flop into the passenger seat. It's even hotter in here than out on the footpath.

"What's wrong with your eyes?" he asks.

"Air conditioning," I say, throwing my rucksack onto the back seat.

He shrugs. This is the first time I've seen him in daylight. He has a moustache and four- or five-day stubble on his cheeks. I'd guess he's around fifty. His hair is greying at the temples and there are fine lines around his eyes. He has the friendly face of a man who takes his kids to watch football or films at weekends and buys them candyfloss. He's wearing washed-out jeans and a cardigan over a grey-and-red checked shirt. Too many layers for this weather.

"I'm not sure I introduced myself properly yesterday," he says, holding out his hand. "I'm Nabil."

"Samir," I say as the car pulls off.

"So Samir, what can I do for you?"

The question catches me off guard, mainly because I don't know the answer yet myself. He approached me yesterday in front of the official taxi rank. The night was orange, humid, and warm, in startling contrast to the cool, neon-lit terminal. He came up to me and offered to take me into town for a fraction of the usual price. I hadn't booked a hotel, so he recommended the Best Western and drove me there. Just before we arrived, I told him I'd need a driver the next day and asked if he could pick me up in the morning.

Nabil noticed my hesitance.

"How about I show you the city?"

We follow the dense flow of traffic. Massive waves of glass and concrete rise up beside us: skyscrapers, banks, hotels, office blocks, and apartment complexes with penthouses, everything ochre-coloured, clean, modern.

"That there," says Nabil, pointing through the windscreen, "is the Mohammed al-Amin Mosque."

I studied my guidebook during the flight here; the

mosque was number six on the map of the city's attractions. "First time in Beirut?" the blonde woman in the window seat beside me had asked as she eyed my book with curiosity. "Yes," I answered, feeling like a damn tourist. "This is my fourth visit," she said. "The first time was in the sixties, before the war. They've rebuilt it beautifully. Really, they did a great job. If you're looking for a good place to go shopping,"—I noticed a reddish-gold bracelet glinting on her wrist as she spoke—"go to Hamra. It's full of designer stores, boutiques, malls, jewellers ..." "Thanks for the tip," I said, swiftly putting on my sleep mask.

Bechara el-Khoury Road takes us right up to the mosque. There is something almost obscenely beautiful about the two blue domes rising from the surrounding sea of ochre. In the early morning light, the stone looks golden.

"I heard the muezzin earlier," I say, as if that's a noteworthy occurrence in a city like Beirut.

Nabil looks at me.

"Are you Christian, then?"

I don't reply. It's been ages since I prayed in a church. I find the hymns oppressive. The way they echo in the hollow spaces of cathedrals and abbeys, reverberating off the intimidating stained-glass windows and marble floors, it makes my chest constrict, and the congregation's reverent silence is always a bit too deferential for my liking. The muezzin's song, on the other hand, has always seemed like the call of home. Anything that sounds, smells, or tastes Arabic has that effect on me. It casts a spell.

"Rafiq Hariri is buried here," Nabil says. In front of us, the mosque thrusts its minarets into the Beirut sky.

I shudder. The assassination of Rafiq al-Hariri changed so much for me personally.

The traffic creeps towards the Martyrs' Monument like a reptile made of tin. Traffic lanes seem to be an alien concept here; the cars simply squeeze alongside each other to form as many lines as will fit. I see traffic lights, but none of them work. A man in tattered clothes carrying a bucket and a squeegee appears and, without consulting us, starts cleaning our windshield. Nabil shoos him away.

"Hariri rebuilt everything. That," he says, drawing a line in the air with his hand, "was the Green Line during the civil war. Christians to the east, Muslims to the west."

The heat is fierce, and we're moving so slowly that no air is coming in through the windows. I wipe the sweat from my forehead.

"I can drive you around for the whole day," Nabil says. "My kids are going to my brother's place after school. I kept the day free for you—I wasn't sure where you wanted to go."

I'm not sure either. None of this was planned. The last twenty years of my life weren't exactly planned either. I don't know if I'm ready for this.

"Can we get out of the city?" I ask abruptly.

Nabil raises his shoulders.

"Lebanon is a tiny country, my friend. We can go wherever we want."

I swallow.

"The cedars," I say. "How far is it to the cedars?"

The city flies past us like a sandstorm. We've taken the Ahmad Moukthar Bayhoum motorway southwards from the mosque. Huge billboards line our route, forming a gaudy avenue—Pepsi, 7up, Armani, Chanel, Rolex, Montblanc, Middle East Airlines, and colossal posters advertising American movies. The further we drive, the shabbier the buildings become. Nothing remains of the warm ochre lustre of the city centre; instead, all I can see is drab grey sandstone. Corrugated-iron shacks are dotted between tower blocks, knots of cables dangle from windows like bird's nests, faded laundry hangs on rusty iron grilles between water canisters and piles of rubbish. The contrast between the glamorous billboards and their surroundings soon becomes absurd. On the footpath, I see three women shrouded entirely in black. Above their heads, a massive poster on the wall of a tower block shows a model lounging seductively in transparent lingerie. VICTORIA'S SECRET, it reads, 25% OFF BRAS AND PANTIES. A few metres on, when I get to see the front of the building, I realise it's little more than a skeleton. Bombed out and empty, the former apartments like missing teeth in the crumbling facade.

Nabil follows my gaze.

"Not everything was rebuilt," he says.

We keep heading south. The city centre shrinks in the rear-view mirror. Soon entire towers fit within its frame. The sea is to the right, but I only catch the odd glimpse of silvery blue, as the road is still densely lined with buildings. Almost every tower block here bears scars; the craters made by rocket launchers disfigure the facades like an ugly rash. I recline my seat, close my eyes and feel the wind stroking my face. All I want to do is sleep.

"Stupid jackass, son of a camel!"

I jump.

"May thousands of flies fart into your father's beard!"

Nabil pounds the steering wheel and beeps the horn.

"What's wrong?"

"He didn't indicate," Nabil complains, pointing to the silver Mercedes with tinted windows that's overtaking the cars ahead of us.

I stare at him. He shrugs.

"I try to set a good example for my kids. I say, if you must go joyriding in my car, then at least follow the traffic laws.

That means you have to indicate. Then they look at me and say, 'Traffic laws?' Do you know how many road fatalities there are here every year? Nearly eight hundred. No one in this country indicates. Most people think that little stalk is an ejection button or something."

"Do you curse like that in front of your kids?"

He shrugs again, but this time he's smiling. It makes him look much younger, almost impish, an adult fenced in by responsibilities and routines who makes the most of the little moments when he can break out.

"Your Arabic is pretty good," he says, nodding at me approvingly.

"Thanks."

"Are you Lebanese?"

Now there are hardly any high-rises to the left of the motorway. They've been replaced by run-down buildings bordering heaps of rubble, and by smaller shacks, with children playing football between the piles of rubbish out front. Dogs doze in the shadows.

"Is this still Beirut?" I ask.

Nabil nods.

"Refugee camps."

"Syrians?"

"Palestinians. Third or fourth generation by now. Syrians too, but there aren't as many of them. Over there," he says, pointing out his window at the corrugated-iron roofs melting into the horizon, "that's Sabra and Chatila."

Sabra and Chatila. Their very names send a chill down my spine.

We drive on in silence. I don't know what to say, and Nabil seems to be reluctant to badger me with too many questions. He has pulled down the sun visor and is staring resolutely ahead. When he catches me looking at him, he glances over and smiles. I turn away in embarrassment. After a while, he starts squirming in his seat. The silence seems to unnerve him.

"So, Samir, what are you here for? Business?" he eventually asks, making an obvious effort to sound casual.

The question was bound to come up sooner or later. Still, it makes me uneasy.

"No."

"Holidays?"

I think about whether to lie or not.

"No. I'm looking for something."

"For a nice hookah?"

"For a person."

He takes his eyes off the road and peers at me.

"Are you a private investigator? Like Sherlock Holmes or Philip Marlowe?"

"No, no, nothing like that."

"I love Philip Marlowe." I believe him; he sounds like a boy squealing, "I love water slides!" He drops his pitch to an unexpectedly gravelly drawl and says, "Heat cloaked the city like melted cheese on a Hawaiian pizza." He draws an arc with his arm as he speaks, as if he's standing on a hill and gesturing at the valley below. "Crazy guy, Philip Marlowe!" he says, laughing.

I don't really want to tell Nabil what I'm looking for, and he seems to have picked up on my reticence. But now the topic is lurking in my head like a spider in a web, and I can't stand the silence any longer.

"I want to get married," I blurt.

"Ah, so you're looking for a woman! Why didn't you just say so?" Nabil bangs on the steering wheel, accidentally sounding the horn. "Would you like me to introduce you to my sister?"

"No," I say. "No thanks ... I already have someone." I pause before adding, "It's a bit complicated."

I can practically see it right in front of me: the pretty blush my proposal painted on her cheeks. I see us standing on the riverbank and her giving me back the ring. I think about the task she set me. About her ultimatum. "We both know you're not ready for this yet," she said. "You need to sort your own life out first, Samir. I don't know what you'll find there or whether you even know what you're looking for. But if this is what you need to do, then do it."—"Don't you want to come with me?"—"No." She paused and added, "There's nothing there for me."—"But I don't know how long it's going to take," I said. "Will you still be here when I come back?"—"It doesn't matter when you come back. The question is *how* you come back."

"It's always complicated," Nabil says, nodding as if he's just solved a difficult equation. So simple, a universal sentence capable of ending any awkward conversation.

"Where are we going?" I ask.

"Didn't we decide to drive to the cedars?"

"Yes, but I mean where exactly?"

"Maasser el-Chouf." He nods towards his side window. I hadn't noticed how much the traffic had thinned. The sparkling blue sea is to our right, and a mountain towers to our left. We turn off into a badly tarred, potholed side road, and soon we are lurching our way up a winding mountain pass.

It takes me a moment to realise the song isn't playing in my head. How strange to hear it again here, now. It's disconcerting. I force myself to keep my eyes open, because I'm afraid that images of a happy childhood will start to flash before me: walks on summer days, singing together. My body rigid, I stare at the radio as it broadcasts first the melody and then her voice: *Sa'aluni shu sayir bi-balad al-'id, mazru'ata 'addayir nar wa bawarid, 'iltilum baladna 'am yakhla'jadid, lubnan alkarāmi wa al-sha'b al'anid.*

"That's Fairuz," Nabil says, adopting the tone of someone who has just had their first sip of an exceptionally rare wine. He turns up the volume. "The Harp of the Orient."

"I know," I say. There's a hairpin bend in the road ahead. Cold sweat breaks out on my forehead, reminding me of the many nights I've woken up screaming. "I know this song."

2

We waited forty-eight hours before calling the police. I knew from films that you're supposed to wait at least twenty-four hours before reporting someone missing. We waited twice as long. I remember the sealed emptiness of the flat as I walked around in my pyjamas the next morning. The kitchen tap was dripping, and there was a bowl of oatmeal and a carton of milk on the table for me. In front of the bowl, a note from Mother: *Back soon.* I remember her returning a little later with Alina in her arms, putting down her shopping bag and casually asking where Father was, her brow furrowing when I shrugged, pointed to the key rack beside the door, and said, "I don't know, but he forgot his key."

It's painful to think that we went tobogganing again after breakfast. We took the car this time, just as Hakim had promised. Yasmin and I giggled and played around in the snow while he sat a little apart and watched us pensively. And it's painful to look back now and understand why his behaviour was so different that day: why he barely spoke a word, said yes to everything we asked for. In my childish excitement over the snow, I didn't give a minute's thought to his tears the night before.

I remember that Father didn't cross my mind the whole day. I had no doubt he'd return that evening, maybe even with another story for me. But it turned pitch-dark outside and I stayed up way past my bedtime, and still he didn't come back. When I finally fell asleep beside Mother on the couch, she carried me to my room. It wasn't until the next morning that I realised his shoes still weren't in their usual place in the hall and his jacket was still missing from its hook.

Apart from the absence of these two items, there was nothing to suggest he wouldn't come back. I simply did not grasp—and in fact, would never fully grasp—that he'd disappeared. When I took Alina from Mother and walked around the apartment gently rocking her, it never occurred to me that she would grow up without a father. Or that he wouldn't see Alina take her first steps, wouldn't hear her say her first word. That he wouldn't be there for her first day at school, wouldn't sit in the audience and clap at her first school play. That he wouldn't be around when she brought her first boyfriend home and danced at the school prom.

Nor would he ever know how I cut my chin the first time I shaved. How my first kiss was with a girl called Hannah, how it was sloppy and tasted of cola-flavoured Hubba Bubba. I'd never have dreamt back then that I'd come to curse my own father for what he did to us, for what he continued to do to us every day in the years that followed, even though he wasn't around anymore. I didn't grasp that life as we'd known it was now over. Even on the second day after he went missing, I had no doubts he'd return. The story he'd told me had been a declaration of love, a vow that nothing comes before family.

The police were perfectly friendly. Two officers stood in front of Mother, questioning her in calm but insistent tones, one of them noting down her answers. Had anything like this ever happened before, had he had an argument with her or anyone else? Did he have friends he could stay with, had he mentioned anything about wanting to go away? And could she provide them with a recent photo? Mother answered all their questions patiently. I sat on the floor in the corner of our living room, eyeing the men and their heavy boots and uniforms. They knocked on Hakim's door afterwards, but I don't know what he told them. Half an hour later, I peeked out the window and saw them get into their patrol car and drive away. Needless to say, the neighbours had spotted the police car and knew that something was up.

Brahim the storyteller had gone missing—the news swept through our neighbourhood like a tsunami. I realised then just how popular he'd been. The baker put a few extra bread rolls and a stick of rock candy into my bag, and strangers stopped me on the street to tell me how their paths had crossed with my father's. Their parting words were always, "I hope he comes back soon, I really do," or "He was—I mean, he is—a great guy, your father." Months later, copies of his photo were still hanging on almost every streetlamp and traffic light. It was as if he'd merged with the town itself. It was as if he'd left not just Mother, Alina, and me behind, but every single person in our neighbourhood.

One day, a group of teenagers stood in front of our building. I recognised them; one was the boy with the horseshoe-shaped scar. When they rang the bell, I opened the window and looked down.

"We're going to look for your father," they said. "Want to come?"

In their black bomber jackets, their arms folded, they stood there in a semicircle like a gang. In reality, they were puppies trying to convince themselves they were bulldogs. We each carried a stick and tramped through a dense little wood, poking around in the snow as we went. That's what you do when someone goes missing; the boys had seen it in films. We walked side by side in silence, the cold air making our noses run. The only sounds came from the frozen ground crunching beneath our feet and our sticks prodding the snow but failing to find anything.

"Remember the time Brahim organised a table-tennis tournament?" one of the boys said after a while. His name was Milan, I think, and he was Czech.

"Yeah," said another boy. "He even got a trophy, engraved and everything."

"I still have it at home," said the boy with the scar. "I thrashed you all."

"Only cos you kept spinning the ball, you moron."

"So? There's no rule against that."

A few more anecdotes about my father followed. They told stories and nodded along like old friends sitting around a campfire remembering the good old days.

I listened, biting back the tears. It had soon become apparent that they never really expected to find Father out here. They'd just wanted to do something, contribute in some small way.

The police came by a few more times to ask questions. They even searched the wood themselves, and a few weeks later, when a walker found a jacket similar to Father's near the lake where we'd launched our little ships, they sent out divers, who found nothing. No one found him. There was still no sign of him after the snow melted, uncovering the fields and the first snowdrops, nor when spring dotted the same fields with crocuses, bluebells, hyacinths, and later lilies of the valley; still no sign of him come summer, when children played football in those fields; and no sign when autumn leaves began to cover the grass. He remained lost without a trace, like a sunken ship.

That's when the nightmares started. The nights when Mother rushed to my bed because I couldn't stop screaming until the light was turned on. The horrible dreams in which I saw Father lying face-down in a grave at the side of a desolate road or bobbing at the bottom of a lake, his eyes bulging and shackles of weeds around his feet. My head was filled with such images because during school breaks, the other boys would speculate about what had happened to him. When they noticed me, they'd elbow each other in the ribs and look down in embarrassment. Some days, Mother would have to come pick me up from the principal's office. With sad, dull eyes, she'd murmur a quiet apology before taking me out into the corridor and forcing me to shake hands with whichever boy I'd got into a scrap with.

It was around then that I started wetting the bed too. This was followed by a series of other firsts: the first Christmas without him, the first New Year's, the first summer, and, eventually, my first birthday without him. I couldn't do anything without thinking that the last time I'd done it, I'd been with him: going to the outdoor pool; buying ice cream in the parlour that sold the crazy bright-blue flavour we used to call Smurf; going for walks and singing out loud. I went through various phases, including one in which I clung to Mother, refusing to leave her side for a second. Afraid that she, too, might shut the door behind her and never return, might vanish like window frost in the sunlight. If she told me before she left the house that she'd be back at seven, by ten past I'd be on the phone, ringing every number in our address book in a panic, trying to find out where she was.

Not even Yasmin could console me. Once, in the cold blue mist of a spring that had arrived late that year, she took my hand, but I shook her off and walked alone across the field, half-hoping she'd follow, half-relieved when she didn't. Whenever she peeked into my room, where I spent much of the time brooding on my bed, I'd pretend not to see her, fixing my eyes on a spot on the floor so that I didn't have to look at her. And I stopped walking to school with her. I'd walk alone instead, looking behind me every now and then to see her following from a safe distance.

She was always tiptoeing around me, ready to step in if anyone started giving me a hard time, always ready to help. But I found her presence painful; I couldn't bear it. Once, when she told me I hadn't smiled in a long time, I snarled back: "That's all right for you to say, you still have a father!" I knew she was hurt, but she didn't let it show, which made it even harder to put up with her, because it showed she was so much stronger than me. I would have liked to behave differently. But I couldn't, because I was afraid she'd ask about the last Abu Youssef story, the biggest secret my father and I shared.

3

Our route is narrow and rocky. Children play at the side of the road, and Nabil does his best to avoid the potholes.

A little while ago, we overtook a roaring, clapped-out delivery lorry as it dragged itself up the mountain. Piled on the flatbed was a metre-high stack of furniture, on top of which perched a girl with black pigtails and a goat, both staring at us in bewilderment. The city lies far behind us. All I can see in the mirror now is the road snaking behind us, and beyond it, the sea. We pass the odd squat house, cube-shaped and whitewashed. The landscape is dominated by citrus groves and boulders. My memory of the city smells fades as we ascend. Pines and broom are dotted across the mountainside, releasing their own wonderful scent.

It's not even sixty kilometres from Beirut to Maasser el-Chouf, yet the journey takes us over two hours. Nabil beeps the horn several times whenever we approach blind bends in case another car is trundling towards us. But the higher we get, the less traffic we encounter.

The air is clear and cold; I could do with another layer of clothing.

"This is the most peaceful place in Lebanon," Nabil says in a relaxed voice, as if he's wrapped in a bathrobe and sprawled on a lounger. "No noise, no cars. It's totally unspoilt around here." He slows down and pulls in at the side of the road. "Here we are." I remember Father telling me many times how, as a young man, he'd sought refuge in the silence of the cedars and looked out on the countryside unfurling below him. And it really is peaceful; were it not for the chirping of crickets, the silence would be palpable.

"There aren't many places like this left in Lebanon," Nabil says. He points up a steep track. "Shall we?"

Here, at a height of almost 2,000 metres, I can see the entire country for the first time. Or at least, that's how it feels. A long, shimmering strip of coast stretching out left and right. Beyond that, the azure sea and foamy white crests of incoming waves. On the shore, miniature harbours and towns gleaming like silvery pearls. Green fields and terraced vineyards on the hillsides. And below me, bathed in the brash midday sun, Beirut, with its sphinx-like, self-assured smile.

The cedars are truly breathtaking. Nabil lets me go ahead and trots behind, his hands clasped behind his back as if he's meditating. For a while, he kicks along a stone. I'm filled with awe. I've pictured this moment so often, seen myself walking along this very route, observed myself as if I were sitting on the branch of a cedar. Now that I'm really standing here on this soft dark-brown earth, I can see how close the reality is to my dreams. Cedars all around me, some over forty metres tall. Their trunks are so thick it would take an entire football team to embrace them. The spicy smell is intoxicating. They've grown old and wise standing watch over the country down the centuries.

"The trees are five to six hundred years old on average," says Nabil. He has stopped a few metres behind me and is smiling, delighted that he can teach me something. "Though some of them are over a thousand years old."

I can't help it; I see Father before me, leaning against a trunk, a blade of grass in the corner of his mouth as he looks down on the city.

"This trunk," says Nabil, pointing to the cedar in front of me, "has split into three sub-trunks. That means it's between two thousand and five thousand years old. It's hard to determine the exact age."

"How come you know so much about these trees?"

Nabil's smile grows even wider. He was clearly hoping I'd ask.

"My father was a cedar guardian."

"You mean a Guardian of the Cedar, during the war?"

"Oh no, of course not!" he says, raising his hands, "We're Muslims."

The Guardians of the Cedars, a far-right, nationalist, Maronite Christian party, were one of the many militias involved in the Lebanese civil war. I know this because over the past few years I've spent more time whispering in libraries and delving in dark archives than I've spent with my fiancée. In 1976, the Guardians of the Cedars took part in a massacre at the Palestinian refugee camp Tel al-Zaatar. Today, they are fighting Bashar al-Assad in the Syrian civil war.

"My father was a repairman, but during the war he had a side line in fruit and cigarettes," Nabil says. "He made a good living. There were always things that needed fixing, and no one was prepared to do without fruit or cigarettes."

I nod.

"Cedar guardian ..."

"Yes." He stops and looks at the trees as if they're close relatives. "The cedars are under threat. The guardians make sure that they survive, plant new trees, and keep an eye on the stock. And, like all guardians, they have to deal with intruders."

"What kind of intruders?"

"Goatherds."

"Goatherds?"

"Yes. They drive their herds into the newly planted areas because every time the forest expands, the goatherds lose pastureland. So, they let their goats eat the saplings." He looks around. "My father became a cedar guardian at some point after the war. He was too old for big repair jobs, and cigarettes and fruit were available everywhere, so he was looking for something else to do."

The trees are so mighty, so noble. It's hard to imagine they might be gone one day.

"Climate change is the biggest threat," Nabil says, reading my mind once more. "The ideal altitude for cedars is between 1,200 and 1,800 metres."

"How high are we now?"

"Around 1,400 metres. That used to be ideal, back when the snow arrived on time and lay on the mountains for ages. The ground stayed damp and cold for several months. Cedar seeds can only germinate when it's cold, which means ..." He looks at me, like a teacher prompting a pupil.

"... that their natural habitat keeps shifting to higher ground," I respond.

"Exactly." Nabil nods. "But the Lebanon Mountains only go so high. If there's no rain in summer, and the trees can't even draw moisture from mist in the spring, sooner or later there'll be no more cedars."

It's a horrible thought. My image of Lebanon is inseparable from these giants.

"They're so beautiful," I say, more to myself than to Nabil. "And they really do look like the ones on the flag."

Nabil nods again.

"That's why we call them 'flag-shaped'. Ground water can only nourish the tree up to a certain height." He looks up at the trunk in front of us. "Eight to ten metres, maybe. Then the tip of the tree dies and the spread of the lower branches gives the cedar its distinctive shape." He traces the horizontal layers of branches with his finger.

We walk for a while, crossing fields and narrow trails. I try to imagine how it might look here one day: the grass tall and wild, the cedars withered or vanished entirely; no more snow-covered mountaintops, just scree and sheer rocks. What would that mean for a country whose identity, whose very name—Land of the Cedars—is synonymous with this tree? The cedar is on everything, from stamps to banknotes. Lebanon—a country without a name?

"Don't look so glum," says Nabil, patting me on the shoulder. "We'll be long gone by the time the last cedar disappears. These trees are much tougher than us. Maybe the sea will reclaim the coast, and everything will go back to how it was in primordial times." He laughs light-heartedly. Strange as it sounds, it's comforting to think that we humans won't be around to see the cedars die out.

Later, we sit on the grass, our backs against a thick tree trunk, and look out to sea. Nabil has fetched savoury pies from the car.

"My wife made them," he says, handing me one. It's filled with spinach and sheep's cheese.

I think of Mother and how she used to make these pies while I tugged at her apron in excitement. When she wasn't looking, I'd stuff my mouth with sheep's cheese before she noticed anything and sneak out of the kitchen, chewing contentedly.

"What else are we doing today?" Nabil asks.

I like the fact that he says "we." But once again, I'm aware that I don't have a plan. All I have is a vague idea, though who knows where it will lead me.

"I need to go to Zahle," I say.

"Zahle," he repeats. "That's sixty kilometres or so. From here we'll have to take mountain roads, though, so it'll take about an hour and a half." He looks at his watch. It must be early afternoon by now. "I'm happy to drive you," he says, "but how much time are you planning to spend there?"

"I don't know." I look down. "Depends on what I find."

4

I'd never bothered much with friends, and now I was paying the price. I spent most of my time alone, obsessing about Father not being here anymore. The silence he'd left behind spread like deadly nightshade.

I'd always found it hard to make friends, even when he was around. The only thing I had in common with my classmates was our route to school. On the rare occasions when I found myself standing around with a group of kids in the schoolyard, I'd keep quiet, my hands in my pockets and eyes on the ground, present but not really there, giving the odd nod, acting as if I knew who'd scored the best Bundesliga goal over the weekend, pretending I'd seen the latest Schwarzenegger film too, and yeah, the explosions were cool, and sure, I'd snuck into the cinema with a friend of a friend who'd bought us tickets. In truth, I wasn't in a football club, I didn't play any instrument, and I didn't have video games at home. I couldn't join in the conversation, but then there had been no need to when Father was around. There had been no reason to concern myself with the outside world. On our street, I had everything I needed to be happy: warmth, togetherness, fun. I had my father and Yasmin, and sometimes Khalil, the diabolo expert. That was enough for me.

But now I couldn't even look Yasmin in the eye. A gulf had opened up between us. I avoided her, partly because I was afraid she'd ask me about the story, and partly because I was beginning to grasp what it must have been like to grow up without a mother. This newfound understanding should have brought us closer together. I could have looked at Yasmin and taken heart: in spite of all she and Hakim had been through, she'd turned out to be a joyful, strong, happy girl. That could have lifted my spirits, given me hope that things would get easier one day. But it never even occurred to me. My fear of getting close to her was mixed with shame, shame that I'd never shown her the kindness she was now showing me. It made me turn away from her even more, until I realised I was completely alone.

After Father disappeared, it felt as if the outside world no longer existed, or at least as if it was oblivious to what was going on in our street. People simply carried on as if nothing had happened. My greatest fear was that no one would remember him, that he'd be forgotten like a rainy day in April, so I saw it as my duty to mourn him for as long as I could. I carried my grief around with me like a bowl of tears, shuffling through the streets with my head down, avoiding eye contact. At school, I spent most of the day staring out the window. The teachers wrapped me in cotton wool, warning the other kids to be nice to me and not to mention Father when I was around. My grades had never been very good, and the teachers were afraid my performance would slide even further if they didn't watch out for me. I tried. I really did. But when I attempted to strike up a conversation with the other kids, to talk about things I thought they'd be interested in, I sensed a barrier going up. Their replies were terse, as if each word was one too many, as if there was a danger I'd take what they said the wrong way. No matter what I did, I would always be the boy whose father had disappeared.

Miss Lisewski, the maths teacher who sang silly songs to

help us remember our times tables, always came over to me at breaktime when she spotted me standing alone in the corner of the yard. She was a tall woman, not very pretty. Her eyes were too far apart. Rumour had it this was the result of an operation she'd had to catch children cheating in exams, especially the ones who sat by the walls. No other teacher embodied their subject quite like Miss Lisewski, whose head was always bowed, like the number nine.

"Don't you want to play with the other children, Samir?" she'd ask. What she really meant was "Off you go, Samir, play with the others!", so I'd do what I was told. I never felt like I was really joining in, though. Despite my lack of talent, I was passed the ball more often than many other kids, and I was never fouled or jostled. The layer of cotton wool around me seemed to unnerve my classmates. They had plenty of opportunities to tease me during these football games, but they didn't dare. Sometimes, as they challenged each other for the ball, I'd look through the tumult of kicking legs and spot Yasmin with a group of girls, watching me. When she caught me looking at her, she'd smile and wave, but I always pretended not to notice.

Laura's birthday marked a turning point. After that, I stopped harbouring any desire to be less alone.

A few weeks after the Easter holidays—our first Easter without Father—I developed a routine for when the final bell rang at school. I'd put my books, pencils, and copybooks into my schoolbag as slowly as possible and stay in my seat until all the other kids had left the classroom. It was the same every day: chairs were scraped back, the volume suddenly rose, rucksacks were opened and copybooks thrown in, jackets were zipped up, and excited conversations were carried out of the room and down the corridor.

I'd usually wait until the teacher asked me to leave, gently explaining that she needed to lock up. If I could still hear my classmates' footsteps echoing in the corridors, I'd kneel to tie my laces. I'd try to waste as much time as possible before starting my journey home. That way no one would see me when I walked out into the schoolyard alone, and I'd spare myself a sight I dreaded: other children running past me into the arms of their parents. Mothers kissing their kids, taking their schoolbags and walking with them to the car park. Fathers laughing and shadow-boxing, putting their arms around their sons' shoulders and driving them to music lessons or football.

At first, I kept a lookout for him. I'd scan the grown-ups deep in conversation as they waited for their children, hoping to spot him among them. I'd convinced myself that the first thing he'd do on his return was pick me up from school. But as time went by, I began to realise that I was no longer sure what he looked like. I still had the photo of him at home in my little wooden box. But he was a young man in the picture, and there were times I couldn't bring myself to look at it. Just holding the box was enough to make me burst into tears. Every time I picked it up, I noticed its smell had become a little fainter, fading just like the picture of him in my head. There came a point when I could no longer call to mind the exact shape of his face. I couldn't remember what his laugh was like. It felt like he was behind a fogged-up window, darting past while I tapped on the pane, trying to get him to stop. No matter where I went, I saw him. If I stopped to look in a shop window, I'd see a reflection of him walking down the opposite side of the street. If I looked out the classroom window, I'd see him standing behind the big oak tree by the fence. And if I missed my bus, I'd see him looking out the back window, waving to me as it pulled away in the pouring rain. That was why I decided to spare myself some pain and wait in the classroom until everyone was gone.

One day, I was sneaking downstairs, my footsteps echoing in the empty stairwell. A usual, I'd dilly-dallied for as long as I could, giving the schoolyard plenty of time to empty before I set off home. But this time, there was a woman standing at the bottom of the stairs. She had paper-white skin, shoulder-length blonde hair blow-dried to perfection, and lips as red as a field of poppies. She looked like a 1950s film star, her pink dress forming a startling contrast to the school's drab grey walls. She studied me with green cat-like eyes. I stopped in my tracks. My classmate Laura was standing beside the woman, blinking at me. I glanced around, but there was no sign of anyone else. It was clear they were waiting for me. The woman put her manicured hands on Laura's shoulders and gently pushed her towards me. Laura cleared her throat and held out an envelope.

"I'd like to invite you to my birthday party," she said. "I'm going to be nine. It's at my house, on Saturday."

The show of friendship caught me so off guard that for a moment, all I could do was stand there and stare.

"Really?" I said eventually.

Laura didn't react. She just kept holding out the invitation. She and her mother resembled Russian dolls, the smaller a near-perfect copy of the bigger one, the only difference being that Laura's lips weren't quite as red as her mother's.

"Oh," I said, taking the envelope from Laura. It was pink, like her dress. "Thanks." It occurred to me that this was the first time she'd ever spoken to me.

"It starts at two o'clock—it says that on the card anyway. We'll have lunch and cake, so you don't need to eat beforehand," she said. "And we'll all play games and things. It'll be fun." She turned to her mother, looking for reassurance that she'd recited her little speech correctly.

"And?" her mother prompted.

"And it would be great if you could come," Laura added. The woman behind her nodded with satisfaction.

Embarrassed, I turned the invitation over and ran my finger along the embossed paper.

"I'd love to," I said and attempted a flustered smile. I'd barely finished speaking when Laura turned on her heel and floated out through the school foyer like a piece of pink chiffon. Her mother glanced at me once more.

"See you on Saturday, Samir," she said and left me standing there alone.

"Laura Schwartz?" asked Mother when I handed her the pink envelope. I'd only noticed how heavily scented it was when I got home. Mother didn't know the names of my classmates. I never talked about school, and it had always been Father who'd gone to parent-teacher meetings. Mother read the card, unable to suppress a little smile. She was clearly proud that I'd finally been invited to a birthday party, but she was trying not to make a fuss. She didn't want to emphasise how unusual it was.

I was pretty proud of myself too. I was delighted, in fact. Laura inviting me to her party seemed like a sign that things were going to get better from now on. Easier. Less lonely. Me, Samir, captain of the Phoenician walnut-shell ships, setting sail for new shores. I'd always secretly admired Laura, possibly because she was so different from me. I'd often observed her in the yard during breaktime and noticed how she drew both girls and boys to her like the sun. Everyone wanted to be friends with her, to be pulled into her gravitational field. Everything came easily to Laura. She glided effortlessly through the corridors, her eyes glazed with the kind of arrogance that comes when your parents tell you you're the centre of the universe. Her house was rumoured to be the nicest in town, not that I knew anyone who'd actually been there. When teachers asked what we'd done during the school holidays, Laura would always be the first to put up her hand. She'd regale us with tales of holiday homes in Miami and Florence, of sailing around the Côte d'Azur with her parents. Her father was an American diplomat, her mother a porcelain doll. Her surname was Schwartz, and she insisted that everyone pronounce it the American way, which I liked because I was fascinated by exotic things. I think the only reason her parents didn't send her to a private school was that they could be sure she'd outshine the rest of us, at least when it came to wealth.

"I bet you'll have a great time, they sound very nice," Mother said, putting the envelope aside. She stroked a strand of hair off my forehead and handed me back the invitation.

I was nervous. I'd never been invited to a birthday party by a kid from school before. It had never occurred to me to invite classmates to my own birthday parties either. I'd always just celebrated with the people from our street, so Laura's invitation was a big deal.

I thought long and hard about what to get her. I figured Laura was the kind of girl who already had everything she could possibly want.

"How about making something yourself?" Mother asked.

I liked the idea of giving Laura something she wouldn't be able to buy in a shop. I decided to bake a cake especially for her. Mother helped me, but I did most of it on my own. I stood on a stool in the kitchen and carefully placed lots of raspberries on the sponge base. I then covered them in cream and wrote "Happy Birthday, Laura" in chocolate sprinkles on top. Finally, I stuck in nine candles, the kind that are hard to blow out.

On Saturday, Mother laid out my shirt and belt and combed my hair before disappearing into the bathroom for what seemed like an eternity. When she reemerged, she was wearing make-up and her pretty blue dress. She smoothed it down one last time as she inspected herself in the mirror. She'd even put on her perfume. It was as if she was the one who'd been invited to the party.

We drove to a part of town I'd never been to before. Big, beautiful houses with white facades lined the street, gleaming like limestone palaces. The air in front of the windows shimmered, ornate columns flanked the entrances, and expensive-looking tables and loungers adorned the balconies. Trees towered over the front gardens, where flowerbeds glowed like rainbows. The smell of freshly mown grass drifted through my open window. We drove past a gardener in a round straw hat who was standing on a ladder and trimming a hedge. This street was another world. Wide and almost clinically clean, it had nothing in common with ours. An alley lined with birch trees. Cadillacs, Porsches, and every Mercedes model imaginable sparkling in covered driveways. My mouth hung open in amazement. Mother parked in a side street, too embarrassed to drive our old Toyota right up to the house. We walked the rest of the way. I held Laura's cake out in front of me, so afraid of dropping it that I started to sweat. I wanted to fit in here, maybe even be invited back sometime, so I had to make sure I didn't mess up this immaculate street with raspberries and cream.

The house was easy to spot. The brightly coloured balloons tied to the garden fence were dancing in the breeze as if they were party guests. The dazzling white house was three storeys high, with arched windows and curved French doors leading out to a balcony on the second floor. A fountain stood in the middle of the wide path sweeping up to the front door. It was guarded by imitation Greek statues, youths in stone tunics armed with bows and arrows. They glared down at me, and I could still feel their eyes boring into my back as we approached the house. Mother walked slowly, looking around her as if she'd just set foot on another planet. We went up the marble steps to the front door. Mrs. Schwartz flung it open before we even had a chance to ring the bell. Behind her, I could hear children shrieking as if they were at a funfair.

"Samir!" she said.

"Hello Mrs. Schwartz," I said, doing my best to pronounce her name like an American.

"Look how cute you are in your shirt! You're adorable," she said, stroking my combed hair like I was a guinea pig. She glanced at Mother, who was standing nervously behind me. "Mrs. el-Hourani, nice to meet you." She took a step out of the hall.

"Hello," said Mother, shaking the proffered hand. "Thank you for inviting Samir."

I'll never forget her standing there, awestruck, between the columns of a house that must have seemed like a palace to her. All done up in her best dress, with her lightly accentuated eyes and her perfume, so smart and pretty: it had been ages since I'd seen her look like that.

"Laura insisted he come," Mrs. Schwartz said. "We're delighted to have him. Laura, Samir's here!"

Laura was wearing a white dress. A garland of flowers sat atop her blonde hair, making her look like a young bride, or a fairy on her way to a secret party in an enchanted forest.

"Happy birthday," I said shyly.

"Happy birthday," Mother repeated and waved at Laura.

Mrs. Schwartz flashed a quick smile. She was the kind of woman who thinks there's a photographer hiding behind every bush, the kind of woman who expects to see her face on the front page of the newspaper the next day. Her smile was a perfectly choreographed dance between the two corners of her tired-looking mouth. Paying no further attention to Mother, she said, "Well then, Samir, in you come."

I stepped into the marble hallway. Through the cut-glass pane in the front door, I caught a glimpse of Mother raising her hand to wave goodbye. It was like looking through a prism.

The walls were covered with pictures of Laura: Laura at the seaside; Laura at the top of a skyscraper, a miniature city behind her; Laura on a ship. She led me through bright, spacious rooms with high stucco ceilings and elegant oak cabinets shining in the afternoon light. Cosy, chintz-covered armchairs were tucked into the corners of the living room beside shelves lined with thick green-bound books. On the other side of the room I spotted a Steinway grand piano and a music stand next to a palm tree that stretched up to the ceiling. I pictured Laura sitting in front of the piano after school, her mother standing behind her as she practised. We passed through some more rooms, past Chinese vases, statues, and a chaise longue adorned with meticulously positioned cushions. I wondered if anyone had ever actually dared to sit on it. A painting of a naval battle hung above the chaise longue. A man was standing at the bow of a ship, brandishing a sword as he roared and pointed towards another ship while thick smoke billowed from the mouths of canons. I followed Laura through this unfamiliar world of wealth. My feet sank into the soft carpet, the air was clear, and warm light shone in through the huge windows.

Light-footed and self-assured, Laura kept striding ahead.

Throughout the house, artefacts from foreign lands were tastefully exhibited on walls and in display cabinets. Laura led me past them as if she were a museum guide. Every now and then, she pointed something out. "My father brought that back from India," she said as we passed a cane topped with a gaudy snake's head. Later, she waved towards a headdress spiked with multicoloured feathers and explained, "In Brazil, newborn babies wear that. Crazy, huh?"

It was crazy indeed. Dumbstruck, I nodded.

"Have you ever been abroad?" She turned and flashed me a curious glance.

I shook my head.

"You mean you've never been outside the country?"

"No."

"Oh my God, why not?" She waved an imaginary fan as if she was about to faint.

"I don't know." I wanted to tell her that living in our street was like living abroad. That it was full of the smells of other countries and that the people spoke lots of different languages. That it was wonderful and mysterious, not like here at all.

"You really have to travel," Laura sighed. "I can't imagine the world without other countries."

"I will, for sure," I said, as if I were making her a promise. "Thanks for inviting me, Laura."

She looked at me for a moment as if she hadn't caught what I'd said. Then she stepped towards me, coming so close that her lips almost touched my ear, and whispered, "The others can't wait to see you."

I'm sure the birthday cake was delicious, but I can't say for sure what it tasted like, as I didn't get any. I behaved exactly the way I'd been taught to. Whenever I would visit Lebanese friends with my parents, I'd always turned down a slice of cake three times. This was considered good manners. At Laura's party, I showed what a polite guest I was by giving Mrs. Schwartz the chance to show what a good hostess she was. But after I turned down the cake a second time, she stopped asking, so I just sat there with my hands folded in my lap, waiting for the game Laura and the others had been talking about so cryptically. Nobody wanted to try my cake, but Laura's mother assured me they would have it for breakfast.

"It's going to be so much fun, this game," said Nico, a boy from our class. A crumb of chocolate cake was stuck to the corner of his mouth. It looked like a beauty spot. Nico was the class clown. He never did his homework; he just copied it from the other kids. He was brilliant at PE and getting into schoolyard scraps, though. He was probably invited to all the kids' birthday parties. "You're in for a surprise," he said with a wink. Laura and the others tittered.

"What are we going to play?"

"Hit the Pot," Laura said. "Know how to play?"

"Yeah, sure."

"But our version has really special presents," Nico said, and everyone started giggling again.

They seemed genuinely pleased to have me there. When I'd walked into the room, they'd all run over to me, shouting "Samir, you made it!"

To my surprise, I was having a good time. This was something new, meeting my classmates outside school. I felt like I was one of them, even though I didn't say much. I mostly just listened, ready to give a polite answer if anyone spoke to me.

When everyone had finished eating, we trooped out into the garden. Laura, who was carrying a pot, a spoon, and a scarf, led the way. We then took turns being blindfolded. The player wearing the blindfold had to crawl around, hitting the neatly trimmed grass with the spoon until they found the pot. Meanwhile, the rest of us helped by yelling "warm" or "cold," but if the player looked like they were going to find the pot too easily, we'd misdirect them a little. It was a lot of fun. Laura hid a different present for each guest under the pot. It was her way of thanking us for coming. Nico got one of those football magazines you stick pictures of players into. Sarah was thrilled to discover a friendship book. Sascha got a little 3D puzzle of the Eiffel Tower, and Sophie, who liked drawing, got a Diddl Mouse notepad. Laura had chosen something special for everyone, something she knew would make them happy.

I was the last to be blindfolded. Up until then, I'd been giving tips with the rest of them and cheering as each player found their prize.

"It's your turn, Samir," Laura said.

"Yeah, Samir, you don't have a present yet." Nico looked at me, his head cocked.

I nodded in excitement and rubbed my palms together. Nico stood behind me as he tied the scarf around my eyes. Everything went black and I felt his breath on my ear. "It wasn't Laura's idea to invite you," he whispered. "Her mother made her." Before I could react, he pushed me onto the ground.

I groped around, blind and confused. I wanted to ask Nico what he meant, but the others were yelling, "Come on, Samir!", so I started crawling across the damp grass. When the children clapped and shouted "Cold!", I turned around, striking the ground with the spoon all the time. The others sounded so loud in the dark. They were screeching like birds of prey. I scrambled around, trying to follow their contradictory directions. *It wasn't Laura's idea to invite you.* What had Nico meant? The heat of the sun was scorching my back, and I had broken out in a sweat under the blindfold. The voices hammered down on me as the spoon missed the pot again and again. None of the other kids had taken so long to find it. I was just about to give up when the others cried, "Warm, warm!" Shortly afterwards, the spoon struck metal.

"God, that took forever," I heard Laura say as I pushed the scarf up off my eyes and saw the pot in front of me. The others formed a circle around me. Nico was standing with his legs spread wide. Laura's eyes had become cold and were fixed on me. The others were staring too, waiting for me to lift up the pot.

Nothing could have prepared me for what I found. Humiliation engulfed me like an avalanche. I tried not to cry, gasping for air in an effort to stop the tears. But they brimmed over anyway, and I crumpled, my strength sapped, mortified that I'd walked right into their nasty trap. How could I have been stupid enough to believe that I was welcome here, that I'd been invited because they liked me? How could I have been naïve enough to think I would find friends here, in a world so far removed from my own?

It hadn't occurred to me that the others would pounce like beasts of prey the moment they'd lured me away from the teachers' watchful eyes. At Laura's party they were taking revenge for me poisoning the atmosphere in our class with my grief. Finally they had a chance to release their pent-up desire to punish me. I sat on the ground, the blindfold still tied around my forehead. My nose ran and I sobbed as fat tears rolled down my cheeks and onto the picture in my hands. It was the photo of Father the police had used when they were searching for him. I cried so hard that the other kids fell silent and stared down at me in horror. I remember Laura's mother eventually pushing her way through the hushed circle. She froze for a second and looked down at me, her hand pressed to her mouth. Then she pulled herself together. "Get back into the house!" she hissed at the others, and she put her hand on my shoulder and told me how sorry she was. I remember how I held the picture tight and couldn't stop crying, and that I was so ashamed about my tears, still clinging on to the picture when Mother rushed across the lawn, hugged me, and kissed my cheeks. I remember keeping my head down as she led me through the living room, where a shocked silence had descended. I remember her nodding wordlessly as Laura's mother opened the front door for us, and how she slid me into the back seat of our car, which sat in the posh driveway all dusty and rusty. I remember vowing to myself never to make friends again, to remain alone forever and to tend my pain and my memory of Father like a garden. All the while I clasped his picture to my chest as if it were a recovered treasure.

5

Weird to think he was born here. This is my first time here, yet every street, every corner reminds me of him. I sense him smiling down enigmatically from the windows, watching me follow the clues, curious to see if I can figure them out. *Follow me*, the walls of the houses seem to say. *Let's see if you can find me.* The traffic rumbles by, restaurant owners smile and point to their menus. So this is where he grew up. This is where he lived, breathed. Being this close to him, I feel his descriptions come to life. As if he's standing right behind me here on the river bank, pointing to the water: *This is the Berdawni. It's a little calmer here in the south. This is where I used to swim when I was a kid. There's a stretch about two kilometres long where the water isn't too deep and the current is steady, perfect for bobbing around in a car tyre ...*

I feel feverishly optimistic. I want answers. I want to forget all the nights I've lain awake, haunted by his face, by the way he looked at us, wet, numb, and haggard, the night before he disappeared. As if we were strangers. I want it all to have been worth it, all these years I've clung to the belief that he's not dead. That he didn't have a heart attack while he was out walking that morning. That he didn't rot away in some desolate bit of woods. I want my own painful explanation to be true: that he simply left us behind like an old coat.

We had approached the city from the north, driving past

endless green hills rising like camel humps out of the rocky landscape, the city stretching out below. Even now, in the middle of summer, the peaks are covered in snow. The Berdawni meanders through the city, carving it up. The business district is in the east. The old quarter is a little higher up, west of the river. Zahle's renowned restaurants are to be found downstream, where rows of vine trellises line the valley.

Zahle is Lebanon's third-biggest city, according to my guidebook, but I knew that already from Father. Its population is almost entirely Christian. You can tell just by looking around. Young couples stroll through the streets hand in hand. The women wear short skirts and leave the top few buttons of their blouses open, prompting the young men sitting on the steps to nudge each other and whisper. It's exhilarating, surreal to walk where he once walked, to see the houses he saw, to breathe the air he breathed.

Schoolchildren in blue uniforms get out of a bus and disappear into a side alley laughing. Entranced, I watch them before walking on. My gaze is drawn to older people in particular. A man shuffles along with a walking stick on the opposite side of the street, and I wonder whether Father ever teased him when they were kids. Did they know each other? Did Father carve his name into the trunk of a tree on the riverbank? What was it like growing up here? Did he take girls out on dates? To a restaurant by the water, maybe? Did he sit in one of the cafés and write stories? Was he standing right here by the fruit stall when he decided to take the job in Beirut despite the war?

Time stood still for me after Father disappeared. As the years went by, my memory of him became hazier, fainter. His contours dissolved. I grew older and changed, but he stayed young. Whenever I thought of him, I saw the same man who'd left us behind, only a more faded version. Here, though, I can't avoid thinking about what he'd look like today. If he did come back here, that is. If he's still alive.

"Zahle," Nabil had said earlier as we rattled along the mountain roads, past makeshift stalls at the side of the road plastered with Pepsi posters and discoloured menus. "The City of Wine and Poetry." Father had never tired of telling me that, but I'd never thought to question it.

"I get the wine part, but why poetry?"

Nabil glanced at me.

"Well, if there's wine, poetry can't be far behind, now can it?"

"I thought you were Muslim."

"That's right."

"A Muslim who drinks wine?"

He put his finger to his lips, signalling me to keep my voice down.

"We're pretty high up here, nearly 2,000 metres—getting closer to Allah. I'll answer that question when we're back in Beirut."

Now, Nabil is following at a discreet distance. He seems to sense that the city has triggered something in me, but he doesn't probe. I, on the other hand, would love to know what he makes of me: a German guy who speaks fluent Arabic comes to Lebanon saying he's looking for someone he doesn't want to talk about, yet he carries on like a tourist, heading straight to the cedars and stopping to gape at every other landmark.

We've been walking for a while since we parked the car. It's not as if I have an address to head to; all I know is that I have to start here. After that? Who knows. There's no plan B. All I have is an idea and a sense of compulsion. The truth is that for twenty years, I've been mired in the past. The only time I thought about the future was when I proposed to her. But if this trip doesn't go well, there won't be any wedding.

"That's Souk al-Blatt."

Nabil rouses me from my thoughts.

"Hm?"

"An old market street." He points towards an alley branching off to the left of the main street. It gives off a reddish sheen in the afternoon light, rusty balconies jut out on both sides, and plaster crumbles off the walls. "In the past—I mean, a really long time ago—merchants from Syria, Baghdad and Palestine used to buy and sell their wares here. The street leads to one of the oldest parts of the city."

"What's it like today?"

"Today it's just old." He laughs. "I've heard they're planning to redevelop it and turn it into a centre for traditional crafts."

"But?"

"But this is Lebanon. I suppose the fact that someone has gone to the bother of planning anything at all is a minor miracle, a cause for celebration."

I look down the alley. Did Father experience the sight and sounds of the markets—traders shouting, customers haggling, the smell of soaps and spices, the jangling of coins on wooden tables?

"We should get something to eat," Nabil says.

He's right. Apart from the pies he shared with me earlier, I've eaten nothing all day.

"Do you know any restaurants around here?"

"No. But if we can't find a restaurant in Zahle, we deserve to starve."

I let Nabil do the ordering. When I open the menu and read the familiar names of the dishes, it strikes me that I've never eaten Arabic food in a restaurant before. There was always hummus, tabbouleh, and kibbeh in my mother's kitchen. The food would be placed in earthenware bowls on the table, a plate of steaming flatbread beside them. Now I really feel like a tourist. If I'm to accomplish anything here, I'll have to focus on the one thing I have. And that's a name.

Nabil eyes me with a mixture of doubt and amusement as I dip the flatbread into the hummus and absentmindedly shove it into my mouth. No doubt it's delicious, but I can't savour the moment. To break the silence, I say, "So what about your family? How many children do you have?"

"Three sons."

"Three boys, wow."

"Yes." He smiles. "We've been blessed."

"How old are they?"

"Fifteen, thirteen, and seven. Jamel is the eldest, Ilyas is in the middle, and Majid is the youngest."

"I suppose they call you Abu Jamel, then?"

Nabil nods.

"That's what most people call me. Do you have children?"

"No."

"If you ever have a son, whatever you do, don't name him Jamel."

"Why not?"

"You know it means 'handsome one'?"

"Yes."

"The problem is, my son knows it too." Nabil laughs, tears off a piece of flatbread, fills it with rice, and dips it into a bowl of labneh. "I never let the boy use the bathroom before me, because once he goes in, it's hours before he comes out again. He stops in front of every damn mirror to check whether a strand of hair has slipped out of place. If he gets one pimple, he doesn't want to go to school. Unbelievable, eh? He steals my cologne, too, but I don't say anything because at least it smells better than the deodorant he buys, which strips the lining right from your nose."

"He's at that age, I suppose."

"He's a good boy all the same. After school, he helps out a friend of mine who owns a shop. They sell all kind of stuff: water, fruit, newspapers, groceries. Masoud says Jamel has been a blessing. Since he's been behind the cash register, the number of girls coming in has tripled. They whisper behind the newspaper stand and buy things just so they can drool over him up close." Nabil chuckles again. I sense his pride, the pleasure he takes in talking about his son. "It's a miracle, really," he says, reaching for the bowl with the vine leaves in front of my plate. "I mean, look at me. He must have inherited his mother's genes."

"What's your wife's name?"

"Nimra."

"What does Jamel want to do when he's older, then?"

Nabil raises his hands in mock desperation.

"I just hope he doesn't decide to be a model or something. He should study something sensible. Finish school and go to university, ideally. Education," he says, looking me in the eye and tapping his index finger on the table for emphasis, "is the key in this country. I put a bit of money aside for him each month. My dream is for him to go to a private university in Beirut."

"Why not a public one?"

"There's only one public university in Lebanon. Students who don't have scholarships and can't afford private university fees go there. But it's not nearly as good as the other universities. I've heard that the professors don't bother to turn up to lectures, that papers lie around for months before they're corrected. Only the private universities offer a decent education."

"Are they expensive?"

"Puh." He shakes his hand as if he's just burned it. "A year at an average university costs around 10,000 US dollars. Some parents beg to send their kids there. Can you imagine?"

"What do you mean, beg?"

"Well, some people try to haggle with the universities like they're at the souk. Lots of private universities offer discounts for good grades: the higher a student's grade, the less the parents have to pay. But it still costs a fortune. So you know what the fathers do? They go to the Gulf States—Dubai, Abu Dhabi, Qatar—because they earn far more there, and they use the money to pay for their kids' studies in Lebanon. And when the kids have graduated, they head off to work in the Gulf States or Europe too. At least, that's what they do if they have any sense." Nabil's tone has shifted from chatty to deadly serious. I can see his sons' education is a huge worry. He's pushed his plate away and keeps glancing anxiously at his hands. "I don't know if I can send all three to a private university. It's not easy. A lot of families have a bit of land they can sell if they need to. We don't, unfortunately."

"Do you work full time as a driver?"

He laughs nervously; he's obviously starting to feel uncomfortable. "I have a few regular customers, some business people I drive around. I don't have the fanciest car, but I've got a good reputation, I'm reliable, and I know all the shortcuts. People know that if Nabil drives them, they'll get to their meetings on time, and word spreads."

I can't help thinking about how he showed up at the hotel an hour and a half late this morning, but I bite my tongue.

"It'll all work out," he says, pointing upwards with his index finger. "Inshallah." *God willing.* "Education is the path to the future. You know, we Lebanese don't have a very high opinion of the past. The future is the only thing that matters."

Now, in the late afternoon, the streets are getting busier. The residents of Zahle are leaving work and pouring out into the streets. People are strolling along the riverbank, almost all the seats outside the restaurants are taken, young men are balancing on a slackline stretched between two trees. Zahle is no great beauty. It lacks Beirut's gleaming hauteur, the sparkle of glass edifices, the magic of the sea, but it exudes a certain charm nonetheless. Very few buildings are more than three or four storeys high. In between parked cars there are donkeys laden with bags, smiling shoeshiners, women standing beside mobile stalls. Red, pink, blue, and turquoise sequinned dresses hang from the racks, and painted clay vases are lined up next to hand drums, piles of brightly coloured tea towels, and postcards of tourist attractions miles away from here: the port at Byblos, the historic centre of Tripoli, the cedar forests. It smells like our street used to. The fragrance of shisha and the aromas of grilled meat, mint sauce, and fresh bread waft past. Nabil turns his wrist and takes a furtive look at his watch. He probably doesn't want me to think he's in a hurry. But I can't afford to waste any more time. I turn to him and say, "I need to find a woman."

He raises his eyebrows.

"I thought you had one."

"Not to marry, Nabil. The person I'm looking for here is a woman."

"Why didn't you say so in the first place?"

"I'm saying so now."

"OK. Have you got a health-insurance number for her?"

"What?"

"Only joking. No one has that kind of thing here." He laughs. "An address?"

"No."

"Never mind. Have you at least got a name?"

"El-Hourani."

"El-Hourani ... it's more common in the south: Tyre, Nabatieh, down that way. I wouldn't say there are too many el-Houranis up here, are there?"

"I don't know."

"What about the first name?"

"Elmira."

"Elmira el-Hourani. Trust me, Samir, you don't need to be Philip Marlowe to track someone down in Lebanon. It's a tiny country. Everyone knows everyone—just watch." He gets up and goes over to a waiter standing in front of a giant menu. The waiter shrugs at first, then he thinks for a moment and points up the street.

Nabil practically skips back to our table, grinning widely. When he gets close, he slows down, narrows his eyes to slits, and says in a gravelly voice, "I'm a lone wolf, unmarried, getting middle-aged, and not rich. I've been in jail more than once and I don't do divorce business."

"Huh?"

"*The Long Goodbye.*"

"Philip Marlowe?"

"Exactly."

"What did the waiter say?"

"There's only one el-Hourani family in Zahle. He doesn't know if the woman is called Elmira. Come on, he gave me directions."

I got the photo out earlier, while Nabil was in the toilet. Not that I needed to take another look at her face; I've examined the picture so many times, I can see it with my eyes closed. But there's something different about looking at it here, in this city.

This time, it's me who's following Nabil. Striding purposefully, he seems to know where he's going. The number of restaurants dwindles as the road becomes steeper and more serpentine. In their place are snack stalls, little electronics shops, haberdasheries, garages. In my mind, I've run through this moment so many times. Will she be pleased to meet me? How am I going to explain what I'm doing here? The feeling is still there, this unhealthy mixture of fear and hope. Fear that he might actually be there, living with her or paying a visit.

Nabil comes to a sudden halt.

"We're here," he says. "This is the house, I think."

We're standing in front of a crumbling facade. "House" is a bit of an exaggeration. It's an old grey wall that seamlessly merges with the walls of the houses on either side, houses that are in far better condition. The wooden window shutters are weather-beaten. A couple of steps lead up to a door that was presumably once green. There's a bell but no nameplate. When I go to ring, I see that the door is slightly ajar. I look at Nabil nervously.

"What's wrong?"

I point at the open door.

He looks at it uncomprehendingly.

"Like I said, everyone knows everyone. Most people don't bother locking their doors."

Our door was open a lot of the time too. It was mostly Hakim and Yasmin who came and went as they pleased, but sometimes other neighbours would poke their head into our flat and call out "Hello?" It was a given that Mother and Father would invite them in and make coffee.

I knock on the door. It opens a little further.

"Hello?"

There's a radio on inside. No one answers, but I hear rapid footsteps approaching. I peep through the gap, so absorbed that it takes me a while to notice a little girl with huge eyes blinking up at me from a good metre below. A moment later, the door opens. Standing in the frame is a young woman. Mid-twenties, black hair tied up in a ponytail. She looks me over suspiciously.

"Hello?"

"Oh, hi," I say. "El-Hourani? Is that your name?"

"Yes." The little girl, wearing pyjama bottoms and a white jumper with a picture of Mickey Mouse on the front, stares at me. The woman pulls the child back into the house by the collar and stands in front of her. She looks at Nabil behind me and then back at me.

"What do you want?"

"Is Elmira here? Elmira el-Hourani?"

"May I ask who you are?"

"Samir. My name's Samir el-Hourani. Elmira is my grand-mother." I can sense Nabil's look of surprise behind me.

"Oh," the woman says, without opening the door any wider.

"Is she there?"

"Who?"

"Elmira."

"No."

"When will she be back?"

"I don't think I can help you." The little girl peeps past her mother's leg.

"Are you ..." I don't know how to put it. My mind is spin-ning—the woman is just a little younger than me. "Are we related?"

She looks surprised.

"I don't think so. Samir? I don't know any Samirs."

"When will Elmira be back?"

"There's been some kind of mix-up," she says. "There's no Elmira living here. I don't know anyone called Elmira el-Hourani."

It takes a moment for her words to sink in.

"I ... but ..." No Elmira? "That's impossible!" I say, louder than I intended. "She must live here!"

The woman shrinks back. I feel Nabil's hand on my shoulder and hear him ask, "Is there anyone else called el-Hourani in Zahle?"

"No," she says. Her voice is softer. She clearly finds it easier to talk to him, but she keeps her eyes fixed on me. "I think I'd know. The name's more common in the south. If there were other el-Houranis living here, we'd know them."

"And there's no one called Elmira in your family?" Nabil asks. His voice is calm and much quieter than usual.

"No, definitely not."

"ok, thanks," Nabil says.

The woman nods hesitantly and steps back.

"Thanks," I mutter. The little girl gives a shy wave just before the door closes.

I don't know why I'm so surprised. After all, this is typical of me. Coming here with nothing solid to go on, looking for an old woman who might be very sick or might even have died years ago. Once again, I've walked into a brick wall with my eyes wide open. I've ignored the bigger picture because I couldn't face the truth: that there was never any real chance of me finding anything here. Even if I did manage to track down my grandmother, there was no guarantee she'd lead me to Father. There's no evidence that he's alive or that he's ever been back to this city, this country. The old green door has closed. I'll never enter this house now. My journey is over before it ever really began.

The sky has turned a surreal shade of reddish gold. It looks like a kitschy painting, the tiny clouds like smudges of grey pencil. It's got much cooler. Nabil walks beside me in silence as we leave the house behind. I shuffle along, my energy sapped.

"Why didn't you tell me you're looking for your grandmother?"

"I didn't know how to." I clear my throat. "Talking about my family was never my strong point." I laugh bitterly. *For God's sake, don't start crying*, I think.

"Might she have moved?"

"She might. But she could just as easily be dead. I don't know."

Nabil nods.

"So what now?"

"I dunno," I say. "Maybe I should just fly home."

It doesn't bear thinking about. I can't go home. I won't have any home if I fly back now. If I phone her and admit that nothing panned out the way I'd hoped, it'll all be over. I'll return to a cold, empty flat and find a note on the kitchen table: *I'm sorry, Samir, I know you tried. That means a lot to me.* That'll be the only trace of her. Her things will be gone, the bed and the bathroom won't smell of her anymore, and the word "future" will be sneering at me from the half-empty wardrobe. Even if I eventually manage to get over her, it won't be long before I've scattered the tiny puzzle pieces out in front of me again, hoping that one of them will lead me to him. That's what really terrifies me: the prospect of an unbearable weight on my chest wrenching me from my sleep at night, a horrible feeling that I missed something here, something that might have led me to him. The same old feeling that's dogged me all these years. And at some point, I'd end up back here, starting from scratch.

"We're fucked, Nabil," I say. "I'm fucked. If you can't find a Philip Marlowe, I'll be back on the plane tomorrow."

"How come you don't have any contact with your grand-mother?" The question barely out of his mouth, he flaps his hands. "No, no, forget it. Sorry, it's none of my business.

"It's OK. I've never met her."

"I don't know any Philip Marlowes," he says, and I can hear how much it pains him. He sounds as if he'd give anything right now to be friends with an ace detective. "Or Sherlock Holmeses. Or Mike Hammers, or Poirots, or Miss Marples, or Columbos ..."

"You've heard of Columbo?"

"Sure," he grins. "Cable television!"

"Looks like we're out of luck then, doesn't it?"

"Know what I think? I think if you're meant to find your grandmother, you'll find her."

"You really think it's that simple?"

"That simple." He points up to the sky again. "Inshallah."

I can't help smiling. I've never really been able to take it seriously, the unwavering, unconditional optimism a lot of people get from their faith. Religion was never that important when I was growing up. I don't think Mother ever prayed until Father disappeared. As a small child, I only went to church at Christmas, to watch the nativity play. I stopped going altogether once Father left, and Mother never made me go with her.

I only register the brisk footsteps when they're close behind us. Nabil doesn't appear to have heard them either, as he hasn't turned around yet.

"Excuse me," the man shouts. "Wait!" He's winded. "Did you just come by our house?" He braces his arms against his thighs and leans over to catch his breath. "El-Hourani?"

"Yes," I say.

The man stands up straight again. Middle-aged, a strong chin, thinning hair. "My name's Aabid. My wife says you're looking for someone called Elmira?"

"Elmira el-Hourani, yes."

He shakes his head, still panting.

"There's no Elmira el-Hourani here."

"So your wife told us."

"Right." He signals with his finger that he needs a moment to gather himself. He takes a deep breath.

"But there is an Elmira. How old is your grandmother?"

"I don't know. Very old, if she's still alive, and probably very frail by now."

The man shakes his head again.

"That doesn't sound like the Elmira I know. This Elmira is old, yes, but strong—she could probably carry much younger women's shopping for them. I don't see her around town much. Her housekeepers run her errands. But she's the only Elmira I know of."

Nabil and I look at each other.

"What's her name?"

"Bourguiba. Elmira Bourguiba."

"Bourguiba? Are you sure?"

The man shrugs and nods.

"Where does she live?" Nabil asks.

The man points past us to the end of the street.

"There?" I ask in disbelief, pointing at the grand house towering behind a brick and mud wall.

6

We never spoke about my grandmother. Mother never mentioned her, and neither did I. I was afraid I'd let something slip. I'd promised Father never to tell Mother or anyone else about the phone calls, so Grandmother became a taboo.

Mother's nerves were shot in the weeks following Father's disappearance. Once, she knelt in front of me and gripped me by the shoulders, her eyes red from crying. "Samir, if you know anything that could help the police, you have to tell me, do you understand? It's really important." But I didn't say a word. I felt her fingers digging into my shoulders and thought about how Father had knelt in front of me just like this the day I made my promise. "You two, you spent so much time together. Didn't he say anything? Didn't you notice anything odd?" I shook my head. I couldn't betray him. It was our secret. Eventually she gave up and left me alone. I took out the little cedarwood box and buried it for safekeeping at the foot of the cherry tree in front of our building. That way, Mother would never get her hands on it. That way, I'd be able keep my promise.

I've often wondered why she didn't pick up the phone and call her mother-in-law. She just never did. As far as she was concerned, my grandmother—a woman I only knew from a photograph—might as well not exist.

I eventually learned how to grieve behind closed doors. Shattered by the experience at Laura's birthday party, I swore I'd never leave myself open to attack again.

The void Father left behind was palpable. It was visible too, especially when it came to Mother. It manifested in many little ways. Long after the initial shock had passed, she refused to even consider the possibility that he might be dead. We were very similar in that respect. I learned a lot from her. I learned to nurture the idea that he loved us even though he'd left us. That he'd come back someday, reappearing as if he'd just been on a really, really long walk. I learned from her absolute devotion to her grief. She kept on cooking for four and setting a place at the table for him. As if he might walk through the door any minute, hang his jacket on the hook, pull off his shoes, and sit down with us, his family. She kept on making kibbeh with toasted pine nuts, the way he'd liked it, even though Alina and I didn't particularly care about pine nuts and she herself preferred kibbeh without. She kept on putting two duvets and two pillows on their bed, and in the mornings, she would smooth the sheet on both sides. When she sat in front of the television in the evenings, she'd curl her legs under a blanket, leaving plenty of space on the right-hand side of the couch, as if he'd just popped into the kitchen to grab a drink. She left room in the fridge for his bottle of beer, and months after his disappearance, his blue tooth-brush was still on the bathroom shelf. Every night, she slipped a hot-water bottle under the duvet on his side of the bed. I think she did it so the bed wouldn't be too cold in the morning, so she could pretend that he'd just gotten up, that he was waiting for her in the kitchen, reading the newspaper over a cup of coffee. One time when she was cleaning the shoe locker in the hall, I noticed that she made sure to leave room for his shoes beside hers. Another time when I went into the shed to get my bike, I saw her standing at the old cabinet, hiding his keys in a drawer. "It'll save him having to ring the bell when he comes back," she said, her eyes downcast, as if I'd caught her doing something shameful. She left his clothes in the wardrobe. He hadn't taken any of them with him. It was as if he'd walked out the door naked, ready to be born into a new life, unburdened by the past, with nothing to remind him of us.

Her appearance changed too. She was thirty-three when Father disappeared. Her skin had been smooth, her eyes sparkling and alive. She had striking, feminine features, and there was something proud and aloof about her, especially when she was sitting at her sewing machine, absorbed in her work. But I soon noticed that her cheekbones had become more prominent, she'd broken out in spots, a haggard pallor replacing her healthy glow. She'd give me a strange, uncertain look whenever I interrupted her thoughts, and I saw that the sparkle had vanished from her eyes. But what shocked me most was that just a few months after Father left, her hair started to go grey.

Father's disappearance didn't affect my sister the same way it affected me. I guess that's why our relationship was so difficult. Of course, it didn't help that she moved to a foster family at the age of nine and found a new father there. She was just a baby in 1992, the year Father left, hadn't even reached her first birthday. And the older she got, the less she could understand why I was so fixated on the man who had ruined our life, a man she had no memory of whatsoever.

It's true to say that Mother played a part in making me who I am today. But that's not an accusation. Who am I to accuse her of anything when I bear the blame for so many other things?

7

"Just a minute, please." The woman standing in the marble-tiled front hall indicates that we should wait outside, then disappears back into the house. We're in a lush garden sheltered by pine and fig trees. The lawn smells freshly watered, and the rising steam is making the air even muggier. The sun has almost set; dusk casts an eerie shroud over the house. The moment the gate in the mud wall buzzed open, I had a sense of déjà vu. I feel like I've seen the house before, just not in this light. *Elmira Bourguiba.* Who is she? Could this really be the right place? An elegant sandstone house with an ornate front door and arched windows screened by latticework mashrabiyyas. Lawn sprinklers, manicured flower beds—it's not at all what I expected. Another thing I find weird is that the city has been completely blocked out. Not even the traffic noise can penetrate the walls. The house's seclusion is absolute.

The woman who opened the door introduced herself as May. Dark skin, bright eyes. She asked what we wanted, and when I said, "I'm a relative," she looked sceptical. She still hasn't reappeared. I dart Nabil a questioning look.

"Sri Lankan," he says. "Pretty common among posh Lebanese people."

"She looks African," I say.

Nabil shrugs.

"Anyone who's anyone has a housekeeper. It started in

the fifties and sixties, when the country was still thriving, especially economically. Back then, most of the house-keepers came from Sri Lanka, so rich people started calling them all 'Sri Lankans'. Once I picked up this business man—you know what he said? 'We have a Sri Lankan from Angola now.' Unbelievable."

I hear footsteps approaching from inside the house. The housekeeper appears, scrutinising us.

"Just you," she says at last, pointing to me. She steps to one side and ushers me in.

"Careful, please. The floor is wet."

The marble tiles are glistening. I know why; Father explained it once. When it's hot outside, you throw water on the stone floors inside. The water has a cooling effect as it evaporates, preventing the house from getting too hot at night.

May leads me down the hall to a large room, signals me to wait, and goes off again. I can see the garden through the mashrabiyyas. Nabil is sitting on the lawn, leaning against the big fig tree. I look around. There are no plants in the room, no photos either. The stone walls are bare and cold. Elmira Bourguiba. Whoever she is, she's not very interested in the past. The grand exterior of the house bears little relation to the interior. An old divan looks lost in the room. Next to it, two chairs at a table that could easily sit six. A glass cabinet with just three plates and three glasses in it. She clearly doesn't receive many visitors. The whole room is pervaded by an unwelcoming sense of emptiness.

I had always pictured my first meeting with my grand-mother as follows: I enter a small room. Candles flicker in the breeze coming in through the open window. There's a smell of herbs and ointments. A woman lies in bed, hooked up to tubes and beeping devices. Her chest slowly rises and falls. Her wrinkled skin is speckled with age spots, her eyes speak of a hundred years of solitude. I step closer, her eyes follow me, though her head doesn't move, and she examines me sleepily. Her fine white hair is a tangled mess. I say her name and take her hand. Her smile is tired, but there's no mistaking her delight that she's finally getting to meet me.

For years and years, I've played this moment over in my mind, imagining older versions of the woman in the photo. Which is why I'm totally unprepared for the reality.

"What do you want?"

I spin around. She's standing there, straight as a rod, a glass in her hand. There's something cool and strange about her narrow, crystalline green eyes. Her face is birdlike, with sharp features and a pointed chin. Thin lips painted on with a fine brush. Her penetrating gaze is directed right at me, her entire bearing is forbidding. Her short, curly hair is black, not the white I expected. The silence that follows her question is deafening. It's impossible to guess her age. My father's mother would be close to eighty by now. If this woman is that old, she must have spent the last forty years doing nothing but taking care of her appearance.

The fact that I recognise her right away is astonishing. She looks the same as she did in the photo of my parents' wedding. Back when the Leitz Prado projected her onto our living room wall, I could sense her air of authority. Here in the flesh, she's even more intimidating, surrounded by a force field that makes me feel small and insecure.

She moves towards me in a slow, almost stately manner.

"I know who you are."

"I'm Samir."

She looks at me with disdain, her fine-boned fingers

twitching around her glass. *Don't waste my time*, her eyes seem to say.

"I ... how are you?"

"You came all this way to ask me how I am?" She exhales sharply through her nose. "After thirty years?"

"How do you know who I am?"

"Please. You've got his eyes."

She's right. It's the only thing about me that still looks like him.

"Did he send you on ahead?"

"Sorry?"

"Here, to me. Did he come with you?"

"What?"

"Are you looking for money?"

"Money? No ... I ..." It takes me a second to realise she's not talking about Nabil. She's talking about Father. The contrast between the woman standing in front of me and the woman I'd imagined has completely thrown me. When I finally grasp what she's just said, my head starts to spin.

"You ... you don't know where he is?"

I detect the first stirring of emotion on her face. Her eyelids quiver, and for a fraction of a second she looks as if she might lose control, but she composes herself immediately. Her voice is even.

"The last time I saw your father, he and your mother were hiding in the boot of a car that was to bring them to Damascus. I wished them luck and closed the boot. They planned to take a plane from Damascus. To West Berlin. That was in November 1982."

I stare at her.

Her flinty eyes stare back. But when she speaks, her voice isn't quite as harsh and pitiless. Then she breaks into a satisfied smile, as if she's predicted every last detail of this encounter.

"So he left all of you too."

A wave of tiredness washes over me.

"May!" my grandmother calls, without taking her eyes off me. Seconds later, the housekeeper is back in the room. "Bring us some wine. The Ksara," she says, still looking at me. "Won't you sit down." It's an order. She points to one of the two chairs at the huge table.

"Yes," I say, my voice sounding thin and fragile. "I've a lot of questions I want to ask you."

The wine is making me drunk. The room is swirling. She's sitting across from me, and I'm finding it hard to look her in the eye for more than a few seconds. She never seems to blink.

"He always said you were sick and that he had to send you money for medicine ..." I say.

"Do I look sick to you?"

I shake my head.

"As I said, I've heard nothing from your father since he left the country with your mother. I never got a cent from him. Your father"—again, the penetrating glare, the strict, chiding tone of her voice—"was very good at taking, but he never gave anything back."

"What do you mean?"

"In this country," she says, "you can accomplish far more with money than you can with weapons. Money and contacts. I had plenty of both, and I used them to save your father's life."

I remember what he wrote in his diary, which I now have.

"I know," I say.

"But do you think he ever showed a moment's gratitude?"

I'm still puzzling over what she said. Where did the money go if she never received it? Had he been putting it aside for his trip? That would imply that he'd planned his disappearance far in advance. A horrible thought. Even scarier is the thought that it would've been easier for someone who'd been saving up for years to vanish into thin air forever, with a new passport, maybe even a new appearance ... I'm afraid to ask the next question, but I've no choice. I've got to know for sure.

"Did you ever phone us at home?"

She looks at me, clear-eyed and calm, like a remedial teacher waiting for her pupil to figure the answer out for himself.

"I might have done if I'd had a number." A smile crosses her face. I can't tell if it's kind or mocking. "I might have picked up the phone if I'd known they'd made it to Berlin and then onwards to God knows where. As I said, their frightened faces in the boot of the car—that's the last I saw of them. And I never heard from either of them again ... or from you, for that matter."

"I'm here now."

"So I see. Was it hard to track me down?"

"It wasn't easy," I say wearily. "But I got lucky. Why did you change your name? Is Bourguiba your maiden name?"

"Change my name?"

"Why aren't you called el-Hourani anymore? Elmira el-Hourani."

She was about to take a sip from her glass, but now she puts it down on the table. Her fingers are bony and old—the only thing about her that seems old.

"El-Hourani," she spits. "*My* name is Bourguiba. Your father's name is Bourguiba." She looks at me triumphantly. "And your name is Bourguiba too!"

"But I'm Samir el-Hourani," I say, taken aback by how whiny I sound.

"Yes, because your father was an ungrateful good-for-nothing who took that damn name," she hisses. "Didn't your parents ever tell you about their wedding?"

"I've seen photos."

"Photos." She laughs derisively.

I reach into my trouser pocket and take out the picture. I put it in front of her on the table. Grandmother turns it around and examines it: there she is with her thin-lipped smile, arm in arm with my father, who's wearing a forced smile and a sharp suit.

"That was taken here," she says, her finger tapping the photo. "Here in this house. We had the ceremony in the garden."

It's dark outside now. I can just about make out the silhouette of the big fig tree in the garden. Of course. Why am I only getting it now? I think back to the other pictures our parents showed us, the humming of the projector as it beamed the photo of our parents' wedding dance onto the living-room wall. It was in this garden. I remember the fig tree, the guests standing around laughing. I get an uneasy feeling as I remember the men standing in front of the brick and mud wall, the men in their khaki shirts embroidered with cedars inside red circles. I picture the gun propped against the tree, exactly where Nabil is now sitting.

I take a mouthful of wine. The realisation that my parents walked across this floor, that Mother got dressed and put on her make-up right here and then stepped out into the sunlit garden, that Father danced with her and kissed her here—it all hits me with an immediacy that threatens to reopen my unhealed wounds.

"A lovely wedding," she says, as if describing a vase of flowers. "Lots of guests and music."

"The musician," I say. "He fled with my parents."

"Is that a question?"

"No. I know they left the country together. What I mean

is, were he and his daughter in the car too?"

"No. Your parents planned to meet him in Damascus, I think. What was his name again?"

"Hakim."

"Hakim. I remember. Your father insisted on him play ing at the wedding. He was good, played the lute, I think, but we could have got someone better. A Muslim, right?"

"Yes."

She wrinkles her nose.

"Terrible, what happened to his wife. But he wasn't the only one. I thought he could probably do with the money. That's why I didn't object when your father wanted him to play at the wedding."

I feel the hairs stand up on my arms. I know what happened to Yasmin's mother. It's in the diary.

Grandmother slides the photo back to me.

"We just had the religious ceremony here. You know that, don't you?

"How do you mean?"

"There's no such thing as a civil marriage in Lebanon. A wedding has to take place in a church, a mosque, or a synagogue to be legal. The state recognises weddings held in registry offices abroad, but you can't get married in a registry office in Lebanon."

"What's that got to do with my parents?"

"Antoine-Pierre Khoraiche of Ain Ebel married your parents. The Maronite patriarch himself, thanks to my contacts," she says, ignoring my question. "Have you any idea what an honour that is? Your father should have shown some gratitude. They disgraced me. Word got out that they'd gone off and got married in a registry office as well, as if the patriarch's blessing meant nothing to them!" Grandmother's eyes remain motionless. Her features are rigid. She emphasises every word in a cutting tone. "The pair of them flew to Cyprus in secret. I don't know where they found the money, maybe your mother had savings. They got married at the town hall in Larnaca. Your father took her name. Then they travelled on to Nicosia, had the marriage officially registered, first by the Cypriot ministry of foreign affairs and then by the Lebanese embassy. They got it all done in five or six hours and were back here that same evening, sitting at this table, and they never said a word." She's trying to sound indifferent, but she can't hide her bitterness.

"But why? I mean, what did they hope to get out of it?"

Grandmother waves her hand dismissively, as if I'm a silly little boy who needs everything explained.

"I've no doubt your mother was behind it. Even at that early stage, she must have intended to talk your father into fleeing. She knew how soft he was, how easy it was to manipulate him." She looks at me. "She had it all planned out. If you flee to another country and want to stay there, it's useful to have a registry-office certificate proving that you're married. You see? Married couples are far more likely to be granted asylum."

It's strange, hearing her tell this story. Grandmother hasn't once referred to Father or Mother by name, as if she can't quite remember.

"I heard about it through contacts of mine. Your father didn't want me to find out. He knew how much it hurt me when he cast off our name. He was my only son."

Was. As if he's dead.

"He knew there'd be no more Bourguibas once I'm gone. That was his way of getting revenge."

"Revenge? For what?" I can almost guess; the answer glimmers between the lines of his diary.

She shoots me a withering look. *How can anyone be this stupid*, it seems to say. But there's no trace of impatience in her voice. She's a master of self-control.

"Revenge for your mother, of course," she says. "I made him marry her."

Water spurts out of the tap, spraying my shirt and the mirror. I let it run into the cup of my palms and dip my face in. The bathroom tiles are decorated with arabesques. I had to leave the room for a bit, to get away from this woman and her wall of icy bitterness. She talks about my father, her son, as if he were a traitor. And about Mother as if she were the serpent that seduced him. I knew from the diary that Grandmother had arranged the marriage. When I first found out, I was horrified. But I thought about my parents, about the way they treated each other—as equals, respectfully and considerately, sometimes even lovingly— and I decided that they must have learned to love each other along the way. Their fortunes had bound them together, their escape from a powder keg to Germany. Before that, their marriage, which shielded Father from the militias and maybe even saved his life. My birth. But Mother as the mastermind of their escape? My father capable of such hatred that he would seek revenge on his own mother? Even worse, that he would one day punish his wife, and me, for chaining him to us?

"So he left you too." When I return to the room, Grandmother is sitting in exactly the same position as when I left. I nod and sit back down at the table.

"When?"

"1992."

"And you think he's here, in Lebanon?"

"I don't know."

"But you thought I might be able to help you."

"Yes." I feel as if I've been caught stealing. "Do you really not know where he is?"

"Believe me, I have absolutely no idea. I slipped the driver an extra twenty dollars and told him to drive over as many rocky bumps as possible. Your father abandoned me. He abandoned you. He abandoned your mother. He's just like his own father: a coward. The kind who leaves everyone high and dry in the end."

Everyone. Not *the people who love him.*

"What about his father?" I never heard my parents mention my grandfather.

She swats the air as if she's trying to get rid of a fly. "He upped and left. Ran out on me while I was pregnant with your father. The apple doesn't fall far from the tree—they were both dreamers, wasters. And the only thing either of them cared about was my money."

She pauses and takes another sip of wine.

"Your mother is well shot of him. I couldn't stand her myself—such a stubborn woman—but I hope she's found someone else in the meantime." I lower my head and take a deep breath, focusing on the fine grain of the wood. *In the meantime.* As if there was any *in the meantime.*

"Can we talk about the hotel?"

She seems a little put out that I don't want to talk about her money anymore.

"The hotel?"

"Father worked in a hotel, didn't he?"

She winces, just for a second, but it's like a mask has slipped. Then she heaves a dramatic sigh, clearly well-rehearsed.

"That's a good example of what a waster he was. He trained to be a hotel manager in Beirut, in 1980, in the middle of a civil war. There were no tourists in the hotels in those days, only snipers who took the lift straight to the top floor. My God, what was he thinking? It was his way of distancing himself from me as much as possible. I wanted him to study abroad—not in Beirut, needless to say—but he refused point-blank. He was always heading off with his pens and scraps of paper, writing poems about trees and grass, about how much he loved his country. Nineteen years old. Other kids his age were proving how much they loved their country by joining the Phalange, Bashir Gemayel's Kata'ib militia—they had offices everywhere, and the queues outside stretched for hundreds of metres. But what does your father do? He heads out to the cedars to daydream. Dreams have never changed a country."

"I thought you didn't want him to join the militias," I say.

"That's not true." Her tone is sharp. "I would have liked to see him fight. Were we supposed to just sit back and let the Druze take over the country? The Sunnis? The Syrians? The Palestinians? The Kata'ib wanted to recruit him. They tried their best. But just imagine your father—he wouldn't have survived a day. He'd have bombarded the Druze, the Amal militia, the PLO, the entire Lebanese National Movement with poems and nothing else. I saved his life."

Up to this point, she's managed to maintain the facade, the wall of composure protecting her. But now it comes pouring out of her, the vitriol, scorn, and contempt. The corners of her mouth twist into a grimace. It's as if a dam has burst into a valley where nothing but poisonous thorn bushes grow. The hatred in her voice when she says the names of the other civil war factions is chilling. As if the wall around her house is too high. As if the news that the civil war ended more than twenty years ago never even made it into her garden. As if neighbours are still shooting each other right outside her gate, as if militia-men are still standing by roadblocks, dragging people out of their cars if their papers declare them to be the wrong religion. As if bodies are still lying on the streets, throats slit and faces shot to pieces.

Now that her eyes are screwed up and her whole face is contorted, I see how heavily made up she is. The rouge on her cheeks just emphasises her pallor, making her look as if she hasn't seen the sun in a long time. My grandmother seems to have withdrawn from life many years ago. Shut away behind her walls, she seems to have become fixated on the story she's been telling herself over and over again, her rage festering away inside. She strikes me as having tried everything to stay young over the past thirty years: the lipstick, the dyed hair, the thick layer of make-up on her cheeks. She seems to have clung to the belief that if she keeps herself looking young, she can stop time from moving on. That way, she'll never get old, never notice how lonely she is. And if her son ever comes home, he'll find the same mother he left behind. That way, it'll be easier to start again.

This woman and I are more similar than I care to admit. Both of us have been abandoned. By the same man. And both of us have suffered at the hands of time.

Her hand trembles when she picks up her glass. She struggles to bring it to her mouth. The fingers of her other hand are clenched into a fist on the table, her white knuckles sticking out. I move to put my hand on hers, but she pulls away. Her eyes have glazed over and are looking through me. She seems to have cast her mind back to a time when the future looked bright.

Nothing has turned out the way I imagined. My own name has been thrown into question. I fidget in my chair. Should I get up and go? I can't. I've got two more questions.

"Teta?" I say cautiously, and I reach for her hand again. This time she lets me. "You said he loved Lebanon."

It takes an age for her to respond. She blinks sadly and nods. She looks exhausted, broken, and very old.

"Do you think he came back here after he left us? Please, I need to know."

She lets out a quiet sob and allows herself a single tear.

"I can't think of anywhere else he would've wanted to go," she says.

At that moment, it seems to hit her: that her son has probably been back in this tiny country for more than twenty years, without ever contacting her. I think it has broken her heart.

I squeeze her hand and she gives a little jump. Her bones are soft, almost malleable.

"One last question," I say. "Is there anyone else who might know where he is? Other relatives? A family friend?"

She stares straight ahead without answering.

Unsure of what to do, I stay seated. If I don't get an answer to this question, it really is all over.

"Teta?"

She doesn't look at me. I push back the chair and rise unsteadily to my feet. Then I put my hand in my pocket, take out the photo I've already shown her, put it on the table in front of her, and leave the room. I don't need it anymore.

May is standing in the hall. She sees me to the door in silence. The water on the marble has long since evaporated. The air outside is cold, and the starry sky catches me by surprise. It's far too clear for my muddled state of mind. I spot Nabil asleep under the fig tree. May nods me a goodbye, but just as she's about to close the door, I hear Grandmother's voice from inside the house, back to its sharp bark—as if the vulnerability of a few moments ago was just a fleeting illusion.

"May," she calls. "Do you remember the man who called here a few years ago? The fat one with the ugly nose?"

May looks at me.

"Yes," she shouts without taking her eyes off me.

"Go get the card he left and give it to the kid. It's on my desk."

8

In the 1990s, the political climate and the world around me changed dramatically. Not that I was paying much attention. I was too caught up in the crazy, lurid decade that marked the end of the analogue era. Swept along by a generation that refused to let anything spoil their fun, ignoring the many warning fingers pointing to the future. We had no battles left to fight. The Cold War was over, the Berlin Wall had fallen, the Twin Towers were still standing. The only obstacles we faced were ones we imposed ourselves.

When I left our house, the world tasted of Center Shock chewing gum, Chupa Chups lollipops, flying saucers, and chocolate marshmallows stuffed inside a bread roll. All of them purchased with fifty-pfennig coins from a grossly overweight man at the train station kiosk who smelled of fried food and ketchup; we called him Jabba the Hutt. I grew up in front of the TV with the *Gummi Bears*, *Darkwing Duck*, and *Chip 'n' Dale*, and later MTV, *Beverly Hills 90210*, and *Baywatch*. By the time I was into *The X-Files* and *Pulp Fiction*, I'd started shaving. My face was changing too. As a boy, I'd taken after Father, with my round head and curly hair. But the older I got, the more like Mother I became. My features became more pronounced and my hair got straighter, changing from black to dark brown. Father's eyes were the only feature I still had. Time had it in for me—having robbed me of Father, now it was robbing me of almost every reminder that I was his son.

The years raced by. The schoolyard began to divide into camps: indie kids, skaters, ravers, hip-hop heads. I hung around on the fringes without really belonging to any of them. As a pimply fourteen-year-old, I sneakily started wearing Father's oversized leather jacket and smearing gel in my hair. I'd skulk in front of the booming ghetto blasters, smoking and coughing and drinking sugary alcopops. We'd stopped swapping football stickers; now we swapped porn. Don't ask me where Sascha got the films. "Trade secret," he'd say. Known as the Porn King, Sascha spent most of his time loitering in the school corridors wearing his trademark popper tracksuit bottoms. He carried on like a drug dealer, darting sideways glances to check no one was coming before producing the video CDs from his rucksack. I wasn't able to watch them at home, but now and again I'd watch them in other boys' basements, where we also played *Monkey Island 2* and *Duke Nukem*, scattering crisp crumbs and inhaling the smell of heating oil. Down here, the sound of the nineties was shoot-em-up video games, the maddening dial-up of a 36k modem, and the startup chimes of Windows 95. Beyond the basement, the nineties sounded like "The Next Episode" by Dr. Dre and Snoop Dogg, "Give it Away" by Red Hot Chili Peppers, or "Insomnia" by Faithless, depending on which party I happened to be at.

I was fourteen when I kissed Hannah during a foam party at our town's ice rink. I knew her from school. I'd lent her my gloves earlier that night, our breath forming little clouds when we spoke. Later, the DJ dimmed the lights, bathing the rink in a red glow. Our clothes were soaked through from the foam. The DJ announced he was going to play "a few slow songs," and everyone moved closer to their partners on the ice. That's when Hannah re-emerged out of the foam. *I feel so unsure, as I take your hand and lead you to the dance floor*, George Michael was singing. Even then, I thought the song was corny. We slid around together for a while, smiling awkwardly whenever we caught each other's eyes and immediately looking back down at our skates so as not to lose our balance. I held her firmly by the waist, making sure that my sweaty hands didn't slip down towards her backside and that I didn't get too close to her and her breasts. Eventually she nuzzled up to me and gave me a long, wet kiss. I'm still not sure what exactly she got up to with her tongue. All I know is it tasted of chewing gum and felt good.

Yasmin was at the party too. She was dancing with an older boy, staring deep into his eyes, arms around his neck. *I should have known better than to cheat a friend and waste a chance that I've been given.* I gazed sappily at Hannah. Later, I plucked up the courage to take her hand, and I continued to hold it when we left the party, only letting go when we spotted her mother waiting in the carpark.

I hadn't entirely kept the vow I'd made after Laura's birthday party when I was eight, as over the years I'd learned how to fit in with the various cliques. But I never did make any proper friends. There was no one I'd spend hours on the phone with, no one I could confide in. I kissed Hannah two more times. I kissed other girls too. That's another 1990s memory: fierce, dimly lit snogging sessions on stained sofas, the sound of thumping basslines in the background. I'm not sure what girls liked about me. Maybe it was that they couldn't quite figure me out. I wasn't like the other boys, who strutted about like roosters the minute they saw a girl with her T-shirt knotted to expose a bit of midriff. I was usually standing in a corner watching, wearing my much-too-large leather jacket and saying little, so maybe the girls saw me as an interesting freak.

I was sixteen when I slept with a girl for the first time. It was at a party. Her name was Mathilda, and she was a year older than me. Wearing a neon T-shirt and red Buffalos, she was drunk, like me. We'd been dancing together, but at some point she disappeared into the mass of sweating bodies. When she reappeared, she walked up to me purposefully and, without saying a word, took my hand and led me to the bedroom of the guy who was throwing the party. She locked the door, kissed me hungrily, undressed herself and then me, and just as I was beginning to understand why people make such a fuss about the whole business, it was over.

That was 22 November 2000, a couple of days after my birthday. The reason I remember the date isn't because it was the first time I had sex. It's because that's the day Mother died.

Over the previous year or two, Mother had transformed. It seemed that the older Alina got, the more Mother changed. Unlike me, she'd eventually accepted that life went on without Father.

One day I was hiding some weed I'd bought from a guy called Gregor when I noticed her standing in front of me. She was holding a laundry basket containing what I could see were Father's clothes. Putting the basket down, she said in a casual tone, "Most of it is too good to throw away. Take out what you want to keep and I'll take the rest to the sports hall."

The only reason I didn't kick up a fuss was that my parents had started out in the sports hall themselves. Plenty more refugees had ended up in our town since then, of course, many of them from Kosovo. There was always stuff about them in the newspapers. I knew Father would have approved of his clothes going to them, so I said nothing and picked out three shirts he'd been particularly fond of.

Mother bought herself a new bed, and Hakim chopped the old one up for firewood. From then on, she slept with just a single-sized duvet. She made herself new dresses and began to use all her wardrobe space, arranging her clothes by colour. Every now and then I'd see her reading on the couch, taking up the full length of it. She opened the windows more often now, bought new curtains, had the flat re-wallpapered and new carpets put down. She started colouring her hair, restoring it to how it had looked before the grey set in.

Mother's dressmaking kept us afloat. She went to craft fairs to sell her dresses and look for new ideas, and when business took off, she started teaching at the local community centre, where chatty mothers piled into her sewing courses. She became more sociable. It started with her meeting up with the customers she'd made dresses for. They then introduced her to other people, who in turn invited her to join their book club. They met on the third Thursday of the month, at a different location each time, and swapped book recommendations. This is how she started reading books in German: *The Diary of Anne Frank* and Kafka's *Metamorphosis*. She'd sit on the couch with her book, a blanket round her legs, chuckling, or furrowing her brow, or looking utterly spellbound. She even managed to plough through *The Magic Mountain*, though she far preferred the Grimm brothers' fairy tales. She was blooming. Whatever she'd found in the fairy tales began to work its magic on her; I noted with resentment that she had mellowed. Sometimes I'd hear her giggling on the phone as if she were a girl again. And she started giving herself little treats: a necklace that had caught her eye, a spa treatment in town. When I came home from school, she'd tell me about her morning in the café, and who she'd bumped into there, or about the old man she'd met while she was out walking who had mistaken her for his daughter. She was bursting with energy. She'd skip around the flat with Alina, just like she used to do with me many years ago. The soft glow returned to her cheeks. She went to my sister's school concerts and to parents' evenings. To Hakim's delight, she bought a children's violin and paid a music student to give Alina lessons. She asked me whether I'd like to take up a hobby too, martial arts maybe, or join a club. I refused.

She'd decided, at the age of forty-one, to start a new life, and she refused to let her son's mistrust put her off. Maybe I was envious of her ability to start again. But mostly I felt she had no right to be happy without her husband.

She made the biggest break with the past in early 1999, when she took an integration course to become a German citizen. She already met all the other requirements for citizenship. She'd been living in Germany for sixteen years. Both her children had been born here, both were at school. A special transitional law applied to my sister, who'd been born in 1992; Mother had been able to have Alina naturalised when she was just two. Hakim had sorted out citizenship for himself and Yasmin long ago, so Mother was doing it for my sake as much as her own.

I didn't want to be German. Ridiculous, really, seeing as I'd been born here and had never once left the country. But I'd been listening to Arabic music for years. I revered a culture I barely knew. I felt Lebanese. What would Father say if he knew Mother was forcing me to become German? Would he stop her? I wanted to have the same citizenship as him. I didn't care that it was a formality, a change in passport I'd appreciate when I was older, according to

Mother. I saw it as my duty to resist, because I was sure that was what Father would have done. But Mother gave me no say in the matter. I began to hate her, not just because she forced German citizenship on me, but also because I saw her decision as a betrayal. As far as I was concerned, it was a blatant attempt to distance herself from her husband as much as possible. By becoming German. By casting off her national identity. That was something he'd never have done.

Needless to say, she passed the test, and when she arrived home, beaming, with the certificate in her hand and a sense of liberation I could barely fathom, I stomped out of the flat.

We had a huge row that day, 22 November. What torments me now is that it was over something really trivial. If only I'd been a bit more understanding. Would it have killed me? It was just a party, and on a Wednesday. Only two more days till the weekend, when there'd be another party anyway. There was always a party going on somewhere, and besides, weeknight parties were never as legendary as the Friday-night ones. But I'd decided that Mother, by making me take German citizenship, had forfeited her right to tell me what to do.

"You're not going to the party," she'd said.

"Yes I am."

"Samir." Her eyes impatient but controlled. "You know I can't cancel my sewing course. And I can't take Alina with me."

"Why not?"

"Because it finishes late and she has school tomorrow. As do you, by the way."

"So?"

"So she's your sister, Samir. All I'm asking is for you to

spend one evening at home with her."

I looked over at Alina, who was lying sprawled on the floor on her stomach, flicking through a book.

"Why don't you ask Nicole?"

"I already did. She can't."

"Ask Hakim, then."

She took a deep breath. I wanted to see her explode, but her voice was quiet.

"You know he has to work."

She was right, I did know that. The joinery where Hakim worked had grown over the years and landed some major contracts, so he'd been working nights over the past few weeks, training a new guy called Hassan. Hakim was on the night shift tonight.

"Samir." She tried to smile. She didn't want to let on how much I was testing her patience, because she knew I would've seen it as a minor victory. This was one of the little games we played. "Alina would be so thrilled if you spent an evening with her. Come on, you're her big brother."

"I can't," I said. "Everyone's going to be at the party." I wanted to get back at her, that was part of it. But I also just didn't like spending time with Alina. Maybe it was the age gap, and the fact that, to my mind, we had nothing in common. She was a sweet kid, well behaved, helped Mother around the house, loved school, and was always bringing friends back to the flat. And she'd been diligently practising the violin. So there was really no reason not to adore my sister. But she made me uncomfortable. Sometimes, as I watched her drawing in her workbook with her coloured pencils, I'd look for traces of our father in her face. She looked more like him than I did. She had his black hair, and her face was rounder and friendly—a pretty girl, especially when she smiled. Because of these resemblances, I found it all the more disconcerting that she never showed any signs of missing him. She simply had no memory of him holding her and humming in her ear until she fell asleep in his arms. She seemed to have forgotten he'd ever existed. Sometimes she'd grab my hand and start chattering about what she'd learned in school that day, how she'd gathered chestnuts and used them to help her do her sums. I never took in much of what she said. I'd catch myself trying desperately to see the world through her eyes, to see if there was any trace of sadness or disappointment in them. But I saw nothing. She enjoyed a carefree childhood under the watchful eyes of our transformed mother and Hakim, who worshipped her and was convinced she had a glittering career as a violinist ahead of her.

What I didn't know was that Mother had a doctor's appointment at five o'clock. For an MRI. A few weeks previously, she'd had mild symptoms of facial paralysis. For a couple of hours, she'd had only partial sensation on the left side of her face. There was no need to worry, the doctor had assured her; it was probably psychosomatic, a trapped nerve caused by stress, though she insisted she hadn't felt so well in years. And the symptoms had disappeared that same evening and never returned. But she'd been suffering from a stiff neck and headaches for a while. "Better safe than sorry," the doctor had said and referred her to a specialist. She planned to drive straight from the hospital to her sewing course in the community centre. As she wouldn't be home until late, she needed someone to keep an eye on Alina and make sure she went to bed.

Mother rubbed her neck and tried again. I could see she was really trying not to lose her temper.

"Can't you do it as a favour to me?"

"To you?"

"Would that really be so hard?"

"Let's just say it's not exactly your most compelling argument."

Her voice remained calm.

"Samir, I know you can't stand me right now. But you should think about how much slack I've cut you over the last while. Your grades are abysmal, all you do is party, you smoke weed ..."

"I ..."

"Please ..." She stretched her palm out towards me. "I'm not as stupid as you think. Do what you like, it's your life, but it would be nice if you could help me out just this once."

"So you're OK with me smoking weed?"

"I'm OK with you testing boundaries."

"What boundaries?"

"The boundaries that exist whenever people live together under one roof, Samir."

"I'm going to the party."

"And I'd like you to stay at home with Alina."

"I'm going to the party."

"Alina would like you to stay at home too."

"I'm going to the party."

"Fine, don't listen to me. But what do you think your father would say?"

This was my weak point. She knew it, and she stuck her finger deep into the wound. I'm afraid I didn't have her level of self-control.

"Father? You weren't thinking of him when you turned us into Germans behind his back. What if he comes home one day?"

"Comes home?" Her voice was raised now too, and her hand was shaking. "Samir, it's been eight years since Brahim disappeared."

"So?"

"So we'll never see him again. When are you going to get that through your head?"

"Like you did?" I snarled. "Do you want me to dye my hair and read shitty books with a bunch of fucking idiots?"

Her eyes widened.

"Go to your room," she snapped.

I really wanted to see her lose it. I wanted to make her suffer. I couldn't take it anymore, watching her breeze around the flat, laughing and daydreaming, while I was doing everything I could to keep Father's memory alive. Otherwise we'd have nothing left to remind us that we were Lebanese.

"Do you really think changing the wallpaper and hanging a few new curtains will get rid of him?"

"Stop." She rubbed her neck again and grimaced in pain.

"I don't care what you do, I'm not going to forget him just because you want me to!" I was spitting venom.

"OK, Samir," she said, her eyes narrowed as if I were giving her a headache, her voice full of disappointment. "I'll find someone else for Alina."

I didn't want her to give up. I wanted to fight, rub her nose in all her wrongdoings, hurt her.

"No wonder he left you," I screamed. "No wonder he couldn't stand it anymore." I'd whipped myself up into a rage. I knew I'd gone too far, but I couldn't stop. My words landed like arrows all over her body. I could see her wince. "I wish he'd taken me with him. I don't care where he is now, I wish I was there and not here. If only *you'd* left instead of him."

"OK," she said. "It's OK for you to think that."

But I could see it wasn't OK. If my words really had been arrows, Mother would have bled to death. Unable to return my glare any longer, she looked at the floor in stunned silence and waited for me to stop screaming at her. I paused for a moment to make sure my next sentence hit its mark.

"I loved him. You never did."

A whack landed on my cheek. Searing pain exacerbated by shock.

"It's my life," she said. Her lips were quivering, her eyes brimming with tears. "I have a right to live it," she whispered.

I turned on my heel, ran to my room, packed my rucksack, stormed past Alina as she stood there staring, and slammed the door of the flat behind me.

After sleeping with Mathilda at the party, I went back to drinking, and when I got to the point where I couldn't drink any more, I kept drinking anyway. I danced, flailing my arms and staggering among the bodies flashing in the strobe light. I could smell their sweat, the alcohol on their breath. I danced until I collapsed and fell asleep on the floor. When I eventually woke up, I scrabbled around for my jacket unsteadily and lurched out of the flat, the frostiness of the November night taking me by surprise. The bus driver eyed me as I unsteadily held up my monthly ticket.

"Don't even think about throwing up in my bus," he said. I grabbed a hanging strap and dropped into a seat. The city sped past me, a slumbering creature, pitch black save for the odd illuminated window and the white beams of approaching headlights. I kept dozing off and jolting awake the moment my head tipped forwards. It was while I was being sick in a bush in front of our house that I noticed the light in our living-room window and cursed.

I tried to slip into the flat without waking anyone, but I knocked over the umbrella stand right behind the door and dragged Alina's jacket down from its hook. It was nearly four in the morning. I just wanted to go to bed, but as I was creeping down the hall, I noticed Hakim sitting on the living-room couch. Beside him was a man I'd never seen before.

Later, I lay on my bed, watching the lights from passing cars dart across my ceiling, and tried to make sense of the hollow feeling spreading inside me. I thought of Alina, asleep next door. It would be a few hours before I could tell her. Lying there, hands clasped behind my head, eyes wide open, I wondered what would happen now, what social services would do with us. And I thought of Mathilda, how she had bitten her lip as she took my hands and guided them over her body. I thought about her hair falling into my face when she bent over to kiss me.

Mother hadn't found anyone to take care of Alina. She'd called practically everyone she knew: friends, customers, and, in the end, Hakim. He contacted his boss, found someone to cover his shift and stayed with my sister while Mother went off to teach her sewing course. It had taken so long to find a babysitter that she'd had to cancel her MRI appointment. If I'd stayed at home, everything would have been fine. The bleeding in her brain would have shown up in the scan, they'd have performed emergency surgery and saved her. But I'd stormed off. Just as she was getting into her car, I'd been cursing the world and feeling sorry for myself. A cerebral aneurysm, the doctor called it a few days later. He'd been talking to Hakim, not me, but I heard him.

It was damp and cold all through November. It had rained, hailed, snowed. The only day the sun shone was the day we buried Mother. It felt like a joke at my expense. I wore a black suit that belonged to Hakim and was far too big for me. Alina stood beside a woman from social services and cried. A few people came and shook my hand, people who'd been fond of her. The man who'd been waiting in our living room with Hakim the night she died was there too. He was very tall and broad-shouldered with grey hair, a few wrinkles, and a kind face. He seemed grief-stricken and awkward, reluctant to approach us, shifting from one leg to the other as the priest spoke. Afterwards, he told me to get in touch if I ever needed anything. "Are you a policeman?" I'd asked that night, after Hakim had told me everything. "I ... em ... no ..." He'd looked at his hands, as if the answer was written there. "Your mother and I ... we ... we knew each other." The hospital had called him because his was the only number saved in her mobile phone. I hadn't even known she had a mobile. I felt so ashamed. All those little details over the past few months—the flushed cheeks, the lightness in her step, the girlish giggling on the phone—in my pig-headed self-absorption, it hadn't dawned on me that she was in love.

Hakim looked ancient and had sunglasses on. Yasmin stood next to me. She was nearly nineteen. Wearing black tights, a black dress, and a black blazer, she held my hand tight the whole time. I didn't try to stop her.

Sometimes I missed it, the magic of our childhood. Sharing secrets, roving about, whispering. But those days had ended when I went into mourning for Father. Then we were just neighbours who got on well, went to the same school, chatted about this and that—anything as long as it wasn't personal. If Yasmin was hurt by my coldness when all she wanted was to be there for me, she never showed it. She was the same bright, kind girl who'd been my best childhood friend. But now there was an unspoken barrier that kept us from talking about us, about me and her and our feelings for each other. We moved in different circles, especially once she started grammar school. While I was hanging around with Sascha the Porn King, she and her friends spent the holidays travelling around the Amalfi Coast in a Volkswagen camper van. She even sent me a postcard.

She had a steady boyfriend. I'd seen him with her, coming and going from her flat. By the time Yasmin turned nineteen, they'd been together nearly two years. His name was Alex and he was German. He wasn't Muslim. The reason I mention this is because, on our street, there were a few Muslim girls Yasmin's age whose fathers would never allow them to go out with non-Muslims. But Hakim was the world's most tolerant father. He supported Yasmin as much as he could, and he never told her what to do. Years later, when I read my father's diary and found out how Yasmin's mother had died, I understood why. Hakim had had enough of dogma. He was done with religion, and so he let his daughter take full responsibility for her life. Yasmin never took advantage of this freedom. She went to parties and had lots of German friends. But she was also a good student, working hard for her final school exams, determined to go on to university. She wore make up and dressed like other girls her age, spent summer days at the pool and evenings by campfires, went on holidays with Alex or camping with friends. I often marvelled at the young woman she'd become. But sometimes I felt the same way about her as I did about Alina. I was baffled by how easy it was for her to adapt, to integrate. Whenever anyone asked her where she came from originally, she'd say, "I'm German. But my father comes from Lebanon."

Nineties Germany seemed oddly unpolitical to me, though in fact there was a lot going on. I sat up and took notice when the refugee shelter in Rostock-Lichtenhagen went up in flames, of course. Everyone on our street was shocked. For a while, it seemed to make the rest of the people in our town more sensitive to the difficulties facing refugees. When I walked past the sports hall, I saw mountains of sacks stuffed with clothes, and lots of volunteers who'd turned up to help. But otherwise, I didn't pay much attention to what was going on in Germany. I didn't care that we had a new chancellor, Gerhard Schröder, who always looked a bit tipsy to me. I also didn't care that scientists had cloned a sheep. I couldn't understand why people were making such a fuss about a dead English princess or about Bill Clinton getting a blow job in the Oval Office. My eyes were always on the East. I paid attention when Israel and the PLO signed the Oslo Accords, and when Bashar al-Assad succeeded his father, Hafez, as president of Syria. I cared that the Syrians were still in Lebanon and that Damascus was essentially controlling Lebanese politics. And that cranes were towering above the skyscrapers in Beirut, transforming the cityscape—I cared a great deal about that.

I idolised Rafiq Hariri, the Lebanese prime minister who used much of his personal wealth to rebuild the country and clear away the rubble that had piled up during fifteen years of civil war. To me, he was a one-man movement, a charismatic orator who brought about a recovery in the land of my forefathers. He had thick black eyebrows, a grey moustache, and silver hair combed back, forelock and all, off a round, pudgy face that reminded me of a French mastiff. He looked like a granddad; I could imagine him enthralling his grandchildren with bedtime stories. He was a single-handed national movement because he knew how to touch the soul of the entire nation. Everyone on our street loved Hariri; even Hakim got over his initial reservations. Hariri opened up Lebanon, got the reconstruction process underway, minimised state influence on business. Thanks to a flat tax of 10 per cent on all incomes, the Land of the Cedars became wealthier. People were happy to overlook the staggering increase in national debt, as the fruits of Hariri's policies could be seen everywhere: new schools, streets, and buildings, regular waste collection ... the list went on.

On 22 November 1998—two years to the day before Mother died—Émile Lahoud succeeded Elias Hrawi as president of Lebanon, thereby becoming Hariri's boss.

"Those Syrian bastards," I heard Hakim say. "Putting that military stooge in so Assad can keep Lebanon under his thumb. Could they be any more obvious?"

I'd been following it on the news. Syria had pushed through an amendment to the constitution that cleared the way for Lahoud to become president. Otherwise he wouldn't have been allowed to run. As a former army commander, he would have had to wait three years before standing as a candidate. Hakim had long been railing against the Syrians and their influence over Lebanon. Whenever we watched parliamentary debates on TV, he'd try to explain what exactly the problem was.

"The Syrian secret service controls everything, sees to it that the cabinet makes the right decisions. The pro-Syrian ministers are given copies of the agenda in advance. The agenda items are listed in one column, and the other column tells the ministers what to say about each item. It's ridiculous, totally frustrating!"

He wasn't the only one feeling frustrated. Rafiq Hariri had had enough too. On 2 December 1998, ten days after Lahoud took office, Hariri resigned in protest over Syrian influence in Lebanon.

My attitude towards Father changed after Mother died. Unconsciously, I think; it was the only way I could cope with losing both of them. I had to choose a side, and so I blamed him for everything that had happened. It was easier than blaming myself. Up to then, I'd been obsessed with honouring him, protecting his reputation, glorifying his memory until he came back. I'd never had any doubt that he loved us. But now I began to resent him. Yes, Mother's death had been partly my fault, but it would never have happened if he hadn't disappeared in the first place. And this blame soon turned into rage. I was sick of being his representative, of keeping a place warm for him, of hoping he'd return. I decided—no, I swore—to chase up every single clue, no matter how tiny, until I tracked him down.

9

I stare grimly at the wall. Blurry scenes from the day flash past. The bustling city this morning, the cedar forest. Grandmother's contorted face. Her voice echoes inside me as if it's being repeated over a tinny loudspeaker. My hotel room is dark. I've closed the window, blocked out the city. Through the thin walls, I can hear the TV in the next room. A presenter moderating a discussion; every now and again, applause breaks out. The air conditioning is blowing a cool current through my damp hair. I took a long shower, washed the day away. Now I'm reclining on the soft mattress with my feet up. I try to make out patterns on the wall—animals, shapes—but I can't. It's a different room from last night, same hotel. Third floor this time, number 302. A different receptionist, same perfume. She saw on her computer that I'd checked out this morning and asked if there'd been a mistake with the booking, if I'd intended to stay more than one night. I said no. How was I to know what awaited me in Zahle and where it would lead? I hadn't known it would lead me right back here. She addressed me as "Mr. el-Hourani" and flashed her receptionist's smile. I smiled back, happy to have a stranger call me by that name. Not "Bourguiba," el-Hourani. That's who I am.

It was dark when we got back to Beirut. Only the odd light was still on in the towering office blocks. Street lamps tinged the pavements beneath the palm trees orange. A handshake with Nabil before we parted, a grateful smile when I paid him the agreed fare for the day, a brief nod to the hotel porter, and I disappeared into the cool lobby. My thoughts are flitting around like a moth. I look at my rucksack over by the wall. The diary's in there. I need to think through the ramifications. I must consider the possibility that it won't be as useful as I thought. Father took Mother's name, and he never even mentioned it in the diary. Which means there may be other things he didn't mention. Or that he lied.

There are earplugs on the bedside table. The hotel management is obviously aware of the poor soundproofing. I jam them in my ears and say the name so loudly that it reverberates inside my head: Samir Bourguiba. I say it over and over. But it doesn't sound right; it sounds strange.

I examine the business card May gave me before she'd closed the front door:

SINAN AZIZ
RHINO NIGHT CLUB
AL SEKKEH STREET, MAR MIKHAEL
BEIRUT
+961 1 701 463

"Never heard of it," Nabil said when I showed him the card in the car. "But that doesn't mean much. Mar Mikhael is the nightlife district in east Beirut. Lots of bars, nightclubs, all fairly pricey. Don't worry, we'll find the place."

What was I expecting when Grandmother had told May to get the card? Not a nightclub, that's for sure.

"Do you know this Aziz guy?" Nabil asked.

The lights of Zahle had almost disappeared; all I could see in the rear-view mirror were little specks burning out like shooting stars. Shortly afterwards, we turned onto a motorway. BEIRUT 53 KM, the signs said.

"No, I've never heard of him."

He asked how the visit with my grandmother had gone, and I told him everything. The car had been shuddering along the poorly surfaced motorway for a while.

"Nabil," I said, "I'm looking for my father."

"Your father? So that's why you're here?"

"Yeah. He disappeared more than twenty years ago. My grandmother ... I was hoping she'd know where he is."

"But she couldn't help."

"No. I'd been hoping to find answers there. But all I got was even more questions."

"Hmm," Nabil kept saying, as I told him about my encounter with my grandmother. It didn't seem to surprise him that my parents had got married in Cyprus. "Well," he said, "it was probably unusual in those days. But today, it's a real industry."

"What do you mean, industry?"

"Lots of travel companies specialise in civil weddings in Cyprus. Fly there in the morning, get married in the registry office, have your marriage recognised by the embassy, spend the afternoon in a hotel room, and fly back in the evening."

"But why?"

"Because there's a niche in the market. Civil marriages are prohibited here. And a religious wedding is only possible if you marry someone from the same religion."

"How many couples would actually want an interfaith wedding?"

"More and more of them. It's becoming an important issue, especially for the younger generation."

"And I suppose the religious leaders see that as a threat?"

"Exactly. It's extremely divisive. Taking marriage out of

their hands would undermine their authority. In a country like ours? Forget it!"

"Why can't there be both? Religious *and* registry office weddings?"

"Because that would be a compromise. And these people don't like compromise. There was this one case that hit the news a little while ago. We have a law dating back to 1936—a leftover from the French Mandate, pre-independence. It allows for civil marriage in Lebanon if neither party has a religious affiliation. This particular couple had their religion removed from their family registers so that they could have a civil wedding. He was Sunni, she was Shia. There was an uproar. The minister for the interior had to decide whether the marriage was lawful or not."

When Grandmother hurled her anger and disappointment over my parents' civil wedding at me, I assumed it was because of the scandal aspect, especially with the civil war raging and religion being so important. All the more so for a woman like her, who obviously cared a great deal about her reputation. What Nabil was telling me came as a major surprise.

"Have people learned nothing from the civil war? Don't they know that they need to put their religious differences aside? Otherwise Lebanon will never be united."

"Samir," he said, looking at me with a smile. "You're a dreamer."

"Why?"

"Because not much has changed, that's why. The Grand Mufti of Lebanon himself weighed in, Sheikh Mohammed Rashid Qabbani. He issued a fatwa. I can't remember the exact wording, but it went something along the lines of: Any Muslim with legislative or executive power in Lebanon who spreads 'the virus of civil marriage' is an apostate."

"He accused politicians of apostasy?"

"Yes, including the prime minister. As you know, the president has to be Maronite, the prime minister has to be Sunni, and the speaker of parliament has to be Shia. So when Qabbani accuses politicians of apostasy, he means people like the prime minister and the speaker. They're violating Islam, he says, so their bodies won't be washed after they die, they won't be wrapped in a shroud, and they won't be buried in a Muslim cemetery."

"You're saying this cleric threatens politicians?"

"Let me put it this way: he advises them."

"So what do the politicians say? What stance do the parties take?"

"None of them will speak out. They all just hem and haw as usual. Hezbollah is absolutely against civil marriage. Nasrallah's authority depends on religion for its legitimacy, so Hezbollah would never agree to a change in the law."

"And the other parties?"

"Very unlikely."

"But ... I mean, how many religious groups are there here? Seventeen?"

"Eighteen."

"Eighteen. So why can't people see this as an opportunity? Allowing interfaith marriages would be a huge leap forwards. Imagine a Lebanon where a child could have one grandmother who's Sunni, the other Maronite, one grandfather Shia and the other Druze?"

"I see what you're getting at ..."

"How could a child like that ever hate anyone because of their religion? Wouldn't a law permitting interfaith marriage have the power to bring all the factions together at last? Unite them into a nation? It would be revolutionary, wouldn't it?"

"Yes," said Nabil. "Revolutionary." It sounded wistful, the way he said it. "But that's exactly what the politicians are afraid of. That's why they're so fiercely resistant. Politics and religion are one and the same thing here. Every single religious leader is terrified of your vision of peace. As long as the land remains divided, people will keep listening to them ..."

We drove the rest of the way in silence. When the lights of Beirut began to appear on the horizon, Nabil phoned his brother to say he'd be by to pick up his children shortly. I could hear them making a racket in the background.

"So, Samir, what hotel should I take you to? Back to the Best Western?"

"Is there a Carlton Hotel in Raouche? Near Pigeon Rocks?"

"A Carlton Hotel? Hmm. I think there used to be, but it's gone now, as far as I know."

"Are you sure?"

"No. Well, pretty sure. Was it quite old?"

"Yes. I'd say it was built in the sixties, maybe even a bit earlier."

"Then I'm certain it's gone now."

"Why?"

"Because all the hotels on the Corniche and around the marina are modern skyscrapers now. Lots of glass. I'll show them to you tomorrow. Developers and investors have been flocking to Beirut since the war ended. Most of them come from the Gulf States: Saudis, Qataris, and so on. They see Beirut as a project. The world's biggest urban renewal project. They've bought up huge swathes of the city. The few buildings left standing after the war were torn down because they were old. Why do you ask?"

It was the hotel Father worked in. I read about it in his diary. "Just curious," I said. "It would be nice to see Pigeon Rocks."

I turn off the air conditioning and put down the business card. SINAN AZIZ, RHINO NIGHT CLUB. The clock says half past twelve. I resist the urge to get dressed and take a taxi there, just show up and start asking about him. I consider phoning the number. It's a nightclub, so there's probably a better chance of someone picking up now than during the day tomorrow. On the other hand, if Father doesn't want to be found, it wouldn't be smart to announce that I'm here in the city. Sinan Aziz might warn him.

I crawl under the duvet. I'll be too warm later, but until then I'll leave the air conditioning off and the window closed. The TV next door is silent now, but a tap is running; I hear the water swooshing on the other side of the wall. I pick the business card up again and place it on the other pillow. As I'm falling asleep, I think of Grandmother and her painful realisation that her son is not coming back. Not if he can help it.

This time I'd set the alarm: nine o'clock. Get up, shower. Breakfast room on the first floor. Crumpled newspapers on a table by the door. Smiling waiters. A European-style breakfast buffet: toast, wholegrain bread, jam, plates of cheese and salami, tomatoes, cucumbers, boiled eggs, fried eggs, scrambled eggs, milk, orange juice (though not freshly squeezed). The guests are in suits, laptops and tablets open, coffee cups and cutlery clinking. To my surprise, I slept through the night.

When I leave the hotel at ten, I can hardly believe my eyes. Nabil is leaning against his car, which is gleaming in the morning sun; he's just washed it. He gives a broad grin and spreads his arms wide.

"Ten o'clock, as arranged."

I feel like patting him on the head.

"I'm impressed."

"Like I said, I know all the shortcuts. Nabil is always on time."

"You even washed the car."

"Well, now that we're official partners, I thought we'd better have a decent detective car."

"We're partners?"

"Yeah, like Holmes and Watson."

"Doesn't Philip Marlowe have a partner?"

"No, he's a loner. But he gets more women than Holmes."

"Oh well," I say, adding in a low voice, "We can't afford any distractions, buddy."

I like joking around with him. Nabil's good humour is infectious. He holds the passenger door open for me. As he makes his way round to his own side, he says, "Pigeon Rocks, you said you'd like to see them?"

"That's right."

"Let's go there, then. I'll show them to you. The address on the business card is to the north of here, and Pigeon Rocks are to the west, but it's not much of a detour. It's just gone ten, anyway. Let's give them a chance to wake up first."

"Good idea."

"By the way," he said, putting on his sunglasses and starting the engine, "I found out a few things about the Carlton."

There's a sheer drop between the land and the sea. It's stunning. The azure sea sparkles, and small white-crested waves break against the craggy cliffs. Many metres below me, jet skis drone and little paddle boats make their way towards Pigeon Rocks, two massive outcrops covered in grey lichen, about fifty metres from the shore. I lean on the railings and close my eyes. The wind caresses my face. The noise of the city's traffic seems miles away. I can't help thinking of that day long ago. Father and me at the lake. Our nutshell-ships. His voice: *May they sail for a thousand years!* I know exactly what he'd say now: *Picture it: Phoenician ships being loaded with cedarwood here before setting sail for Egypt. The most advanced civilisation in the world.* I've been doing my best to blot out the fond memories these past few years. I wanted to be angry with him. But now I can't stop them flooding back. I see a whole fleet of red-sailed wooden ships on the sea and I remember an entry in his diary:

> I'm not supposed to be here. Fariz, who's on cleaning duty up here today, gave me the key. The roof is out of bounds for us. Too dangerous with the snipers. But I checked with a few people, and they all said there haven't been any militiamen around today. I love the view from up here. If you look east towards the city, you can barely see through the smoke billowing up from the streets. But if you look west, all you can see is the sea. You can forget about the explosions for a while. And if you look slightly to the right, you can see Pigeon Rocks, so resolute, I wish I was one of them.

I survey the hotels and the penthouses on the opposite side of the street. Their glass facades reflect the coast. My gaze drifts upwards, and I imagine Father on the roof of the Carlton, looking west. A burning city behind him and nothing but sea and limitless sky ahead.

"What did you find out about the Carlton, then?" I ask Nabil, who's leaning on the railing beside me. He's pushed his sunglasses back into his hair, and his chin is resting on his palms.

"Let's take a wander," he says.

The Corniche is teeming with people out for a stroll. Parents pushing buggies, lovers twisting into poses for seaside selfies, and street traders who've spread out their wares: knock-off Louis Vuitton handbags, recent Hollywood releases burnt onto DVDs, Rolex watches, disposable cameras. The promenade is lined with palm trees. Old men sit on benches reading newspapers and shelling pistachios. A little boy wearing faded running shorts and a Messi football jersey runs barefoot across the hot asphalt, a bunch of roses in his arms.

"Syrian," Nabil says. "A refugee."

"How can you tell?"

"The Corniche is full of them. Especially in the streets where the bars and hotels are." Nabil points to a trader flogging sunglasses to a couple. The man is trying on a pair; his girlfriend, unconvinced, shakes her head. "They're all refugees. The boy is probably here on his own or else with his mother. The Syrian refugees are mostly women and children. Their husbands are either fighting Assad or dead, or they've fled to a country where it's easier to find work. They send money back to their wives. The kids have to pull their weight too, if their families are to keep their heads above water."

I've heard about it in the news. Lebanon, with a population of barely four million, has taken in more than a million refugees.

"They either stay in the old refugee camps, where a lot of Palestinians live—you know, on the outskirts of the city—or they find hovels in town with no running water, no electricity."

"And how do the Lebanese feel about them?"

"Well, there's no such thing as *the* Lebanese. What about the Germans? Do they have a problem with refugees coming into their country?"

"Some do."

Nabil looks at me.

"What's the population of Germany?"

"Around eighty million."

His eyes narrow, his forehead wrinkles.

"So, proportionally, you'd have to take in nineteen million refugees to match us."

I nod.

"Good luck with that," he says, and smiles. "But to go back to your question, some Lebanese people have a problem with the refugees, of course. Syrians have always been a sore point in Lebanon. The Syrian army left the country less than ten years ago, and now their civilians are coming over here. The Syrian military didn't exactly endear itself to people here. Most Lebanese associate the Syrians with years of repression and tyranny. And don't forget, there's some evidence that Syria may have been behind Hariri's assassination; we still haven't got to the bottom of that. We all loved Hariri. The Lebanese government is split into two camps: the Sunnis and Christians in one, and Hezbollah, which is Shia, in the other. The Sunnis are supplying weapons and munitions to the opposition in Syria, while Hezbollah has joined forces with Assad to fight the very same opposition. The Lebanese civil war has basically shifted to Syria, you see? Now we've got all the people you see on the news, people lying on blankets in the camps and so on. But there are plenty of rich Syrians who fled here too, and they're renting entire floors of hotels, and penthouses like those." He points towards the buildings across the street. "There are loads of wealthy Syrians here, but they're not included in the official refugee statistics. They're different. They just feel like they've come home."

"What do you mean, come home?"

"Lots of Syrians regard Lebanon as part of 'Greater Syria.' As far as they're concerned, we never achieved independence. If you ask them, they'll say, 'We've just moved a little closer to the sea.'"

I study Nabil's face as he speaks. He's talking faster, eyes flashing, gesticulating wildly, his hands taking on a life of their own. He reminds me a little of Hakim: they're both laid-back, even-tempered men who transform into fiery orators whenever talk turns to politics. In fact, Nabil is similar to most Lebanese people in that regard. No matter how many thousand kilometres lie between them and their homeland, they'll have an opinion on what's going on there. Whenever Nabil starts talking like this, I feel like a schoolboy who's diligently studied for an exam only to find that it's on an entirely different subject. I've tried to keep up to speed all these years. I've read and watched so much about the civil war, and about the developments since the war ended, but now I realise that I never learned how to see the bigger picture, how to connect the bits of information. I just noted the details without questioning them or really understanding their significance. I know facts, figures, dates. I gathered knowledge on Lebanon obsessively because I wanted to find out about my roots, about Father. But I never related that knowledge to today. What was it like for him when that bomb went off? When this or that happened in Lebanon, what was his reaction in Germany, his country of exile? Those were the only questions I ever asked.

I remember a common scene in our town: me standing in a crowd in front of the sports hall. Almost everyone from our street would be there, plenty of Germans and Kosovans too. We'd block the entrance so that the police couldn't get into the hall. We did this whenever we got word that someone—or even an entire family—was going to be deported, very often to Hungary, as this was many refugees' first port of call on their journey to Germany. We'd link arms and form a chain. It wouldn't have been hard to break us up, but I think a lot of the officers were secretly impressed. Sometimes we were successful, some-times we weren't. But at least we felt that we'd tried.

I wonder how this small nation copes with the flood of refugees. I feel ashamed to be a citizen of a country where so many people demonise asylum seekers, a country where refugee shelters are going up in flames again.

"Believe me, this crisis is unprecedented," Nabil says after a pause to draw breath. "We've been coping with it up to now. How? By doing what the Lebanese do best: denying reality and rallying to help. But it's all going to blow up in our faces sooner or later. I don't mean *collapse*, I don't mean *fall apart*. I mean it's actually going to explode, the whole powder keg."

"What makes you say that?"

"Well, there's the political conflict, for one thing. But leaving that aside, the people who tolerate Syrian refugees in Lebanon will soon be outnumbered by those who want the Syrians out. And why? Because the Syrians aren't given work permits. Many of them work illegally, getting paid far below the minimum wage. So employers are hiring Syrians, and Lebanese people are losing their jobs. Remember what I was saying yesterday about education? Hardly any of the refugee children go to school. They have no con-tact with Lebanese kids, so neither side will ever get over their prejudices."

Nabil's bleak vision jars with this sunny day, with the holiday atmosphere of the promenade.

"So it'll be like years ago, when the PLO started flexing its muscles," I say. This was history. I was back on familiar ground. The Palestinian presence in Lebanon since the late 1940s had contributed to the outbreak of the civil war in 1975. The refugee camps became a state within a state and were used as bases for PLO attacks on Israel, which turned the entire country into a target for Israeli retalia-tion.

"Yes," says Nabil, nodding gravely. "The Palestinian camps are nearly as old as the Republic of Lebanon itself. The refugees lead their own lives there, their communities are very tight. But the Syrian refugees today … they're a different kettle of fish."

We continue along the promenade. The modern buildings on the other side of the street all face the sea. Spiral-shaped towers, polished facades, uniformed doormen hauling heavy suitcases out of limousines and onto shiny gold trolleys. All I see on our side of the street are relaxed faces, street traders, and fruit sellers. This is the Beirut tourists come to see. A beautiful day without a cloud in sight, not even far out above the sea. I've got used to the fact that Nabil has cast himself not only as my detective partner, but also as my tour guide. I guess it makes a welcome change from driving bankers to and from meetings, listening to them gabbling on their mobile phones. He's having fun, but it's hard for me to swallow the fact that I'm a tourist in my parents' country.

"It used to be full of wooden huts here," he says. "Sort of mini-kiosks. In the seventies, especially. Right along here, where we're walking now. The tourists loved them, because they were directly across the street from the hotels, but everything was a fraction of the price they charged at the hotels."

"Yeah, I've read about the huts. What happened to them?"

"I don't know whether the hoteliers managed to get them banned or whether the traders just packed up and left once the tourists stopped coming." Nabil stops and points to a building across the street. "Anyway, that's where the Carlton used to be."

The box-shaped building is around a dozen storeys high. It looks pretty new but lacks the showy architecture of many other buildings facing the promenade. A simple high-rise: grey concrete, identical balconies.

"There's an apartment building there now. You wouldn't think it to look at them, but the apartments cost a fortune because of the location."

"What happened to the hotel?" I ask.

"It was pulled down. Pity. It was nothing to write home about architecturally, but it was a renowned hotel at the time. It was the place to go. That's where the pool used to be." Nabil points vaguely towards the forecourt. "It was on a slightly raised terrace, so you could lie by the water and look out to sea. People used to rent it for parties and weddings. I found a few facts and figures—want to hear them?"

"Sure."

"A hundred and forty rooms, all with a sea view. Ten floors, five stars. A panoramic restaurant and an American bar with chesterfield sofas and imported whisky. The hotel closed down in 2002. There was talk of renovating it, but Jamil Ibrahim, a prestigious architecture firm here, bought the property and tore the building down in 2008. At first they wanted to build a new hotel: pure decadence, taps made of gold, that type of thing. Like in Dubai."

"So what happened?"

"Someone must have decided it was a stupid idea and built apartments instead."

I can picture it perfectly. The hotel with the Carlton sign glowing on the roof; golden lamplight at the reception desk; a huge multi-tiered chandelier in the foyer; a wide carpeted staircase; polite, friendly staff; waking to a view of the sea; a piano player in the restaurant; socialites in sunglasses chatting over cocktails by the pool. Father described it so vividly in his diary, I feel as if I've been there myself. So much happened here. Hakim and Father's first meeting at a lavish wedding. The photo of Father in uniform standing beside the other man. So many other things happened here too ...

Two men charged in and opened fire in the lobby. Yunus, the kid at reception, was killed. He only started here a couple of weeks ago.

"You look like you've seen a ghost," says Nabil, patting my shoulder.

A ghost. He's closer to the truth than he realises.

"I don't know about you ..." he says, as he puts his sunglasses back on in an attempt to look tough. "But I'm dying to find out who's waiting for us in this nightclub."

10

Mother's death was too catastrophic to take in. Too abstract, like a mathematical formula I didn't understand and would never figure out. From the moment they buried her, I was consumed by a desperate longing for her. The longer she was dead, the more alive each one of her gestures, words, actions seemed. And the more suffocating the dark, heavy shroud around me became.

The neighbours came by. Wearing sombre expressions, they shuffled around our flat as if they were visiting a museum or a cemetery, and whenever they noticed me staring at them, they looked away in embarrassment or put a hand on my shoulder. One day, men in work boots spent a whole day coming and going. Equipped with measuring tapes and cordless screwdrivers, they dragged cupboards, cabinets, and furniture out with them. The sound of hammering, drilling, and banging filled the rooms until the flat had been cleared. I looked at the marks on the carpet and the dusty traces of our furniture on the wooden floor. The walls were cold and ugly. Even the curtains were gone. Mother's room: empty. The living room: empty. The kitchen: completely dismantled. Nothing left but a few boxes in my room.

I spent the days immediately after the funeral in a haze. Incapable of making decisions, disoriented and scared. The future seemed more terrifying than ever, like a snarling monster. I had no idea how we were going to manage. The only thing I knew for sure was that Alina and I couldn't stay here.

Painful as Mother's death was for me, its impact on my sister was frightening. In the initial aftermath, she suffered from uncontrollable crying fits. She refused to sleep in her own room and insisted on crawling into Mother's bed, where traces of her sweet smell still lingered. Then she started sucking her thumb again. She wanted to be with me all the time, refusing to leave my side, clinging to my leg or hand or insisting that I carry her, wrapping her arms around my neck and burying her face in my shoulder. Five days after the funeral, she came out of her bedroom in her pyjamas and started shouting for Mother. She went from room to room, looking around and calling for her, as if she'd just woken up to find that Mother wasn't in the bed beside her. It was both heart-breaking and unnerving. I put my arms around her and held her tight. There was nothing I could say. All I knew was that things were spinning out of our control. Yasmin had started to stay with us at night. About two weeks later, Alina was doubled over with such awful stomach cramps that we had to call the doctor.

Social services came not long after that. One of them, a child psychologist, explained what traumatic grief is. She sat in Hakim's tiny living room across from me and him. Her hair was soft and silvery, her eyes green and clear, her voice quiet but determined.

"It's very important that Alina receives proper care," she said, looking at us as if to check that we were following what she was saying. "Children who have lost one or more parents can develop severe difficulties in forming relationships. It's a natural defence mechanism—the attachment system shuts down to prevent an overreaction to the loss.

Alina hasn't quite got to that point yet, but she's showing all the classic signs of traumatic grief: overanxiousness, clinginess, searching for the deceased parent. In some children, this can develop into suicidal tendencies."

Hakim and I exchanged looks. The woman's words hung in the air like a wrecking ball.

"We need to talk through the next steps," she continued, glancing at the two social workers nodding beside her. Talking through the next steps was probably their job, but they seemed to be leaving it to the psychologist for fear of freaking us out even more. "I know this is a terrible loss, and I understand how difficult it is to even contemplate the future, but I have to ask whether you've thought about what you're going to do."

I was still stuck on the term "traumatic grief." Had I suffered a similar trauma when Father left? I'd been eight, the same age as Alina was now. Maybe Mother's death would send me over the edge completely. Was I going to wind up in a padded cell?

Hakim cleared his throat. He looked worn out, but when he spoke, I was startled by how steady and resolute his voice was.

"Mrs. el-Hourani made arrangements," he said. "As I'm sure you know, Mr. el-Hourani isn't around, so he's unable to fulfil his parental responsibilities. Mrs. el-Hourani drew up her will a few years ago. It says that I should become the children's guardian in the event of her death."

The psychologist gave him a surprised look, then turned her attention to me. I did my best to hold her gaze. Hakim had told me about the will the day after the funeral. I just nodded silently, relieved that I didn't have to do any thinking myself. But hearing it again, here in his flat, in such familiar surroundings, I felt a stabbing pain. It made me realise how far apart from each other we'd grown, Mother and I. She'd ultimately managed to shake off her grief and look ahead, even to the extent of confronting the prospect of her own death and its consequences for us, while I'd let myself be sucked into the vortex of the past.

"May I see the will?" one of the social workers asked. He was sitting behind the psychologist and hadn't uttered a word until now. "It doesn't have to be right now, but we'll need to check it at some point, as I'm sure you understand."

"Of course," Hakim said.

The psychologist looked at me.

"Samir," she said quietly. "In principle, the family court is bound by your mother's will, but since you are sixteen, you have a right to object to the guardianship."

I shook my head. I wouldn't have dreamt of objecting. The idea of moving in with Hakim was comforting. It was the only place I could imagine living now.

"That sounds like a good solution," the psychologist said. "When will you be finished with school?"

"Next year."

"So you'll get your diploma?"

"Yeah."

"Good." She smiled at me encouragingly. "There's just one thing," she said, and I could tell bad news was coming. "As I've said, the family court is generally bound by the parents' will—as long as it is in the children's best interests." She paused to let her words to sink in. "I believe this guardianship is in Samir's best interests. In any case, he won't require a guardian for very long. I'm sure he'll do some kind of apprenticeship when he finishes school, start earning his own money, get his own place."

I couldn't believe that this woman was making plans for me. I couldn't even think as far as the next day.

"Alina's case is different. She's going to need psychological support. I'll have to write a report for the family court.

It's very important that you listen carefully to what I'm about to tell you." She paused again. She'd emphasised the words "very important" by tapping the side of her hand on her thigh. "We," she said, turning to the two social workers and then back to face us, "are of the opinion that Alina will not find the stable environment she needs here."

Hakim leaned in and tried to say something, but the psychologist raised her hand to signal that she wasn't finished.

"Immediate family members and close friends are often under severe emotional strain themselves. The death of a loved one is a deeply distressing experience. It can impact their ability to care for others."

Hakim looked at me helplessly and put a hand on my leg.

"But the will appointed me as guardian for both of them," he said.

"I know." The psychologist remained unflustered. I wondered how many times she'd had this conversation. Living rooms, sad faces, the same wretched routine. "But we have to consider the child's best interests. It's crucial that we provide Alina with a secure environment to grow up in. An environment with the steady structures she needs to lead a normal life. It's not just about psychological support, it's about giving her a stable home and a sense of order."

"A stable home?" Hakim asked. His voice was steady, but I could see his foot shaking underneath the table. "I brought up my daughter on my own. She's going to sit her university entrance exams in spring and start her studies next year. I can do this. I've known Alina since she was born ... I'm like a father to her."

"We don't consider this a stable environment for the girl," said the other social worker, the woman. It was the first time she'd spoken since she arrived. I wished she'd kept her mouth shut. Her voice was formal, bureaucratic, devoid of empathy.

"So what kind of environment do you have in mind, exactly?" Hakim asked.

"A foster family." The social worker answered as if she'd just been asked what she had for lunch. She might as well have been saying, "Burger and chips."

"A foster family?"

Hakim's foot was shaking more violently now. How was he managing to sound so calm?

"We believe it's what's best for the child," the psychologist said. "I believe it's the most sensible decision."

There were so many questions I could have asked, but it felt as if the visitors' voices were incredibly far away, in another space and time. A foster family. A new home. A new father, a new mother. Maybe new brothers and sisters too. I knew they were right, but their plan was no less appalling for that. They wanted to simply transplant Alina's life. I thought about her gentle face. She had our father's features and his long, straight hair. I was going to lose her. Like we'd lost our parents. I was going to lose her without ever really knowing her. All those times she'd just wanted to hang out with me. *Will you take me to the playground, Samir? Will you stay for my birthday party? Will you tell me a story?* I'd never really been the son my mother had needed, and I'd never been the brother Alina had wanted. Now both of them were gone. Out of reach. All that would be left of the family that had moved here eight years ago was a dim memory.

I'll never forget when they drove off with her. She was slumped in the back seat, staring at her hands. A little black-haired bundle. I wanted her to bang on the windows, to cry and make a scene, but she just sat there listlessly.

She looked right through me as Hakim, Yasmin, and I watched the car pull away and leave our street. She didn't even wave.

We'd gone for a meal beforehand. After endless telephone calls, the time had come for them to come and get Alina.

"Why are you sending her so far away?" I'd asked after finding out where the foster family lived.

"Because your sister will be happier in a totally new environment. It'll help her recover," they'd said.

Her new parents had invited us out to a restaurant. He was the minister in a tiny parish somewhere in the north of Germany, "just sixty kilometres from the sea." She was an art teacher, "but only part-time." They did their best to hide their discomfort. They talked about their big house— Alina would love it, they said—and the beehive in their garden. They weren't bad people, they were actually quite nice. But I couldn't eat a thing, and neither could Hakim or Yasmin. We all just pushed our salads around our plates.

"We have a son, Marcel," they said. "He's eight, the same age as Alina. And we have an adopted daughter called Sulola. She's from Nigeria."

I didn't believe they were really going to take my sister away and raise her until I watched them drive off with her.

It felt like they'd torn off a piece of my own flesh. I missed Alina with every fibre of my being. Her happy-go-lucky laugh, her adorable capacity to lose herself in a book, the way she bent her wrist when she was writing so that, being left-handed, she wouldn't smudge what she'd just written. The way she brushed her teeth in a circular motion, just as she'd been taught, and burst out laughing when the foam from the toothpaste made her look like she had rabies. The way she sang and danced. There was so much I wanted to say to her. And so much that would remain unsaid.

Six months passed before I sent her the first of only a few letters. Yasmin used to phone her now and again, Hakim too, but I couldn't bring myself to call. So I wrote a few lines about how I'd be leaving school soon. Mostly, though, I asked about her. How she was doing, how she was settling into school, how she liked the sea.

She wrote back, but she never said how she was doing. Her childish scrawl just described what she saw:

The house is lovely, the teachers are nice. We even have a dog. His name is Moses. He's cute, but he's not allowed to sleep in the house. He has his own little house in the garden. I've been to the beach. But I couldn't swim, because the water here is too cold. My violin teacher's name is Viola. She has really long fingers. If I practise a lot, I might be allowed to play in a concert. When you come to visit, I'll play something for you.

I took Hakim's bedroom, and he slept on the living-room couch. It was a temporary arrangement. Yasmin would be moving out and starting university in the summer, so I'd take her room, if I hadn't moved out by then myself.

It was both nice and weird to be so close to Yasmin again. Weird mainly because Alex, her boyfriend, never left her side. He was nice enough to me, but I always got the sense he was keeping an eye on me. That he was suspicious of the past Yasmin and I shared. If the two of us were alone in a room when he came in, he'd make a show of putting his arm around her waist or giving her a casual pat on the backside. And when he was looking for her, he'd never just call her name, he'd shout something like, "Can you come here a minute, honey?" We spent many evenings in front of Hakim's TV with bags of crisps, cartons of ready-made sangria, rented videos. Yasmin and Alex didn't do too much cuddling and kissing when I was there beside them, but later, when I lay in bed staring at the wall, numb with loneliness, I'd hear rustling and muffled panting next door, followed by the sound of them tiptoeing to the bathroom.

When we were kids, Yasmin never made me feel like I was two years younger than her. Going on expeditions through dark corridors, climbing trees, jumping in puddles, whiling away rainy spring afternoons together—it's all blended into one fuzzy memory. The two of us in cahoots, united, inseparable.

But now, eight years later, it was hard not to notice the age difference. Puberty had taken me hostage, scattering angry red spots on my forehead and making my voice croak, whereas she'd become a woman. Everything about her was womanly: the way she smelled, walked, talked, dressed. I loved being around her, even though it made me painfully aware of how young, short, and inexperienced I was.

While I half-heartedly studied for my exams—I couldn't have cared less about school and my classmates and their banal chatter—Yasmin spent her afternoons swotting for her university-entrance exams in the library or with a study group. She wanted me to go with her—after all, it didn't make any difference where I studied—but I refused. I knew I wouldn't be able to resist glancing over at her, watching as she tucked her hair behind her ear like a little girl. I was stunned by how time had transfigured her. If I looked closely, I could still see that wild, fearless glint in her eyes, and it made me think of the tomboy who used to charge through undergrowth, beat a path through the thicket. But these days, there was something perceptive about her eyes, too; she always seemed present and curious and genuinely interested. I could be talking about something completely trivial, but the way she listened and nodded and asked questions made me feel like I was interesting, and my mind would go back to those wonderful afternoons on our steps when I used to relay Father's stories and her pupils would reflect the worlds I was creating. We used to be able to tell at a glance what the other was thinking, or we'd start a sentence with the exact same words at the same time. There were rare moments when it was still like that. Then it felt like nothing had changed, like our closeness had stood the test of time.

I never went into the library with her. But I'd meet her outside later. After school, I'd study in the canteen, spending half the time checking the clock above the vending machine. When at last it was time to go, I'd make my way to the library, an imposing stone building with decorated columns. Statues of two bearded men observed each other in front of the entrance: Plato and Socrates. I'd stand under their eyes on the steps, waiting for Yasmin to emerge, grinning, with a clear plastic bag full of books and notes.

One day we were strolling through town. The air was close and the streets were still shiny after a May shower. The pavements were crowded. People had closed their umbrellas, but they kept eyeing the sky with suspicion, ready for the next downpour. Our exams were just a few days away. We walked in silence side by side, going nowhere in particular. That was another great thing about being with Yasmin: our silences were never uncomfortable.

"Are you all set?" she asked after a while. The humidity had made her hair a little frizzy.

I shrugged. "I'll be fine. What about you?"

"Yeah, I'll be fine too." She smiled. "You can do it. I'm not worried about you at all."

I wasn't worried either. In fact, I didn't give a toss how I did in the exams.

"Are you looking forward to moving on?" I asked, without really thinking about what I was saying. "Starting uni, I mean?"

"Yeah." She smiled again. "Do you think I'll make a good psychologist?"

The question surprised me. She was usually so focused and ambitious, she didn't need encouragement from anyone else.

"Absolutely." It just came out of my mouth, but I really meant it. I knew she'd be a brilliant psychologist. She was such a good listener, someone you knew you could trust.

"Well, psychotherapist, to be precise. Five years of studying and then another three to five years of training."

"Wow, that's a long time." Five years seemed like forever to me, eight to ten were unimaginable. "And where? Will you go to uni here?"

"I don't know." Her voice had become more serious, tinged with a sadness that was unusual for her. "It's not easy to get a place. I'm just going to apply everywhere and then see what the Central Admissions Office says."

I nodded slowly.

"You'll be offered a place, don't worry."

"We'll see."

Yasmin looked at the ground as we walked on. Her mood had darkened, and it seemed to have affected the sky above us. The slate-grey clouds had thickened and merged with the horizon. *It's going to rain any minute,* I was thinking, when Yasmin started to cry.

"I'm looking forward to something new, I am. New people, student parties, all that stuff. A change of scene."

"But?"

"But it's hard to face leaving. I've never been anywhere else."

Hard. The prospect of Yasmin leaving wasn't hard. It was

unbearable. I didn't know how I'd have got through the past few months without her, and the thought of a future without her close by made my stomach tighten.

"Think of it as an adventure," I said. I smiled, hoping it didn't seem too forced. "I'll look after Hakim, don't worry."

She didn't reply, just took my hand and didn't let go as we continued on our way, her fingers interlaced with mine. It was an innocent gesture between friends who'd been brought together by ill fortune, who'd just realised that things couldn't stay this way forever. Yet my heart was thumping and a warm sensation tingled up my spine. I hoped I hadn't gone red.

We fell silent again. Our shoulders grazed, and we were connected not just physically, but by the knowledge that we had to savour this moment, that we mightn't get another one like it. We'd left the pedestrian zone far behind by now. We walked through estates, past houses with little gardens and flowers drooping after the rain. We just kept walking, with no real destination in mind.

"What about Alex?" I asked eventually. I held her hand tighter, afraid that the mention of her boyfriend might make her withdraw. But it didn't.

"He'll go to whichever uni takes me. He wants to study sports, and he can do that practically anywhere." Then she added, "Even so ..."

"That's good," I said. "You won't be on your own."

But it wasn't good. It was wrong, unfair, cruel. With a pang, I realised that they'd move in together, share a life. He'd be there when she needed someone to talk to. Alex, not me.

"Yeah, at least I won't have to worry about keeping a long-distance relationship going on top of everything else. The thought of it: having to phone him every night, heading down the motorway on Friday afternoons, spending

Friday evenings adjusting to each other again, spending Saturdays thinking about Sunday, then back on the motorway again. I'm not cut out for it."

"Out of sight, out of mind, eh?"

"That's not it. I just think it's really, really hard to keep your feelings for someone alive if you hardly ever see them. Anyway, it's beside the point—he's coming with me."

She sounded relieved. I lowered my head. If she did move away, what she said would apply to our relationship too.

"What about you?" she asked.

"I don't know yet. Haven't really thought about it. I'll find something."

"I've no doubt you will."

She squeezed my hand again.

By now, the houses had been replaced by blocks of flats. We'd somehow walked all the way to the edge of town. Desolate fields, pylons, bottle banks. I was thinking about how long it would take us to walk home when Yasmin suddenly stopped. I looked at her and she was beaming. Tower blocks rose up ahead of us, concrete behemoths as grey as the sky. An old wall, wet and covered in moss, blocked our view of the courtyard.

It hadn't changed much. Just more graffiti, more broken glass by the kerb, more ivy and spider webs around the entrance. Like a long-abandoned ruin, an enchanted Elysium, our Atlantis.

Yasmin let go of my hand and looked at me. Her eyes were transformed, as if someone had pulled aside a grey curtain to reveal a brightly lit stage. She didn't have to say anything, I knew exactly what she was thinking. We walked up to the rusty gate, creaked it open, and walked into the courtyard. The same old swing was there, but the paint had peeled off and the corroded chains looked like they were about to fall apart. The same teenagers, huddled and smoking. They would have seemed so grown-up back then, the kings of the flats. But now they were just kids brought together by boredom, the last guardians of a forgotten temple. We felt like ghosts who'd travelled back on a shimmering time stream.

"Come on," Yasmin whispered. Her cheeks were red with excitement as she made her way up the stairs gingerly, as if her footsteps might wake us from our beautiful dream. It was so potent, this physical sense of all the years that had gone by. We sneaked through the corridors beneath broken lightbulbs, running our fingers along the walls and listening to the sounds coming from behind the doors: TVs, low conversations in exotic languages, the faint beats of unfamiliar music—like when we were kids. I didn't notice at first that Yasmin was no longer beside me. I turned around, and it took a moment to spot her on her knees, holding her nose to the crack of one of the doors. She beckoned me over and patted the floor beside her. I knelt down beside her, put my nose to the door and inhaled the strange aromas.

"African," she whispered.

"Are you sure?"

"Yes. What can you smell?"

I sniffed again. Yasmin had always been better at this game than me.

"Onions?" I whispered back.

"Definitely. And chilli. A trace of cardamom. A pinch of pepper—black, I think. Sweetcorn too, but I could be wrong about that. A few peanuts, maybe, and definitely a handful of baobab leaves, cassava root, and ground fenugreek."

I gaped at her.

She stared back, deadly serious, but couldn't keep a

straight face for long. She dissolved into snorts of laughter and had to press her hand against her mouth to keep the noise down. I started laughing too. An absurd scene, two overgrown kids on their knees in the dirty corridor in front of a stranger's flat, sniffing at the door. Just like in the old days. Yasmin grinned at me. Bright and clear and carefree. We were back in our world. Right then, it didn't matter where life might take her; we felt so close that no distance could separate us. I grinned back. I could smell her skin, the fragrance of her body lotion, a delicate mixture of honey and musk. Our cheeks were almost touching. We heard footsteps behind the door and sprang to our feet. Giggling, Yasmin pulled me along after her, and we made it around the corner before the door opened.

We leaned against the wall, shoulder to shoulder, laughing and trying to catch our breath. Then we played the game again, kneeling, sniffing, guessing, standing up, going to the next door. Until we eventually got to number 37. A damp doormat, a tarnished doorknob, a nameplate without a name. We looked at each other. If Yasmin was anything like me, thousands of images were flashing through her mind: Mother combing her hair, the two of us exchanging conspiratorial glances across the dining table, Father reading aloud to us as we cuddle up on the sofa in our tiny living room. Instinctively, my fingers stroked the old wood in the doorframe. I felt as if I could reach out and touch the past. Memories of a world that wasn't yet so big that we'd get lost in it. Yasmin put her hand on mine, held it tight, and kissed me quickly on the lips. It was longer than the blink of an eye, but not long enough for me to be immersed, to really feel the warmth of her lips.

It was late by the time we'd ambled home beneath a slightly brighter sky. We ate with Hakim, but we didn't talk much. He eyed us curiously but knew better than to ask why we were so quiet. Alex came by later and gave me a high five. Yasmin flung her arms around his neck and they kissed. I can't remember what film we watched. We sat on the couch, Yasmin in the middle with her head on his shoulder and a hand in his lap. She stroked his fingers absent-mindedly. I sipped beer out of a can and tried to concentrate on the film, but I couldn't, because my foot was under the coffee table and Yasmin's little toe was touching it.

We both passed our exams. Yasmin got straight As, I scraped by. Not that I cared. I was just surprised, seeing as the numbers and words on my exam paper had all been a blur and I'd guessed most of the answers. That was in July 2001. I was finished with school. I sent Alina a letter with a photo of a smiling me holding my exam results. She wrote back a few weeks later.

Hi Samir,
Your suit is lovely. Marcel wears a suit when we go to church on Sundays. I like it there because everyone sings together.
I painted Moses a picture and hung it up in his kennel.
There are pictures hanging up all over the house, but he's not allowed in. Everyone is nice to me here and at school.
I like school and I'm glad I'm not finished like you. We're going on holiday in August. I can't wait, I've never been on a plane before. There are beaches where we're going, but it'll be warmer there, so we might be able to go swimming at last. I'm sending you a photo too. The girl next to me is Louisa. We're in the same class. If you come visit, you'll get to meet her.

I didn't recognise the dress Alina was wearing. Her long hair had been plaited into pigtails, and the innocent smile on her face as she looked into the camera made me want to cry. I probably would have, if Hakim hadn't knocked on the door. He had his jacket on, a well-stuffed sports bag in each hand, the car key wedged between his fingers.

"Coming?"

I shoved the letter and the photo back into the envelope, nodded, and took one of the bags from him as we made our way outside. Yasmin and Alex were already sitting in the car.

I timed the journey: it took exactly five hours, thirteen minutes, and twenty-four seconds to reach the car park outside Yasmin's student residence. It was half a country away. En route: smelly service areas, the heady odour of petrol stations, and changing landscapes: fewer mountains, more trees. I thought back to the day Yasmin had got her letter. Her eyes had widened as she read it and she'd thrown her arms around me before running out of the room to tell Hakim.

We carried their luggage down a narrow path to their rooms. A student-run residence: two rooms, furnished; one kitchen and two bathrooms to be shared with the other students in the residence; washing machine and dryer in the basement; a bike rack. The two of them went ahead, hand in hand, looking around excitedly and whispering. Washing hung from makeshift lines outside some of the doors, students sprawled on blankets on the lawn, reading and smoking. The flat was small, impersonal, and not very clean, but I knew Yasmin would make it feel like home in no time.

Hakim hugged Alex goodbye and wished him luck. Then he put his arms around Yasmin and held her while Alex and I stood by awkwardly. It seemed as if he'd never let her go. I had a lump in my throat as I said goodbye. I twisted my mouth into a smile and put my arms around her. Not for too long, just a short, friendly hug. I'd pictured this moment so many times, ever since she'd opened the acceptance letter and I'd sunk into conflicted gloom, pleased for her but feeling as if it was the end of the world for me. I'd even prepared a little farewell speech thanking her for everything she'd done for me over the past few months, promising to write and visit. But I was too embarrassed to deliver it here in the car park with Alex and Hakim looking on.

"All the best," I said. "Take care."

She nodded, welling up. It was late summer, hot and muggy, the end of another August and the start of something completely new, a cloudless day that was much too bright for what was happening.

"You too."

They waved as Hakim and I drove off. I raised my hand briefly, then looked straight ahead at the hot air shimmering above the road. I felt neither sadness nor hope. Just emptiness. Had I known it would be years before I saw her again, I might have turned around for one last look.

11

Sunlight slants in through the slats of the shutters, landing on high tables and a bar. Dust motes dance in the narrow strips of light. Animal-shaped shadows fall across the posters on the wall advertising parties past and future. There's a smell of sweat and alcohol and smoke. The sticky floor is littered with cigarette butts and plastic glasses, and a disco ball rotates above our heads.

"We closed four hours ago," the man says. Ripped muscles are visible beneath his tight black T-shirt. Dark brown eyes, full lips, a round, bald head, and a bull neck. He's twice as broad as me. "We don't allow anyone to see the club like this."

A few minutes ago, we were standing outside. Though the footpaths were almost deserted, it was obvious that Mar Mikhael is a nightlife district. Clubs and bars on both sides of the street, brightly coloured buildings, graffiti, low-hanging bunting. Everyone we do see looks like an artist, street entertainer, musician, dancer, or fire-eater. The clubs have English and French names: Studio 43, Behind the Green Door, Floyd the Dog, Electro Mechanique, L'humeur du Chef. It took us a while to find Rhino Night Club. Crumbling, overgrown with ivy, and with a plain sign above the door, it looked more like a run-down youth centre.

I rang the bell three times before the man finally appeared. He waved me away and pointed to his watch: we're closed.

He turned away, and I rang the bell again.

The glass door opened. Forbidding biceps, surly voice.

"What?"

"I'm looking for Sinan Aziz."

"And you are ...?"

"Samir el-Hourani. This is my friend Nabil."

"We're not open till later."

"I need to speak to him right away."

"I need to go to bed right away. Come back this evening."

"Are you Sinan Aziz?"

"No."

"Is he there?"

"He doesn't like visitors. Not at this time of day, anyway."

"Can you just tell him I'm here? He might make an exception."

Raised eyebrows, a sceptical look.

"Now why would he do that?"

"I've got this card."

A gale of laughter.

"You're joking, right?"

"No, why?"

"That's just one of our business cards. They're all over town."

"But I was given it in Zahle."

"So what?"

"By my grandmother. Sinan Aziz brought her the card himself."

A short pause.

"What do you want me to tell him?"

"Tell him Brahim Bourguiba's son wants to talk to him."

The club is bigger than it looks from the outside. It's not very wide, but it goes right back, like a train tunnel. The man leads us across the dancefloor, past a little stage. Cables and other technical equipment are lying around on the floor.

"We have live music on Fridays," he says.

We turn into a narrow corridor and pass the toilets. The sign on the gents says "Rhinos," and it's "Rhinas" on the ladies. At the end of the corridor, a flight of stairs leads to another door.

"Go on up," the man says. "That's his office."

We enter a dimly lit room. The curtains are drawn, and a small lamp bathes a desk in a sepia glow. My eyes need a moment to adjust. Behind the desk sits a dark, hulking figure. I can hear him breathing heavily.

"Sinan Aziz?" I ask.

"Come in," the figure says. His voice is preternaturally deep and booming, as if it's coming to us from the depths of a ravine.

As I walk towards the desk, the giant rises slowly to his feet. I can't see his face. The breathing turns into puffing and panting as he comes out from behind the desk. He must be at least two metres tall, his footsteps heavy and ungainly. He seems to take up the entire room.

The first thing I notice when his face finally emerges from the darkness is his eyes: narrow, inquisitive slits. His cheeks are doughy, and a cunning smirk plays around his thin lips, like he's just figured out how to cheat an opponent at cards. He towers so high above me that I have to tilt my head back to look at him. He's smiling, but it fails to hide his tension. He's like a deceptively lumbering animal that could rear up at any moment and charge through a wall.

Grandmother's words ring in my ears: *The fat one with the ugly nose.*

Without that nose, Sinan Aziz would be fairly average-looking. Exceptionally tall and heavy, yes, but there would be nothing remarkable about his long, heavy-chinned face were it not for the nose. It juts out sharply like a horn and has massive nostrils. Now that he's right in front of me, a wild suspicion begins to creep over me.

"I'm Samir," I say.

He offers his paw.

"Sinan Aziz."

We stare at each other for a second. Then he lets go of my hand and points to two chairs in front of his desk.

"Have a seat."

"Should I wait outside?" Nabil asks me.

"No. He's a friend," I say, turning to Aziz.

Aziz shrugs and lumbers back behind his desk. I quickly explain why I'm here. That I'm looking for my father, that my grandmother told me to come here. He listens in silence, his skin glistening in the dim light.

"So you've showed up here hoping I can help." Aziz cracks an oily smile, revealing a set of crooked teeth. "Let's see what I can do."

"How do you know my father? If you know him, that is?"

Aziz gives a sluggish nod, as if the answer's obvious, as if it's a stupid question. Listening to him talk, watching him move, I get the same feeling I had yesterday in Grandmother's garden. A vague sense of déjà vu. This is the first time I've met this man, yet I feel as if I know him.

"I used to work with your father."

"In a nightclub?"

Aziz bursts out laughing, his belly wobbling like a bowl of jelly.

"This place is only eight years old. I never had anything to do with clubs before that. We worked together in a hotel. The Carlton."

"The one on the Corniche?"

"There was only one Carlton in Lebanon."

"So you were colleagues?"

"That's what I just said."

My creeping suspicion is becoming a certainty. I stare at him in amazement.

"Me and him, we didn't have that much to do with each other." He opens a little metal case, takes out a cigar, cuts the end off, and lights up. "Brahim dealt with the guests: in the restaurant, by the pool, at weddings. Always on the front line."

He purses his lips and releases little rings of cigar smoke.

"Did you work on the front line too?"

He snorts.

"You must be joking. I generally helped out in the kitchen or cleaned rooms once we were sure the guests had left the building. I was never the best-looking guy, not even back then, and our manager was a bit … difficult."

"How do you mean?"

Aziz waves dismissively.

"It's ancient history. I haven't thought about it in years."

"I'd like to hear about it, though. If you don't mind."

He examines me suspiciously, his eyes becoming even narrower.

"His surname was Abdallah. He wasn't your typical hotel manager."

"Why not?"

"Have you ever been personally welcomed by the manager when you've arrived at a hotel?"

I shake my head.

"Well, it happens in a lot of hotels. The manager gets a call from reception telling him that new guests have arrived. So he goes into the foyer, shakes their hands, wishes them a pleasant stay. They tend to be slick operators, the kind of guys who could charm the birds out of the trees. Good talkers, well dressed, real ass-kissers."

"What about Abdallah?"

"Abdallah wasn't like that at all. The entire left side of his face was covered in burns. Don't know what happened to him. In the wrong place when a grenade was thrown, I guess. Anyway, he was always holed up in his office—he only ever came out to threaten us, to tell us we were too slow, too dirty, too fat, too lazy. He'd dock our pay whenever he felt like it and then claim the guests had complained about their food or the state of their rooms. 'You're no better than the filth you clean up.' That was one of his favourite sayings. He treated us like slaves." Aziz looks me in the eye. "Your father was the only one he left alone. He was the one who welcomed new guests, shook their hands. 'Our manager, Mr. Abdallah, sends his apologies. He would have liked to welcome you himself, but he's in an important meeting. If there's anything I can do for you, please let me know.' Good-looking guy, your father. People liked him. As I said, we didn't have that much to do with each other. Different shifts, different interests. But Brahim was a happy-go-lucky kind of guy. Everything was a game to him. He got more tips than anyone else. He was charming, well-spoken, knew what the guests wanted before they knew it themselves. The minute their glass was empty, Brahim would be standing behind them with the right wine. He had them wrapped around his little finger. Excellent businessman."

"My father? Really?" I'd never thought of him as a businessman. The only hint of business acumen I ever saw was when he tried to haggle with the shop assistants when we were out buying groceries.

"You and your father. You didn't know each other very well, did you?"

"I'm not sure anyone really knew him," I say.

"The people who stayed at the Carlton were pretty loaded. Most of them came from the Gulf States, money was no object. But they were incredibly bored by their wealth. Brahim knew how to use that boredom to his advantage."

"How?"

"By making them feel like they were caught up in a big adventure. The main characters in an incredible story, born under a lucky star. If he saw one of them standing alone in the corridor for even a second, he'd sidle up and ask if he could do anything for them, if they needed anything. 'I bet you like whisky,' he'd say. To which they'd usually answer, 'My God, it's eleven in the morning, do I look like an alcoholic?' and try to send him on his way. But then Brahim would say, 'I don't mean right now.' He'd move a bit closer and lower his voice." Aziz leans his massive body across the desk and brings his face up to mine. "'I mean in general. You look like someone who appreciates a good whisky. We both know it's completely overpriced here in the hotel. The usual brands—Copper Fox, Baker's, Blanton's—I mean, the whisky's fine, but it's nothing special. I know it's not about the money for you, but let's be honest: you don't like people taking advantage, do you? Of an honest man like you?' He had their attention then. Brahim was able to speak these people's language. 'But I can get you the best whisky in town. You've never had a whisky like it. Incredibly rare—priceless, in fact. But I can get you a whole bottle for five hundred dollars.' The guests would get wary then, start to suspect he might be trying to pull a fast one. So what did your father do? He banished all their doubts with a story. A story so absurd it could only be true in a city as crazy as Beirut at that time. 'In the east,' he'd murmur, 'there's an old cellar. Hidden within the Phoenician city walls. The entrance is blocked by nondescript metal fencing. You'd never notice it if you didn't know it was there. Behind the fence there's a long passage leading to a labyrinth of old escape tunnels dug thousands of years ago. You won't find this forgotten labyrinth on a map, though. Nobody really knows where all these tunnels lead; there's just too many of them. If you don't know your way around down there, you can forget it—you'll never get out. Have you heard of the Oxford family?' Needless to say, the guests would shake their heads, so then Brahim would say, 'The Oxfords came to Beirut in the late 1930s. Before independence. The grandfather was a renowned American archaeologist, became rich and famous after he dug up dinosaur bones in Argentina. He came to Beirut to examine Phoenician burial sites. During one of his expeditions into the underground labyrinth, he stumbled upon a kind of vault at the end of a tunnel. A big cellar full of old casks. Several hundred of them, by all accounts. After some investigation, he realised they hadn't been stored down there by the Phoenicians—that would have made them more than a thousand years old. No, there's a way of estimating the age of these things, and he discovered that the casks had been down there for about a hundred years. And that could only mean one thing: that the Ottomans had hidden them there when they occupied Beirut. As you know, Lebanon was under Ottoman rule until 1860. Anyway, when old Mr. Oxford took a look inside the casks, he could hardly believe his eyes.' At that point, Brahim would pause and whisper, 'Whisky. More than a hundred years old.'"

Sinan Aziz roars laughing again and his stomach bumps against the table, causing it to shake precariously.

"Imagine!" he says. He laughs even louder and bangs on the table with the palm of his hand. "Ottoman whisky! Anyone with an ounce of sense would have dragged your father by the ear into Mr. Abdallah's office. But these guys were so bored, so seduced by the idea of getting their hands on something really rare and special that they believed his ridiculous bullshit."

I can't say I blame the tourists. Father could certainly spin a yarn. No doubt they'd have thrown themselves out of a tenth-floor window if his story had demanded it.

"So what happened then?"

"That's when Brahim needed an accomplice. He'd tell the guests he needed them to keep a lookout while he went off to west Beirut to get the whisky from a middleman. He'd give them a pair of binoculars and a radio, and tell them to warn him if they spotted any roadblocks or snipers on the roofs. 'How are we supposed to know if there are snipers around?' the guests would ask. Brahim would send them off up onto the roof with me or another colleague, and we'd make sure they were facing east, towards the city. Of course, we could only do that when we were sure there were no snipers on our roof. Meanwhile your father would amble out of the hotel, cross the street to the little wooden huts on the Corniche, and buy a bottle of whisky for three dollars. You should've seen it, those guys in their fancy white suits. They thought they were players in some cloak-and-dagger operation, standing around on the roof while their wives were getting hammered by the pool. They'd radio your father, 'All clear, no road blocks in sight,' and he'd radio back, 'Good. Remain vigilant, I'm nearly at the Green Line.' And all the time he'd be standing right in front of the hotel, eating an ice cream."

"And he never got caught?"

Aziz shook his head admiringly.

"The whisky was vile stuff. Brahim just poured it into old brown bottles, no label, nothing. I don't know if the guests ever tried it, their Ottoman whisky. They probably thought it was too precious to drink. And if they did try it, I'm sure they convinced themselves that it was this special Ottoman note that gave the whisky its distinctive flavour."

I have to smile. If Father had one talent, it was storytelling. In a painful kind of way, it's wonderful to hear that he'd always been a master of the art.

"If anyone had got wind of it, we'd all have been in deep shit," Aziz says. "Abdallah would've killed us. Had us lined us up against the wall and shot. But no one ever did find out. Partly because Brahim never set off straight away to get the whisky. He'd always wait two or three days, depending on how long the guests were staying. He'd tell them it took a while because his middlemen couldn't go down into the secret passages whenever they felt like it, they had to wait until the coast was clear. Having to wait convinced these guys they were getting their hands on something really special."

"So what did he do with the money?"

Aziz grins again, and I notice a gold tooth glinting in his mouth.

"He blew it all on us. Maybe he was trying to keep us sweet, I don't know. Brahim was the only one who got on with Abdallah. It made the rest of us a bit suspicious. We never knew how much we could tell your father. But then there was a general atmosphere of mistrust during the civil war. You know the Lebanese. We're open and friendly. But not during the war. You didn't know who you could trust, so you had to be careful. Religion wasn't a major issue in the hotel. Among the employees, I mean. Religion was used by the militiamen as an excuse to butcher each other. Meanwhile, among the civilian population, Christians, Muslims, and Druze were generally getting along fine, just as they always had. But you always had the sense that things could get ugly very easily. A slip of the tongue, a minor car accident, an argument, and you wouldn't be a neighbour anymore, you'd be the Muslim, the Christian, the Druze, and people would be quick to hurl accusations around. But Brahim didn't care what religion we were. He was generous, bought us all drinks. I think he just liked a good knees-up, really."

That's comforting to hear too. It sounds like the man I knew. Father wasn't fake, he didn't lie to us.

"I remember this one evening," Aziz says, scratching the back of his head and looking at the wall above my head, as if he's just spotted a portal leading him back to that evening. "The reason I remember it so well is that I only went out with your father twice. We rarely worked the same shifts. I heard about most of his exploits from others. But this one time, we were in a disco. Brahim paid for all the drinks, and we were pissing ourselves laughing at a Saudi he'd scammed out of five hundred dollars with his whisky racket. We'd just been to the theatre. The play we'd seen was the talk of Beirut. In fact, the entire country was up in arms about it. It later became famous throughout the Arab world and ran in Beirut for years. One matinee performance and one in the evening. Constantly sold out. It premiered in 1980 at Cinéma Jeanne d'Arc in Hamra, in west Beirut, where they sometimes put on plays. Tickets were like gold dust. The waiting list was six to eight months. But we were determined to see it."

"Why was there so much hype about it?"

"It was by Ziad Rahbani, who was a star even before he wrote it. The son of Fairuz, the singer—you know Fairuz. But Rahbani wasn't famous just because of her. He was multitalented in his own right: an author, pianist, columnist—there was nothing the man couldn't do. But he surpassed himself with *Film Ameriki Tawil*."

I catch Nabil nodding out of the corner of my eye and turn around.

"You saw it too?"

"Oh yes," Nabil says. "Everyone saw *Film Ameriki Tawil*. It was the sole topic of conversation at the time, so you had to see it if you wanted to join in."

Aziz looks at me and points at Nabil. *Told you*, he seems to be saying.

"So why was it the talk of the town?"

"It's set in a lunatic asylum," Aziz says, "sort of inspired by *One Flew Over the Cuckoo's Nest*. You could say it's a metaphor for the civil war. Religious paranoiacs and neurotics everywhere. An outrageous comedy, took the piss out of everyone and everything. Showed how absurd the war was. Can you imagine what it was like? People making their way through Beirut; burning buildings and gunfire on some streets, totally quiet on other streets. It's dangerous to be out and about, but no one wants to miss out. So everyone's flocking to Cinéma Jeanne d'Arc to see a play about a war they've just walked through."

"The best thing about it was the characters," Nabil says. "They were just like us. One character, Hani, lives in constant fear of being stopped by the militias. So he runs around the ward showing people his ID and refusing to go away until they give him permission to move on. Another character ... what was he called again?"

"Abed?" Aziz suggests.

"Abed, that's it. Abed is a writer who wants to write a book about the civil war. He wants to reveal the truth about the war, about the conspiracies behind it, but he never figures out the truth, so he can never start his book."

"The play is full of characters like that, characters that everyone recognised." Aziz smiles. "Another one is terrified of Muslims, so he refuses to talk to strangers until they tell him what religion they are. Like I said, tickets were like gold dust, but somehow Brahim managed to get his hands on some. There were four of us: me, him, and two other colleagues. All in our best suits. We split our sides laughing, it was the best evening of my life. Afterwards we were pretty hyper, first in the disco, then in the taxi on the way back to the hotel. We jabbered about the play non-stop, but Brahim ... I don't know ... He was unusually quiet, deep in thought."

"Why?"

"I don't know. I wanted to include him, so I said, 'Brahim, what was your favourite bit?' And he looks at me and says, 'The beginning.' 'The beginning?' I ask. 'You mean the first dialogue?' 'No,' he says. 'I mean the beginning. When the announcer takes the stage.' I look at him and ask, 'Why was that the best part?' And he replies, 'The play is full of truth, but the truest bit is right at the start.' Brahim used to speak in riddles sometimes. For some reason the very start got him thinking."

"What happens at the start?"

"Not much," says Nabil. "The play opens with the sound of bombs going off and the Lebanese anthem playing. An announcer comes on and says, 'It is the year 1980 or 1979, but it could just as well be 1978.' That's all he says. That's all he needs to say. Everyone knew what he meant: the war had reached a stalemate. It was Rahbani saying that the war was going to drag on for at least another ten years, that's how we interpreted it. He turned out to be right."

"It made an impression on all of us, but it seemed to affect Brahim the most," Aziz says. "He was quiet for the rest of night, sat in the corner as we were playing cards, lost every hand."

I prick up my ears.

"Cards?"

"Yeah, we played a game in my room that night. We had a regular cards night, but your father was there only that

one time. No wonder he lost—I was basically unbeatable."
Aziz grins again. "This nightclub has been my job for the
past eight years. It's honest work. Before that, I was a professional gambler, spent five days a week in the casino.
One day eight years ago, I made a fortune. When I woke up
the next morning, it hit me: that's it, I'll never need to work
again. But I'm not the kind of guy who can sit around on
his ass all day. So I opened this nightclub, and I've been
here ever since," he says, gesturing around him with both
arms.

My eyes are drawn to a row of photos on the wall behind
Aziz's head. One shows him standing in front of the bar
with his arms around two beautiful blonde women. He's
still talking, but I'm barely listening. In this dark office, it
dawns on me.

Rhino Night Club. We had a regular cards night ... I was basi-
cally unbeatable.

I stare at him as he keeps on talking. My temples are
throbbing. Aziz's voice is far away, barely audible. I feel
weightless; the realisation is so powerful that it yanks me
back to my childhood. So many images flashing past:
Father sitting on the edge of my bed, his eyes sparkling,
telling a story in a soft voice.

"The rhinoceros—it's you!" I blurt.

Aziz stiffens.

"What did you say?"

"I know who you are," I say, "You're the rhinoceros who's
unbeatable at cards."

He frowns, looking at Nabil as if I'm out of my mind.

"Father spoke about you," I say. "Well, not about you directly, but about a rhinoceros that never loses at cards."

Aziz's bewildered expression softens a little.

"Rhinoceros," he says. "I haven't been called that in a
long time." He leans over again, casting a massive shadow

over the desk. "Rhinoceros was what the other employees called me in the Carlton. I told them I didn't like it, so they started calling me Rhino instead, which I thought was cool. It sounded kind of American. People still call me that today."

It feels as if the characters in Father's stories have come to life, as if they've escaped from my imagination and are now leading real lives of their own. But what really stuns me is the fact that Father never once mentioned Sinan Aziz or the rhinoceros in his diary. I've always assumed he made up this part of his story just for me. That the rhinoceros and camel were products of his imagination, nothing else. The thought that they're real people, people I can track down, gives me a tingling sensation in the pit of my stomach. I've always known that Father found inspiration for his stories in real life; he'd done that back when he told stories to the kids in the sports hall. But sitting so close to Sinan Aziz, knowing that I could reach out and touch the rhinoceros, a character from one of Father's last stories, is overwhelming. It makes Aziz seem slightly surreal, like something out of a fairy tale.

"So he talked about me, you say?"

"Not directly. I didn't know you used to work together. But he more or less based a character in one of his stories on you."

Aziz doesn't seem to know whether he should be amused or baffled.

I'm itching to ask the next question. It feels like I'm closing in on Father, and the suspense is killing me.

"Sinan," I say. "Why did you go see my grandmother a few years ago? You gave her the card. Why?"

The giant leans back in his chair, and his face disappears into the shadows again.

"I'm surprised that wasn't the first question you asked,"

he says. "What can I say? I was hoping to find Brahim."

I jump out of my seat.

"Why?"

"Take it easy. I've already told you I barely knew your father. That's the truth. I haven't seen him since 1982; he just disappeared off the face of the earth. But that wasn't unusual back then, there was a lot of coming and going in that hotel."

"And then, almost thirty years later, you suddenly decided it would be nice to see him again?"

His voice remains calm.

"You're barking up the wrong tree. I'm not interested in Brahim. I never really knew him and I'm not about to change that now." He examines me for a moment. He seems to be considering whether he should say the next sentence. "There's something you should know: you're not the only one looking for your father."

"What's that supposed to mean?"

"Brahim and I," he says, his eyes still fixed on me, "have a mutual friend."

"A mutual friend? Who?"

"I can't tell you. He's a bit of a recluse. I hadn't seen him for years. He'd disappeared too, left the hotel not long before your father. And then one day he showed up here, asking whether I knew where Brahim was. Which of course I didn't, but it wasn't hard to track down his mother. So I visited her and asked her to call me if her son ever turned up."

"This friend. What does he want with my father?"

Aziz doesn't answer right away. He nods towards my chair, I sit down again and he exhales slowly, his nostrils flaring.

"He wants to forgive him," he says eventually.

Nabil is looking at me. He seems to be unnerved by the

turn the conversation has taken. He's had his hands clasped the whole time, and I can see a film of sweat on them.

I do my best to keep my voice steady. "What does he want to forgive him for?"

"It's up to him to tell you," Aziz says, folding his hands over his belly. "If he wants to. Some stories should only be told once."

The sunlight is so blinding when we leave the club that I have to shut my eyes. For a while, all I see are orange dots. The city has woken up. Mopeds are rattling across the asphalt again, tables and chairs have appeared on the pavement and are already occupied. Waitresses ferry trays of tea and fruit juice. Young people wander past, and nearby a mime artist stands stock still on a bucket, a hat on the ground in front of him.

The door has just closed behind us, yet my encounter with Aziz already feels like a dream.

He said he'd call the man. And if he's willing to meet me, he'll let me know. Aziz promised this before he showed us out of the office

We head back to the car.

"How are you doing?" Nabil asks. "Are you all right?"

"Yeah," I say. "Ever feel like you don't know if you're awake or sleeping?"

"Sure."

"That's how I feel right now."

"If you're sleeping, you're dreaming of me." Nabil laughs. "I'm honoured."

Back in the car, I get the diary out of my rucksack. A bit I'd forgotten about has just popped into my mind. I flick through the diary until I find the entry:

Beirut, 4 September 1980

8:30 p.m.

I got a promotion today. Well, not really a promotion, but I've been given an important new responsibility. Abdallah called me in. I thought he wanted to talk about the wedding tomorrow. Whether I've been in touch with the musicians, whether the seating arrangement has been sorted out, whether we've got everything ready downstairs. I know how important the weddings are. For the hotel's reputation—and because they bring in a lot of money, of course.

– Close the door, he says when I come into his office.

Mr. Abdallah always keeps his curtains drawn and the little lamp on his desk on. Because of his burns, maybe?

– You wanted to see me?

– That's right. I hear you're doing a good job here. You're reliable, the guests like you.

– I do my best.

– Don't be so modest. I have a job for you. You know how much I've got on my plate.

He points to a pile of envelopes on the desk.

– If I have to get up every thirty minutes and run downstairs to welcome guests, I won't get through half of these.

– I can imagine.

– So I'd like you to greet the guests in future.

– Certainly, if you wish.

– I don't wish anything. I'm telling you, this is your job from now on. Any objections?

– No, Mr. Abdallah.

– Good, then get back to work.

His eyes look almost white in this light. He looks at me impatiently.

– Thank you, Mr. Abdallah.

I'm almost at the door when he calls my name again.

– Brahim!

I turn around. A strange smile plays around his lips. The left half of his face is illuminated by the lamp, and the burned skin gives off a greenish sheen, glinting like scaly armour.

– Brahim, he says, you've been working here for more than six months now. From now on, I'm going to address you by your first name. That's not something I do with everyone.

I know he doesn't do that with everyone. Sometimes when he's bawling out the others, he calls them animals.

– I want you to address me by first name too, he says, his eyes flashing.

There's something creepy about him, something sinister, reptilian. I shudder inwardly and nod.

– Good, he says, his smile turning into a sneer. Then call me Ishaq.

12

"This was under E." Chris said disapprovingly, waving a book in my face. His black horn-rimmed glasses had slid down his nose, making him look like a moronic Harry Potter. "The lady back there chased me up and down the aisles until I found it for her."

I looked over his shoulder. An elderly woman in a dark jacket, grey hair peeking out under a black cloche hat, was standing at the loans desk. In one white-gloved hand she held a black umbrella. She was impatiently tapping the counter with the index finger of the other.

"Is that Mary Poppins?" I whispered.

"Could be, forty years on. Look—you put the book back on the wrong shelf. See, it belongs under F. For begins with an F."

My eyes fell on the title: FOR YOURSELF: THE FULFILMENT OF FEMALE SEXUALITY.

Chris shrugged.

"She said it's for her niece."

"Sorry," I said. "I wasn't concentrating."

"It's OK. But be careful." He pointed his thumb over his shoulder at the endless aisles of shelves. "If you put books back in the wrong places, we'll never find them again. It was sheer chance that I found this one."

"Thanks," I said, because I knew that's what he really wanted to hear. And though it stuck in my craw, I added, "You're the best."

Chris was nearly forty but looked more like eighteen. He had a very high voice and walked with a bit of a stoop, which I put down to the fact that he was always poring over books. The way he shoved his glasses up his nose every other second, I reckoned he'd end up with arthritis in his finger. Chris was my boss. The kind of boss who makes you wonder what kind of demeaning things he must've had to do before someone showed mercy and elevated him to his current position. He didn't command the slightest shred of authority—as evidenced by old ladies chasing him up and down the aisles, and junior staff and visitors alike addressing him by his first name. For me it was important to be on good terms with Chris. I didn't want him watching my movements too closely because I'd be finished if he ever found out what I got up to down in the archive or on the computer in his office.

"Any plans for this evening?" he asked casually, after handing the female sexuality book to the old lady.

"I think Aurea wants to go out for dinner."

He frowned for a second, as if considering what day it was.

"Aha," he said. "And what are you going to give her? Flowers?"

I hadn't bought anything. In fact, I hadn't really been planning on giving her a present at all.

"Yes, flowers."

"Very good. Old school—I'm proud of you." He laughed. The way he said it was unintentionally funny. You'd swear he was Casanova giving his naïve grandson a few tips on seduction.

The thought of spending the evening with Aurea was giving me a headache. It didn't suit my plans at all. What I really wanted was to keep doing what I was doing in the archives. She'd caught me on the hop when she casually suggested doing something on Valentine's Day, but then I'd just smiled and said, "Whatever you like."

"How old are you, Samir?" asked Chris. We were piling returned books onto a trolley.

"Twenty."

"Ah, twenty—the right age to be celebrating Valentine's Day," he said. He gave me a chummy dig with his elbow. "Why don't you leave early today. Use up some of the overtime you've clocked up over the last few weeks."

"No need, thanks. We're not meeting until this evening."

"Samir, you need time to go home and smarten up. Then you pick her up and take her out. That's how it's done."

"Thanks, really, but I've got it under control."

He looked at me over the rim of his glasses.

"What if I make that an order?"

What an absurd idea. Even a two-year-old wouldn't take an order from Chris Poliak.

"I'll put these books back first," I said to change the subject. "Who knows, maybe I'll finish the job early."

"OK." Chris pushed his glasses up his nose. "But make sure you put them back in the right places."

The light from the tall library windows fell on the long wooden shelves. The trolley glided over the marble floor, and all around me I heard the muted whispers of library users. I loved that sound, but I loved the smell of the books even more. There was something comforting and magical about it. The scent of countless stories slumbering between book covers, waiting to be read. A mysterious pheromone designed to lure the right reader to the right book. The older the books, the stronger the scent. Whenever I could, I detoured through the section where nineteenth-century books exuded the smell of yellowed pages and thick leather bindings. My romantic sentiments conveniently filtered out the fact that the smell was really a sign of age and decay. The library's directors had decided to move with the times and had begun digitising the collections in order to preserve them. For weeks now, dozens of interns weighed down by books had been staggering through the main reading room and disappearing through a door that said STAFF ONLY. Behind that door, stairs led down to the archive, which was almost twice the size of the public space upstairs. Here the interns scanned the books page by page.

All this activity didn't suit me one bit. The scanners and photocopiers were constantly going; I kept bumping into baby-faced interns in the corridors; someone was always calling for a technician because a copier was on strike; and if I was at a copier myself, a queue of people would form behind me in no time. The whole operation was a nuisance. The more people there were down there, the greater the danger I'd be found out. And the archive was only half the story. I'd be out on my ear if anyone knew what I got up to on the computer upstairs.

I thought back to the day I'd first set foot in the library. I'd stood awestruck in the huge entrance hall, between the stone columns that supported the gallery, and gazed at the brimming book shelves. The respectful hush was irresistible; I had to go in.

My original reason for going to the library had nothing to do with books. I went because I missed Yasmin. There was something comforting about going to the places she'd liked. I'd started having breakfast once a week in the café where I'd often seen her sipping her coffee. I'd been to the swimming pool several times; I didn't really like swimming but I knew she liked the pool. I tried to see these places with her eyes, to imagine what it was like when she heard the rattles and hisses of the coffee machine or inhaled the chlorine fug of the pool. When I went to the cinema, I picked films I thought she'd have gone for. It was the same with the library. I wanted to get to know the place where she'd spent so much time during the last days we shared. I wanted to sit where she'd sat, read what she'd read. It was like following a faint trail of perfume before it faded altogether.

We wrote to each other and spoke on the phone now and then. We talked about her studies, about people she'd met, about how she was getting a student grant now. The first semester, she didn't come home at all. Alex was going to uni there too, and she was completely wrapped up in her new student life. She went off travelling during the semester break and didn't come home the second semester either. Hakim visited her occasionally but I never went with him. I couldn't bear the idea of seeing her for a couple of hours and spending the whole time thinking that all too soon I'd have to leave her again. She went to the USA in her second year, spending a semester at San Diego State University. She sent me a photo, taken from behind, of her looking out over a fabulous Pacific bay. It was a nice photo, but I was far more interested in who she was there with and who had taken the picture. Alex had stayed in Germany, I knew that much. When she sent that photo, I was half way through my own professional training. I was going to be a "Specialist in Media and Information Services." It was a silly job title—"Librarian" sounded a lot better. It was a three-year programme divided into practical and theoretical elements. I did the practical apprenticeship in the library and the theory in the vocational college. I got a job in the library when I qualified, and I'd been permanent for six months now.

The minute I'd walked into the airy space between the entrance-hall columns, I'd known that this would be one of my special places, one of the few where I felt at ease. The library was perfect in many ways. It was a repository for all the stories born out of the imaginations of the world's great storytellers. Being close to their stories meant being close to Father. I knew he'd have liked this place. I also knew that Yasmin had liked it here, which made it even easier for me to like the library.

But what clinched it was something else. I had wandered almost reverently up and down the aisles, past Fiction, Biography, and Reference to Non-fiction. Overwhelmed by the sheer number of books, I skipped a few shelves until— as if fate had led me there—I ended up in front of a section labelled MIDDLE EAST. I traced the titles on their spines in amazement:

Der alte Libanon
Coexistence in Wartime Lebanon
Pity the Nation—The Abduction of Lebanon
Syrien & Libanon
Constitutional patriotism in Lebanon

It was a shock to see so many books on Lebanon and Lebanese history. I'd always assumed that no one except the people who live on our street had any real interest in the country. How wrong I was. And how lucky. The library was somewhere I could feel close to those who meant so much to me, but it was also somewhere I could quench my enormous thirst for knowledge. There was nothing for it: I had to apply for a place on the librarianship course.

I was dreading the evening with Aurea for the same reason that I dreaded us being anywhere other than her flat—I was afraid she'd suggest going to my place. I liked Aurea. I really did. Her parents were Portuguese but she'd been born in Germany like me. She was twenty-three, had dark, animated eyes, was a dance teacher by day and studying for university entrance exams by night. We'd been sleeping together for about six months, which was presumably long enough to call whatever we had a relationship. Six months was a record for me. I'd been with various girls over the years—I'd even managed to string along two girls at the same time for a while without either of them finding out. But I'd never really had a proper relationship. Any time I'd felt they were beginning to get serious—or were about to break it off—I did a runner. Even today, the thought of being abandoned makes me do things I hate myself for.

None of the girls had ever set foot in my flat. Not even Hakim had been in it since the day I moved in. I'd started my librarianship course at the end of 2001, a few months after Yasmin had gone to uni. The following summer I'd moved out of Hakim's. It was now 14 February 2005. For three years I'd put off potential visitors with a litany of excuses, because I knew that anyone in their right mind would get an awful shock.

"Samir!"

Chris was waving from the other end of the aisle. I put the last book back on the shelf and made my way towards him. I could tell from his grin that I wasn't going to like what was coming.

"A visitor for you," he said, thumping me on the shoulder. "I think you should finish up now."

"But I can't," I protested, "I still have things to do."

"Yeah, yeah." Chris patted my shoulder, propelling me forward at the same time. "Tomorrow is another day."

Aurea was standing at the loans desk. She had a scarf wrapped round her neck, her eyes were shining from the cold outside, her cheeks glowing. She beamed when she saw me.

"I figured I'd just come and collect you," she said.

"What a nice surprise," I lied and gave her a quick peck.

"How about a walk before dinner? It's pretty cold out, but the air is so crisp and clear."

"I'm not sure I can get away this early."

I hadn't noticed Chris standing only a few metres away, pretending to leaf through a magazine. Now he turned to us.

"Of course you can go, Samir. Enjoy the rest of the day, you young things," he said, shoving his glasses up his nose and turning to Aurea. "That was a great idea, to show up here. Fresh air is just what young Samir needs."

I could have throttled him.

Aurea beamed even brighter. She'd probably been a bit unsure; now she was relieved to have the boss's official blessing.

"Right. Let's be off," she said cheerfully.

I forced a smile but I was sweating from every pore.

"OK. I just have to get my jacket." I needed to get down to the archives in a hurry.

"Your jacket's here, Samir," said Chris, full of bonhomie. He held out the jacket so that all I had to do was slip into it.

Bloody idiot, I thought. I did my best to suppress my rising panic.

"Do you want to go ahead?" I asked Aurea. "I think I left my mobile downstairs. I'll run down for it and catch up with you."

What a lame excuse. But the moment I said it, I realised that my mobile really wasn't in my jacket pocket. Where had I left it? My thoughts were racing. What if I didn't get another chance to go downstairs?

"Do I have to call security to get you out of here?" Chris laughed and looked at Aurea to see if she liked his joke. But she was giving me a sceptical look.

In that instant, what could only be my mobile phone

began to ring. Some readers shot indignant looks at the signs with the crossed-out mobile phone symbol. I patted my trouser pockets. Nothing there. I checked my jacket pockets. Not there either. Several heads had turned in our direction.

Chris raised his hands in a placating gesture and whispered impatiently out the side of his mouth, "Is that your phone?"

I went round to the other side of the loans desk. There it was, ringing away, exactly where I'd stood piling books onto the trolley earlier.

"I don't believe it!" I said, with a little too much hysteria in my voice. "It's here, not in the archive!"

Aurea watched the whole scene with a curious air. The phone stopped ringing as soon as I picked it up. I checked the display.

"Who was that?" she asked.

"Hakim," I said. "That's odd. I've got several missed calls from him."

"Right. Out with the pair of you now," said Chris.

Aurea took my hand and pulled me towards the exit. Distracted, I shoved my mobile into my jacket pocket.

The air was cold and bracing outside. It was late afternoon, twilight on the way. Everyone was wrapped up, their frozen faces framed by hoods or woolly caps as they walked along the street preceded by the white clouds of their breath.

Aurea latched onto my arm and nestled into me. We were still standing on the steps outside the library.

"Gorgeous, isn't it?" she asked.

"Yeah. Good idea to go for a walk."

My temples were throbbing. I tried to convince myself that Chris wouldn't go downstairs again today. Why would he? He hardly ever went down to the archives. The other thing bothering me was all the missed calls from Hakim.

"Hold my gloves for a sec, if you don't mind," I said.

I rang Hakim's number but he didn't answer.

"Maybe he's got something on this evening and just wanted to let you know, in case you were going to drop by?"

"Unlikely," I said.

We went down the steps and crossed the plaza. The farther we got from the library, the more I felt the nausea rising. I scrabbled for an excuse to go back, but Chris was bound to intercept me and usher me out again.

"... for dinner?" I tuned in at the tail-end of Aurea's question.

"Hmm?"

"Where do you fancy going for dinner?"

"I ... em ... I don't really know. Any suggestions?"

"What are you in the mood for?"

"I'm easy." I was really nervous now. Too many open questions. I hated not being in control. Things were getting out of hand.

"I was thinking we could eat somewhere near here and go to your place after?" she said shyly.

My flat was certainly closer to town than Aurea's, or rather, her flat was so far out in the sticks that it would have been daft to insist on going back to her place.

My mind was too muddled to make excuses. I was in trouble and something was up with Hakim.

"OK. Why not?"

"Great! I didn't bring my pyjamas, though," she said, "but maybe I won't need them." She grinned mischievously and stood on tiptoes to give me a kiss. Her lips were cold but the kiss was warm and tender.

"Listen," I said. "I'm worried about Hakim. Would you mind if we check in on him?"

Aurea seemed put out.

"Well, OK" she said. "I don't suppose it matters where we go for a walk as long as we're together, right?"

I didn't want her tagging along. Hakim rarely phoned me, never mind five times in a row. Something must have happened.

"I think I know why he's been ringing," I blurted, delighted with my brainwave. "I'm such an idiot. I left your surprise present at his place yesterday. I bet that's what he wanted to tell me!"

"A surprise?"

"Yes, for Valentine's Day. Did you think I wouldn't have anything?"

She stopped in her tracks. I didn't expect my words to have such an effect. There were tears in her eyes.

"Why are you crying?" I asked.

She brushed the tears away, embarrassed.

"Well, you know ... Me and you ... I didn't really know where you stood ... We never really talked about whether we ..."

"Whether we're a couple?"

She nodded.

"Of course we are!" I burst out without thinking. I'd already hung myself out to dry, so it didn't matter what I said next. "That's why I want us to have a really wonderful evening ..."

"So do I," she sighed, flinging her arms around me.

"But not without the surprise! Listen, I'll just run over to Hakim's and get it. Please—I really want you to have it today. In the meantime, you can pick out a fab restaurant. I'll ring you, you'll tell me where you are, we'll have a lovely time, and afterwards ..."

Oh God, what was I doing?

"Yes," she smiled. I kissed her before either of us could

say another word, took her head between my hands, and wiped her tears away with my thumbs.

"Twenty minutes," I said, already pulling away from her. "I'll be back in twenty minutes."

"OK. See you soon," she replied, waving at me. I felt rotten, seeing her so moved.

By the time I reached our old neighbourhood I was lathered in sweat. I shelved all thought of how to extricate myself from the mess with Aurea. Right now it was Hakim who mattered. If it turned out there was nothing wrong with him, I'd even fit in a quick detour back past the library.

I stumbled through the front door and climbed the stairs. As usual, Hakim's door wasn't locked. I could hear the TV when I went in.

"Hakim?"

No answer. I knew my way. Down the hall and turn right into the living room.

"Hakim?"

He was sitting silently in front of the TV. His face was frozen, his eyes fixed in an expressionless trance.

"Hakim, what's the matter?"

I heard sirens, took in what was on the TV screen and nearly jumped out of my skin. As if on auto-pilot, my hand reached into my jacket pocket. I rang Aurea without taking my eyes off the TV.

"I'm in Lemar," she announced cheerfully as soon as she answered. I could hear voices and the clatter of cutlery in the background. "It's an Afghan restaurant. OK?"

"I can't," I heard myself say.

"What do you mean? Samir?"

"I can't come to meet you," I said in a flat voice.

"But ... But ... Why not?"

"I've got to go."

"Samir. Tell me ..."

I hung up. Right then, I didn't care how Aurea would take the brush-off. I didn't even care if they found out what I'd been up to in the archives. I just stood there watching the images flickering on TV. Rushed, shaky shots trying to capture what was happening: shattered glass, blackened walls, smoke and flames, and wounded people everywhere in dirty, blood-soaked bandages. The explosion had blasted a deep crater in the street, and thick smoke was billowing out of it. Emergency services were trying to get near the flames, past burnt-out skeletons of cars and screaming people holding their heads in disbelief.

"Beirut," I said, dropping my mobile.

Still no response from Hakim.

"What happened?" I asked, though I guessed the answer already.

Hakim spoke without looking at me.

"Hariri," he said. "Hariri's been murdered."

13

I hang up. Now that the tension's gone, I'm overcome with exhaustion. I haven't shaved since I got here. My cheeks are stubbly and my hair is glued to my head with sweat. I haven't slept in two days, or left the hotel. I didn't even go down for breakfast. Instead, the plates piled up on the desk. I got to know every detail of this room. I waited with feverish impatience for him to call. I only rang her once, late at night, when I figured I'd be least likely to miss a call from him. She sounded alarmed but I told her I had a lead, that it was good news for us, for me.

Then he rang, just a few minutes ago.

"Hello?"

"Samir?"

"Yes."

"Sinan Aziz."

"That took ages."

"I'm not a magician. Our friend is not easily contactable. If you knew how he lives, you'd be congratulating me on how quickly it happened."

"Does he want to meet?"

"I don't know if he *wants* to, but he's willing to."

"When?"

"Tomorrow."

"Where?"

"He lives in Brih, a small village in the Chouf Mountains."

"What's his name?"

"I can't tell you."

"Why not?"

"Because I don't know if he'd want me to."

"So how am I supposed to find him?"

"Believe me, once you get to Brih, you'll find him."

"What's the address?"

"I don't know."

"Are you doing this on purpose?"

"No. I've better things to be doing than giving you a hard time. There are no street names in Brih."

"So am I supposed to knock on every door and say I'm looking for a man but I don't know his name or what he looks like?"

"It might be enough to knock on the first door you see and say you're looking for a man who's a Christian."

"A Christian."

"Just trust me. You'll find him once you get there."

14

We felt the explosion on our street. Its shockwaves made our houses tremble. Even here, thousands of kilometres away, we knew that the crater this bomb left in the heart of Beirut was more than a hole in the ground. It was an abyss, a burning, soot-black chasm, and the world stared into it from the edges, terrified that it could cause cracks that would lead first Beirut and then the whole Middle East to collapse.

People poured out onto our street. No one wanted to be indoors. Everyone needed to talk, to be with others. A cold fog dimmed the street lights, giving the whole scene a funereal air. I stood with my hands in my pockets among numbed people speaking to each other in a mixture of grief, horror, and outrage. Someone had propped a framed portrait of Hariri against a tree. We lit candles and placed them beside it. Some folks kept saying, over and over, how much they loved him. Others said they'd always known he'd die like this—he had been too outspoken in his criticism of Syria; Bashar al-Assad didn't tolerate enemies. And in hushed tones some sombre-faced people were predicting exactly what would come to pass in the following weeks.

I first heard the term Cedar Revolution in a TV news bulletin. Thousands of people were gathered on Martyrs' Square in Beirut, waving red-and-white scarves and holding pictures of Hariri aloft. Estimates suggested over fifty thousand people. They were chanting Hurriya, Siyada, Istiqlaal—freedom, sovereignty, independence; and Haqiqa, Hurriya, Wahda wataniya—truth, freedom, national unity. The demonstrators consisted of the anti-Syrian opposition and its supporters, as well as pro-Hariri supporters waving their blue ribbons. There had been anti-Syrian protests before, in the 1990s, but they'd been violently suppressed. Now Christians, Sunnis, and Druze were demonstrating side by side, and no one was stopping them. They all shared the same goal: complete withdrawal of the Syrian army and resignation of the pro-Syrian government under Omar Karami, who had become prime minister after Hariri's resignation. Grief over Hariri's murder was tempered with a sense of optimism that spread throughout the land. A breath of spring air heralded big changes, the quiet promise of a future, rumours of freedom and democracy, the abolition of a pseudo-state, the end of the post-war era—the end, indeed, of a pact with the devil. No substantial evidence was found to prove that the Syrians were behind the assassination, but international pressure was huge, and demands for Syrian withdrawal from Lebanon became increasingly loud. So how did the demonstrators defend themselves against the all-powerful state that had decided their fate for decades? They toppled their own government because it served Syria. After Hariri had resigned in 1998, he became prime minister again in 2000. President Émile Lahoud, who had been installed by the Syrians, did his best to force Hariri onto the political side lines; Hariri resigned again in 2004 and was replaced by pro-Syrian Omar Karami. Now, Hariri's violent death posed a threat not just to President Lahoud but, more importantly, to his protectors, the Syrian army.

In the turbulent weeks following the assassination, the

deep divisions in Lebanon became apparent to the whole world. The desire for radical change was enormous, yet only a few days after the Cedar Revolution had begun and demands for Syrian withdrawal had grown louder, hundreds of thousands of people took to the streets demanding that the Syrians stay. For many years, the Shias in Lebanon had been at the bottom of the pile socially, economically, and politically. Despite being the largest religious group, Shia Muslims lived a marginal existence on the southern outskirts of Beirut and in the south of the country, where the problem was not Syria but Israel. Yet they had been gaining power since Hezbollah—originally a militia during the civil war—had become a political party after the war ended. Now the Shia regarded the protests against the Lebanese government and its Syrian protectors as a provocation. The prospect of Syrian withdrawal posed an unspoken threat to the Shias' growing influence, as it could lead to the disarming of Hezbollah, the only militia that had refused to lay down its weapons when the civil war ended.

Hezbollah had forced the Israelis to withdraw from southern Lebanon in 2000, which had been celebrated as a kind of liberation at the time. Many seemed to have forgotten that it was Hezbollah in the first place that had largely been responsible for the 1996 Israeli invasion of southern Lebanon. This was in retaliation for Hezbollah rockets fired into northern Israel. Now, even though most of the Christian parties and the other civil-war militias acknowledged Hezbollah's role in liberating southern Lebanon, they felt very uneasy when they saw huge numbers of pro-Syrian demonstrators—up to eight hundred thousand, mainly Shias—rally to Hezbollah leader Hassan Nasrallah's call. Hezbollah now seemed a much more threatening power, instrumentalised by outside forces, and the only militia that still had all its weapons.

In the end, the Cedar Revolution succeeded. The last Syrian troops left Lebanon on 24 April 2005—about two months after Hariri's assassination—and the anti-Syrian demonstrators were hailed as heroes of democracy. But until that time bombs kept exploding.The unrest was accompanied by assassinations too. Most of the targets were in the anti-Syrian opposition camp, and the assassins were believed to be part of pro-Syrian terrorist groups trying to prevent a Syrian withdrawal. On 2 June, a car bomb killed Samir Kassir, a prominent journalist whose anti-Syrian views were well known. Lebanon wasn't just rumbling now, it was quaking. The government was under pressure, and despite its assurances, the threat of civil war was more real than it had been since the last one ended.

I followed the developments compulsively, always thinking of Father. I wondered what his reaction would be if he were here, watching it on TV with us, or, if he really was in Lebanon, what his reaction was there. It was impossible not to think of him, especially when the government eventually resigned and a general election was called. It would be the most important election since the one in 1992—the first election I was old enough to remember, and the beginning of those strange weeks that culminated in Father's disappearance.

Living at Hakim's couldn't make up for what I'd lost. I missed Mother, Alina, and Yasmin terribly, but so did Hakim, and somehow this created a bond between us. We spent many an evening in his living room, playing backgammon on an ornate board or sharing a water pipe. As the smoke wafted around us, we'd reminisce about the happy days when all six of us were together.

Hakim was born in 1943, which made him fifteen years

older than Father. To my eyes he'd always seemed like an eccentric granddad, partly because of his gait. His slow shuffle, hands behind his back, made him look like a learned professor on the brink of a great discovery. His face was full of wrinkles, as if life's events had etched lines on his skin the way a prisoner marks off the days in his cell. Hakim always spoke in calm, even-tempered tones, rarely raising his voice. Even if he was cursing or discussing politics, he would speak impulsively but never rashly. In spite of his rather fragile appearance, he was a pillar of strength in the years after Father disappeared, and I never forgot that. He had helped Mother with everything, from filling out forms to doing the shopping to minding Alina. In those turbulent years, he was our anchor. He never tried to replace Father—that would have been impossible, as he well knew. Hakim didn't tell us stories. Nor did he put us to bed; he left that to Mother. He was simply there, radiating calm and reassurance, and when the satellite dish on the roof broke down at one stage, he bought a new one and asked Khalil to align it—to 26 degrees east.

As for me, at first I was afraid all the time. Afraid to look him in the eye. Afraid to ask if he knew more about Father's disappearance than the rest of us did. Afraid he might say he knew nothing. Afraid he might say he knew everything but wouldn't tell me. I just didn't have the nerve. I slunk around, keeping a close eye on him, eavesdropping on his conversations with Mother. But Hakim never gave anything away. It was a long time before I let him get close to me again, though there was no going back to the easy intimacy of before. I buried the farewell scene I'd witnessed in the stairwell deep in my memory. Soon I couldn't even be sure that it hadn't all been a dream.

After I moved in with Hakim, it took a while for us to get used to each other. Then Yasmin moved out, leaving a huge silence that we had to fill. We weren't like father and son, yet I felt that Hakim was the one person who understood the enormity of my grief and knew how to relate to me. He was my legal guardian but he didn't lay down any rules. When I got up, I'd find the breakfast table set—Hakim would be long gone to work. When he came home in the evenings, he'd change the shirt that smelled of timber and sawdust, tell me about his day, and slip in a few questions about what I'd been up to.

"This and that," I'd usually reply, and that seemed enough. He never asked me where I hung out all day, and I never told him that I spent much of my time retracing his daughter's footsteps. Maybe he guessed. He never put pressure on me to get an apprenticeship or a place on a training course, nor did he lecture me about the importance of that kind of thing for the future. Some might say he was a little too hands-off, but I was grateful that he accepted me as I was.

When I told him I'd decided to become a librarian, he was delighted, giving me a big hug and telling me I was doing the right thing. Hakim was glad to have me around, glad that the flat wasn't empty. Ever since he and Yasmin had fled to Germany with my parents, Hakim had never strayed far from us. He was around when I was born and when Alina was born he was part of the family, He missed Yasmin terribly. He didn't talk about it much, but I often caught him in the living room, looking at photos of her as if they were precious paintings. He missed Mother and Alina too. The whole house was quieter without them. The toing and froing between our flats was gone, the creaking stairs, the carefree laughter he'd hear before they appeared around the bend of the stairs. All the more reason for him to look after me: I was all he had left.

"There's no need to move out," he said sadly when I told

him of my plan to find a place of my own. This was a few months after I'd started the librarianship course. "There's plenty of room here for the two of us, and we get on well."

That was true, of course, but I had begun a new chapter in my life and it felt right to stand on my own two legs as I embarked on this adventure.

One day shortly before I moved into the small flat he'd helped me find, I saw Hakim standing by the cherry tree on the patch of grass outside our building. He was running suspicious fingers along its trunk.

"It's canker," he said, wincing. "Come here. Take a look."

He pointed at the bark, much of which had turned dark brown, with some reddish-orange patches. The wood was dry and cracked, and lumpy growths had appeared in places.

"Is canker kind of like tree cancer? I didn't know trees could get cancer," I said.

How many times had I walked by that tree without noticing the changes. It made me think of Father explaining the satellites with cherry stones from this very tree while Alina sat on the grass watching us.

"It's not really cancer," said Hakim. "The cells don't multiply uncontrollably. It's actually a fungal infection."

"How does the tree get it?"

"Through little wounds in the bark caused by frost. I'm afraid we'll have to cut it down. It would probably still flower this year, but the cherries could develop fruit rot."

The thought of this tree dying saddened me. On the one hand, it was logical—predictable even. The bitter truth was that everything connected with this house seemed doomed. On the other hand, this tree held more than just my memories within its branches, as I had buried the little cedar box between its roots. It had seemed like a safe hiding place for the slide.

Before the tree was felled, I dug out the box. I had wrapped it in newspaper, but moisture had got in and stained the cedar. It didn't smell the same either. The sharp woody scent had faded into the earth, been washed away by the rain.

I regarded the demise of the cherry tree as a sign. That slide was part of me, was meant to be near me at all times. It was also inextricably linked to the events surrounding Father's disappearance. So I decided it was time to ask Hakim what Father had said to him that night.

He didn't seem surprised. We were sitting across from each other in the living room. My things were boxed up in the hall. That evening, for the first time, I'd be getting the keys to a flat of my own. Steam rose from the tea we'd just poured. Hakim didn't bat an eyelid.

"Were you watching us?"

"Yes. I followed him. You remember the state he came home in that evening? Soaking wet and scared out of his wits. Remember what a fright we all got? I was worried, I wanted to keep an eye on him."

Hakim always wore glasses at home. The warm steam from the tea fogged up his lenses when he put the cup to his lips.

"He went and got something out of the basement. He had it with him going into your flat, but his hands were empty when he came out. What did he give you?"

Hakim scrutinised me thoughtfully. Without a word, he got up and went to his bedroom. He came back shortly afterwards and put a photo album on the table.

"This is what he gave me."

I recognised many of the photos in the album. Photos of my parents' wedding, the same ones Father had shown us that evening. But there were other pictures, ones I hadn't seen before—pictures of Hakim playing the lute, his head inclined dreamily, and pictures of Yasmin as a child, playing in a sandpit in Lebanon.

It was a long time ago, that evening. All I'd seen was the vague outline of that rectangular object, since it was hidden under a cloth. It's possible that it was the same size as a photo album. But there was something fishy about it all the same.

"If this album was there all along," I began, "why did he bother with the slideshow?"

Hakim smiled and watched me go through the album page by page, inspecting each glued-in image.

"That's what I said too. No need for the slides. 'Why don't we just show the kids the album?' I said. But Brahim insisted on putting on a show for you. You know how much he loved to perform. He really wanted to have a Leitz Prado bang in the middle of your living-room table!"

"But why did he give the photo album to you?"

"I've no idea," sighed Hakim. "Your father was like a brother to me, as you know. We were great friends. These photos are souvenirs of our friendship. And they're the only pictures of me playing music—he loved my music. In fact, we only met because I was a musician at the time. Maybe that's why he gave me the album." He seemed sad now, a bit helpless, and he avoided eye contact. "So, your father came to me that evening. Yasmin was already asleep. I asked what was wrong. I'd got just as much of a fright as you when I saw him standing there like that in your flat. Yasmin and I were worried. But he didn't offer any explanation. All he said was, 'I've got to leave, Hakim.' He didn't tell me it was for ever. I thought he meant a couple of weeks. I was convinced the whole time that he'd be back any minute. I don't know what kind of trouble he was in."

"And you didn't ask him where he had to go?"

"Of course I did." Hakim sighed again. The memories seemed painful. "He couldn't tell me. I was sitting exactly where you are. He kept pacing up and down, and all he said was, 'I've got no choice, do you see?' He kept repeating that, as if he had to convince himself as well as me. I begged him to tell me what kind of trouble he was in. I wanted to help, but he brushed me off. I couldn't get the slightest bit of information out of him—you must believe me. He took me completely by surprise. I couldn't believe it next morning, when he was gone. We were friends, Samir. I loved him."

Hakim's expression changed. He looked as if he'd been dreading this moment for years.

"When he was leaving your flat, I heard him make you promise something."

I tried to make eye contact with Hakim. I was remembering the two men crying.

"What kind of promise was it?"

The old man bowed his head.

"He asked me to look after you all." He drew a deep breath full of regret. "He wanted me to make sure you were all ok while he was away, to make sure nothing happened to you." Hakim seemed dejected and uncertain. "Considering everything that's happened since, I didn't do such a good job, did I?"

The day after the attack on Rafiq Hariri, I got up very early and went to the library. I needed to get there before anyone else. It was 15 February 2005—three years since that conversation with Hakim. I'd spent the night at Hakim's; I couldn't face the loneliness of my own flat. Our old street seemed the only safe refuge at that moment, a bulwark of solidarity. For the first time, I'd understood why people need to gather in churches or public spaces when disaster strikes, to light candles, lay flowers, reflect in silence. The crowds mourning on our street had eventually broken up. Everyone had gone home. TV screens continued to flicker in the darkness of the night. The portrait of Hariri remained propped against the tree, a film of frost forming on it. Hakim eventually fell asleep in front of the TV. I put a blanket over him. His rib cage rose and fell evenly. His head was on a cushion, his feet sticking out over the end of the couch. He looked utterly exhausted. I sat up for a little while, staring at the endless loop of images from Beirut—the smoke, the flames, the shattered glass, the news analysts' worried faces. I didn't hear what they said. I had turned the sound down on the TV. And I'd put my phone on silent because Aurea wouldn't stop ringing.

It was strange to hear my footsteps echoing off the library walls. Normally, I'd never be the first in. Chris sometimes wore the same clothes two days in a row, so I suspected that he slept in the library the odd time, but he wasn't in yet. I went down to the archive. To my relief, everything was exactly as I'd left it—newspaper all over the floor, ancient articles on yellowed paper. How could I have been so careless? I set about covering my tracks, folding the newspapers and putting them back on the shelves.

The morning passed without incident. Chris wasn't due in until lunchtime, as he had a meeting somewhere else. The usual pensioners came in to pore over the papers through their reading glasses. Hariri's murder was headline news. The front pages all showed the bomb crater in Beirut. Around eleven, a group of bored schoolchildren came in for a tour. I showed them around the public areas, explained how they could use the computers to search the catalogue and borrow books, told them about the reference-only collection and interlibrary loans and the DVD collection. That last bit got them interested. When

Chris arrived at 1 p.m., his jacket was soaked, his hair was dripping, and his glasses were blurred by raindrops.

"Forgot my umbrella," he said, shrugging.

"How was the meeting?" I asked nonchalantly.

"OK. We're definitely going to be one of the venues for Literature Night in May. Who we'll be getting for the readings isn't decided yet. How did your evening go?"

"Lovely," I lied.

He studied me briefly, then nodded.

"Terrible about Hariri. I heard it on the news. You must have got an awful shock."

"Yes, but who didn't?"

"I'm not that well up on him," Chris said, "but he seemed like a good guy. He did a lot for the country, didn't he?"

"Yes, he was a really important figure after the war."

"Let's hope there isn't worse to come. There's always some kind of trouble down there." He hung his wet jacket on the back of the chair. "They were saying on the radio that it might have been the Syrians. What do you think?"

"It's certainly a possibility."

"I remember the eighties—when I was your age. There was a civil war in Lebanon. Then Bashir Gemayel was murdered. I reckon the impact of that must have been similar. The first thing they said was the same then too: 'It was the Syrians!'"

I nodded, adding gruffly, "History repeating itself."

I didn't really want to discuss Hariri or Gemayel with Chris, even though I'd read a lot about Gemayel and his assassination. In fact, I definitely had no desire to discuss Gemayel. I remembered all too well the day, not long after I'd started my library training, when I'd opened one of the books on the civil war and hit upon a particular page. I got the shock of my life. It's impossible to describe the confusion I felt, the surprise, the goose pimples. I stared in disbelief at the picture with the article: there he was, the Lebanese president, the man who had been leader of the Phalange militia and founder of the Forces Libanaises. The photo showed a handsome young man with a full head of black hair, dark eyes, and an engaging smile waving at a crowd. It was Bashir Gemayel. The same man who was on the slide, standing in his uniform beside my father.

That evening I strolled home under a leaden sky. The whole town was wrapped in a pall of February grey. The shutters were down on most of the shops, smoke drifted from chimneys, and puddles formed on the footpaths. The umbrellas of people dashing home through the rain were the only splashes of colour.

Despite the gloom on the streets and the horrific events of the previous night, I felt relaxed and surprisingly optimistic. No one at the library seemed to suspect me of anything. Little did I know this was the last time I'd feel relaxed and optimistic for a very long time. If I'd known, maybe I'd have slowed down, despite the rain dripping from the greengrocers' awnings, and breathed in the clear air after the rain stopped. Maybe I'd have enjoyed, just a little longer, the feeling, that everything had worked out OK. How was I to know that Hariri's assassination would trigger a series of events that would have serious consequences for my own life?

One immediate consequence was that Aurea broke up with me. When I got home, she was huddled on the front steps.

"You never rang back," she sobbed. Her hair was dripping wet, her hands shaking, but I didn't dare give her a hug. "Will you not tell me what's going on?"

The rain pelted down on the steps and the railings.

"No," I said. "I can't."

I could see that Aurea was struggling and I felt bad. I would have liked to make more of an effort, for her sake, for both of us. She could have caught me at the library. But the fact that she was here meant she was testing me—if I finally let her into my flat, it would be a sign that I still cared. But I couldn't, not even when she was sitting here on the doorstep, soaked to the skin. It had to end here and now. She'd left me no other choice.

"You can't." It was less a question than a flat repetition of my answer. "You promise me a surprise and then leave me sitting on my own in a restaurant. On Valentine's Day. And you don't feel you need to explain that?"

"I can't," I repeated.

"I don't suppose you're going to ask me in now either?"

"No."

"Is it that you've already got a girlfriend?" she said. "Do you live here with her?" She pointed behind her at the front door. There were eight names beside the bells. "Is that why you never wanted me to come to your place?"

I said nothing. It was better for her to think that. It might make it easier for her to get over me if she thought I was a complete bastard. I really would have liked to ask her in, but it was out of the question.

"What age are you, Samir? Sixteen? Grow up, for God's sake!"

"I'm sorry," I said.

"Well I'm not!"

She shot me one last disappointed look before brushing past me and trudging off into the rain, shoulders hunched, hands shoved into her pockets.

That was the first knock-on effect of Hariri's murder in my own life. The second—an almost absurd twist of fate— had significantly wider implications and was far more destructive. For at the exact same time as I was dripping up the stairs to my flat, Chris, who was still in the library, thought of something. He told me what it was later, when he asked to see me in his office. Being the sort of guy who likes precise details, Chris had gone down to the archives, to a dusty shelf way back in the reference holdings, looking for an old newspaper dated 15 September 1982. He wanted to read up on the details of Bashir Gemayel's assassination, to see if there were any parallels with the attack on Hariri. He found the newspaper, but not what he was looking for. Which is how he caught me out in the end.

15

The Volvo's engine labours on the steep ascent. The rock face is lined with scree, the road winding up in hairpin bends. The landscape of the Chouf region is full of paradoxes—rocky wilderness punctuated by grassy meadows where goats graze among low pomegranate trees. Mostly what we see is pines and juniper bushes, though. We hear the crickets singing on the slopes.

I keep going over what I've found out so far. The lizard-like Ishaq who liked to keep animals with unusual talents was really Ishaq Abdallah, the manager of the Carlton Hotel. The Ishaq of my father's stories had only one weak spot, his fear of fire. That made sense, since a fire had left half of the real Ishaq Abdallah's face covered in scaly scars. The rhino who was unbeatable at cards is none other than Sinan Aziz—I met him myself. I've been fidgeting in the passenger seat ever since we left Beirut. If my hunch is right, I already know the name of the man we're on our way to meet.

"People are desperately poor up here," says Nabil. The car jolts over the bumps, the engine howling as he drops down the gears, gravel crunching under the tyres. "There are tiny villages all over the place. People can't afford diesel or gas to heat their homes in the winter, so they cut wood illegally."

He points out the occasional tree stump along the road.

We've just overtaken a man struggling up the hill on a rickety bicycle in the scorching heat. He was dressed in a grey tunic and a white hat shaped like a slightly tapered cylinder.

"The Chouf is Druze heartland, has been for hundreds of years," says Nabil. "Their territory extends as far as the Syrian border."

I don't know much about the Druze. Just a few facts gleaned here and there. It seems like a fascinating religion.

"How many Druze live up here in the mountains?"

"About two thousand. Of course, there are also Druze in Beirut and other cities, but most of them live in the many villages of the Chouf."

One source I read said that the Druze in Lebanon have the right to administer their own affairs and even have some of their own laws. I ask Nabil if this is true.

He nods.

"They are bound by Lebanese civil law, of course, but they have separate jurisdiction in terms of family law. They regard themselves as Arabs, but not as Muslims."

I'd read that the Druze are descended from the Fatimids, a branch of Shia Muslims in eleventh-century Egypt, but their teachings also contain elements of Greek philosophy, Hinduism, and Christianity. They believe in reincarnation, for example. They even believe that a Druze who suffered a violent death can, in their reincarnated life, remember their parents from the previous life.

"How come most of them live up here? Were they given this territory?"

"Yes and no. There used to be plenty of Christians up here too." Nabil paused. "Not anymore."

Sinan Aziz's words come to mind. *It might be enough to say you're looking for a man who's a Christian.*

"It's a dark chapter in our history." Nabil strokes his

beard with one hand, steering the car round a narrow bend with the other. If I stuck my hand out the window, I could break off a sprig of juniper. "The government is making all kinds of efforts to bring Christians back up to the Chouf."

"Why?"

"So that they can come home," says Nabil. "The ones who were driven out."

Goats on the roadside eye us indifferently as we rumble by. To our right, the land falls sharply away. Hills and rocky mountains rise up to the left. Far below, Beirut glistens like a string of pearls, with the sea beyond.

"It's a resettlement plan imposed by the government. Forced reconciliation, you could say." Nabil looks at me. "In Brih, for example, Christian and Druze families used to live side by side. That's how it was in nearly all the mountain villages. But during the civil war almost a quarter of a million Christians fled the area ..."

The civil war again. It's an omnipresent theme, the after-effects of which can be seen up to today, though they're not always obvious. They can be hidden by cranes, cement mixers, and the noise of construction sites that promise new beginnings.

"The trouble between the Druze and the Christians all started around the middle of the nineteenth century," Nabil explains. "There was a brutal massacre of Christians in Damascus. Then a massacre of Druze by Christians in Lebanon. Neither side gave any quarter. During the civil war, Christians and Druze fought over control of the Chouf. There was another massacre in 1977, in Brih. Men with machine guns attacked Christians at prayer. More and more families started to flee the Chouf, most of them heading for Beirut."

"So this resettlement programme is meant to bring the Christians back?"

"Exactly Brih is one of the last places where this 'recon-ciliation'"—Nabil supplies the air quotes—"has yet to happen. Very few Christians have come back here, partly because most families have created new lives somewhere else in the meantime."

"How do the Christians feel about it? Do they want to move back?"

"They're divided. It's like this, the Chouf was their home too. The older folk remember happy childhoods, family gatherings on the terrace, the Druze from next door coming over for dinner and vice versa. Who wouldn't want to go back home?"

"But?"

"But there's a law which protects displaced people from paying rent on their current homes. That would all change if they agree to resettle, unless they're lucky enough to find their original houses still standing."

There's a goat in the middle of the road. It doesn't even look up when Nabil swerves, driving with one wheel up on the grassy verge until we've passed the animal.

"It's a tricky subject one way or the other. The government's going to build a church in Brih, to help the returnees settle in. A school might make more sense, if you ask me. OK, we're here."

Nabil steers the car round the last bend. Ahead, the village nestles in a narrow mountain valley. The blue of the sky lends intensity to the green of the vines on the terraced slopes and the whitewash of the houses dotted around us.

My pulse quickens when we park the car and walk past the first few houses. The unpaved surface crunches underfoot. There's hardly a soul to be seen. An old woman in a flowery apron is hanging washing on a line. Two dogs are lazing in the sun, flies buzzing around them. A little boy wearing nothing but a nappy is sitting on the ground beside the dogs and drinking from a water bottle that's nearly as big as himself. Half the water ends up down his tummy. He laughs and waves at us as we pass by. I wave back. The village looked idyllic and unspoilt as we approached it. Close up, it's clear that many of the houses are unfinished projects. Crumbling terraces, unplastered walls, clouds of dust, peeling yellow and blue paint. Brih is a ghost village. A miniature, sleeping Beirut. Rebuilding started, then stalled. New storeys sit half-finished on top of old walls.

"Are you from the phone company?" The old woman hanging up the laundry is looking at us.

"Sorry?"

"Are you from the phone company?"

"No."

"Hmmm. I didn't think so."

I look at Nabil. He shrugs.

"They were meant to come two weeks ago," the woman continues. She takes a white blouse from the laundry basket and hangs it up without looking at us. "'Three months', they said. 'You'll have new telephone cables in three months.' So they said. But nothing's happened yet."

"I'm sorry, we don't know anything about that."

"Not to worry," says the woman, continuing to hang up her washing. "We don't even have a phone. But it'd be nice if they told the truth for once. It's always the same—they make a promise, or announce something, and nothing happens ... Oh, hello!" She looks up, addressing someone behind us.

"Hello," a man's voice says, before we've turned around.

"They're not from the phone company," she informs him. "I already checked."

I can't see the man's face at first, as he's looking towards the ground. All I see is the top of his head and his fine grey hair. His back is badly bent and his shirt cannot conceal a big hump. He lifts his head and looks at me.

"No matter," he says. "So you must be Samir ."

I'm not surprised; I'm transfixed. Images flash through my mind. Childhood memories pull and swirl. I see myself in the shade of the cherry tree. I take Yasmin by the hand and lead her to the steps in front of our building. We are six and eight. *Ready*, I ask Yasmin, and she nods, barely able to contain her excitement. She sits on the top step and I stand below, like an actor in a play. Yasmin is my audience, her eyes a thousand bright lights. I remember exactly how I felt—paralysed by stage fright, bursting with excitement, presenting a story. *Today*, I announce with a big smile, *I'd like to introduce you to someone, a friend. His name is Amir, and he will be joining Abu Youssef on many an adventure.* I look up at her and, in Father's voice, tell her about the camel Amir, Abu Youssef's faithful friend. I see Yasmin's pleasure and bask in her applause. The images keep coming. Now it's like a curtain has been pulled back to reveal Brih as the real setting of my father's stories.

"Amir," I whisper. I don't mean to, but my voice won't come out.

He smiles. A gentle smile reserved for special occasions.

I'd like to step towards him, run my hand over his head, and stroke his wrinkled face. I'd like to touch the hump that bears down on him. I want to feel him and see if he's real. But I can't move. I'm rooted to the ground.

He holds my gaze and keeps smiling until I'm able to stir.

"Come," he says. "You must have hundreds of questions."

His house is one of the few in the village that isn't a building site. From the outside at least, it looks finished and lived in. The facade is bright yellow, and the polished stone floor of the terrace gleams in the sun. Basil, mint, and a few other herbs grow in window boxes. We're sitting outside. A lizard darts under a stone. The breeze stirs, carrying the scent of lavender across the open space. A glass of lemonade with ice and a slice of lemon sits on the table in front of me. A few hundred metres away, I see Nabil disappearing behind a wall. He's taking a walk around the village.

Amir sits across from me. His whole demeanour is that of an old man. His hand shook as he poured my lemonade, and his eyelids twitched. Yet his voice is steady, more like a man in his mid-thirties. A pleasant, firm voice. It's hard to look at him and not think of the comical camel. I still feel as if I've walked through a magical wardrobe or a tunnel to a parallel world in which all my favourite childhood characters are real. If this is a dream, I'm not sure I ever want to wake up.

"Nabil was telling me about the resettlement programme," I say. "When did you come back?" I feel I can talk to him like an old friend I haven't seen in years, not a man I'm meeting for the first time.

"I never left," he smiles. "Except for that brief stint in the hotel. Sixteen months in all. The Chouf is my home. I was born in this house and lived here with my parents. I went to work in the Carlton in March 1981 and came back in September '82."

"You were up here during the war?"

"Yes. We ended up being the last Christians in Brih. Now there's only me."

"Where's the rest of your family?"

"All gone. I have no brothers or sisters, so it was just the three of us, my parents and me. When I moved to Beirut, they came with me. They didn't feel safe on their own up here. Not that they had it any easier as Christians in west Beirut, but at least the city was bigger than the village, more anonymous. We got a flat in the west of the city. I had a room in the hotel, so I gave what I earned to my parents for their rent. When I stopped working in the hotel, there was no money, so we moved back to Brih. At that stage there were already fewer Christians."

"So you haven't lived anywhere but here since 1982?"

"No. I only left Brih once in all that time."

"To go to Beirut and ask Sinan Aziz about Father?"

"Exactly."

"Why did you give up the job in the Carlton if it meant you and your parents would have to move back here?"

"It wasn't just the money," he says. "There was something else."

He looks straight at me with his warm eyes, though it seems an effort to keep his head up. I'm guessing that he sees something of the young Brahim in me.

"Aziz said you were looking for Father because you wanted to forgive him for something. What happened between the two of you?"

Amir reaches for his glass and drinks.

"A few years ago, I heard about the resettlement programme, the same one you mentioned. Civil servants and government ministers came up here to tell us about it. They said more than three thousand Christians would be returning within two or three years, that it was time for Druze and Christians to make peace up here. That's when I thought of Brahim. I liked the idea that we could make peace, even after all these years. All the houses being refurbished or rebuilt in this village used to belong to Christians. They're going to build a church, lay telephone cables, modernise the hospital, and so on, and so on. The idea is to restore Brih to how it was. I know that won't be easy. I also know that it's mostly about politicians trying to make themselves look good with a flagship project. It's fraught with difficulty as far as the people on the ground are concerned. Still, I like the idea of people coming back. Brih is their home. Some might be friends of mine from way back, people I was in school with or grew up with. It's never too late to forgive one another."

"What did Father do to you?" I ask again.

"It doesn't matter now, Samir," he says gently. "I didn't find Brahim. His own mother doesn't even know where he is. When I asked Sinan to call and see her, a couple of years ago, she was under the impression that he was in Germany. The fact that you're here suggests otherwise. What happened between us formed a dark cloud. That cloud has passed."

"I think he's here," I say.

Amir nods slowly.

"I think so too."

"Why?"

"Because I can't imagine him lasting any length of time away from Lebanon. He loved every stone and every tree in this country." There's wistfulness in Amir's voice, as if he's remembering bygone times with Father.

"Were you good friends?"

"I don't know whether he thought of me as a friend," he says. "But we liked each other a lot. On our days off, we'd often head up to the cedars. Brahim loved it up there. He even showed me his poems once. I'm no expert, but they seemed good to me."

The question is still bothering me, so I try again. "Whatever he did to you, it must have been pretty bad if you weren't able to let it go for thirty years."

Amir studies me silently.

"I understand your wish to know," he says. "But I'm not going to tell you what happened, Samir. Your father was a good man and I'm not going to tarnish your memories of him over one mistake. Tell me—when was the last time you saw him?"

"1992."

"Were you born in Germany?"

I nod.

"1984."

"When did your parents leave here?"

"They fled in late 1982."

"And this is your first time here?"

"Yes."

"How do you like it?"

"I don't know. It's very different to the image of Lebanon I had growing up."

Amir laughs. He puts a hand to his ribs, as if laughing hurts, but it sounds sincere.

"When was the last time you saw him?" I ask.

"Brahim? Mid-September '82. He was still working in the hotel when I left. He was due to get married soon after."

"Did he ever show you stories, apart from the poems? Stories he wrote himself?"

Amir thinks.

"I only remember the poems, but it wouldn't surprise me if he wrote stories too. Brahim was a brilliant storyteller. He could talk a tourist into shelling out five hundred dollars for a three-dollar bottle of whisky."

I can't help but laugh.

"Aziz told me about that."

"Why do you ask? About stories, I mean?"

Amir seems attentive and alert, his gaze warm and steady.

"Because I know you," I say quietly. The memories are so powerful I'm afraid I'll lose my voice. "I've known you for a very long time. Father told me stories about you."

Amir blinks.

"Stories about me?"

"About you and Sinan Aziz. You were characters in his stories."

"Really?"

His eyes light up. He seems genuinely surprised, and his old face flushes with boyish excitement.

"Imagine that," he says, raising a hand and scratching his forehead in amazement. "That he didn't forget me, I mean."

I shake my head.

"He definitely didn't forget you."

"What kind of a character was I?" Amir still seems amazed.

Now that I see him opposite me, his hump rising behind his head like a mountain behind a tree, it seems mean of Father to have compared him to a camel. But Amir has a right to know.

"You were Amir, a camel who was the servant and faithful friend of Abu Youssef, the protagonist of these stories."

I was afraid he'd be disappointed or hurt, or indignant even. But his face becomes even more animated before I've finished the sentence.

He bangs the table with the palm of his hand and bursts out laughing.

"That's brilliant!" he says. "Were they bedtime stories?"

"Yes."

"Fantastic. Did he write them down? Do you still have them?"

"He just told them to me."

I'm relieved that he's so pleased.

"That's really amazing. And? Am I how you imagined me?"

"Well, I didn't know that any of you existed in real life," I say. I feel like a little boy whose toys have started talking to him from the bedroom shelf. "I thought you only existed in his stories."

"Well, I'm here, as you can see," he says with a laugh.

"Tell me, what kind of adventures did they have?"

"All sorts of adventures. You and Abu Youssef, you were famous throughout the land. You were hailed by everyone, from kings and sheikhs and princesses to the ordinary folk, and they all wanted your autograph."

He beams with pleasure.

"I like the sound of that," he says. "Thanks for telling me. It's amazing, isn't it—we forget so much as we grow older, but the stories we heard as children stay with us all our lives, don't they?"

"That's true," I say. "And these were pretty special stories."

I take a quick gulp of lemonade before the ice melts entirely. There's no sign of Nabil. He's probably snoozing under some tree.

"Amir," I say. "There's something I have to ask you."

"Ask away." His voice is still bright with pleasure.

I'm not sure how to phrase the question. It's been keeping me awake ever since that meeting in the Rhino Night Club. The feeling is so strong that I haven't been able to shake it off.

"Sinan Aziz was a rhinoceros who was unbeatable at cards," I begin. "You were a camel, the hero's trusty servant. There was an Ishaq in one of the stories too, a slave driver who could change into a lizard."

Amir's face suddenly darkens.

"Ishaq," he whispered.

"Yes."

"A slave driver, you say?"

"That's right."

"And he could turn into a lizard?"

"Yes. At full moon."

"Very apt."

"That's what Aziz said too. Did you leave the Carlton because of Ishaq?"

"Partly." Amir nods, embarrassed. "But that's all in the past. Let's not go into it."

"All I want to say is this: Ishaq was in these stories ..." I speak slowly to make sure he's with me. "Sinan Aziz was in the stories. You were in lots of his stories ..." I pause for a moment. "Amir." I look him in the eye, trying to keep his full attention. "All of these figures are real people."

"Yes," he says uncertainly. "I understand."

"So," I say and take a deep breath. "Who is Abu Youssef?"

The crickets' singing has grown louder. It's everywhere, a cacophonous concert resonating in the valley. The dogs that were dozing on a terrace now pad sluggishly down the road. A man comes out of the house across the way, looks into the sun, and nods at me before heading off into the village. Amir reappears with a fresh jug of lemonade. I had gone inside to use the toilet, then sat down outside while he was refilling the lemonade. The inside of his house took me by surprise. All the rooms were bare. No furniture except for a mattress in one room. I didn't see any sign of a TV, a telephone, or a computer. I remembered what Sinan Aziz had said: *If you knew how he lives, you'd be congratulating me on how quickly I found him.*

It's sad to think of Amir all alone up here. He doesn't seem too bothered by it, but this reclusiveness seems at odds with the jolly camel who loved crowds, loved signing his autograph and being the centre of attention. It's as if real life had let him slide once the stories about him stopped.

"I've been thinking," he says, putting down the jug. "There was a guy called Youssef in the hotel. I didn't really know him but maybe he and Brahim were friends. That could have fed into the stories. It's one possibility, though I never saw the two of them together, and Youssef was only there for a short time. Which is why there may be another explanation ..."

"Which is?"

"There's nothing special about the name Youssef. It was a very common boy's name in Lebanon at that time, still is today. Let's say you were telling a story about France and you wanted your hero to symbolise the French people, to be a typical Frenchman, you'd call him François, right? François and Youssef are symbolic, they're everyman. Brahim may have given his hero that name deliberately. He's a prototype, you could say, the classic Lebanese: friendly, hospitable, loves parties, an adventurer like his Phoenician ancestors. And of course, there's bound to be a lot of Brahim in this character too."

Amir smiles at me. This second explanation sounds very plausible. I know how much Father loved Lebanon. It would be just like him to create a symbolic character whose name would be instantly recognisable as Lebanese.

"It makes sense for a dreamer like him," says Amir, who has obviously read my mind.

"Yes, it does."

He nods his head in satisfaction.

"Not every question is as complicated as we think. Am I right?"

"Definitely," I say. We clink glasses.

"Can you tell me more about my father?"

"Of course." He massages the back of his neck with one hand while he speaks. "When I started at the hotel, in March 1981, Brahim and Sinan Aziz were already there. I often worked with Sinan. I don't know what Brahim told you about Ishaq, but at the time, Sinan was not exactly slim, and I had this hump. Ishaq didn't want the guests to catch sight of either of us. We were good, hard-working employees at a time when not many people wanted to work in hotels, so he couldn't easily replace us. We were good enough for menial tasks, but we didn't look the part in a fine hotel. It was the Carlton, after all, a prestigious Beirut institution. Ishaq was pretty brutal. He'd make us do the worst possible jobs for days on end. One day he roared at me, 'You're damn lucky there's a war on in Beirut. We used to have Cirque du Soleil round the corner. They'd have loved to get their hands on a talking camel like you.' Your father cheered me up later. 'Technically, you are a dromedary, as you only have one hump. He should have referred to you as a talking dromedary.' I had to laugh, the way he said it. He never treated me any differently on account of my appearance, and we were probably a bit closer because we were both Christian."

"Was religion an issue among the staff, then?"

"No. But we were afraid it might become one. It wasn't that there were bombs going off all the time in Beirut. It wasn't the kind of war that had everyone rushing to the cellars as soon as the alarm sounded. The trouble was often confined to particular streets, so chances were you'd hardly notice it. Weeks would go by without any shots fired, but then the gunfire would break out again. A lot of it was about gaining control of entire districts. It wasn't just Christians fighting Muslims fighting Druze; everyone fought everyone if they thought they had something to gain. For us, it was more a war of fear. We kept hearing about road blocks, about militias randomly stopping people in the street and taking them away, or shooting them on the spot and dumping them in the sea. The thing we all worried about most was one of our workmates' relatives being abducted or killed. Things could have turned sour if, for example, Christian militiamen had murdered a Muslim colleague's cousin. Then we wouldn't have been just workmates any more, we'd have been *Christian* workmates.

Religion would have become important all of a sudden, even though it was largely irrelevant in our daily interactions. Brahim understood perfectly how to leave what was going on outside the hotel where it belonged—outside. He did it by treating everyone exactly the same, even though he had special status himself. The tricks he played on the rich tourists meant that he always had money, and he shared it with us. If Ishaq withheld a portion of our wages, Brahim would sometimes lend us that amount and more. He always had money to spare because he worked where the best tips were to be had. He really was very popular, your father. When I started working there in 1981, he was already a minor celebrity. He was the one who represented management, who'd welcome important guests when they arrived, shake their hands. He was the man to talk to if you wanted your wedding in the Carlton. He handled all the details—the number of guests, the menu, the wines, the lute player, the mini fireworks display by the pool. He was indispensable, really."

"You said he was very popular among the staff. Because he shared his money, you mean?"

Amir shakes his head emphatically.

"No, no. It was his whole manner. The kind of easy-going light-heartedness he had about him was pretty rare in Beirut at the time. The fact that he shared his money with us helped, but it wasn't the main reason for his popularity."

"What was the main reason, then?"

"Sooner or later, word got around that Brahim's mother was very wealthy. As a matter of fact, your father didn't actually need to work at the Carlton at all. He could have left Lebanon and studied abroad. But there he was in the hotel with us, and he didn't seem to care about money. The rest of us would have seized an opportunity like that with both hands. We'd have packed our bags and waited somewhere else for the war to end. Studying abroad would have been like winning the lottery. Your father was different, though. Perhaps it was foolish of him, but we all admired Brahim's rebellious streak."

Rebellious. That's the word I was looking for. Suddenly, I remember the print in my pocket. I slide it across the table.

"Can you tell me anything about this photo?"

Amir's fingers draw it closer. He studies it silently for a while. Then, in a quiet voice, he asks, "Where did you get it?"

"It's from an old slide," I say. "I've had it for a long time. I had a print made a couple of years ago. His disappearance has something to do with this slide."

"Really?"

"Yes. I don't think I was ever meant to see it. He showed us the slide by accident one night and my parents had a big row over it afterwards. Mother accused him of breaking a promise. She was under the impression that he'd destroyed the slide years earlier, and she was furious that he still had it. I took the slide and put it in a safe place."

I look up to see if there's any reaction from Amir, but he's just looking at me, waiting for the rest of the story.

"While they were arguing, Father said something to Mother: 'The photo means something to me.' I'm convinced that this slide triggered something in him. He behaved strangely from that evening on, and a few weeks later he was gone."

Amir rests a bony hand on mine. His skin is warm and his grip so firm that I look up in surprise.

"I'm sorry, Samir," he says. "I'm so sorry your family had to go through all that."

I try to smile gratefully but I'm not sure I succeed.

"Do you know anything about this picture?"

Amir's hand loosens its grip on mine. He holds the print

in both hands and studies it at length.

"I recognise the scene, but from a different angle," he says, frowning. "I haven't seen this picture before. See the photographer at the left edge of the frame? I've seen the photo he took."

"You mean there's another photo?"

"You know who that is, standing beside your father?"

"Bashir Gemayel."

He nods.

"Brahim was very proud of that photo. Of the original, I mean. He even had it in his room, over his bed."

"Do you know when it was taken?"

Amir wrinkles his forehead.

"It must have been April or May 1982." He examines the photo closely, as if that might elicit the exact date. "But there's something about your theory that doesn't add up."

"Which theory?"

"Your theory that this photo triggered something so momentous that he decided to leave his family."

"What doesn't add up?"

"I'm not saying it's not possible, but it would surprise me."

"Why so?"

He points at the picture.

"Haven't you ever wondered why there are so many other people in the picture, looking on in the background?"

I had actually wondered about this, but eventually I'd put it down to Bashir Gemayel's celebrity status.

"The whole thing was staged."

"Staged? How do you mean?"

"Well, like I said, it was April or May 1982. A Wednesday, I think. Just a regular morning in the hotel—guests lounging by the pool, staff taking in grocery and toiletry deliveries at the rear entrance. This happened every Monday, Wednesday, and Friday. My colleagues were helping to unload supplies. I was assigned to the laundry, so all I can tell you is what others told me later."

"Please. Go on," I say. "It might help me piece things together."

"That morning, Brahim got a call from reception to say that a VIP had arrived. So he went down to greet the guest on behalf of the management, as he always did. He was more than a little surprised to see Bashir Gemayel standing there. This was west Beirut, after all. Bashir was founder and leader of the Christian Forces Libanaises. He was the enemy, at least as far as the ruling militias in west Beirut were concerned. Bashir showing up in the Carlton wasn't exactly the eighth wonder of the world, since he was well guarded, but it was very unusual all the same. Your father greeted the guest. Bashir turned to him. 'Are you the manager?' he asked. Brahim explained that Mr. Abdallah was tied up but sent his apologies. Then Bashir said to his people, 'Let's do it here.' He pointed at Brahim. 'Give the uniform to this young man.' One of Bashir's men handed Brahim a Forces Libanaises uniform, with the cedar in a red circle on the jacket. Your father put it on. They even tucked a gun into his belt. Then they positioned Bashir and Brahim in front of the staircase in the foyer, under the chandelier, and a photographer took pictures. When it was over, Bashir only wanted the gun back. They said your father could keep the uniform. The whole thing took no more than fifteen minutes. Then they all trooped out of the hotel and drove off."

"But that doesn't make sense," I say.

"We didn't think so either," says Amir with a knowing smile. "But three days later someone brought a copy of the Forces Libanaises paper to the hotel, spread it out on the table, and there was the photo, on the third page. The caption read, 'Our leader, Bashir Gemayel, welcomes the 25,000th recruit of the Forces Libanaises.' Your father was given a completely fictitious name too. D'you see? It was a propaganda photo. Who knows, maybe it was pure chance that they were driving by the hotel that day and got the idea for a photoshoot. The foyer was very grand, after all, just the right backdrop. Brahim was simply in the right place at the right time; that's how the photo came about, and this shot"—Amir points at the print on the table between us—"was probably taken by a colleague who happened to be in the foyer at the time. It was full of people, as you can see."

What Amir says sounds credible, but I still feel a piece of the puzzle is missing. Father's reaction to this photo was so out of character. I can't see how such an apparently casual incident could have had such a dramatic effect on him.

"It doesn't surprise me that your mother asked him to get rid of the slide, though," Amir continues. "Your father is wearing a Forces Libanaises uniform and standing beside Bashir Gemayel. He even has a gun in his belt. If your parents had been stopped at a road block manned by Muslim militias and your father had this photo on him, you can be sure they'd have taken him prisoner or killed him." Amir sees my uncertainty. "Thirty years," he says. "Time passes and we begin to question things. We see puzzles even where the answers are plain to see. We don't want to accept that the solution is usually simpler than we think—we wish it were more complicated. We wish there were countless obstacles to overcome before we can find the answer. And you know why? Because overcoming these obstacles gives us time—time and an excuse to keep pondering the question, even though we've long since realised there's nothing more to it. The irony is that the longer we think about it, the more discrepancies and questions arise. And at the end of our lives, we realise that all we've found is new mysteries and no new answers, apart from the one simple answer, the one that seemed far too easy at the outset."

"Maybe you're right," I say.

"I know I am," says Amir, handing the photo back with a smile.

"Did my father admire Bashir, I wonder? I'd like to know why this photo was so important to him, like you say. There must have been a reason why he kept it and hid it."

"I don't think he admired him," says Amir. "But I do remember him saying something odd when I asked him about it. He said, 'What makes the photo special is what's going on around it.'"

"What's that supposed to mean?"

"Everything and nothing," Amir laughs. "Brahim was a poet, and poets have a knack of expressing even the simplest things in complicated language."

"Could he have been referring to what Bashir stood for? New hope?"

Amir puffs out his cheeks and exhales sharply.

"That's a tricky one," he says, tilting his head in a gesture that brings Amir the camel to mind. "Bashir Gemayel was a symbol of hope for most of the Christians. Some of the Muslim population would have been able to live with him as president too. But he was hated by many. You mustn't forget where he came from. His father was the leader of the Kata'ib Party, from which the Phalange militia emerged. They were Christians with far-right or at least very conservative leanings. Bashir then formed the Forces Libanaises, which was meant to unite all the Christian militias, namely his father's Phalangists, the Ahrar militia, the Guardians of the Cedars, and a few others. Bashir had no scruples. In order to gather all of these organisations under one umbrella, he had prominent members of other parties and militias killed, including Tony Franjieh, son of the former president, Suleiman Franjieh. The Forces Libanaises did not become a party-political organisation until after the civil war. Bashir was one of the key figures in all the bloodshed, at least up to 1982."

"I know the story," I say. I had researched all the facts for myself. The Cedar Revolution twenty-three years later ultimately benefited the Forces Libanaises, who were openly anti-Syrian. Prior to that, their influence had been significantly curbed by the pro-Syrian parties. I had read a lot about Bashir Gemayel, especially after I found out that he was the man in the photo. Many Lebanese people had hoped he would be in a position to rid Lebanon of all external influence, particularly that of the Syrian army. In his speeches he evoked a state in which Christians and Muslims would live peacefully side by side. He spoke simply but passionately. He had charisma and his messages were clear. Those who wanted to keep him from the presidency were worried about his closeness to the Christian militias from which he came. They accused him of selling the country to Israel, of practically inviting Ariel Sharon to invade in order to evict the PLO, who had been using Palestinian refugee camps in Lebanon as command centres for their raids on Israel. The Israelis invaded southern Lebanon on 6 June 1982 and subsequently laid siege to west Beirut. They wanted to banish the PLO from Lebanon once and for all. On 20 August, a multinational force of French, Italian, British, and American soldiers landed in Beirut to oversee the negotiated withdrawal of the PLO. More than ten thousand Palestinian fighters came out of the refugee camps and left Lebanon, among them their leader, Yassir Arafat. The multinational force stayed on to oversee the controversial election of Bashir Gemayel to the presidency on 23 August.

"Do you remember the attack on Bashir?" I ask.

Amir nods slowly.

"Of course. It didn't come as a total surprise. Celebrations broke out in east Beirut the minute he'd been elected, horns beeping, guns firing in the air. In west Beirut, meanwhile, Muslim parliamentarians who'd voted for Bashir had their apartments torched. It was clear that some people weren't happy with the outcome of the election, even if Israel and the US tried to convince themselves otherwise. So what happened on 14 September '82 didn't really come as a total surprise. Bashir would have been the youngest president ever in Lebanon, but he hadn't even been sworn in. Brahim and I were in the hotel that day. I was working in the kitchen and your father was on pool duty. Bashir was on his way to the Phalange headquarters in Ashrafieh, east Beirut. It was a Tuesday, the day the party leadership gathered for its weekly meeting at 4 p.m. Bashir's people had begged him not to attend. They were concerned for his safety, as everyone and anyone knew he'd probably show up at HQ. But Bashir insisted. As president-elect he had to resign as leader of the Phalange, but he was determined to say goodbye to the men of the Forces Libanaises in person. After all, he owed his political success to them. He began his speech at exactly 4 p.m. Ten minutes later we heard an explosion. It was so massive that the glasses in the kitchen and on the poolside tables shook. We even heard that it set the chandelier in the foyer swaying. We all went out on the street. A big cloud of smoke was billowing over Ashrafieh. Sirens wailed all over the city as ambulances raced to the source of the cloud. Rumours of an assassination spread all over town within fifteen minutes. At first, people said he'd survived. Some heard he'd been taken to hospital with an injury to his left leg. Others claimed he'd emerged unscathed from the rubble, though no one really believed that. Fifty kilos of TNT had been detonated in the apartment above the party headquarters. The whole house lifted off the ground, apparently, before imploding completely. Not much chance of anyone coming out of that alive. In east Beirut, church bells rang out to celebrate Bashir's survival, and the Voice of Lebanon heralded the resurrection of the nation over the airwaves. It was chaos. No one knew where Bashir was, no one could find him. A few hours later, the radio station stopped broadcasting and all we heard was white noise. We went back to work, but someone always had one ear pricked to pick up the latest news. Early the next morning, Chafiq Wazzan, the prime minister, announced that Bashir was dead. They'd managed to get him to hospital, but his face was so badly mangled no one could identify him. It was his wedding ring that eventually led to his identification. Beirut has always been good at stirring up rumours, so you can imagine what it was like next day. You couldn't walk past a newspaper kiosk, a supermarket, or a street corner without hearing the same snatches of conversation: Who were the assassins? Whose interests did Bashir's death serve? Speculation was rife, and the answer was, it served the interests of many. A lot of Christians remembered the bloody power struggles during the founding phase of the Forces Libanaises. Then you had the Muslim militias. Bashir's aggressive campaign to deal with the Palestinian question by evicting the PLO and all refugees from Lebanon had earned him many enemies in this sector. He wasn't popular with the Syrians either. Two days after the attack, Habib Shartouni was arrested, and he confessed to the crime. He admitted that he'd been given the bomb and the long-range detonator by a man called Nabil al-Alam. Shartouni was the perfect man for the job: his grandparents owned the apartment above the Phalange HQ, so he could come and go as he pleased, despite the heavy security around the building. Al-Alam, who had excellent connections to the Syrian secret service, disappeared over the Syrian border immediately after the assassination. Even though he'd confessed, Shartouni was never charged, not even when Bashir's brother Amin became president soon afterwards. Perhaps it suited Amin that way. It might even have added to Bashir's martyr status."

"How did my father take the news?"

"He was devastated, of course. We all were. The multinational force had pulled out after Bashir was elected, so Beirut was a vacuum in security terms, totally out of control and left to its own devices. Brahim was constantly pacing up and down. I took him by the arm and said, 'Brahim, everything will be OK.' But he said, 'You know that's not true. They'll want to avenge him. Something terrible is going to happen.'"

"He was right about that," I say.

Amir nods. His eyes mist over, as if memories are unspooling in his head.

"Sabra and Chatila," he whispers. "The Israelis knew something was going to happen too. They decided to march right into Beirut. Officially, they were meant to be protecting Muslims from Phalange revenge attacks."

"Officially?"

Amir shrugs.

"Who knows for sure. What was clear was that the Israelis weren't happy about Bashir's death. They'd shared a common purpose with Bashir when it came to the Palestinians; both wanted them out of Lebanon and as far from the Israeli border as possible. The PLO had made a big deal of withdrawing from Beirut at the end of August, but the

Israelis claimed there were still terrorists in the camps. So they moved in and surrounded the Palestinian refugee camps. What happened next is common knowledge."

On 16 September 1982, Israeli soldiers let Phalange militiamen enter Sabra and Chatila, and did nothing to stop them from murdering women, children, and old men. The Phalangists rampaged through the camps for two days, massacring anyone who crossed their path.

"Can you tell me any more about my father? What was he like between May and September?"

"He was worried about your mother, naturally," Amir says. "That was a bad year for Beirut, even worse than the previous years. Your parents were due to get married in early October '82. Not in Beirut, in Zahle. But all hell had broken loose in Beirut, which is where your mother lived too."

"Did you know her?"

Amir gives a bashful smile.

"I never met her, but I sometimes felt like I knew her."

"How do you mean?"

"Brahim used to visit her, even before they were married. The marriage was arranged by your grandmother, but I think he really liked your mother in spite of that. He often went to see her, usually in the evenings after work. He'd be back in the hotel before his shift began in the morning."

"How do you know?"

"Because I went with him the odd time."

"You went with him?"

"Yes, as far as her flat. I often went to the same part of town in the evenings, because my parents lived there, and in west Beirut it was safer to walk in pairs."

"But you each made your own way back to the hotel?"

"That's right." Amir nods. "Brahim was clearly head over heels. Even though he hadn't chosen your mother himself, he couldn't conceal his happiness. It was lovely to see him like that. He practically floated along the footpath, singing away to himself, a twinkle in his eye."

There's something poignant and beautiful at the same time about this image of my father. It adds a reassuring little piece to the puzzle of my parents' life. Beirut was quaking, rumbling, and burning, but nothing could stop my father from secretly visiting my mother. He had protested when Grandmother forced this marriage on him. But had he been putting on an act? Maybe part of his rebelliousness meant he had to criticise every decision his mother made. He couldn't give her the satisfaction of being right.

"And you really never met my mother?"

"No," Amir shakes his head. "But Brahim said she was really beautiful."

"Yes, she was."

"I went as far as the house a few times. Your father, madman that he was, climbed up the drainpipe to get to her balcony. Then the door would open and he'd disappear inside. Fairytale romance." Amir smiles pensively. "It was lovely to watch him when he knew he'd be seeing her later on. He'd whistle to himself, and once I even caught him dancing with the hoover. What passion he had. I was happy for him."

I try to imagine Amir back then, to picture the friendly face of his youthful self.

"It's a wonder he never got caught," Amir says. "Brahim didn't just climb up the drainpipe. He had to climb back down too. Things didn't go too smoothly one time—he fell and fractured his foot. Don't ask me how he made it back to the hotel alone at daybreak. He worked all day, despite the injured foot, until someone found him at the bottom of a staircase. He told everyone he'd fallen down the steps. No one knew the truth except me. The fracture didn't heal all that well. Left him with a bit of a limp."

So that was the real story behind his limp. He'll have it for the rest of his days. A comforting thought. No matter where he is, every step will be a reminder of the nights he spent with Mother.

"Why weren't you at their wedding?" I ask.

"I thought we agreed not to talk about that," Amir replies, mildly. "The wedding was in the first week of October, in your grandmother's house in Zahle. I'd left the Carlton a few weeks previously. Let's leave it at that."

When we started talking, I was keen to find out why my father and Amir fell out. Now I'm not so sure. What I've been hearing about Father casts him in a better, softer light. I picture him climbing up the drainpipe under cover of darkness, reaching one arm out for the balcony railing. I picture Mother waiting for him inside. He swings his leg gracefully over the balcony. Then he signals to his friend, waiting below, and Amir slips into the shadows. I see Beirut shrouded in darkness. Amir and Father slinking through the streets. Two accomplices who must not be caught. I see Father caressing Mother's face and kissing her. I see them talking about their wedding, the future ahead of them, the children they might have one day. I see them holding each other tight while the city quakes and rocks. And I see him stealing out onto the balcony at dawn the next day, before anyone catches the lovebirds.

Suddenly I understand that the purpose of my journey is not to find Father after all. It is to find out more about him, to fill in the gaps, to release him from the prison of my thoughts. And although I now accept that I may never find him, I am flooded with a warm, true feeling that I haven't felt for ages. It must be happiness, this overwhelming lightness that's sweeping everything heavy away. Amir has closed the circle for me. The stories from my childhood have come to life here, and Amir has led me to the place where the last goodnight story took place. Even the golden balcony was real. Father's last story was about us, for us.

I feel Amir's hand resting on mine, and I meet his gaze. You were my favourite companion, my best friend, I think. We were separated when I was a little boy, but time has brought us together again.

Amir is right. There are no puzzles for me to solve. My search ends here. When I left Germany and set out on this quest, I never dreamed I would achieve as much. If black moments plague me again, I'll remember this day. If doubts beset me at night, clawing at me and whispering in my ear, I'll think of my old friend Amir. I'll turn on my side and inhale the smell of my wife's hair. I'll kiss the nape of her neck and listen to her breathing. I'll put my arm around her, feel her warmth, and keep telling myself, I'm here, with you, it all turned out well, who'd have thought?

"I wish I could tell you where to find him," says Amir. "I'd love to see him again too. But I've a feeling he doesn't want to be found. There's no trail leading to him. You could look for other trails, and I'm sure you'd find them. You could even follow them, but every time you reached the end, you'd see that you're back at the same crossroads where you started. You could spend your whole life like that, convinced that you're looking forwards, whereas in reality you're looking back. There is no road leading to him. They all lead back to the beginning. And that's where you are. You and only you. And it's up to you to decide what happens next." He squeezes my hand. "May I give you a piece of advice?" he asks.

I nod.

"Go home, Samir. Take all the positive things with you, all the good new thoughts. Leave your fears behind. Keep telling yourself you're not the only one who remembers your father. Lots of people out there met him, and in one way or another, he affected them all. They know his name. They know who he was, and that's what keeps him alive. Hold onto the idea that he was a good man, and above all, hold onto this thought: no matter what drove him away from you, it wasn't your fault."

16

"Excuse me, can I get this bound, please?"

It was a routine request, typical of my monotonous duties. I barely looked up when I heard the woman's voice. I'd been working in this copy shop since early 2008. Three years had passed since I'd lost my job in the library, since the assassination of Hariri. A rainy summer had come to an end. Now it was autumn, and golden leaves lent the town a magical glow. The copy shop was not far from the vocational school where I'd done my librarianship course. It was on a narrow street between the train station and the cinema, next door to a pizzeria where up to thirty teenagers would congregate at lunchtime for the student deal—a small pizza with a soft drink. The library was only a stone's throw away. I sometimes saw Chris passing by on his way to work, lost in thought, leather briefcase under his arm. The shop's main customers were from the vocational school, though we occasionally got students from the university who wanted to get their seminar handouts copied or theses bound. At work, I wore a black cap and T-shirt with COPYCENTER printed on them in green. The back of the T-shirt bore the shop's slogan: COPY THAT? I used to pity the poor suckers at supermarket check-outs who said nothing all day except, "Do you have a loyalty card?", "Would you like a receipt?", and "Have a nice day." I wasn't much better than them now. It had only taken three years and a couple of poor decisions to slide down the slippery slope.

When Aurea had left me standing on the steps outside my house that time, I'd gone in, closed the door and headed for the stairs. As usual, I checked my letter box on the way. I hardly ever got post, apart from junk mail and payslips from the library. Even Alina had practically given up writing. But on this cold grey evening there was a postcard. A picture of a historic town somewhere in northern Germany. Lots of half-timbered facades with brightly coloured shutters. A photo taken on a fine summer's day. An inviting small-town idyll, the green patina of a church spire gleaming in the distance above the rooftops.

Dear Samir,
I looked at an apartment here today. I'm moving here in the autumn. Do you like it? :) This is where I'll be doing my further training—the clinic specialises in trauma therapy. I'll miss uni (though not Statistics), but I'm looking forward to getting practical experience. I won't make it home this summer, I'm afraid. First I've got to finish my thesis, then I'll be moving house. At least we'll both be spending lots of time in a library. ;) I hope you still like it there. Come and see me some time?
Yasmin

The writing was clear and unadorned. Purposeful, like Yasmin herself. My finger traced the slight grooves the biro had left on the card. Three more years, then. Three more years she'd be beyond my reach. Yasmin had outgrown our town. She had outgrown me too, and the longer I didn't see her, the wider the gap became. She became a work of art constructed from my memories, shining brighter and brighter the more I missed her.

I only saw her at night now, when I was tossing and turning in my sleep. We'd stroll together in a dreamy blue light, walking on water. I often walked on water in my dreams. On particularly restless nights, the sky above me would turn black, and walls of waves would tower over me as high as mountains. I'd wake from such nightmares drenched in sweat, gasping for air in my dark room, terrified I was drowning. The dreams were more bearable if Yasmin appeared in them, because she'd take my hand and lead the way. She always wore a white dress, the hem just skimming the water. Her hand was soft and reassuring, her stride unerring. I always woke up before we arrived anywhere, but when Yasmin appeared in my dreams, at least I woke up feeling that there was a shore somewhere.

Three years of restless nights, rain-dark silence in my flat, and sluggishly meandering from job to job until I ended up in the copy shop. That's where the time had gone.

"Excuse me, can I get this bound, please?"

My eyes fell on the stack of paper in the cardboard box the woman was holding.

"Sure," I said, still not looking up. "We can do perfect binding using thermal glue, and you can choose softcover or hardcover. Alternatively, we have spiral binding or comb binding, which ..."

"Hardcover, please, and the best quality. It's a gift for someone."

"No problem," I said, taking the box from her and glancing at the title page of a thesis: "Trauma and Identity: Subject Formation in Refugee Children in Germany."

I raised my head. She was looking straight at me.

It's hard to describe what I felt at that moment, except that it was something deep and true. The years had woven a magic spell, and here she was now, all grown up and radiant. Her hair was shorter, her face more striking, more self-assured, more beautiful than ever. Somewhere between studying, writing her thesis, moving, and doing her practical training, she had become a woman. Twenty-six and almost too beautiful to behold. I was speechless, terrified it might just be a dream, that Yasmin would vanish if I so much as moved a finger to touch her. I stood there in my silly uniform, taller, and skinnier than the boy she once knew.

"Samir?"

The affectionate way she said my name gave me a jolt of pain and joy. I closed my eyes for a second. Her voice was gentle and full of surprise. Her eyes flickered, as if she was trying to figure out what I was doing here. Then she ran her hand along my cheek, slowly, as if she were blind.

Embarrassed, I lowered my eyes, although every millisecond I wasn't looking at her was precious time wasted. How long had I been waiting for this moment? How many hours had I spent staring at her postcard on the wall above my bed, its colours fading with the years?

If I'd managed to get out of bed in the mornings, it was only because I remembered there was a world out there in which she left her traces. Now she'd blown in here in her warm yellow coat like an autumn leaf.

"Samir." Her eyelids quivered.

I swallowed. I couldn't speak.

Eight years. It was eight years since we'd said goodbye in the car park. Eight years since we'd gone back to the derelict estate where we used to live as kids. Eight years since that fleeting kiss at the door of our old flat. "Yasmin." I was nearly choking. Next thing, she was hugging me close. After years of exhausted drifting, a wave was carrying me to shore. Mustering the last of my strength, I wrapped my arms around her and buried my head in her shoulder. She was my island.

We strolled through town beneath a leaden autumn sky. Its dark border of cloud looked as if it had been drawn in heavy pencil strokes. Yasmin had linked her arm in mine. Our shoulders touched, and I stole sideways glances at her. Every now and then, she brushed a stray lock out of her eyes, just like she used to when she was a kid. Around us were winding streets and alleys, autumn window displays and the metallic rumble of cars hurrying over the cobbles. Inside, I felt like lights were exploding. My heart was pounding and my hands were clammy.

Yasmin took it all in, amazed to see how much things had changed. To her, it must have seemed like a major transformation. She kept stopping in surprise, noticing a building where before there'd been nothing, or something completely different. For her, the town still held the nostalgic scent of the past. All I'd been able to smell for some time was decay. I still couldn't believe she was really here.

"This is where Aimée used to live," she said, pointing at a big hole in the ground behind a construction fence. "Remember? Aimée from primary school?"

"Yes ... They're going to build a carwash there."

I vaguely remembered Aimée. She and her family had left years ago.

"I've been away for an eternity, haven't I?"

A whole ocean away, I thought; you were as far away as the other side of the ocean.

Before we'd left the copy shop, I'd printed and bound her thesis. A corner of the black hardcover was sticking out of her bag.

"When did you get here?"

"This morning."

I nodded and did my best to sound casual.

"How long will you be around?"

The doors of a bus hissed open beside us. A man helped a woman and a buggy in. The bus rolled on.

"I don't know yet," she said. "The clinic where I've been working has offered me a proper job. I'm probably mad not to have accepted straight away. I've made lots of friends there, I like my colleagues, I've grown fond of the patients, it's a fantastic clinic with good promotion opportunities."

"But?"

She looked at me. A falling leaf had landed on her hood.

"But my father has been on his own for such a long time now. I think I'd like to be near him for a while. So I might apply for a job here as well." She didn't sound entirely convinced. It was as if her heart was influencing this decision more than her head.

"Refugee children," I said. She looked blank for a second, until I nodded at her bag.

"Oh." She smiled. "Right."

"What's it about exactly?"

"It's about the subjective experiences of different generations of refugees." We crossed to the other side of the street because the pavement was blocked by construction work. "And about their identify formation as children, to what extent the trauma of displacement played a role in that. These are children who are catapulted into a different life overnight. They have experienced terrible things in their home countries, and very often during the flight to safety. They grow up in an environment where they are confronted with the life histories and refugee experiences of previous generations, so they are exposed to different kinds of cultural memories. I'm particularly interested in how these children develop individual subject positions. However ... Sorry, I've been working on this for so long that I tend to speak in academic jargon," she laughed. "What I wanted to know is what makes these children who they are, and how much of what they embody might be attributable to behaviours and attitudes they have assumed subconsciously."

"Wow," I said, lost for words.

"There you go. But it's crazy, isn't it? These people go through hell to get out, then they meet people in the host country who'd as soon send them back to hell. That's a further stress factor."

"You're right. It's not much different here."

The sports hall was still serving as a refugee reception centre. You'd see them in town from time to time; they couldn't help standing out. You'd also see the disparaging looks on people's faces as they gave them a wide berth. Only recently, two Syrians who'd been in the sports hall were deported to Hungary, because they'd been fingerprinted there in transit. I wondered how much Yasmin's own background had influenced her choice of research topic.

"Have you seen him yet?" I asked.

"Father? Not yet. I'm going this afternoon."

"He'll burst with excitement."

"I reckon he's expecting me already. After all, tomorrow's the big birthday."

Hakim was going to be sixty-five. I'd been to see him quite often over the last three years, but it was true—he did seem rather lonely, and he seemed to have shrunk a little, especially since his retirement two years earlier. He spent a lot of time in the shed and going for long walks, collecting wood for the figurines he carved. It was obvious that he missed the joinery and the routine of work. The thought of Yasmin back in her old home for a few days was immensely reassuring.

"Your room is just as you left it," I said, rubbing my nose. "Well, almost—I got rid of your boy-band posters."

"I never had boy-band posters," she replied, laughing out loud and digging me in the ribs. "I was nineteen when I moved out."

She still wore the same perfume. It triggered a storm of images that threatened to overwhelm me.

"I know." I glanced at her from the side. The lightness of her step was infectious. "Maybe it was a cool surfer with no T-shirt on."

"You had no right to do that," she said with mock indignation. "I was going to take that poster with me to my new place."

"I think it's still in a box somewhere."

"I certainly hope so, for your sake."

We passed jogging fathers pushing buggies, two homeless guys fighting over a beer bottle they'd found in the litter bin, old ladies lugging shopping bags with lettuces and radishes poking out the top, and a stag party whose hapless groom was trying to engage passers-by in conversation.

Yasmin's arm was still linked in mine. Our shoulders still touched. We jostled and teased a bit, checking whether we were the same children, just in grown-up bodies. Then we walked a few steps in silence.

"It seems a long time ago, doesn't it?" she said after a while. Her tone was pensive, and she smiled shyly, as if she'd only just realised that we'd grown older.

I said nothing.

"It's so good to see you," she said, her eyes focused on the toes of her shoes. She was balancing on the kerb, still holding my arm.

"Likewise," I said, going weak at the knees.

We were strolling down an old street of half-timbered

buildings with garlands strung between them. It was the last bastion of small retailers, sewing and alterations workshops, little shops selling artisan chocolates and hand-carved wooden toys.

"I've never believed in 'out of sight, out of mind'." She was looking at me now. "I thought of you so many times, wondering what you were up to." She stopped to buy a little bag of chocolates. As she stashed the sweets in her handbag, she asked, "How come it's been so long since we last met?"

Because I couldn't bear being reminded that I couldn't be with you all the time, I thought.

What I said was, "I don't know."

"Father came to see me loads of times—you could have come with him."

Was there a hint of accusation or disappointment in her voice? She was right. Hakim had gone to see her often, and he'd always asked if I wanted to come along. But I'd never gone with him because the thought of seeing her again was inevitably linked to the knowledge that we'd have to say goodbye.

"I know. I'd like to have gone with him ..." I left the silent *but* hanging. "Why didn't you ever come home?"

A gust of wind swept the leaf off her hood.

"It was all so new and exciting," she said. "I was afraid I'd miss something. When I left here, I was scared of the unknown, but within a week I couldn't imagine how I'd stuck it out here for so long without once getting out. It was a whole new world. I loved it. My timetable was full, seminars all day, then studying, writing presentations ... Weekends were really busy too. We often went camping, or visiting other cities—I've been nearly everywhere in Germany. Then there were lectures and exams. When I moved in 2005, Alex couldn't come with me. He tore a knee ligament and missed two whole semesters, so he was still catching up by the time I moved. So I ended up in a new job, a new town, and a long-distance relationship."

"Oh," I said. That bit was news to me.

"That's right. Me in a long-distance relationship." She kicked a stone and sent it skittering across the cobbles.

"If I remember rightly, that was something you couldn't even imagine before."

"Yes." She sounded sad. "But sometimes you don't have a choice."

Alex hadn't entered my mind in a long time. He never featured when I thought of Yasmin or dreamed of her.

"How is he?" I didn't really care, but the conversation seemed to prompt the question.

She shook her head. "It didn't work out."

"Sorry about that," I lied, extending a silent thank-you to the universe.

For a moment, she seemed reluctant to talk about it. Then, before I had a chance to say anything else, she continued. "At some point I just felt there was nothing holding us together any more, if you know what I mean. I was in the clinic, dealing with horrific cases every day, and at the weekend I'd be back into student parties, snogging in the dorms, mouldy dishes in the communal kitchen. Maybe it's unfair of me, but I felt too old for that. And Alex didn't want to grow up. He loved the idea of being the eternal student, having poker evenings in his dorm, that kind of thing." She shrugged her shoulders. "And you? Have you got a girlfriend?"

"No." I paused. "It didn't work out."

The wind had blown her hair into her eyes. She looked at me through the strands. I was a whole head taller than her now.

"D'you want to talk about what happened?"

"I don't know ... I reckon we just didn't have enough ..."

"No, no." She had a firm grip on my arm. "I mean d'you want to talk about your job, why you're not at the library anymore?"

We had slipped back into our old companionship so easily. I wondered if it was a sign. If eight years had made no difference, if we didn't feel the least bit strange in each other's company, surely we were meant for one another? If anyone else had asked me that question, I'd have skirted around it, made up some excuse, like it wasn't the right job for me, or I was going through a phase, figuring out what I wanted to do. But Yasmin wasn't anyone else. Even if she didn't see it that way, she was my soulmate, the stronger part of me.

"Because I fucked up," I said. "I fucked up and got fired."

She pressed her lips together. To my relief, she didn't press me any further.

"Hakim doesn't know," I added, embarrassed.

Her eyebrows arched almost imperceptibly.

"Were you planning to tell him?"

I let out a big breath.

"The reason I didn't tell him is because I was afraid of letting him down," I said. "He went to so much trouble for my sake. I didn't want to upset him."

"I don't think you could ever let him down," said Yasmin, her tone implying I was an idiot to even think that. "He loves you. He often said to me, 'I miss you, Yasmin, but I'm glad I have Samir. He's like a son. He looks after me. He works hard. He does his own thing, like you.'"

Like a son.

"You don't have to fess up on his birthday, but how about next week?"

"I can't."

"Why not? I'm sure he'd rather hear it from you than find out some other way."

"Are you going to tell?"

She shook her head, but her face clouded over. I was forcing her to keep a secret from her father.

"No. But I don't understand why you …" She slowed her pace and looked at me. "How long is it since you got fired, Samir?"

"A while," I said.

"How long is a while? A couple of months?"

I shook my head.

"Three years."

Yasmin stopped short and fixed me with her gaze.

"Three years? What have you been doing since then?"

"This and that."

It was the truth, if not the whole truth.

Isolated raindrops started to fall from the dense clouds. They weren't landing on us, but suddenly Yasmin was on edge. She stepped up the pace and headed towards the café where she'd always liked to hang out.

"Let's get a hot drink," she said, gesturing for me to follow.

Soon, two cups of hot chocolate were steaming in front of us. We hadn't spoken since giving our order. It was as if we were waiting for a third person to arrive before resuming the conversation. Something subtle had changed, I realised. In the old days, a silence between us had never bothered me. It had never been uncomfortable. But now, because I found myself wondering what Yasmin thought of me, the silence was making me a little uneasy. Still, it was good to be sitting opposite her, looking at her without having to twist my neck. I could see that the carefree expression on her face had given way to earnestness.

"How are you, Samir?" she eventually asked in a gentle voice.

"I'm fine."

Yasmin gave me a silent look.

"Are you analysing me now?" I asked uncomfortably.

She shook her head.

"No. I'm worried about you."

"There's no need to worry."

"Don't you have any dreams? Three years, Samir." She held up three fingers, spelling it out. "Three years? I mean—don't you want to make something of your life, achieve something? Earn some decent money and finally get out of this place, see something new, maybe settle down somewhere else?"

Normally I'd have felt cornered, forced to defend myself. But I knew she was right, so I just shrugged and looked down.

"Don't do that," she said, reaching for my hand.

"What?"

"Don't shut me out. Please. I've been away for a long time, but I'm not a stranger, Samir. We've known each other our whole lives. You're important to me." In different circumstances, those last few words would've had me jumping for joy. But there was a pleading note to her voice. Yasmin was worried about me. That was scary.

"I find it really difficult," I said awkwardly. I looked up but couldn't face her scrutiny for more than a few seconds. I cleared my throat. Where had this tightness come from?

"Talk to me, then."

Had she always had that tiny mole just above her lip? Outside, the rain was heavier and the sky had darkened, while inside all was a warm glow. The lamps were reflected in the lustre of the newspaper racks and the handle of my teaspoon. The coffee machine gleamed in the corner of my eye, and Yasmin's eyes were two big pools of expectation.

"I wake up in the mornings and everything feels empty," I began nervously. "I spend a lot of time on my own. It takes enormous effort to get to work. I don't even go through the park any more. I can't bear to see families."

Her fingers were touching mine, but it felt like I had gloves on; her body present, yet somehow far away.

"When I walk through town, I have to keep my eyes fixed on the ground. Every time I pass a shop, I think: here's where Father and I bought ice-cream, here's where he lifted me up on his shoulders. I even go to the supermarket in a different part of town because I don't want to go to the old one where we used to do the shopping together. I have no friends. I mean, I don't really go out. I've had a few flings, but I can't bear the thought of anyone leaving me. I find it really difficult to think about tomorrow. The day after tomorrow is an eternity away. Next week is practically non-existent." Where was all this coming from? It was years since I'd spoken about myself, to anyone. Now the words were rolling off my tongue like heavy stones. "I can't get a decent night's sleep. I wake up at three or four in the morning, coated in sweat. I have these dreams. There's no land in them"—*just a hint of land when you are in the dream.* "I see my parents everywhere. My mother is every mother waving to her child at the school gates, wiping the corners of her baby's mouth as they sit on a park bench, tucking in her baby in its buggy as they walk along the street. And my father," I stirred my chocolate awkwardly. Yasmin was still holding my other hand. "My father is every father cheering his son on at football, reading him a story, driving him to his school graduation party and telling him he can get drunk if he wants, because life is too short not to celebrate. I see them *so often*, these fathers and sons. I really *see* them, in shop windows, on billboards, on the bus, at the supermarket check-out, at the take-away. And this town," the hand holding the spoon began to shake, "this town seems so cramped, so small. I see the same people all the time, it's so monotonous, but at the same time, I don't feel able to leave. There doesn't seem to be any way out. I can't even think where I'd go. It's like ... I feel so ... so ..."

"Alone?"

I nodded silently. At the table next to us, a man got the bill. Coins clinked onto a plate. Behind me, a newspaper rustled.

"Every single person I've loved has disappeared at some point. I have no contact with Alina any more. I'd like to take responsibility for her, but I don't even know what she's up to, how she's doing. She's seventeen now—seventeen! I know how this all sounds," I said, sighing wearily. "Like I'm afraid of life. And I am, to some extent. But it's not just that I'm afraid."

"What else then?"

"I'm angry. I try not to be, but it doesn't work. I'm mad at myself, because I keep wondering what I could have done differently. But if I go back farther—and no matter what way I look at it—I always come back to him, to Father. I'm mad at him for what he did to me. Worst of all, I know he's still alive, living somewhere far away from here."

She sipped her chocolate.

"He is? How do you know? Did he make contact?"

"No." I shake my head again. "I just sense it. You know the way you might be thinking of someone and then the phone rings, and it's them? It's kind of like that. Like he's thinking of me the whole time. I'm always thinking about him, but the phone never rings. I'm not religious, but sometimes I wonder if this is some kind of test. And if it is, what's my mission?"

"Why do you think him disappearing means you have a mission?"

"Because I feel like there's something I missed. That I should have been able to prevent it. Or that I've had it in my power for a long time to find him. Except I'm still here."

"Do you want to find him?"

Now the rain was hammering against the window. Someone burst into the café. A cold blast of wind ruffled newspapers and serviettes until the door closed again.

"Not a day goes by that I don't think about finding him. Not a single day."

Yasmin's voice was clear, and there was no hint of judgement in her next question. "If you did find him one day, what would you say to him?"

I looked at her.

"I'd ask him why. Why he left just like that. Why he did that to me, to us. Why he did that to us."

Yasmin dunked the biscuit that came with her hot chocolate. She looked into my eyes and lowered her voice.

"Have you ever talked to anyone about this? Like now, with me?"

"No," I murmured. I had actually thought about seeking help a few years back, but my idea of psychotherapy was one big cliché—a bright room with large potted plants in the corners, floor-to-ceiling bookshelves, someone taking notes in a leather armchair, me on a couch opposite them, talking about my life. About my parents. About Father. About him making me promise never to tell. But telling a therapist would have been breaking the promise.

"Did you ever try writing it down?"

"Writing?"

Yasmin nodded. Drops from her dunked biscuit fell on the white china.

"The letters you wrote me were really beautiful," she said. I swallowed.

"You use such beautiful language, and the imagery is so alive. I read them over and over."

"Really?"

"Absolutely. I wish you'd never stopped writing," she said awkwardly.

I hadn't stopped. But she didn't know that. At home, in a box, were hundreds of unposted letters to her.

"You have a talent for writing, for storytelling. I think it would help you." She was looking straight at me. "What do you think?"

"I don't know. I mean, what would I write about?"

"About yourself? It's just a thought, but it often occurred to me when I was reading what you wrote. I think you're an even better storyteller than your father."

She blushed as she smiled. She'd read and re-read my letters—why had I never posted the rest? It would have been one way of remaining close to her.

One day you'll put your own children to bed and tell them stories, Father had said.

"Alina would be thrilled to get a story from you too," Yasmin said. "A story from her big brother. She'd love that."

"Alina? But we never even talk to each other."

"So what? She often talks about you."

In my fidgety state, I'd torn my serviette into little pieces. Now someone yanked the café door open, and a blast of cold wind sent all the serviette confetti flying.

"You've been in touch with her?"

"We never lost contact," said Yasmin, as if it was the most natural thing in the world. "We write, we phone each other, that kind of thing."

"How is she?"

As always, my throat constricted at the thought of Alina. For all I knew, she was my only living relative in this country, yet she still seemed out of reach.

"Her family is great. She's happy there. She's gone a bit Christian, but that's hardly surprising when her foster father is a minister. She goes to church fairly regularly, and on parish youth outings. But she doesn't lay it on, the religious stuff, if you know what I mean." Yasmin laughed. "She often asked me about you, wanted to know how you were doing, what you were up to. So you're wrong if you think Alina doesn't want any contact with you. It took her years to get back on her feet. Hours and hours of therapy. She thought you were in therapy too. Told me she'd love to see you again sometime, do something with you, see how you turned out. When ..." Yasmin looked at me, holding my hand tight as she spoke. "When you're feeling better."

Maybe Yasmin was the safe shore I'd imagined all these years. She was certainly bringing me the first bit of good news I'd had in ages.

"Alina," I mumbled, as if it was some fairy creature's name. "She's well, you say? I mean, what's she up to, what's her favourite subject in school, does she have a boyfriend?"

"I think she's in love," Yasmin said, smiling.

"Really?"

"Well, she was asking me for tips—dos and don'ts for your first date. What does that tell you?"

I couldn't help but smile. Since Mother's death, if not before then, every day had seemed an endless struggle. Now, to my surprise, the years seemed to have flown. My little sister had blossomed into a young woman who was beginning to live her own life.

"So she thinks of you as her big sister?"

"I don't know. Maybe."

"I hope she does."

Saying nothing, Yasmin smiled.

"And she'd like to hear from me?"

"Definitely."

"I thought she'd blame me."

Yasmin had just put her cup to her lips but set it down again. "Samir, no one blames you for anything! What would they be blaming you for anyway?"

"My mother ..." It was barely a whisper.

"Samir, Rana was ill. None of us could have saved her. Alina knows that too."

I said nothing. Then I asked, "And she wants to see me?"

"You don't have to meet right away. How about a letter? Or a story? And then a phone call? These things take time, Samir. But you're only twenty-four—or you will be in a couple of months. Twenty-four! I don't want to sound like an old woman, but you have your whole life ahead of you. There is no question that you've been through a lot. No one has any doubts about that." Now she leant in and laid both hands on mine. "I don't have any doubts about that. I know how you feel. I grew up without a mother. I never knew my mother, so I didn't have the kind of bond you had with your father, but it still wasn't easy growing up without a female role model. Father was brilliant. He did more for me than anyone could have expected. What I'm trying to say is: I know exactly how you feel. But I also know something you still have to learn: Life goes on. It's a cliché, but wherever there is darkness, there will always be light."

I wished she'd keep talking and never let go of my hand. I could have stayed like that forever, slumped in my chair, the smell of hot chocolate wafting up from our cups, Yasmin's face opposite me, the one thing that counted. But she paused, and I knew I had to say something.

"What if I can't see the light?"

Her eyes moved up from my hands, locking my gaze.

"Then you need someone who can show you where it is."

The rain had become even heavier, lashing against the window panes. The outside world floated away in a blur.

"What time is it?" asked Yasmin.

I looked at the familiar clock behind the coffee machine. "Nearly three."

"I want to be at Father's by four at the latest. Why don't you come with me?"

I had been planning to visit him today anyway, to see if he wanted any help. His birthday was going to be celebrated whether he wanted it or not. The neighbours had invited themselves weeks ago.

"OK, I just have to get changed first." I was still wearing my copy-shop uniform.

"Do you live near here?"

I nodded.

"Between the library and our street. About ten minutes from here."

Yasmin signalled to the waiter and dug her wallet out of her bag.

"Right," she said. "I'm going with you."

A wall of stale air hit me when I opened the door to my flat. The walk here was like a blurry film with distorted noises and voices. The sound of passing cars became a roar, the acoustic signal at the pedestrian crossing seemed more shrill than usual, every light dazzled and fractured, and the clacking of our footsteps seemed to come from another world. Loudest of all was the pounding of my heart. I could feel Yasmin's arm again, linked in mine under the umbrella, but it felt very far away. As we walked to my flat through the easing rain, I felt like I was looking down at us from above. The closer we got to my place, the more I tried to calm down, to reassure myself that it was OK to take Yasmin there.

Of all the people who had left me, she was the only one who had come back. How could she release me from my prison if I didn't let her in?

In a state of numbness, I saw my flat through her eyes. A dark, oppressive, cramped space. Stuffy. Incredibly untidy.

The shutters were closed as usual. Slivers of light filtered through. Yasmin went in first, her eyes trying to adjust to the dark. My heart thumped even louder when she stopped and looked around in disbelief. I could only see her from behind, but I sensed her shock.

The bands of diffused light showed up screaming headlines on yellowed newsprint pinned to the walls:

NO PEACE FOR LEBANON

CIVIL WAR

INVESTORS ABANDON BEIRUT

BASHIR GEMAYEL KILLED IN BOMB ATTACK

WHAT WENT ON IN SABRA AND CHATILA?

CEDAR STATE TOPPLES TOWARDS THE ABYSS

Crisscrossing each wall, and stretching from one wall to another, were long threads held in place with thumbtacks. Like a giant spider's web, they linked details in the newspaper articles. Years, dates, placenames, people's names, all circled and flagged with exclamation marks. Further threads led from there to other articles around the room in which the same names occurred. No matter where you looked, you saw words, images, newspaper cuttings. Even the ceiling and the furniture were covered in clippings—the backs of chairs, cupboard doors, the table top. It was like being trapped inside a giant newspaper, or in a hidden chamber behind a bookshelf, a place where a secret society was hatching dubious plans. Or like one of those classic movies in which the despondent detective, abandoned by his wife and children, spends his evenings staring at pieces of evidence pinned to the wall, whiskey in hand. A storm rages outside. He knows he's missed something. It's probably staring him in the face. He paces up and down in a drunken stupor, the cop who's lost everything because he's spent half a lifetime obsessively chasing a serial killer.

On the largest wall, at the point where all the threads met, was the photo of my dreamy-looking father beside Bashir Gemayel. Above Father's head was a sheet of white paper with a big question mark on it. I could hear Chris's disappointed voice again: *Why didn't you just photocopy the pages?* Eyes downcast, I'd answered: *It wouldn't have been the same.* No originals, no authenticity.

"I thought I had a right to it," I whispered, shuddering at the thought of the years I'd spend crawling around in here.

Yasmin still had her back to me, but I could see her covering her mouth in shock.

"Really, no one else was interested in this stuff," I continued in a whisper. It was the same excuse I'd used to justify my actions to myself. "I traced it all on the computer."

Yasmin's face was ashen. She looked at me in horror, struggling for words and failing to find any.

She stood frozen in shock and confusion. I put my hand on her shoulder and she jumped, then looked at the wall again.

"What have you done to yourself?" she asked in a trembling voice.

I swallowed, struggling to find an explanation.

"This … It really hurts to see this." Yasmin reached a hand toward one of the threads crisscrossing the room. It trembled at her touch. "I mean, how can you live like this?"

"I've been hoping to find a clue."

She turned to face me. Her pupils were enlarged by the dark. I could see the flicker of pity in them.

"You're breathing, Samir," she said bitterly. "But that's not living."

I nodded in silence. What could I say? She had exposed it for what it was—a crazy web of delusion. There we were, surrounded by the images we'd seen projected on the living-room wall all those years ago, like waymarks on a three-dimensional timeline. I had wrenched Yasmin back into the painful past. It was too much for her.

"I'm sorry," she said, laying her hand briefly on my shoulder as she turned away. "I can't do this."

She ran out of the flat. Seconds later, I heard her footsteps hurrying down the stairs.

I stood frozen to the spot. The sound of the door closing at the bottom of the stairs jolted me into action.

"Yasmin!"

I charged out of the flat, ran down the stairs two steps at a time, and yanked the front door open. Outside, the air was fresh, the sky clear, the pavement still glistening with rain. To the right—nothing. To the left—a flash of Yasmin's yellow coat, the echo of her footsteps.

"Wait!" I cried, my heart pounding. "D'you remember the secret?" I could not, would not lose her now. "D'you remember?"

She stopped and turned.

"His treasure," I said, all out of breath. "The secret everyone talks about? Remember?" Was that a smile on her lips? "You do remember," I said. "I know you do."

She was half facing me, half about to walk on.

"What about the secret?" It was the little girl from back then who was asking.

"I know what it is," I said, full of excitement. "I know the secret."

The wind blew autumn leaves and images from our childhood towards us. Then she turned fully round to face me.

I looked at her.

"From the south to the north, from the Chouf to the sea, from Beirut to Damascus ..." I began breathlessly.

"... rumours abounded," continued Yasmin.

I nodded. "From Tyros to Tripoli, behind walls and shuttered shop windows ..."

"... behind the fruit vendors' crates at market stalls and in front of the columns of the palace ..."

"... everyone was talking about his secret ..."

"... a treasure that he guarded and protected ..."

She was standing in front of me now.

"... even from Amir, his best friend ..."

"... And everyone wondered what it could possibly be ..."

"... that Abu Youssef was hiding up there in his little house," I whispered.

The old magic was there in Yasmin's eyes. The curtain was drawn back, revealing the wide stage, the lights, the set.

"So you know the secret?"

I nodded.

"I was afraid to tell you before."

"I didn't know he'd told you."

"He did. On that last night."

Her cheeks were rosy, her hair curly from the damp air.

"You don't have to tell me."

I do, I thought. I have to. We drifted apart once already because I never finished the story.

Yasmin's hand was cold as I led her back to the entrance to my building. She sat on the dry top step. I stood at the bottom and told the story, raising and lowering my voice, gesticulating with my arms. I knew it inside out, every word. The sentences and images tumbled out of my mouth and into her ears, transporting her back on a time stream. I could see it in her eyes, a warm glow that came from deep inside.

This wasn't our old building. It wasn't our old street. It certainly wasn't our old life. But we were here. We were sharing what we had in common. We were eight and ten, and I was taking her back to that night, to the last time everything was still all right.

17

I'm around three years old and I've never been taller. From my lofty perch on his shoulders, I look down on a world full of small grown-ups and even smaller children. I am a giant. I'm the tallest of them all. I can see the roofs of the cars and the clouds reflected in them. I'm flying, defying gravity. If I reach out, I think I could touch the treetops or even the sky. Then two strong hands grab me, lift me up, and set me down. I feel the ground under my feet again and look up. Father is looking at me. He's got a red baseball cap on to shield his eyes from the sun, and his black hair curls out from under it. He pats my head and strokes my cheek. I wonder what it must be like to be that tall, what it must feel like to be able to reach out and touch the sky. As I look at him, he smiles a mysterious smile. That's my earliest memory of him.

Beneath my window, the lines of traffic wind down the street like ants. Miniature people. Toy cars. The curtains flutter in the breeze. My hair is still wet from the shower. For my last night, I requested a room on the top floor, so that I could see the panoramic view one more time. The towers in the city centre are all in a cluster, each glitzy facade reflecting the next. To my right, beyond the blueish domes of the al-Amin Mosque, I can make out the harbour. Straight ahead, I see a maze of huddled houses, roofs with clothes lines, satellite dishes, water tanks, and potted plants. Mosques and church spires serve as reference points in the landscape.

My first morning here was one overwhelming impression after another: noise, smog, heat. Now I know I'll miss Beirut: this vibrant, yearning, crazy city that's forever in flux; this melting pot of cultures, religions, and languages. Beirut is pure joy and pure sorrow all at once. Beirut is forgiveness. Beirut is limping, confused, and scarred, but still dancing. Beirut is like me.

Last night, when we got back from Brih, the city had transformed itself yet again. It welcomed me with open arms. The palm-fringed promenade was alive with crowds of young men and women in trendy clothes, all heading for the brightly lit beach bars and nightclubs. Music and laughter rang out everywhere.

My rucksack is packed. I pick it up off the bed and leave the room. In the lift, I see my face in the mirror. Dark rings under my eyes. Tiny pupils. A weary but contented expression. I'll sleep on the plane.

The receptionist wants to know if everything was to my satisfaction, if I was happy with my new room, and she hopes I'll be back again. Hotel staff push luggage trolleys through the foyer. Some guests in leather armchairs sit crouched behind their laptops. A familiar scene. I'm scanning the lobby for his face. It's half past eight. I'm too late. He's not here.

"Eight o'clock. No problem," he'd said as we parted company last night. It was three or four in the morning, in a dark side street. We were both drunk, leaning against a wall not far from the bar. "I'll get you to the airport on time." I took a taxi back to the hotel, Nabil staggered off into the thrum of the night. My head hurts, but I have to laugh. What a mad night we had!

"We should celebrate," Nabil had said as he steered down the bumpy road. Brih, tucked into its valley between the mountain sides, had disappeared as soon as we'd rounded the first bend. I was relishing the absence of the heaviness I'd felt for so long. I was breathing easily, thinking of Amir and what he'd said to me: *Take all the positive experiences with you. No matter what drove him away from you, it wasn't your fault.*

I felt in control.

"We've solved the case!" Nabil repeats emphatically, as I'd failed to react the first time he spoke. I had told him about the photo and how it was all staged by Bashir Gemayel. About my father visiting my mother on the sly, climbing up the drainpipe. About Amir coming to life.

"That's the best story I've heard in a long time," exclaimed Nabil, banging the steering wheel. "You should move to Beirut, Samir—we could have so many adventures together. You'll get married. Why not bring your wife here? We'll open a detective agency downtown ... We'll need a logo. How about a magnifying glass? Too hackneyed? What? You're heading home tomorrow? What a shame. Then we definitely have to celebrate tonight!"

"How do you celebrate solving a case?" I asked. I took a swig of lukewarm water from the bottle under my seat.

"Don't ask me." He shrugged but continued enthusiastically, "That was my first case. We have a 100-per-cent success rate. Not bad for beginners, huh?"

"Absolutely. We're a hard act to follow." I laughed, shoving the bottle back under the seat.

"Damn right. Although ..." He scratched his head. "Strictly speaking, you solved the case on your own. You asked all the right questions. So the plot structure is as it should be."

"The plot structure?"

"Well, it's ultimately the detective who solves the case, not his assistant."

"But Nabil, you're Philip Marlowe, not any old assistant."

"Maybe so, but you're Sherlock Holmes. He is a little more famous, let's face it."

"So that's why you had a snooze under a tree. You wanted me to solve the case."

Nabil laughed.

"Exactly. I knew we'd have something to celebrate this evening, so I was taking a little nap in advance."

Later that evening, the air was cooler but still pleasantly warm. We could hear the babble of voices, the music from the bars. In the narrow streets, shoulders rubbed shoulders, aftershave mixed with perfume. Outdoor tables, neon lights, floodlit facades.

"I suggest we start at the beginning and drink our way to the end, bar by bar. That's the simplest thing." Nabil's face broke into a grin when he saw my surprise. Uruguay Street, downtown Beirut, where revellers are drawn to the nightlife like moths to a flame. There were no seats at the outdoor tables, so we found a table inside. The warm air in the pub was loud with the chatter of voices, the clinking at the bar, and the music from the speakers. Nabil ordered for the two of us. As the barman nodded and turned away, Nabil closed the drinks menu and said, "The answer is no, by the way."

"The answer to what?"

"You asked before if I drink wine. The answer is no."

"OK," I said. "But you just ordered two arak. Is it alcohol-free here?"

"No, but arak is different," says Nabil. He looks like a teenager who's bought alcohol at the petrol station for the first time. "It's transparent. Less conspicuous."

"Less conspicuous?"

"Yes. It looks like water." Nabil points at the ceiling. "Allah is way up there, and it's very crowded down here. If he were to look at my glass from up there, it looks completely innocent."

"I get it." I had to laugh.

I would miss Nabil as well. Something about this friendly faced guy who's playing keyboard on the table-top right now reminds me of an air-traffic controller who works diligently all day, only to throw himself into whatever adventures life has to offer by night, his tension dissipating as he navigates the crowds. He had done it again—taken me to one of the most touristy bits of Beirut. This time it didn't bother me, though. I was completely at ease.

"So, what's next for you?" I asked.

"Me?" He raised his palms. "Well, I'll start looking for an office, for when you move to Beirut. Somewhere downtown, twenty-fifth floor or something like that, panoramic view for ourselves and the clients, a fountain in the courtyard, golden taps." He winks. "No, I'll do what I always do. Drive. I'll continue to solve cases on the side, assuming something interesting comes along. And sooner or later I'll buy the car Philip Marlowe drives in the movie of *The Big Sleep*. Have you seen it?"

"No."

"Robert Mitchum. Brilliant."

"What kind of car is it?"

"A 1930s Chrysler. I might have to break into a museum." He laughs. "On the other hand, the way people drive in Beirut, you wouldn't want to take such a beauty out on the road."

Electronic music was thumping out of the sound system by now, and the atmosphere was more club than pub. Fortunately, we had a spot by the wall, so the speakers boomed the music out over our heads. Unlike the other customers, we didn't have to shout to make ourselves heard.

I followed Nabil's gaze as he scanned the pub. Most of the tourists seemed to be from the Gulf States, but there was also a table down the back where some English and Russian guys seemed to be having an international drinking contest. It was hard to tell whether their faces were red from the drink or the sun.

"It's good to have the tourists back," he said, perhaps because he'd seen me staring. "In 2006, after the Israelis bombed us, we thought it would take forever for tourism to recover. The airport, the city, everything was in ruins again. Everything we'd rebuilt since 1990 was in danger. But somehow it all worked out." He smiled. "Things always have a way of working out."

"We should drink to that," I said.

Nabil looked around for the waiter.

"If we ever get a drink."

"More tourists also means more clients for us," I said.

"See?" He laughed. "That's what I like about you. I like the way you think. I'm glad we met. You're a good person, like a brother to me, *habibi*."

He put his hand on my arm, and I was a young boy again, back home on our street, where men I hardly knew embraced me and called me *habibi*, and that was perfectly normal, perfectly OK.

"Let me tell you something, Samir," Nabil continued. "It's been thirty years since I had a holiday. Thirty years. My children have never been outside this country; my wife and I only once. We went to Syria, back when Damascus and Aleppo had more markets and bazaars than bullet holes. I told you about the money I've been putting aside for Jamel's college fund, didn't I? Now your story has helped me reach a decision."

"Really? How?"

"I'm on the go all day—don't get me wrong, I don't mean this evening or the week I just spent with you, I mean in general—I work like mad. I hardly see my kids. I work so that they'll have a better future. I want Jamel to go to college. So I spend fourteen hours a day driving strangers around, and most evenings I go to the airport hoping to pick up a fare into town. When I get home, the kids are either asleep or heading out the door. I only see them in passing, like ships in the night. I hope this isn't too close to the bone, Samir," he said, hesitating briefly, "but I don't want my children to get to your age one day and have to go looking for strangers to find out what kind of guy I was. You know what I'm saying?"

I nodded.

"Does that sound wrong?"

"Not at all."

"So maybe a holiday would be a good idea. Pack up the whole family and head off. Spend some time together. Maybe I'll even read stories to them." He smiled, but it was an absent-minded smile. The waiter brought the arak and we raised our glasses.

"A toast to everything working out in the end?"

"No," I said. "A toast to fathers."

"ok. To fathers. Look ..." He wiped his mouth with the back of his hand and pulled a crumpled brochure out of his trouser pocket. "This is what I was thinking of: Turkey. Not too far away but still a change of scene."

The colours were so faded, he must have been carrying it around for ages. It was like a treasure map. The picture showed a hotel resort. The photographer had presumably chosen the most flattering angle, but it was still pretty obvious that the pool was tiny and the hotel a big concrete box. Two stars, no private beach access, and at least thirty kilometres to the nearest tourist attractions. But I could tell from the way Nabil put the brochure on the table and pointed at it that this place held untold promise, the answer to all his cares.

"It looks great," I said. "Go for it, Nabil."

"I will," he said, tapping the brochure. "Splashing around with the kids, relaxing, reading, time out, hanging out together." Then he looked at me. "Those stories meant a lot to you, didn't they?"

"My father's stories? Oh yes, they meant the world to me."

"My father told us stories too, during the war. It was nice, because you could forget everything else for a while. So I know what you mean. Do you know 'Kilun 'indun siyara wa jidi indu hmar'?"

"The children's song? Of course!" *Kilun 'indun siyara wa jidi indu hmar.* Everyone has a car, but my Grandpa has a donkey. "My parents often sang it with us."

"We used to sing it with our kids too," said Nabil. "I'd love to sing children's songs again. I'm not great at telling stories, but one thing I'm good at is making up children's songs."

I pictured him gathering his family together for a sing-song over the next few evenings. I could almost feel my melancholy ache return, but Nabil shook off the wistful mood and clapped his hands.

"And you? After you get home, when will the wedding be?"

"The date isn't set yet," I said, then adding confidently: "But it will happen."

For the rest of the evening we just enjoyed ourselves and drank arak. With each round, we became more relaxed and more talkative. At some stage we moved to a different pub and switched to beer. Nabil ordered his in a juice glass. He put a finger to his lips and said, "Strictly between you and me."

After a while, some Americans—all wearing red T-shirts with a university logo—decided it would be a good idea to move the tables and clear space to dance. We watched them for a bit, and next thing I knew we were joining in, absorbed in the bass and the melody, swinging our arms and legs, singing along way too loud and totally out of tune. I laughed and laughed, happier than I'd been in a very long time. I was suspended between the warm sense of having finally arrived and the pleasant anticipation of getting home, throwing my rucksack in the corner, and proudly announcing that I'd done it, that my journey had been a success.

Later, beneath an orange moon, we sat on a wall which, according to Nabil, was part of the old Phoenician fortifications. We dangled our feet, drank cans of beer, and sang children's songs into the cloudless night, as if it was the last summer of our youth, as if we knew it too.

I'm pretty sure this is the hottest day of my life. It's early morning and the thermometer has already hit 35 degrees. I've left the cool foyer, and it's like walking into a hot, damp towel again. The young man in hotel uniform holds the door for me, smiling stoically even though his brow is beaded with sweat. Nine o'clock. No sign of Nabil. Maybe he overslept. He probably shouldn't even be driving, but I doubt if anyone gives two hoots about that here. I'm beginning to get worried. My rucksack could go as cabin baggage, but I will still need time to get to the airport and clear security. To make matters worse, the traffic in front of the hotel has come to a complete standstill. Cars are stuck at all angles, suspended in chaotic motion, their occupants gesticulating on their phones and blowing their horns, although the traffic has nowhere to go. I look for Nabil's Volvo in this sluggish chaos, but I don't see him.

No wonder it's taking him so long. Bechara el-Khoury Road is completely backed up.

"Would you like us to call a taxi?" the porter asks.

"No, thanks. I'm waiting for someone."

Though I can't wait much longer, I'd like to see Nabil before I leave. We'd deliberately kept our goodbye brief last night.

"It might be a good idea to phone the person you're waiting for and arrange to meet somewhere you can reach on foot." He nods towards the street. "You won't be getting out of here in a hurry."

Have I still got Nabil's business card? It's probably in my wallet.

"Where would be a good meeting point?" I ask, fishing out my wallet and looking for the card.

"If you head south in this direction and turn left at the second side street, you'll see Saint Joseph University. It's about a fifteen-minute walk. There's a big car park and it's very close to the highway. You're going to the airport, right?"

"Yes."

I take out my mobile and enter Nabil's number. After a few rings, it goes to voicemail.

"Hmm," I say. "Thanks for your help."

At the university, I manage to pick up a taxi. As we take the slip road up to the highway, the driver says something about a leaking gas pipe, a construction site, the worst traffic jam for months. I listen with one ear, the other glued to my mobile. Again, no answer, then voicemail.

I'd woken up feeling so relaxed I was almost euphoric. I'd forgotten what that felt like. The path Amir had described finally seemed to point in one direction, straight ahead. But it feels strange to set out on this path without saying goodbye to Nabil. It feels like unfinished business, the wrong way to start. I don't want to leave Lebanon with a bad feeling.

I try one more time. Still no answer.

A horribly familiar feeling takes over: wishing I'd done things differently. We'd been so close last night, like old friends. It was the perfect moment to say goodbye. We were on a high after a successful journey and a good night out. We'd shared songs and stories under the night sky. That called for a hug, a heartfelt "Thank you," a "Good night"—but no, we'd simply said, "See you tomorrow!" A taxi had pulled up beside me and Nabil had vanished into the night.

I can tell from the road signs and low-flying aircraft that we're approaching the airport. The thought that Nabil might be at the hotel right now, asking for me, is unbearable. He might even follow me to the airport and miss me by a hair's breadth. Or he might be at home, sick or in trouble.

In west Beirut it was safer to walk in pairs—that's what Amir had said. He had accompanied his friend, my father, through the bombed-out streets of Beirut. Was it remiss of me to let Nabil head off alone? Should I have told him to take the taxi, to make sure he got home safely? Nabil is my friend. I've never had any friends, which is why I'm so sure of it now. It's a new feeling, a beautiful one. But there's something else as well—a growing sense of foreboding, a fear I cannot name.

Certainty is everything. I can't live without it. My fear might be unfounded, but right now it's stronger than me. I know exactly what'll happen if I go home with a new mystery, if I don't make sure he's OK. Father let Amir down. I can't make the same mistake.

"Excuse me …," I say to the driver and lean forward to hand him Nabil's business card. As the airport fades from view, I keep repeating it to myself: Friends don't let each other down.

The balconies on the building are all the same, grey on grey. The stairwell has trapped the heat of the day. The first-floor passageway is like a shabby hotel corridor: a sequence of worn timber doors, a lift that doesn't work. I'd rung the bell downstairs, and now a stranger is waiting in the open doorway, blinking at me.

"Hello," I say, slightly out of breath. "I'm looking for Nabil?"

The man examines me briefly. He doesn't ask who I am, just shakes his head and swallows.

"Nabil," I say. "Is he in?"

He doesn't seem to be able to look at me any longer. He looks down, lets out a deep sigh.

This body language is disturbingly familiar. It reminds me of the night I sat sozzled opposite Hakim in our dimly lit living room. He was telling me what happened to Mother and he couldn't look me in the eye.

"The police say he was drunk at the wheel," the man whispers. "A terrible accident."

He puts a finger to his lips and silently invites me in. The hall is dark. The air is stuffy and stale, but I can smell food too—mujaddara and fried onions. The man beckons me, again without a word, and quietly leads the way. Is he a brother of Nabil's? On the hall cabinet there are photos of Nabil, his sons, and his wife, typical family photos, soft focus against a blue background. The man walks down the narrow corridor and opens a door. When I go in, I see a man with a long beard sitting on a chair. Three boys and four men sit at his feet. The man who escorted me points wordlessly at the floor: *Please, sit down.* Apart from the man on the chair, they all raise their heads and nod when I enter the room. Then they look away again. The hush is reverent and broken only by a deep, continuous murmur. The man with the beard is quietly reciting verses from the Koran while the others listen.

I feel like an intruder in this stillness. I want to get up and leave. These people are strangers, though I know this is where Nabil's family lives. The three boys have to be his sons, Majid, Ilyas, and Jamel. The last has big brown eyes and perfect skin—the handsome son, exactly as described by his proud father. When our eyes meet, I think I see a flicker of recognition behind his palpable grief. Jamel's brothers look at me too, and for a fraction of an awful second I think I can read their whole future in their eyes, a future full of unanswered questions.

The murmured words from the Koran drift over my head. I rest my back and my head against the wall. Nabil's sons turn their attention back to the old man. No one shows any further interest in me. All eyes are on the man, who's now reciting the 36th surah, *Ya-Sin.*

It reminds me of the day Shahid al-Nur died, an old Lebanese man who lived on our street. I was six or seven at the time. Father held my hand as we made our way to the flat. "We have to be very quiet and respectful," he told me. "The flat will be a place of mourning for three days. Shahid's family will have arranged for the sheikh to come. He'll read the Koran from beginning to end over the next three days, and the others will listen."—"But we're Christians," I said. Father nodded. "That doesn't matter. A friend has died." The atmosphere was similar that time. The flat full of neighbours, friends, and relatives. Intense silence. Men and women in separate rooms. I clung to Father's hand and sneaked a look at the sheikh. He was wearing a white djellaba under a brown kaftan, and on his head a turban-like 'imma. His words were clear, and he had an aura about him that was more solemn than sad. "Poorer families can't afford a sheikh to read from the Koran when someone dies." Father had leaned down and was whispering in my ear. "In that case, neighbours or friends do the reading."

I've only just noticed the bead curtain separating this room from another. The window is tilted and an afternoon breeze rustles the strings of beads. I can see shadows on the far side. I think there's a woman sitting on the bed, wearing a black abaya and hijab. It looks like there are four women sitting on the floor. In addition to the men's voices murmuring in this room, I can now also hear a woman's voice reading quietly from the Koran.

It's weird. Suddenly I feel safe. Nabil is dead, but I've had a gentle landing. By rights, I should be bawling my eyes out and falling to my knees, begging his family to forgive me for not protecting him. Instead, I feel calm. Surrounded by his family, I feel in good hands. My heartbeat settles, my breathing becomes steadier, and I listen to the holy verses. They don't mean anything to me, but they convey a sense of security, as if something is guiding me, telling me not to worry.

"Inna nahnu nuhyi al-mawta wa naktubu ma qaddamu wa atharahum wa kulla shay'in ahsaynahu fi imamin mubinin," murmurs the man on the chair. *Indeed, it is We who bring the dead to life and record what they have put forth and what they left behind, and all things We have enumerated in a clear register.*

Nabil's young sons sit cross-legged side by side, their backs to me. The men, unshaven and dressed in dark-blue trousers, are seated around them as if to protect them.

They have friends and relatives here, I think. They are not alone. They have support, people who will help them.

Nabil's brother looks over at me. Here, in the pale light, it's impossible not to see the resemblance. He mouths my name: *Samir?*

I nod slowly.

He joins his hands, closes his eyes, and makes a little bow. *Thank you.*

I tilt my head in the direction of the bead curtain and mouth: *Umm Jamel?* Jamel's mother?

He nods.

I look back at him and put my right hand on my heart. I don't know how else I can show that I'm sorry.

The words of the old man fill the air. They float through the room, and somehow it reminds me of how Father used to gather us around to tell us stories.

I sit on the floor for another while. When I eventually stand up, no one turns round. All I see are the narrow, drooping shoulders and bowed heads of Jamel, Majid, and Ilyas. Their uncle stays where he is too, but he smiles briefly to say farewell. Slowly I open the door and step into the dark corridor. The last words I hear are: "Wa in nasha' nughriq-hum fala sarikha lahum wa la hum yunqadhuna." *And if We should will, We could drown them; then no one responding to a cry would there be for them, nor would they be saved.*

18

My throat was in a knot. I was hot and dizzy, barely able to breathe. The tiny window let little light in. The walls, the table, everything was spinning. I could hear the murmur of the people gathered outside.

"Hang on." said Yasmin, "Let me open a button."

She came closer, undid my bow-tie in a few quick moves, and opened the top button of my shirt. Then she stood on her toes and kissed me on the forehead.

"Better?" she asked calmly.

I nodded. She took a step back and inspected me with a smile.

"You should wear a suit more often."

Her hair was plaited at the back and she was wearing a daffodil-yellow dress that fell just above the knee. A silver necklace and a flower pinned to her dress completed the outfit. She looked like spring.

"Have you got the ring?" she asked.

I patted the pockets of my jacket, my cufflinks flashing silver as I moved.

"Yes, I've got it." The little box was safely in my inside pocket. I looked at her. "You look fantastic!"

"So do you." She could tell I was nervous. "I'm really proud of you."

"Thanks." I smiled awkwardly.

Yasmin moved in and brushed some fluff off my shoulder.

"There's no need to be nervous. Enjoy today. Enjoy every minute of it. Be glad that we're here. You made it. The two of you really deserve this."

I was just about to put my arms round her when Marcel stuck his head round the door.

"Ready?" he asked.

I remember it all—the light streaming through the high church windows, the decorations on the altar, the wooden benches creaking beneath the weight of the wedding guests. Alina wore a white dress with a long train. Behind her veil, her grey-green eyes shone with excitement. I remember the collective gasp when the organ began to play and the guests turned round to catch their first glimpse of the bride. She stood at the entrance with me, the daylight behind us projecting our shadows up the aisle. I can still see the beaming, emotional faces. Alina's foster mother giving us a little wave, seventy-year old Hakim surreptitiously brushing away a tear. Marcel and Sulola, Alina's brother and sister, seated up front with Yasmin, proud smiles on their faces. Alina's foster father, performing the marriage ceremony himself.

The young woman beside me was beautiful. The same shy, reserved beauty our mother had. I couldn't take my eyes off her. Because I hadn't been there to see this beauty unfold, and because I'd had no idea what to expect, its effect had been all the more dramatic when we were reunited. Since then, I'd often searched her features for the little girl I'd known, catching the occasional glimpse of her when Alina talked excitedly or laughed out loud. I remember her trembling slightly as she took my arm, and I remember the little pools of light on the floor as I led her to the altar. I remember my heart thumping and the joy I felt in that moment, a pure joy free of doubt.

During the wedding banquet, Alina sat between me and her husband, Hendrik. They'd been together for three years. Alina was twenty-two. We chatted about their honeymoon plans, about the delicious meal, about Hakim's moving speech. He had insisted on saying a few words in the church, extolling Alina's virtues, telling us how musical she was, even as a child, his voice breaking with emotion now and again. When a choir sang with violin accompaniment a little later, he shed a few more tears. I felt really proud. I was her brother. She was my sister. Alina Elbrink— no longer el-Hourani. But we were still family.

Later, when we were all gathered round the bride and groom as they danced in each other's arms, I squeezed Yasmin's hand in gratitude; she had never left me on my own on this journey.

When it was time for the father-daughter dance, Alina came to get me, a smile on her face. I rested one hand on the small of her back and led her with the other. We twirled before the eyes of the assembled guests, until everything around us spun by as fast as the previous five years.

The old uneasiness was still there, but in brighter moments I felt more in control of it. I still thought of Father frequently. I railed at him, cursed him for his absence, wished he could see how hard I was trying to glue the pieces of our family together again. I no longer had photos and newspaper articles and threads on my bedroom wall. I wasn't even living in that flat any more. But I was still driven by the idea of finding him, of tracking him down and confronting him. I had a burning desire to see the country we were from, to travel in his footsteps in Lebanon. Me, Samir, captain of Phoenician walnut-shell ships, heading off in search of the unknown. Nothing had changed that longing, not even the fact that Yasmin and I were together now.

The magic of storytelling had helped us find our way back to one another. Not immediately. Not right there on the steps, where I finally told her Abu Youssef's secret, fifteen years too late. The process was a gradual one. In the end, it was my stories that made her fall in love with me.

She was the reason I started to write, and once I'd got going, she encouraged me to keep at it. I soon figured out that in order to write, you had to allow yourself a life with stories. And in order to experience anything, I had to get out of the house and pay more attention to the world around me, not focus on myself and my past.

For the first time since leaving our old flats, I became more aware of my surroundings and discovered magical places outside of town. Yasmin and I went off exploring. We'd cycle along the river until we'd left the town behind us, pick a grassy spot to spread our rug, and I'd try to describe what we saw as clearly and in as much detail as possible. Then I might take a blade of grass and twirl it round her belly button, or move up and trace the contours of her smile. In the evenings, we went to funfairs, milling among the crowds and taking in the garish lights of the rides and shooting galleries, the barkers' cries, the smells of candy floss and chocolate bananas, the giant teddies at lottery booths, the shining eyes of children.

My first story was about a boy who fell in love with a girl. He had a serious illness, the symptoms of which only disappeared when the girl was near him. So, in order to survive, he had to make her fall in love with him. It wasn't a great story. It was full of awkward imagery, and the characters were too obviously based on us, but Yasmin liked it, and that was how I got going. When I was visiting Hakim, I'd sometimes slip the pages of a new story under her door. Then she got her own flat, and eventually I moved in. A couple of days after I'd given her a story, I'd ask what she thought of it, and she'd say, "I haven't touched it. I'd much rather you read it to me."

When I read to her, it was as if the magic of our past had survived everything. We were children again, transported to another world for hours on end. Nothing could have brought us closer. We were like two gentle spirits hovering around each other, and though there were some very dark stories that I never showed her, it wasn't long before Yasmin and writing were the twin mainstays of my life.

At this stage, Yasmin was working in a trauma therapy practice about twenty minutes' drive from town. She had her own patients and her own office, and when she had the time, she volunteered as a contact person for refugees in the sports hall.

To this day it's a mystery to me why Chris didn't press charges when he fired me from the library. At any rate, his lenience—or negligence?—meant that I had some chance of starting over.

The library where I got my new job was in a different town, thirty minutes away by train. It was smaller than the other library, but that meant I had greater variety in my work.

In the first couple of years, our relationship was characterised by the lightness, the tingling passion of young love. Everything is magical and new until that first flush gives way to a bigger, deeper love that's perhaps a little less exciting. After Alex, Yasmin had had a few fleeting relationships, but none that lasted. For both of us, it was completely new to be in a relationship with someone we'd known our whole lives, and to discover that there was so much we didn't know about each other. Little things, mostly—for example, Yasmin liked to perch on the edge of the bath and hum to herself while she was brushing her teeth, and after showering, she'd go to the bedroom wrapped in a towel and get dressed there, whereas I always took my clothes with me to the bathroom. She noticed that I always got out of bed left foot first, put on my left sock first, and my left trouser leg too. I noticed the way her body would give a funny little jerk just as she was about to fall asleep. They were just little things, trivial quirks and foibles, but they gave us plenty of laughs.

Yet the curse remained—never being able to trust my luck, never allowing myself to be happy for too long, always suspecting disaster lurking behind every beautiful day, every wonderful moment. And paradoxically, the more I came back to life in the present, the greater my desire became to find out once and for all why Father had left me almost twenty years earlier.

Strolling through town one day, the last-minute offers and pictures of palm-fringed beaches in a travel agent's window caught our eye.

"Wouldn't you like to go to Lebanon some time?" I asked Yasmin. "To see where we're from, get to know the home country?"

"This is our home," was all she said. She buried her hands in her jacket pockets and gazed at the turquoise sea on a poster.

Broaching the subject of a trip to Lebanon was tricky. While for me it was the country my father was from, where I suspected he was now, and also the land of the Abu Youssef stories, for Yasmin, Lebanon was where her mother had died.

"There's nothing there for me," she'd always reply. Maybe she was throwing cold water on my longing for Lebanon because she wanted to cure me of this obsession. Maybe she felt I was having a relapse. In any case, she made her position pretty clear. "When our parents fled to Germany, they had next to nothing. They fled in the hope that we, their children, would have better lives. By deciding to come here, leaving everything behind, they gave us the gift of a home. They made it possible for us to lead lives we would never have had if they hadn't left." She paused, brushed her hair out of her face, and continued in a quiet voice. "There's nothing waiting for me in Lebanon. This is my home. I want my father to be proud of me. I want to show him that giving up his former life for my sake was not in vain, that I'm grateful to him for all the good and the bad."

It was only a matter of time before I slid back into old habits. Once an addict, always an addict. It started with me staying at work a little longer to pore over books. I knew the sickening pleasure of it would be short-lived. Now that I was in charge of acquisitions at the library, I made sure that the holdings on Lebanon grew slowly but surely. I knew it was wrong but I couldn't resist. I no longer stole anything, but I read as much as I possibly could. More and more often, I lost track of time, buried in books, and arrived home late to find Yasmin gone out and a plate of cold food waiting on the kitchen table. In the mornings, I took a roundabout route to the station, just so I could hear the muezzin's call at the mosque, and if I was at the market, buying from one of the Arab stallholders, I'd insist on speaking Arabic.

Yasmin had a wide circle of friends, but I didn't find it easy to fit in. When we were younger, we used to go to clubs and bars, but now we were at the stage where most of our friends were getting married, having babies, or inviting each other to garden parties. The topics of conversation would be the weirdos next door, or work, or the best barbecue lighters, or prenatal courses—all of which seemed utterly banal compared to what was going on my mind. I felt more like a hanger-on than a genuine companion, so I'd stand on the periphery swirling my glass, sucking ice cubes, and smiling politely until it was time to leave.

The signs were there, some more obvious than others, and it seemed like I was heading in the wrong direction again. Something inevitable was brewing. We both felt it.

"You seem so unsettled again these days," Yasmin said one night. We were in bed, staring at the dark ceiling.

Unsettled. That was the word she used to describe my mood. She turned over on her side. I curled into her, put my arm around her, and breathed in the smell of her hair, her skin. But even then I wasn't fully with her; my mind was already on a journey.

"We will continue on this path. We will shoulder this responsibility and accept the sacrifices and consequences that come with this responsibility." Hezbollah leader Hassan Nasrallah was speaking on TV. A coffin draped in a yellow flag was being carried through Beirut. Hundreds of people were lining the streets and reaching out to touch the coffin, which held the body of a Hezbollah fighter who had fallen in Syria. Men had been coming home in coffins for weeks now. I'd been following it on the news. Lebanese Hezbollah were fighting on Assad's side in a civil war that was none of Lebanon's business. This really exposed their masquerade for what it was. Up to this point, Hezbollah had always used the fight against Israel to justify their existence and their arms, but the Syrian civil war was nothing to do with that.

"They've no choice," said Hakim, who was sitting in front of the TV in his living room. "If Assad weren't in power in Syria, Hezbollah would have a serious problem."

Yasmin was on the couch, flicking through a brochure.

"Because of the direct support that Assad gives them," I said.

Hakim nodded and poured water from the terracotta jug straight into his mouth. Then he wiped his lips with the back of his hand.

"But primarily because of Iran. Syria is the link between Lebanon and Iran. No one supports the Shias in Lebanon as much as those two countries. If Syria falls into the hands of the rebels, the supply lines will be cut off."

The fighting had spread all over Syria at this stage. Hundreds of thousands of civilians had fled to Lebanon. TV images from the border area showed shivering women and children who'd been caught in unexpected snow. Syrian refugees led camera teams through their miserable makeshift huts in Beirut, past dripping water pipes and jury-rigged power lines. Northern Lebanon became the stronghold of the anti-Assad activists, who were training fighters and preparing for a war on his regime. This led to many bloody encounters right on the border.

None of that put me off. The sense that Lebanon—like me—was walking a dangerous tightrope only strengthened my desire to go there. Lebanon had become a refuge for so many millions. Why not for me as well?

Yasmin and I had been having more arguments, and they were getting fiercer. The contrast between the trajectories our lives had followed since childhood was never as stark as in these heated moments.

"You have Baba,"—her father—"you have Alina, and you have me, Samir. But you still feel something's missing?" This was only a few weeks after Alina's wedding.

"I'm sorry," I replied. But that's what I always said, so it just made Yasmin angrier.

"If you were genuinely sorry, you'd make some effort to change," she said. "But I hardly see you. You come home at all hours and won't tell me what you've been doing. It'd be nice to spend the evening together sometime, just you and me watching a movie on the couch, but you're glued to the news all the time. Your eyes, Samir—you should see that look you get as soon as you hear the word Lebanon. I can't understand why you're still like this. Tell me, why is all that so much more important than you and me?"

I couldn't explain it. But I had a gut feeling that things would only get worse if I didn't go looking for Father. Nothing would change if I didn't at least try to find answers to the questions that plagued me. Yasmin knew it too.

My gut also told me that I didn't want to lose Yasmin. Even if I couldn't always show it, I loved her with every bone in my body. She had hauled me ashore but I had to go the last bit of the journey on my own, hoping she'd be waiting at the other end.

Almost exactly a year after I'd led Alina to the altar, I went to Hakim and asked for his daughter's hand in marriage. Of course, Yasmin made all her own decisions, but somehow it felt like the right thing to do. No matter how progressive he was, or how laid-back his attitude to German customs and mores, in his heart of hearts Hakim was still proudly Lebanese.

He had got a whole new lease of life when Yasmin moved back. He laughed more, became more agile, and now and then I'd see him in the shed, clamping a plain length of wood in the vice. His hair had turned from grey to white and was unrulier than ever. After I made my request, he stood up, joints creaking, and came over and kissed me on the forehead. Then he stood there and just looked at me.

"You and me, Samir ...," he said after a while. "Many's the time I wished we'd been closer." I went to speak, but he held up his hand. "Sadly, I failed to keep the promise I made your father. I tried to rescue you—I do realise what all those years have done to you—and I failed, I know. But Yasmin ..." He took my head in his hands and looked into my eyes. "Yasmin is the light you have always been looking for. If she can't rescue you, no one can." Without taking his eyes off me, he continued in a slower and quieter voice. "Ana fakhur fik ya ibni." *I am proud of you, my son.* "I have no right to ask you to promise anything, since I didn't keep my own promise. But you are asking me for my daughter's hand. She is the brightest star in my life, which is why I have to say this to you: If you wish to marry Yasmin, you must promise to love her as she deserves to be loved: unconditionally, truly, every minute of every day until you die. And you must not be a burden to her."

"I love her," I said, looking straight at him. "I've always loved her."

Hakim's old hands moved from my face to my shoulders.

"I know," he said, with a smile and a sigh. "I've always known it."

Yasmin followed the clues in the stories. It was a paper chase. I led her back to places that played a special role when she was growing up. They had become special places for me too. The first story took her to what had been her favourite café. The waiter handed her a menu in which she found the second story. It was about a mermaid who had left the sea years ago but longed to return to it. This led Yasmin to the old swimming pool. The man in the ticket booth, a secretive smile on his face, handed her the key to a locker, where the third story awaited her. In it, a girl is in the library studying for a difficult exam when a lonely genie suddenly emerges from the pages of a book and offers to sit the exam for her if she'll promise to visit him regularly and keep him company. When Yasmin got to the library reading room, she made a bee-line for the spot where she used to study. There she found a piece of paper with F.ELH 2008 written on it. The F was for Fiction, so she went to that section, then started looking under E until she found a slim folder labelled EL-HOURANI between the numbers 2007 and 2009. In it was the final story, "The Paper Flower." It is narrated by a flower that has grown out of the grey asphalt in a run-down housing scheme. The flower feels lonely, even though she is much loved. She is the only splash of colour in a sad wasteland, which is why the residents are so fond of her. As the flower grows older, her colours fade, and the people are afraid she will wither and die. But the flower doesn't mind, since being lonely seems a worse fate. The desperate residents call on a magician, who tells the flower that he could turn her into a paper one. She would no longer have a conscious mind, but she would bloom for ever and light up the lives of the residents, who had nothing else. The flower agrees.

Yasmin took the bus to our old address. Time had not been kind to it. The grey blocks of flats loomed like dinosaur skeletons. The perimeter wall had even more holes than the last time we'd been here, and it was covered in graffiti. The playground swing was rusting away. When Yasmin went into the courtyard, the little kings of the streets just stared at her silently. Then they went into a huddle, whispering among themselves. After a few moments, a wide-eyed girl ran to Yasmin and handed her a red paper flower. Yasmin took the flower and unfolded it. *Come to the river*, it said.

I was waiting on the riverbank when she appeared between the trees and clambered down over the rocks and fallen branches. Behind her, beneath a grey sky, was the backdrop of our childhood, but Yasmin's bright coat and eyes lit it all up like the flower in my story. She smiled at me, her cheeks rosy from the treasure hunt.

My hands shook as I slipped the ring over her finger and looked at her with misty eyes. She nodded, and we quietly embraced while the river rushed by. She took a step back and studied her hand in the dappled light.

"It's a gorgeous ring," she said. "And I do want to marry you, Samir." She paused and looked around the familiar setting. "But I can't." She took off the ring, reached for my numbed hand, and placed the ring in it.

The look on her face was tender, sad, and beautiful.

"I love you, Samir," she said. "You mean everything to me. But we both know you're not ready for marriage yet."

Something snapped somewhere and landed with a dull thud.

"But I love you. I always will," I said quietly.

"I know," she said, stroking my cheek. "I know. But I'm thinking of the future." Her hand moved to my shoulder and brushed off a leaf. "What if we have children, Samir? Can you handle that kind of responsibility? Will you be able to be a good father? Or will you always be afraid of making a mistake because you so desperately want to be the father you miss? You're with him most of the time, even now, I can tell. I see it in your eyes when you're watching the news, when you pass a man on the street who looks like him. You look for him everywhere."

I lowered my gaze and felt grey again, as grey as the blocks of flats behind us.

She sighed.

"You must go on this journey. We both know it. I can't imagine anything better than having you by my side for the rest of my life, but you need to sort out your own life first, Samir. I thought I could help, that I could give you what you're missing, but I can't. Only *he* can. I don't know what you'll find there or whether you even know what you're looking for, but if that's what you need in order to change, then you have to go there."

I nodded. On the one hand, it was what I wanted, even if the chances of finding Father were slim. But I could feel my chest tightening at the thought of my future happiness with Yasmin hinging on this journey.

"Don't you want to come with me?" I asked. The water rushed downstream, and I already knew the answer.

"No." She paused. "There's nothing there for me."

Would we ever stand here again, by the water? Or would we look back one day and wonder how we ever ended up on this riverbank?

I wanted to take her hand, but she had clasped her fingers.

"Will you still be here when I come back?"

Yasmin looked at me. Her eyes were full of uncertainty, but her voice was steady.

"I'll wait for you, and if you need my help where you're going, I'll give you as much support as I can." She took my hand and squeezed it. "It doesn't matter *when* you come back," she said. "The question is *how* you come back."

19

He'd still be alive if I hadn't come here. I stagger like a drunk through streets flanked by housing blocks. He died because of me. I've no idea where I am. It's late, I'm exhausted, but I daren't close my eyes. My T-shirt is stuck to me, my eyes are dry from the heat, my tongue feels thick in my mouth. When did I last have anything to drink?

My rucksack is weighing me down. My shoes are covered in dust. I reach into my pocket and find the ring. *Yasmin.* It feels heavy on the flat of my palm. The little diamond has an orange glint from the street lights.

I texted her earlier. I couldn't phone. How could I have explained it? *Still in Beirut. Will be in touch. S.* She was probably already waiting at the airport by then.

The traffic rushes by, I turn into a side street, lean against the wall to catch my breath. I put the ring back in my pocket. How on earth did I get into this mess?

The guilty mantra goes round in my head—I shouldn't have left him on his own, I should have taken the keys off him. *He died because of me.* I'm falling into a black hole. There's nothing to catch me, and when I land, I'll be back in Germany, sitting on the side of the bed, more broken than ever, and Yasmin will be packing her bags. Because I'll have disappointed her yet again.

After an eternity of wandering aimlessly, I collapse onto a chair in a bar and put the rucksack down beside me. The music is Arabic, not club music. I still haven't a clue where I am, but I can hear the sea, so the Corniche can't be too far away. No tourists here. I stand out, feel eyes on me. Puffs of smoke from shisha pipes on the tables. I order a beer. It arrives lukewarm. I am dazed. I open my rucksack and root for the diary. Maybe the weight of it in my hand can restore the sense of safety I'd felt among the mourners at Nabil's, before I left the house and fell apart outside, alone again.

I'd always thought of it as a treasure map that would show me the way, a secret book full of codes to be cracked, sentences pointing to Father like road signs. But I'd over-estimated the importance of the diary. Or had I? Part of me still feels it must be more than a collection of anecdotes. I can't explain why. But now, as I leaf through it and look at Father's wobbly writing, it's not telling me anything. All I can hear is Amir's voice: *There is no road leading to him. They all lead back to the beginning. And that's where you are. You and only you. And it's up to you to decide what happens next.* But the voice is very far away, and Hakim's whisper takes its place: *If he left any clues as to where he is or why he had to leave, you'll find them in his diary.*

Two men are staring at me. When I look over, they raise their glasses. I raise mine in return and they look away. I drink the beer in one go. The alcohol and the heat are making me feel a bit woozy. I think those guys are talking about me. They keep looking over. When I count out the money and leave it on the table, one of them digs the other in the ribs and they quickly finish their drinks.

I stuff my wallet and the diary into the rucksack. The photo of Father and Bashir is tucked into an inner slip pocket. By the time I stand up, the men are gone. I didn't even see them leave. I can feel the other customers' eyes on my back as I walk out onto the street.

The sea must be very close. I can smell it as well as hear it. The air is moist and salty, just how I imagined it as a child. The lights of the buildings towering above me eclipse the stars in the infinitely black sky.

My mobile vibrates. It's a text from Yasmin.

I'm worried. Text me, please!

I hear footsteps behind me.

20

I bolted upright. I'd been lost in thought, sitting in the dim light shimmering through the closed curtains. Something important was about to happen, I could tell. Hakim avoided my gaze. He'd come back to the room with his head down and lowered himself wordlessly into his armchair. He hesitated briefly before placing the object he'd been carrying on the table. We both stared at the black cloth it was wrapped in. There was shame in Hakim's eyes.

It was a sunny day, and he'd been working in the shed when we arrived. Hakim waved. He removed his coarse apron and brushed the sawdust off his clothes before hugging us.

"Congratulations," he exclaimed, giving Yasmin a kiss. "I'm so happy for the pair of you."

There was an awkward pause. Yasmin and I kept looking at each other as we tried to explain the situation with a minimum of words. Clearly ruffled, Hakim looked at Yasmin's hand, which bore no sign of an engagement ring.

"What? No wedding?" His disappointment seemed to grow from one second to the next. He looked at me. "You want to go to Lebanon?" The way he said it, you'd think it had never occurred to him that I might one day want to set off in search of Father.

"I have to go," I said.

Hakim nodded and took a seat on the stump of the cherry tree.

"It's not the same country your father spoke of with such passion," he said in a quiet voice. "Nor is it ever likely to be that country again."

"I know," I said. "But I have to do this all the same."

"Where will you begin? Lebanon isn't a big country, but without a starting point, you'll be a long time looking."

"I'll start in Zahle," I said, because it was the only thing I knew for sure. "I might find my grandmother there. If she's still alive."

Hakim avoided our eyes. Sitting there staring at his hands, he looked like a little boy lost in the body of a very old man.

"Zahle," he repeated tonelessly. "I've often wondered, like you, whether Brahim is still alive and where he might be." Hakim paused. "At one stage I even wanted to go looking for him myself ..." He smiled hesitantly. Then he looked at Yasmin. "And you don't want to go with Samir?"

"No," she said, looking from Hakim to me. "He has to do this on his own."

Now I was in Hakim's flat, a few days later. He'd phoned and asked me to come alone. When I'd taken a seat in the living room, Hakim had disappeared, returning with the object now sitting on the table, wrapped in its black cloth. It all came flooding back, the silence, the cold, and the tiredness I'd felt as I waited on the stairs that very last night. For a long time, it had been just a blurry image at the back of my mind, like a faded painting, but now I could see it clearly again, the object Father had retrieved from the basement and taken to Hakim's that night.

Hakim cleared his throat.

"I lied to you ...," he said in a shaky voice. "When you asked before, about what Brahim had given me that night, I couldn't tell you. I wasn't ready." The object on the table looked as foreign and immovable as a standing stone somehow fallen from the sky. "He asked me to mind it." Hakim's voice was barely audible. He was genuinely ashamed. "I asked him why he didn't give it to your mother, or to you and Alina. But Brahim said, 'I'm giving it to you. If and when you feel Samir needs it, please pass it on to him.' Then he made me to promise to take good care of it."

Hakim was clearly struggling. I knew exactly how he felt. Father had extracted a promise from him. No one knew what that meant better than I did.

"This is not the photo album you showed me before," I whispered.

He shook his head in confirmation. Without a word, he reached for the black cloth and pulled it aside. There on the table lay the diary.

I could barely hold back the tears. Opening it and seeing Father's handwriting after so many years was such sweet pain. It reminded me of the notes he used to leave on the kitchen table if he had to go out in a hurry, so we wouldn't worry. I also had a really clear memory of looking for a note when he wasn't there the morning after that night. I flicked through the diary pages. Dates and names leapt out: *Rana, Hakim, Beirut.*

"I think you need this now," said Hakim. "Maybe your father foresaw this moment. Maybe he knew you'd go looking for him sooner or later. It's better to start your search knowing more about him." He paused. "Maybe this will help you to understand some things better. And maybe Yasmin will say yes when you get back."

I kept looking at Father's writing.

"Have you read it?"

Hakim didn't answer.

"Does it provide any clues to what happened?"

I forced myself to look up for a moment, to engage

Hakim, but he kept his eyes on the diary.

"It's only a hunch. But if he left any clues as to where he is or why he had to leave," Hakim took a deep breath before finishing the sentence, "I reckon you'll find them in his diary."

21

Bright lights, throbbing sounds. Beirut by night, a sparkling beauty, a twinkling tiara, a breathless trail of flickering lights. As a child, I loved to imagine myself here someday. Now there's a knife stuck in my ribs, and the pain shooting through my chest is so intense I can't even scream. *But we're brothers*, I want to shout, as they tear the rucksack off my back and kick me till I sink to my knees. The pavement is warm. The wind is coming in from the Corniche; I can hear the sea lapping at the shore and music drifting out of the restaurants along the street. I can smell the salt in the air, and the dust and the heat. I can taste blood, a metallic trickle on my lips. Fear wells up inside me, and rage. *I'm no stranger here*, I want to shout after them. Their echoing footsteps taunt me. *I have roots here*, I want to cry out, but all I manage is a gurgle.

I see my father's face. His silhouette framed in the bedroom door, that last shared moment before my sleepy young eyes closed. I wonder whether time and regret have haunted him.

I remember the verse the old man with the beard had muttered: *... then no one responding to a cry would be there for them, nor would they be saved.*

Then I remember the rucksack. But it's not the money or my passport I'm thinking of—they're gone. It's the photo in the inside slip pocket. And his diary. All gone. The pain is so bad I almost pass out.

I am responsible for a man's death, I think.

Then, as the blood seeps out of my chest: Pull yourself together. It must mean something. A sign.

The men's footsteps fade and I am alone; all I can hear now is my own heartbeat.

A strange sense of calm comes over me. If I survive this, I think, it will be for a reason. My journey won't be over yet. I'll make one last attempt to find him.

III

You'd have to be blind not to see what's going on.
Something terrible is about to happen.

1

The first thing I notice is the absence of noise. For the first time in ages, I'm surrounded by fresh air. The scent of orchids wafts by, and the smell of soil is so strong I can practically taste it. There's something bright and cheery about this place. A few olive trees here, a row of cypresses and pines there, shading the benches underneath them. Everything faces the sea. A rugby team is training on a pitch. To the left, where sea and coast meet, a lighthouse stands tall. Winding paths form a network of arteries running through verdant lawns lined with neatly clipped hedges. An oasis hidden behind ochre walls, guarded by a security man dozing at the gate. From his little gatehouse, a path flanked by flower beds leads past stone buildings to a large green, where young people sit beneath palm trees, their heads buried in books.

I sit on a step, squinting into the sunlight, and watch the orange spots floating behind my eyelids.

Four nights ago, I found myself in a strange bed. The wind had carried the sound of people partying in through the window, jolting me awake. The apartments across the street cast light into the room, turning my fingers silver as I ran them along the bandage wrapped around my chest. It hurt so much to breathe that I winced. Piles of books and a laptop on a large desk, notes on the wall, a poster of the Vitruvian Man. I hoisted myself into a half-upright position, resting my lower back against the pillow, and tried to remember how I ended up here.

Now I hear footsteps behind me and feel a hand on my shoulder.

"What did the doctor say, Samir?" Wissam asks. He's wearing shorts and an Abercrombie T-shirt, a pair of sunglasses pushed back into his hair.

"The wound looks fine," I say. "He praised your handiwork."

Wissam shakes his head. "You were lucky. A couple of inches in the other direction and they'd have got your lungs." He gives me his hand and pulls me to my feet. As I stand in front of him, the sun hidden behind his head, I have a flashback of him bending over me on the street, a street lamp behind his head, just before I blacked out. "Shall we?"

I nod and turn to face the building I've been waiting outside: "AMERICAN UNIVERSITY OF BEIRUT—MEDICAL CENTER," it says above the sliding glass doors. Wissam is a medical student in his fourth semester. God knows what would have happened to me if he hadn't come along. He managed to stop the bleeding there on the street before taking me back to his place, where he disinfected the wound and stitched it up. I didn't come to until that evening.

I asked him why he hadn't just taken me to a hospital. "You didn't have ID and I didn't have much cash on me. They'd have sent us away," he said. It was him who set up the appointment at the university clinic. "We need someone else to take a look at you. You can stay here until you're sorted," he said, gesturing at the apartment. "Stay as long as you like, ahlan wa sahlan."

His apartment is big: two bedrooms, a modern kitchen, and the bathroom faucet has far better water pressure than at the Best Western Hotel. Downstairs in the foyer, a security guard keeps an eye on the people coming and going. Wissam lives in the middle of Hamra, west Beirut, in a sparkling glass complex just a few minutes' walk from the American University.

We stroll across the campus. Near the main gate, the bell tower of College Hall extends its long neck. A row of pointed lancet arches marks the entrance to the hall: Moorish-style architecture, elegant and sophisticated. The entire campus exudes an air of gentility and self-assurance.

"We've had your credit card blocked," Wissam says. He's taken out a piece of paper, a to-do list. Some of the items are already ticked off. "I wasn't sure what to do about your mobile phone. Have you got a contract?"

"No," I say, "Prepaid."

"OK." Wissam ticks another thing off. "I called the embassy. They'll need a passport photo. We can take care of that later—there are photo booths here on campus. We'll go to the embassy with the photo tomorrow, you'll have to sign a few forms, and they'll issue you with a temporary passport in around ten days. Your fiancée will need to fax the embassy copies of your ID and birth certificate."

"Thanks so much, Wissam."

He shakes his head. He always does this when I try to thank him.

"It'll give you a little more time to find your father, won't it?" he says.

"Yeah," I say and think: ten days. My new deadline.

Wissam said I was calling out for Father in my sleep that first night, so I told him all about my search. About why I'm here. He's been so kind, the way he's taken care of me, but I hate feeling so helpless. Wallet, passport, ID, everything's gone. I've even had to borrow a T-shirt from him.

"Where are we headed?" I ask. The doors of the building

on the right have flung open, and students are streaming out.

Wissam puts his list back into his pocket.

"Rassan's waiting for us at the main gate."

I've only seen Rassan once. Last night, in Wissam's apartment. He called around to see how I was doing, and because there was something the two of them wanted to talk to me about. Rassan is studying here too, sociology, fourth semester. His parents live in the US, where his father is an architect. These two students were the first to rush over to me after I was attacked. Rassan helped Wissam get me back to his apartment.

"I'm glad you're doing better," Wissam says, putting a hand on my shoulder. His relief is palpable.

"I can't tell you how grateful I am," I repeat. "What would I do without the two of you?"

Wissam smiles nervously.

"It's the least we can do."

After our talk last night, I know what he means.

The sea is to our left. The water glitters, a light breeze blowing up the hillside and rustling the leaves of the olive trees. The campus is like a catwalk: men and women dressed to the nines in designer clothes accessorised with expensive bags. I'm surprised at how much skin some of the female students show. They wear miniskirts with high heels and T-shirts slit open at the sides to reveal their bras. In their midst, veiled women are also making their way to lectures. Students of all religions attend the university. There's a vibrant mishmash of cultures, a babel of languages: Arabic, English, French—sometimes all from the same mouth.

I wonder if Nabil was ever here. If he dreamed of sending his sons here. If he'd have been able to afford it.

"How much does it cost to study here?" I ask.

"Depends on what you study." Wissam puts on his sunglasses as we reach a large square. "Between six and eight thousand US dollars."

"Per semester?"

Earlier, in the car park, I noticed the Porsches, the Jaguars, the black SUVs. This, the top university in the country, is reserved for the financial elite, and they don't try to hide how rich they are. I imagine all the students here live in apartments like Wissam's. He's been paying for everything. Over breakfast today, I promised I'd pay him back as soon as I could, but again, he just shook his head. "What happened to you is our fault. I want to make it up to you."

Last night, we were sitting in Wissam's dimly lit apartment, an untouched plate of sandwiches and sliced tomatoes on the table between us.

"We've got something to tell you," he said, in a tone that made me sit up and pay attention. "Rassan and I didn't just happen to be nearby when you were attacked on Tuesday." The two of them glanced at each other and then at me. Rassan nodded silently. "We were in the bar across the street."

"I know," I said. "You already said."

Wissam's hands were clenched into fists, his knuckles white.

"Right ..." he said. "But we were there ... for a reason." He hesitated. Was he embarrassed about something?

"Go on."

"And when we saw what had happened and ran over to you ... Well, at first we thought ..." He looked over at Rassan, who finished the sentence for him.

"At first we thought you were someone else."

"Someone else?"

Wissam ran the back of his hand across his nose. "We'd

arranged to meet a friend. It was too dark to see you properly, and you're about the same height as him, similar hair. Your clothes weren't really his style, but we figured it might have been a disguise."

"Why would your friend come to meet you in disguise?"

Wissam got up and started pacing the room. Rassan watched him in silence and then turned to me.

"Because he had a feeling it might happen."

Wissam went over to his desk by the window and looked down at the street.

"What might happen?"

"The attack," Rassan said quietly. "We thought our friend had disguised himself to avoid being recognised."

"Recognised by who?" I kept looking back and forth between the two of them. Slowly, very slowly, it began to dawn on me. "Let me get this straight," I said. "You're telling me I was mistaken for someone else?"

Wissam nodded from the window, half of his face in the dark.

"It may not have been you they were after."

"Who were they after, then?"

"Our friend," he said.

"But why?"

He turned away from the window and looked at Rassan.

"We'd better not say any more," Wissam said curtly. He looked like a stranger in his own room. "Not here, anyway."

They feel guilty, I thought. They've been going out of their way to help me because they think they're partly to blame.

"What's wrong? Why can't you just tell me the whole story?"

Again, it was Rassan who answered.

"You never know who might be listening in." He seemed much calmer than his friend. "Stand up." Tilting his head, Rassan signalled that I should join Wissam by the window.

"See the car?"

A silver Mercedes was parked in the pale beam of a street lamp. Through the tinted windows, I could make out the silhouettes of two men.

"They're here every night," Wissam said. "They never get out of the car. When I come back from uni every day, the space is empty, but they always arrive shortly afterwards and stay for hours."

"Who are they?"

"Could be anyone," he said tonelessly. "Hezbollah, Amal, Forces Libanaises ..."

"They're spying on you?"

Rassan came over to the window and stood on the other side of me.

"Yes, they've had us under surveillance for a few weeks now. Wherever we go, that car follows us."

"They're not very good spies," I said. "Kind of conspicuous, aren't they?"

"That's exactly what they want," he said. "They want us to know we're being watched."

"But why?"

"Intimidation," Rassan murmured, scratching his beard. "Pure intimidation."

The two silhouettes in the car hadn't moved, yet I got the sense they were looking up at us.

"Anyway, we have to be careful not to talk about him here, not to talk about any of it," Wissam said, turning away.

But a little later, as we were seeing Rassan out, I couldn't stop myself asking.

"Why would any of the political parties want to intimidate you? Are you in some kind of trouble?"

I wasn't really expecting to get an answer.

"They want us to stop," Rassan whispered.

"Stop what?" I found myself whispering too. Could the apartment really be bugged?

He scrutinised me for a moment. "They want us to stop searching for the truth," he said and stepped out into the corridor.

Rassan is standing in the shade near the main gate, chatting to a girl. When he sees us, he apologetically gestures to her and rushes over to us.

"How are you, Samir?" he asks. "What did the doctor say?"

"I'm going to be fine."

"Great! I've got a surprise for you later. You're going to like it." He winks at Wissam, who nods approvingly.

"Listen," Rassan says. "About last night. I know it must all be a bit overwhelming. But I want you to know we're not involved in anything illegal. It's complicated. What we're doing isn't against the law, but no one wants us to do it. Before you were stabbed, we thought they were just trying to scare us, to let us know they were on to us, you know?"

I nod, though I don't really know what he's talking about.

"We don't know if the attack was connected," Wissam says. "But if it was, we've entered a new phase. If they've resorted to violence, a line has been crossed. Which means we have to be more careful than ever."

"Your friend," I say. "What exactly did he do?" Could there really be a government conspiracy to knock this guy off? It sounds like something out of a novel.

"We doubt that they actually wanted to kill you." Rassan raises his hand to reassure me. "We think they wanted you to survive."

"Survive?" I try to recall the men's faces, but that night in the bar I was too absorbed in the diary. "ОК, then let's assume they wanted to attack him, not me, and let's assume they only wanted to injure him. Why? Seems a pretty drastic way of scaring someone."

"It is," Wissam says. He starts wringing his hands again. "But we're pretty sure all they wanted was the rucksack."

We pass through the arches of College Hall and emerge out the back of the building, where a narrow path leads down through bushes and undergrowth. Wissam leads the way. I don't know where he's taking us. The last few days have been like a horrible film. Being mugged and stabbed has left me in a state of shock and humiliation. What hurts most, though, is losing Father's diary and the photo. At night, I see Nabil's sons in my dreams, sitting cross-legged, listening to the old man with the beard. I see Nabil's wife, a grieving shadow behind the beaded curtain, and I feel guilty.

"Is your friend a student here too?" I ask.

"No," Rassan says, bending a branch out of his way. "He's studying history at the Lebanese University. That's where students who can't afford private university fees go—it's public. But the politicians wield enormous influence there. The campus is right down in the south of the city, in a totally different Beirut—you'd find it hard to persuade a taxi driver to take you from here to there. It's another world. LU students hardly ever come here, and we never go there."

"So how did you meet him?"

"In our library," Rassan says. "He was dressed a bit ... scruffily, let's say. Worn-out shoes, a dirty shirt. He stood out like a sore thumb here."

"What was he doing in the library?"

"Looking for something he couldn't find at the Lebanese University."

"A book?"

"Support," Rassan says. "The LU is a state university; in other words, the lecturers work for the state. He can't trust anyone there—the staff would run straight to the authorities and report him. His project would have been sabotaged before he even started."

I'm about to ask what the project is when Wissam comes to a sudden halt and I almost bump into him.

"It must be this one," he says.

We're standing in front of a green bench nestled between two mighty spruce trees. The bright walls of College Hall can be glimpsed through their branches. Wissam leans over to read the brass plaque on the backrest and laughs. "Our friend is quite the poet."

I step closer to the bench and read:

OUT OF SUFFERING HAVE EMERGED THE STRONGEST SOULS;
THE MOST MASSIVE CHARACTERS ARE SEARED WITH SCARS.
— KHALIL GIBRAN —

"What are we doing here?" I ask. "What's that supposed to mean?"

Rassan nudges me out of the way with his arm and kneels down.

"Let's see what he's come up with this time," he says, running his hand along the underside of the seat. Suddenly he pauses, then pulls out a scrap of white paper. He unfolds it, reads it, and gives it to Wissam, who takes a quick look before passing it on to me.

HORSH BEIRUT. TOMORROW NIGHT—that's all it says. I'm bewildered.

"This is how you communicate?" It seems a bit over the

top, carrying on like characters in a spy movie. "Wouldn't it be easier to just phone each other?"

Wissam and Rassan give each other a grave look. Before they have a chance to shake their heads, I realise how ridiculous my question seems to them. They really believe their phones are bugged.

We're almost back at the main gate when Rassan taps me on the shoulder.

"Just a minute," he says and disappears in the direction of the lockers.

I sit beside Wissan on the library steps. The sun is blazing, and little beads of sweat drip from my forehead into my eyes.

"Horsh Beirut," I say. "What's that?"

"It's the safest place in the city," he says.

"And your friend's going to be there?"

He nods.

"Everyone's going to be in Horsh Beirut. There are loads of us."

"How long have you been living in Lebanon now?"

"I only came back two years ago," he says. "I moved to France with my parents when I was ten and came back here to study. The original plan was to leave as soon as I finish. It's so hard to find a decent job here. There are far more opportunities for young doctors in other countries. In fact, there are more opportunities for all graduates in other countries. My plan was to go back to France, maybe the US."

"So what happened?"

"What happened is we met our friend, and he talked me into helping him with his project." Wissam's voice is tinged with regret. I can tell he's deeply disturbed by what happened to me. Not just because an innocent bystander was hurt, but because one of his friends may have been the real target. I imagine he's worried that his name might be on a list somewhere. He seems to be realising that this is not a game.

"What kind of a project is it, exactly?" I ask. "You said it's all above board. So why are you being followed by the authorities?"

Looking straight ahead, Wissam wipes the sweat from his forehead with the back of his hand.

"You know, I'm not that afraid of what might happen if we fail." He slowly turns to face me. "I'm more afraid of what might happen if we succeed."

We sit for a while in silence. The heat shimmers above the asphalt, a gardener clips a hedge, students giggle and spray each other with water, someone dives to save his laptop. Just before the silence grows uncomfortable, Rassan's grinning face emerges from a crowd of students. He walks towards us carrying a large plastic bag.

"What have you got there?" I ask.

"Your surprise," he answers, beaming. "But hold your nose. It stinks."

"Stinks?"

"Yeah, I fished it out of puddle. It was hidden behind a pile of rubbish sacks."

"You shouldn't have."

Rassan laughs.

"All right, no need for sarcasm. You missed it that night, but while Wissam was pulling the knife out of your chest, I was running after the attackers. I didn't manage to catch them, but I was pretty sure they'd dump your rucksack."

It hits me like lightning. "You found my rucksack?"

Rassan reaches into the plastic bag.

"I did, but be warned: your wallet, passport, mobile phone, everything's gone. So they know who you are."

"You really managed to find my rucksack?" I repeat.

"Well, what's left of it."

The fabric is discoloured and gives off a disgusting fishy stench. The zip is half open, and as Rassan passes me the rucksack, the diary falls out into my lap.

"I wish I had better news for you," Rassan says, "but I think your boxers are still in there. At least you have a change of underwear now."

I barely register his voice. I stroke the pages. Father's writing is blotched and barely legible in places. The cover is greasy and the pages curl at the edges. I hear Hakim's voice echoing from far away:

If he left any clues, you'll find them in his diary.

Ten days, I think. Ten days to find him.

2

Beirut, 3 August 1982
2:00 p.m.

**Pity the nation divided into fragments, each fragment
deeming itself a nation.**

It's as if Gibran prophesied the war.
   Today was not a good day. I was up on the roof for a while
earlier. Road blocks and sirens everywhere. Shots echoing
throughout the city. Men with guns on the streets. Barking
commands at each other, pointing in various directions, getting
into cars and disappearing off between the tower blocks.
Columns of smoke in the south. The refugee camps are being
shelled. The Israelis are in Beirut now. Their tanks rolled down
the Corniche a few weeks ago, and there hasn't been a day without gunfire since. They've laid siege to west Beirut and they
mean business: Bourj al-Barajneh, Mar Elias, Sabra, Chatila—all
the camps are surrounded. The PLO will never survive this. The
situation's been getting steadily worse, but today was the worst
we've seen in a long time. We don't dare step outside the door
on our own anymore. We bring a workmate with us even if we're
just going for a smoke. It's too dangerous otherwise. Every time
we hear a car screeching to a halt beside us, our blood runs cold.
There's been an abrupt rise in the number of kidnappings.
Almost every family in the city is looking for a loved one. The

newspapers are full of missing-person ads. More and more bursts of gunfire since this morning. They stopped for a little while earlier, but they're at it again now. You can hear them even when the windows are closed. Word is that the French are going to help with the Palestinian militants' withdrawal, the Americans and Italians too. Apparently talks are underway. No one knows when they're going to arrive, though. Or whether they'll arrive.

4:00 p.m.

Thy lips, O my spouse, drop as the honeycomb; and the smell of thy garments is like the smell of Lebanon.

Time becomes such a relative concept when you don't know if there will be a tomorrow. Two months to go until the wedding. Mother still believes she's saving my life. They've showed up at her gate countless times, armed with rifles.

– Your son, we could really use a man like him, they said to her.

Long after I'd moved to Beirut, they kept calling on Mother.

So I'm going to marry Rana. I know Mother was overreacting. Those men have never forced anyone to join them. All they wanted was money. But she can't stand not being in control. So many sons are dying. She calls on the neighbours, brings cakes, sits in their living rooms, mourns with them. And all the time she's thinking: *I never want to see you in my house. I never want you to kiss my hand and tell me how sorry you are.* Just knowing that I'm in Beirut, beyond her reach, must keep her awake at night. So she tries to pull strings, to protect me as best she can. Sometimes I don't know whether it's about me or about proving to herself that she still has influence. It's a smart move in any case. A cousin of Rana's father is an officer in the Forces Libanaises. Contacts. You've got to have the right contacts.

– Marry this girl and they'll stop asking you to fight with them, Mother said.

– Why would they do that?

– Because they won't want to make his daughter a widow.

They say that it's our national duty to fight. As if there is such a thing as "the nation"! Sometimes the front runs between balconies. Where yesterday neighbours were sharing coffee and sugar, today they're throwing grenades. Yet hardly anyone knows what they're fighting for, or even who's fighting who. Alliances have changed so many times that it's every man for himself at this stage. Everyone claims to be fighting for the country they're destroying. It makes no sense to appeal to our duties as Christians, Druze, Muslims. Who wins if we're all wiped out in the end? Jesus Christ? Mohammed? How will we ever look each other in the eye again?

5:20 p.m.

A beard does not a prophet make.

Young men with rifles slung over their shoulders are patrolling the lobby. I wonder if they know the old saying. They have blank eyes and full beards. I was in one of the bedrooms when they drove up and jumped out of their jeeps, laughing. I can hear them now, stomping around and checking people's papers. Usually it's over pretty quickly. It's all a game. A brief show of force. *In this part of town, we're the ones in charge*, that's what they're saying. *Here, in west Beirut, we call the shots, not them. And we'll protect you, don't worry.*

They've been coming more often since Bashir Gemayel announced he's going to run for president. I'm not afraid of the checks anymore. There have been so many. When they come to the hotel now, my only concern is: I hope the door isn't locked.

These days, there are few rules that can't be bent. There's just one rule that must be followed to the letter: the door to the cellar has to be left open. The security check is just a pretext. They come here to help themselves to our liquor. In the evenings, after a hard day's fighting, they want to get plastered. I've seen them so many times, racing through the streets in their jeeps, firing into the air, and celebrating the fact that they've survived another day. The most expensive bottles are stored right at the back. They never delve that far, they just take whatever is near the front. We just need to avoid pissing them off by making sure they can get into the cellar.

There's going to be a wedding in the hotel tonight, no matter what happens today. Weddings provide some of life's most wonderful moments. We may not be a nation, but we do have a national identity: *Shoot at us all you like, destroy our homes. But you can't destroy our lust for life.* It's what sets us Lebanese apart. We've just been making the final preparations for the wedding. The tables have been set, place cards and all. The candles are ready. Later, we'll light the torches around the pool. In the dining room, everyone will get up out of their seats and dance. They'll sing and celebrate and be enchanted by Hakim's lute.

– You know this will be our sixtieth wedding together? I asked him as we were preparing.

– I like that, he said. Let's not measure the length of our friend-ship in years. Let's measure it in weddings.

Soon I'll be married myself. What then?

10:30 p.m.

Hakim never showed up. I don't know where he is. We haven't been able to get in touch with him. There was no wedding today. The door to the cellar was locked. Something went wrong.

3

Lights flash past, illuminating the pages of the diary. Beside me in the backseat, Rassan keeps turning his head to look out the rear window. The silver Mercedes is nowhere to be seen. It pulled out as we left the underground car park of Wissam's apartment building, and for the first few minutes we could see it glinting among the dense traffic behind us. But at some point on our southward journey, we managed to lose it.

The cityscape is different here. There are no glossy billboards. It's mostly Shias who live here, and the buildings are emblazoned with huge posters featuring Hezbollah's yellow flag. The further south we drive, the poorer our surroundings become.

The diary, heavy and dirty, is on my lap. Frowning, I stare at the entry I've just read. I want to focus on the last few months before my parents got married. These are the most critical. I read the entry again and reappraise it in the light of everything I've learned from Grandmother, Aziz, and Amir. It would appear that Father didn't even trust his own diary. There are gaps, contradictions. He never once mentions Aziz or Amir. He talks about Bashir, but he doesn't say anything about the photo that meant so much to him. If there's an answer, it won't be in the lines he wrote; it'll be between the lines. I circle the following sentence: We don't dare step outside the door on our own anymore.

Kidnappings, roadblocks, indiscriminate killings of people who belong to the "wrong" religion, street battles for west Beirut. If the situation in the city was so cataclysmic that he didn't dare step outside the hotel, why did he risk going to meet Mother so often? After all, it was just another ten weeks until their wedding.

And why didn't he ever mention these meetings in his diary?

"We're here," Wissam says.

He parks at the side of the street and glances in the rearview mirror. Shabby blocks of flats loom to our right. The walls are riddled with bullet holes, some of them fist-sized. To our left, across the street, is darkness.

"Where are we?" I ask. When I squint, I can just about make out barbed wire separating the darkness from the street. Below the street lamp a few metres ahead of us, a man in fatigues is on patrol, a machine gun slung over his shoulder.

"Horsh Beirut," Rassan says. "Our meeting place."

"This area was heavily shelled by Israel in 2006," says Wissam. "It's a Hezbollah stronghold."

"What exactly is Horsh Beirut?" I ask.

"It's the biggest park in the city," Rassan says, darting a look across the street before he reaches behind the back seat, pulls a leather briefcase out of the boot and gives it to Wissam. "Seventy-five hectares. Closed to the public for more than twenty years."

I look over at the barbed wire again. Behind it, dark bushes rustle in the wind.

"It must be completely overgrown by now," I say.

Rassan looks over my shoulder and scans the opposite side of the street again.

"Yes, it's been completely forgotten," he says as he begins counting a wad of banknotes. "It's right here under people's noses, but hardly anyone even knows it exists."

"Why is it closed?"

"The official version is that people might trample on the seedlings, that the park needs time to regenerate. But they've been saying that for years." Rassan holds out his hand, and Wissam passes back more banknotes.

"What's the unofficial version, then?"

Rassan stops counting for a moment and looks at me.

"The park is in a strategic location. It separates major Shia, Sunni, and Christian districts from each other. The government is afraid these communities would run into each other in the park. Though they would never admit as much. Here we are, in front of one of the biggest city parks in the Middle East, and no one's allowed in."

"So they're afraid the park could become a flashpoint?"

"Maybe." Wissam turns around to face us. "But what scares them even more is that the various communities might actually get on. Talk to each other. All our problems, all our prejudices, are rooted in the fact that Beirut has no real public life. Nowhere for people from different backgrounds to mix. Everyone stays in their own part of town, with people of the same religion. People spend a lot of time talking about the other communities, but they never talk to them."

"Done," Rassan says. He flicks the wad with his thumb and puts it into a bag before opening the door and crossing the street to the man with the machine gun.

"Ready?" Wissam asks. "We'll have to be quick."

I nod.

Rassan throws the bag into a bin and walks past the watchman.

"Let's go!"

We get out and cross the street. The watchman raises his head and looks at us. For a fraction of a second, I'm terrified he's going to point his gun at us. But he just looks away and ambles towards the bin. The coast is clear.

"You've got to love the local customs," Rassan says, giving me a wink as we step through a circular hole in the barbed wire and enter the park.

Branches snap under our feet as we pick our way through knee-high grass. I'm reminded of the peaceful afternoons spent with Father by the lake: the autumn wind ruffling the fields, the trees creaking under the weight of their fruit, the constant hum of dragonflies in our ears.

Eventually we arrive at a clearing where there's a little more light. A half-moon hangs over the city. Dusky, velvety fields stretch as far as the eye can see. The trees extend their branches like tentacles, and the sweet, heavy scent of overripe fruit suffuses the air. The noise of the city has faded away; all we can hear are pigeons fluttering up from behind a rock and cats wailing somewhere in the darkness.

"This way," Wissam whispers. Briefcase tucked under his arm, he shines his smartphone torch down a gravel path. Mosquitos immediately start buzzing around the light.

The park expands in all directions like a dark carpet. The lights of distant buildings glimmer at its edges. After a few minutes of picking our way through a dense copse of trees, we find ourselves in another clearing.

"Over there," Wissam says, pointing to a circle of light.

"They're here already," Rassan says.

We wade through thick grass, and as we approach, I see it's a circle of candles, their flames flickering beneath the night sky. It reminds me of a summer camp in a teen movie: kids strumming guitars and telling stories around a campfire, marshmallows on sticks, an ocean of stars.

There must be around a dozen young people sitting in the circle. Their eyes are all on a single shadowy figure.

Wissam taps me on the shoulder. "Here," he whispers.

We sit down. People scooch over to make room. They look me over and give me a friendly nod. Wissam puts the briefcase down on the grass in front of him and turns his attention to the young man speaking in the centre of the circle. It all seems a bit like a secret ceremony.

The young man is wearing sandals, loose linen trousers, and a tatty shirt. There's something about him that instantly fascinates me. Maybe it's the sharp lines of his nose and chin. They give him an air of elegant severity, but there's a gentleness to his warm tenor voice. Then there are his eyes, dreamy and otherworldly one minute, crystal clear and resolute the next. He's alarmingly thin, yet he has enormous presence. Every movement he makes crackles with energy.

"I'm scared," he's saying. "I look at us, the students, our country's educated elite, and I'm scared."

A blade of grass blown into a candle flame flares and crackles as it burns.

"We don't learn how to think for ourselves anymore," the young man says, looking around at us. "We're brainwashed. Our religious leaders do the thinking for us. Young people drive around the streets honking and chanting, 'We'll give you our blood, our souls, o Nasrallah, o Jumblatt, o al-Rai.' And I have to ask myself, when have our politicians ever given their blood for this country?" He stands still, clenching his fist.

There's a murmur of agreement. Wissan and Rassan pensively nod as the man continues.

"The Shia student tunes in to the Hezbollah radio station over breakfast and learns that Israel is the enemy and that's why he has to go fight in Syria. The Sunni opens his newspaper and reads that he should steer clear of Haret Hreik and Ghobeiry, because that's where the Shia live, and they want him dead. The Christian watches TV and learns that he should stick to Mar Mikhael and Ashrafieh, because that's where he can go for a drink with his own people. University students are hurling stones at each other because they disagree on how to celebrate Ashura. Young women are turning their eyelashes into a political statement, tinting them the colour of their party. We're as divided as ever." Though his voice sounds so light, it carries on the wind, and his audience hangs on every word. "We've no sense of solidarity," he says, his tone becoming more urgent. "And a nation that hasn't had a shared revolution of its own will never be able to shape a brighter future."

Someone quietly calls out "Yes!" and a murmur starts rippling around the circle again, but the moment the man raises his hand, silence descends.

"We need this book," he says. "All the people who were involved in the war have to talk to each other. Our job is to make sure they do that. We must be courageous; only then will others find the courage to confront the past. This revolution is essential, but I know it won't be easy. We keep meeting with resistance. We ask for documents, photos, papers, and they say, 'Forget the past'. But how can we forget the past when there are parents who still don't know where their children are? When there are children who don't know where their parents are? Whether they're still alive. Whether they're buried somewhere."

A shiver runs up my spine during the intense silence that follows these words. I lean over to Wissam and whisper in his ear, "Who are all these people?"

"Students," he whispers back. "All religions. From various universities, most of them humanities students. They're all taking part in this project." He puts a finger to his lips. "We can talk afterwards."

"We're living in a country that's unable to write its own history because its people can't agree on a shared history." The young man moves silently through the grass, looking each person in the eye. When he comes to me, our eyes lock for a moment. "You all know my history," he says. "I was directly affected. Many of you are still affected by it today. They're trying to scare us off, but they can't prevent us from carrying on. They can make things difficult for us, but that won't stop us. We'll keep gathering information. We'll keep talking to witnesses, rooting around in archives. We won't rest until we've got everything we need." He pauses and looks around again. Then he turns around to face us. "Wissam, Rassan," he says, and the two of them look up. "Any luck?"

Wissam picks up the briefcase and holds it up.

"It wasn't easy. They asked a lot of questions. I imagine that it's going to be harder from now on to get stuff there, but it's a start, at least." He reaches into the briefcase and pulls out two sheets of newspaper. In the candlelight, the paper gives off a yellowish glow. I've spent enough time in archives to know that the pages are originals. Wissam stands up and clears his throat, and everyone turns to look at him.

"We went to *An-Nahar* and *As Safir*," he says, adding, possibly for my benefit, "*An-Nahar* is the Christian newspaper, based in east Beirut; *As Safir* the Muslim one, in west Beirut. That's where we found these." He lays the two pages out on the grass, and the students cluster around to examine them. It's as if, after years of teetotalism, a drop of vintage wine has fallen on my tongue, triggering a desire for more. I feel faint when I read the newspaper's date: 14 April 1975. The day after the civil war began.

I lean close to Rassan's ear. "You're writing a history book?"

His eyes gleam in the candlelight.

"Lebanon has no coherent history book. We're writing the first one. And it's going to include the issues that have been taboo until now, that have never been addressed. We want to reveal the contradictions." He points to the newspapers.

The coverage in both refers to the previous day's event, the event that triggered all-out conflict in Lebanon. Armed Christians had ambushed a bus full of Palestinians in east Beirut in retaliation for Palestinian guerrillas opening fire on a congregation gathered outside a Christian church earlier that day.

The front page of the newspaper on the left, An-Nahar, says, "27 Palestinian Guerrillas Killed in Bus Ambush in East Beirut." The page on the right says, "27 Martyrs, Our Palestinian Brothers, Killed Yesterday in Christian Attack in the East." Two voices. Two views.

"Thanks, Wissam and Rassan," the young man says. "Could you take the documents to our archive in the next day or two? The amount of material we have is growing all the time, so it's really important that we're well organised. We can't just throw everything into a pile, as that will cost us months when we get down to the writing part. We need people to sort what we've got chronologically and thematically. Missing-person ads, reports, witness statements, confessions, tape recordings, videotapes. We need to label everything, archive it, keep it all in order."

All eyes are on him. But I keep staring at the newspapers on the grass, pieces of history that so clearly illustrate what went wrong, what's still going wrong. I observe the young man commanding his audience's attention with the tiniest of gestures. I see the zeal in their eyes, their conviction, their faith in what they're doing. A realisation has been creeping up on me the last few days, and now I'm forced to face it, a realisation that the Lebanon Father told me about no longer exists. While I was growing up and grieving, it disappeared. I would've had to come here years ago to see Father's Lebanon. Though perhaps the Lebanon he loved had disappeared long before that; perhaps it was already gone by the time he left for Germany. Father came back here, though—I can feel it, deep down. The question is why, when he knew his country would never be the same again? All the young people gathered in this forgotten park in the heart of the city are light years ahead of me. They grew up after the war, in a Beirut that had been reduced to rubble. While I've been visiting archives to look back, they've been digging up the past because they want to look forward.

By the time the last candle goes out, almost everyone has left. The moon looks down on the park with a lopsided grin, and a flattened circle in the grass is the only sign we were here. As Wissam and Rassan talk to the young man, he notices me watching him and raises his index finger. Wissam falls silent and turns to look at me. The young man walks over. He has dark brown eyes, and when he smiles, little dimples appear on either side of his mouth. "You must be Samir." He takes my hand, squeezes it, and places his other hand on top. "Welcome," he says. "I'm Youssef."

4

Beirut, 15 August 1982
7:30 a.m.

**Everyone I meet wonders
what the sense of it all is.
And I want to call out to them: Lebanon doesn't make sense.
This country is a mystery to those who love it.**

You hear stories every day. About people who've been kidnapped, murdered. You read about them in the paper, hear
first-hand accounts. You look out at the destruction, broken
windows, blown-up pieces of concrete. Yet you still feel as if
it's got nothing to do with you. As if the war is happening miles
away, as if you're not right in the middle of it. You hear that
they're stopping people randomly on the streets, checking their
IDs and religions—and shooting anyone who happens to have
another faith. It's dreadful, you think, but it won't happen to me.
Or anyone I know. Until one day it does happen and you're
completely blindsided.

   This is one of the stories I was told: Early on the morning of
3 August, a young man—a Muslim—left the flat he shared with
his mother. She was sick, so his sister had come round to look
after her. The man went up onto the roof of a building a few
streets away and took up his position. He was a sniper. Late that
afternoon, as the sun was sinking, he spotted an unveiled woman

hurrying across the street. He pulled the trigger. Smiling, he watched her sink to the ground and bleed to death on the concrete. No one came to her aid. When the young man returned to his flat that evening, it was filled with neighbours and friends of the family. They told him his sister had been killed by a sniper as she was on her way to the pharmacy to pick up medicine for her mother. She hadn't worn her veil so as to escape the attention of the Christian snipers who'd been firing on this part of town for weeks. The young man broke down. He'd murdered his sister.

There's nothing I can say to console Hakim. He has buried Fida, his wife. He wants to leave the country. That's what he told me. It might be irrational, but the war suddenly seems more real than it did before. The press didn't pay much attention to her death. It was just one of many. Another sad statistic, another notch on the wall. But for me, the war now has a face I know.

6:15 p.m.

Abdallah is still apoplectic over the cancelled wedding. I say that deliberately: he's apoplectic over the wedding, couldn't care less about the rest. He's been stomping through the corridors, purple with rage, telling us how much money we've lost him.

This is what happened on the evening of 3 August: Two men charged in and opened fire in the lobby. Yunus, the kid at reception, was killed. He only started here a couple of weeks ago. A little earlier, I'd come downstairs to the lobby to find militiamen kicking up a stink because they hadn't been able to get into the cellar. The door was locked, they said. They saw it as an affront. They ranted and raved for a while and then stormed off. Not long afterwards, though, two of them returned and started shooting.

Abdallah is determined to find out who locked the door. He spits venom, screams at us all, even me. Lines us up, shoves his

scaly face right into each of ours, and snarls, "God help whichever one of you useless parasites locked that door."

Two things have been on my mind since that day. First, what
will I tell Hakim if he asks me to leave the country with him? And
second, while I was bending over Yunus as he lay bleeding
behind the desk, I felt a hard object in my pocket. It was the key
to the cellar.

The problem is, there's only one key.

5

Lights throb and bodies writhe in time to the music. Everything's dancing, twirling. Strobe lights flashing, bass, shoulders rubbing against each other, sweat, a frenzy of movement on the dancefloor, the steps, the tables, the sofas. Colour everywhere: low-cut sequined tops, lipstick on collars, glittery fingernails, frozen-fruit daiquiris.

"You can't leave Beirut until you've had a night on the town," Wissam said earlier, handing me one of his shirts as Rassan nodded enthusiastically.

An American girl is standing in front of me, blonde, soft-skinned. She'd be kind of hot if she hadn't spent the past five minutes yelling in my ear in English, "Beirut is awesome!" and jerking her head to the music like she's having an epileptic fit. "The country is really fucked up, but the nightlife is crazy! I've been to a lot of countries, but there's something special about the vibe here, isn't there?"

I nod.

"Where are you from again?"

"Germany."

"Oh, I love Germany! Are you here for the nightlife too? Berlin has awesome clubs, but you can't compare ..."

I take a sip of the drink Wissam bought me earlier. Beats thunder from the speakers. It's "International DJs Night," and right now, DJ Hammer from Wuppertal is on the decks.

"I love the Lebanese," the girls shouts. "They're so open-minded."

"Yes," I shout back. "Very nice people."

A mirror slopes from the ceiling, doubling the size of the crowd. Smoke machines shoot swirls of fog into the air. Everyone whoops and throws their arms about. I spot him emerging like a phantom from the haze, his hands buried in his pockets. He smiles when he sees me. The fog makes my eyes water, I blink a couple of times, and when I look up again Youssef has vanished.

"Too bad there aren't any nice beaches in the city, like in Barcelona," the American shouts. "But the parties are amazing, the people here are so full of energy."

"Yes," I shout back. "It's because they know they could die tomorrow."

"They what?"

"They could die," I say, running my thumb across my throat. "They know the whole country could burn down again tomorrow."

I find Youssef outside. He's leaning against the wall, scratching at the stamp on his wrist. He's wearing one of Wissam's shirts too, and he's visibly uncomfortable in it. There's something more dignified about him when he's in his scuffed sandals and old clothes. Now he looks a schoolboy whose mother has just cut his hair.

"Well? Is it what you expected?"

"Yes," I say. "It's impressive." I'm not sure what else to say. I haven't been into clubbing for years and I'm relieved to be out in the fresh air again.

It's two days since we left the park through the hole in the fence. I haven't seen Youssef since, but the image of all those people hanging on his every word has stayed with me. There's so much I'd like to ask him, but now that he's right in front of me, I don't know where to begin.

"What about you?" I ask. "I guess you think clubbing is a waste of time?"

Youssef shakes his head.

"Trying to enjoy life is never a waste of time."

"But?"

"But there are things I enjoy more than clubbing." He smiles. "People would say that's unusual for a Hamoud."

"Is Hamoud your surname, then?"

Just then, Wissam staggers out of the club, a blonde girl clinging to his arm. It takes me a moment to realise it's the American who was yelling at me earlier. She shoots me a look as if to say, "Your loss," and they start kissing. Shortly afterwards, Rassan stumbles out.

"Samir," Wissam says when the girl lets him come up for air. He nods towards her and raises his shoulders.

"Got it," I say. "I won't be home for at least another three hours."

Grinning, Wissam gives me a thumbs-up.

"Hey, Rassan!" he shouts, switching to English so that the girl can understand. "Samantha wanted to know why we're not afraid about the Islamic State being only two hours away from our borders. Tell her why conquering Beirut will be impossible for IS."

"Too much traffic," Rassan deadpans.

Wissam bursts out laughing, and the girl creases up too. Youssef looks at me.

"His favourite joke," he says.

I find myself laughing along with them.

Later, after Wissam and the girl have sped off in a taxi, Youssef and I stroll through the streets. Rassan went home on his own. It's way past midnight, and soon the sun will be coming up. Somewhere along the way, we fell silent, but it doesn't appear to bother either of us. It reminds me a little of the silent longing Father and I shared by the lake more than twenty years ago. And why wouldn't it? Youssef and I share a sense of yearning, I think. Even in the park, when I only saw his face by candlelight, I sensed a connection between us. I see in him qualities I always wanted to have myself: self-assurance, focus, vision.

"Can I ask you something?"

"Sure."

"Aren't you afraid of them? Of them catching you, I mean?"

"Oh." Youssef laughs, a strangely happy laugh. "I've no doubt they'll catch me in the end. But I'm more worried that we won't have finished the book by then."

"The book ...," I'm not sure how to put it without causing offence. "Do you really think it'll change things?"

Youssef stops and gives me a friendly look. It's as if it's never even occurred to him, the possibility of no one reading the book, of it having no real impact, of it never even getting published. "I know it will, Samir."

"How far have you got with it?"

"Not very far." We cross the street. To our right, the domes of the al Amin Mosque rise out of the orange mist cloaking the city. "It's a race against time," Youssef says. "The witnesses are becoming forgetful, getting older and less reliable. They're dying. Only a few of them are willing and able to corroborate their versions. Documents and papers haven't been stored properly, so they're disintegrating. There's a lot of stuff that's simply unusable."

"I read somewhere that several archives were destroyed."

"That's right. The parties knew there'd be questions asked after the war, so they blew up the archives themselves. Who knows what they destroyed. But there's another reason why we're running out of time." With every sentence, the urgency in his voice increases. I'm fascinated by the transformation. His expressive features harden, the gentle, friendly look in his eyes turns piercing, almost fanatical. "The security situation is worsening every day. Not just in Beirut. The whole country is fragmenting into religious conflict zones. State institutions are basically powerless. In the south, Hezbollah is fighting Israel, in Syria it's fighting the rebels. An Islamic front is forming in the north—young men are driving jeeps around Tripoli, waving the Isis flag out the window. And then there are all the Syrian refugees coming into the country."

"Like the Palestinians did years ago."

"Exactly. I was in Tripoli not long ago, visiting missing-persons' associations to gather material. You know what I saw in Bab al-Tabbaneh? Assad supporters and opponents fighting. Right in the middle of Lebanon! Kids picking sticks up off the street and pretending they're guns. That's what they're learning from their fathers."

"You're afraid the younger generations are going to make the same mistakes."

"The mistakes are already being made. The problem is the complete lack of trust. Have you visited the AUB campus? It gives the impression that people are living in harmony, but that's only because the AUB brings people together. Outside the campus, there's hardly any friendship or trust or solidarity between people of different religions. That's very dangerous. There are eighteen religious communities here, and they're all terrified of each other. Each community thinks the others are trying to wipe them out. And each community feels abandoned, like it's been left to deal with the trauma of the civil war by itself. Someone has to help them see that they've all experienced the same pain. That everyone—literally everyone—has suffered."

I think back to what it was like growing up on our street. It seemed like we all lived happily side by side. Maybe people had to leave the country before they could overcome their differences. Or maybe I didn't understand what was really going on; I was just a kid, after all. Who knows what people were saying about Yasmin behind closed doors because she didn't wear a headscarf, because Hakim let her do whatever she wanted. Who knows what people were really thinking about Mother after Father disappeared.

"Anyone who wants to understand our history has to fight their way through a thicket of censored accounts, half truths, suppressed experiences," Youssef continues. "This book represents a huge opportunity for us. As long as every teacher keeps on giving his own version of the war, there'll be a fundamental gap between the truth of the Muslims and that of the Christians. It goes right back to the nineteenth century. The Christians welcomed the French, saw them as friends, while the Muslims saw them as colonial invaders. No wonder we have no shared account of the civil war."

"Selective memory," I say. "My fiancée has written about it, in relation to the children of refugees."

"Precisely. Children, teenagers, they're all growing up with selective memories of past injustices. As a result, they identify only with the religious community in which they grew up. We, the Christians; we, the Alawites; we, the Shias; we, the Druze; we, the Sunnis. When what they should be saying is: We, the Lebanese."

He looks at me, his cheeks red.

"My father would've liked you," I say. "I'm pretty sure of it."

Youssef puts an arm around my shoulders.

"Tell me about your father," he says. "Who is he?"

"I wish I knew who he is," I say bitterly. "I've been trying to figure it out for over twenty years. In some ways, my search is a bit like yours—time is running out, and I'm not sure there are any useful clues left."

We turn our backs on the mosque and head towards the port. On the horizon, a narrow band of light appears above the mountains behind the city.

"I'm sure my father would support your project if he knew about it," I say. "I think he'd also see it as the key to returning the country to its former glory. Vibrant, cosmopolitan, free from fear. He told me about it many times."

"What about your mother? Does she want you to find your father?"

I shake my head.

"She passed away."

"Mine too."

The mountains are suffused with a warm gold that makes the city gleam like a treasure chest. Light pours across the roofs and onto the sea as we walk along the waterfront.

"I grew up in a village," Youssef says. "I used to hate Beirut. The others loved coming here: the sea, the shops, the cinemas. But the city never appealed to me. Now, though, I can't imagine living anywhere else. I like the contradictions. I like the houses with bits of bullets still lodged in the walls, all just a few metres away from a shiny new shopping centre. I like that the streets in Hamra are deserted when the muezzin calls, and at exactly the same time the squares in the east are packed."

"Hmm," I begin, hoping I don't sound too sceptical. "But aren't those the kind of contradictions you're hoping to resolve?"

"Yes, eventually. But while we're working on the project, the contradictions are a daily reminder of just how important this book is."

"When do you hope to finish it?"

Youssef picks a flat stone off the ground and skims it out to sea. It bounces on the surface three times before sinking.

"Depends on how much resistance we face," he says and turns to me again. "I know I sound like a dreamer, Samir, but I'm not." Ironically, though, he does have a dreamy look on his face as he gazes past me at the city. "Rassan, Wissam, and the others are passionate about the idea, and I'd be lost without them. It's really important that students from all kinds of backgrounds work on the book, that they come from different universities, different religions. That's the only way to make the project a truly collective effort. But I'm under no illusions. I'm the only one who's not studying at a private uni. When the others graduate, they will be welcomed abroad with open arms. And I can't blame them if they go. I'm not saying that it's all just a bit of fun for the others. They care deeply about the project, and they know their involvement places them in danger. We're making good progress at the moment, but that'll change. It could take years to finish our book. But I will finish it."

Youssef and I really are similar, I realise with a mixture of affection and compassion.

"You're not convinced, are you?" He buries his hands in his trouser pockets and looks ahead. "You don't believe our plan's going to succeed."

"I hope it does."

"Can I ask you something?"

"Of course."

"When you first arrived here, did you think you were going to find your father?"

"Yes."

"And do you still think that?"

"I don't know. At times I've wondered whether finding my father was ever my real purpose. I thought I had to make this journey in order to put him behind me once and for all."

"But you feel like you might not succeed."

"I just want to know what happened to him."

"And deep down you feel you might get this one chance that could change everything for you."

"Exactly."

"And this feeling is much stronger than the rational voice telling you it's impossible, that you'll never achieve your goal."

"Yes, that's how it seems."

"That feeling eclipses everything else, and it seems like the whole purpose of your life was to lose him in order to go search for him." He pauses. "You feel that your mission is to find him."

I nod.

"It's the same for me with this book," Youssef says. He takes his right hand out of his pocket and opens it to reveal a piece of paper. It's been carefully folded but is obviously old and tattered.

"What's that?" I ask. Youssef doesn't answer, just holds out the paper.

I unfold it. It's a piece of newspaper. On the left, there's a picture of a man's face. It's a composite sketch, not a photo, badly drawn and faded.

"What is it?" I ask again, but my question is answered when I read the text beside the picture:

This man was last seen on Friday, 17 September 1982. He left his apartment in Mseitbeh, Beirut, and never returned. Anyone with information on his whereabouts is asked to phone 00 961 01 273881.

The morning wind ruffles Youssef's black hair and the collar of his shirt.

"A missing-person ad?"

He nods.

"Who is it?"

Youssef takes the paper from my hand and looks at it intently. He's clearly very familiar with this man's features. A smile flickers across his face. "That's my father," he says.

6

Beirut, 31 August 1982

Time's vagaries crush us like glass; thereafter
We'll never be remoulded as one piece.
Abu al-'Ala' al-Ma'arri

We sat on the roof facing north, watching the ships depart.
Truck convoys guarded by French soldiers, who arrived on the
twenty-first, have been trundling into the port, men in khaki
uniforms jumping out and boarding the ships. More vehicles have
been lining up outside the port. Rumour has it that Sharon is in
town to witness the PLO withdraw himself.

In years to come we'll still be talking about all this. About the
last few days in particular. A wind of change is blowing, I can feel
it, but I can't tell if it's for better or worse. Bashir Gemayel: our
new president. His dream: a unified nation. Hakim is not convinced.

—November, he said a couple of days ago. I'm leaving this
country with Yasmin in November. I'll play for you on your wedding day, but then I'm packing up the lute for good.

He's beating himself up about his wife. He was away from
home too much, he says, too wrapped up in himself.

– The only thing that matters now is my daughter, he says.
Look around you. There won't be a building left standing by the
time the war is over. Nor a family that isn't mourning. I don't want
her growing up here, not here.

My wedding day. I can already see our first dance. I'll have Rana in my arms. Maybe we can pretend we're alone, even with the others gathered around. Mother. All the people she'll invite. The men Rana's father will bring.

Our team is shrinking day by day. Abdallah is taking great pleasure in firing people at will.

– One of you is going to go every day, he tells us. I'm going to send someone packing every single day until you tell me who locked the door.

The bullet holes in reception have been plastered over; it's as if Yunus never existed. The guests keep coming. Who in their right mind would want to visit Beirut right now? I lie awake at night and think about what it all means for me. Abdallah is waging war on us. He's docking our pay.

– Until I've recouped the money you useless animals lost me, he says.

We're being worked into the ground. The others are exhausted and scared. Many of them are their family's sole breadwinner.

I can't come clean. He's trusted me for so long. If he finds out, I'll lose everything. And I can't be a husband if I'm not earning. Not earning would mean moving back in with Mother. There's no way I can tell him.

7

We watch the taxi drive off, leaving us alone in a wasteland around twenty kilometres outside Beirut. Drought
has cracked the earth into honeycomb patterns. The road
shimmers in the heat, melting away into the distant hills.

"What exactly are we doing here?" I ask. Youssef doesn't
reply.

There's something he wants to show me. I look around.
Nothing but sand, withered bushes, and fly-tipped rubbish bags. Further ahead, there's something that might
once have been a little cabin. We start walking towards it.

"There was a time when I came here nearly every day," he
says.

"Why? There's nothing here."

"Because this is where I got the idea for our book."

The road doesn't seem to lead anywhere. In the haze
behind us, Beirut looks like a blurry ghost town.

"Where are we?"

"Almost fifteen thousand people disappeared during the
war," Youssef says, as if he didn't hear my question. "There's
been no trace of them since."

"Youssef, why are we here?"

"After the war, they set up a commission to find out what
happened to the missing. It was a farce. The head of the
commission was a police officer, the others were military
and security personnel. The only evidence they looked at

was what the relatives had gathered themselves, and eventually they came to the conclusion that none of the missing persons were still alive. They advised the relatives to have their loved ones declared dead, despite there being no proof."

We've almost reached the cabin. In the blinding morning light, it looks like the forgotten hideout of a band of robbers.

"Several mass graves have been uncovered in recent years. In any other country there would have been uproar. People would want to identify the remains, find out who killed these people. But not in Lebanon. Here, no one wants to talk about it. We're afraid of what truths might come out, afraid of upsetting the apple cart." He goes up to the cabin and runs his hand over the wood. "For the sake of peace, we keep our mouths shut." He looks me in the eye for the first time since we arrived here. "The question of the disappeared never became a national issue," he says. "But it's going to be the most important chapter in the book. We want to include everyone who was involved in the war. Our government and our people just as much as the Syrian regime and the Palestinians. What makes the question of the disappeared so complicated is that many of those responsible for their disappearance are now running the country."

"This has to do with your father, doesn't it?" I say. "What happened to him?"

Youssef looks at the ground. "My mother refused to have him declared dead. Who would want the father of her son declared dead without any proof? The commission kept telling the relatives that no one had survived. It was 1992, the war was over, end of story, they wanted everyone to forget about it and move on."

"So what happened next?"

"Just a few weeks later, fifty-five missing persons returned home from Syrian prisons. My father was one of them."

Youssef's eyes have lit up. A smile hovers on his lips as he recalls the day: a winter morning, a streak of gold above the mountains, dew on the fields, the houses still shrouded in fog. A man in heavy boots walks into the village. A knock at the door, the boy wakes up.

"This is where he was kidnapped," Youssef whispers, as if he's losing his voice. "There used to be a Syrian checkpoint here. He doesn't like to talk about it, finds it too difficult. But from what I've gathered, he was arrested here and taken to Anjar."

"The military base?"

"Exactly. They accused him of spying for Israel and agitating against the Syrian presence in Lebanon. Then he disappeared and was gone for ten whole years."

I feel a sharp stab. Is it my wound playing up or is it envy? The loneliness I've felt for so many years is more than social isolation. It's always been bound up with a sense that no one else can relate to my pain, that no one else really knows what I've been through. Irrational, maybe, but it's made my sense of isolation complete.

I stare at Youssef.

"What went through your head?" I ask. "Tell me. I want to know what it was like, that moment."

"It didn't feel real." His soft, light voice is so quiet now that I have to move closer. I don't want to miss a word. "In all the years he was gone, my mother never stopped talking about him. So when he finally walked through our door, I felt like I knew him. We both cried. Though we were basically strangers, he told me he'd thought about me every day. He said I looked exactly as he'd imagined. His disappearance caused my mother so much pain and suffering, more than I could ever describe. And I cursed all those years he wasn't around. But in hindsight, I'm glad things happened the way they did. Know why?"

My throat feels tight, and when I speak, my voice sounds strange, fragile.

"Because of the book," I say. "Because if things had been different, you'd never have started writing this book."

Youssef nods.

"I hope with all my heart that you find your father," he says. "If deep down you feel that he's here, then I'm sure he is."

We're standing in the middle of the road. It could be the exact spot where Youssef's father was dragged out of his car all those years ago. So many images appear in the hot, shimmering air in front of me. Father standing in the door that last evening. The emptiness of our flat the next morning. Mother's expression, bewildered at first but not yet panicked, only turning sad later. Youssef's mother, who I see before me though I've never met her: black hair, soft pale skin, the same expression, the same emotions.

"How old were you when he was kidnapped?" I ask.

A car appears at the point where the road meets the hills. It's coming towards us.

"In 1982?" Youssef says, squinting at me. "I wasn't born yet."

8

Beirut, 15 September 1982

Treason, Sire, is a question of dates.
Talleyrand

6:00 a.m.
It's just been announced on the radio: Bashir didn't survive the attack. I don't know how much more bad news I can take. There's no end to it.

3:45 p.m.
The news is barely out and Israeli tanks are rolling into Beirut again. They're sealing off the refugee camps. They say it's to protect the Palestinians from Christian retaliation. But you'd have to be blind not to see what's going on. Something terrible is about to happen.

5:20 p.m.
They have their suspicions. My workmates. I reckon they know who locked the door. Or is it just fear making me read things into their glances? I thought it over last night. There's a way out. I've got a meeting with Abdallah in two hours.

9

My pulse racing, I stare at the lines in the diary until they swim before my eyes.

"I said what had to be said," I mutter, absent-mindedly scratching my neck.

"Huh?" Wissam says. A confused expression crosses his face as he finishes his coffee. Without looking away from me, he puts his dishes in the sink and grabs his bag from the worktop.

"Everything OK?" he asks.

"Yeah, all good."

"You look a bit pale."

"I'm fine."

He glances at the clock above the door. "I've got a lecture at ten. We can meet on campus later if you like, grab lunch in the canteen. Otherwise, see you this evening. Oh, and here." He reaches into his bag and produces a mobile phone and a cable. "I got the phone you wanted," he says. "It isn't a smartphone, but you just need it to make calls, right? I'm not sure how long the credit will last if you phone Germany, though." He slings the bag over his shoulder, and his T-shirt creases beneath the strap. "I've saved our numbers in your contacts. If you're planning on hanging out on your own again, we need to be able to get in touch with each other."

"Thanks."

"No problem. Noura will pick you up in the late afternoon."

"Noura?"

"Yes, Noura." Wissam narrows his eyes. "You met her over lunch one time, remember? And she was in the park that night. Are you sure you're OK?"

"Yes, don't worry."

"She'll show you the archive. Can't wait to hear what you think."

I don't reply. Wissam hesitates in the hall and then shakes his head. "OK then, Samir, see you later."

The moment the door closes, I go back to the diary. I told Wissam I woke up an hour or two ago, but the truth is, I didn't get a wink of sleep. I feel dreadful. I spent the whole night marking passages, circling sentences, filling the margins with notes. Sticky notes poke out from the pages, flagging comments such as "See entry of 3 August" and "Contradiction!"

I've been agitated for the last two days, since that conversation with Youssef. Breathless with envy, admiration, and affection for him. I keep picturing him in his doorway in his village, his father kneeling in front of him. I try to imagine how he must have felt: a weird sense of familiarity, and a weight being lifted off his shoulders, years of pain vanishing in an instant.

We'd taken a taxi back into town, shaken hands, and said goodbye. I'd walked in a trance to Wissam's apartment a few streets away. He wasn't there when I arrived. Instead, I was greeted with a snooty smile from Samantha, who was flouncing bare-legged around the kitchen, wearing one of Wissam's T-shirts. I went into my room, took the diary out of my rucksack and didn't look up again until it was so dark I had to turn on the light. Yesterday, too, I poured over the entries and chewed the end of my biro until shadows fell on the pages. I was so preoccupied that Wissam eventually asked if I was pissed off with him over Samantha. I was wired, fuelled by the fear that I'd never experience the kind of moment Youssef had described.

The realisation hit me while I was reading. I tried to shake it off, but the shock stopped my heart for a moment, and when it started up again, it felt like a fist punching my chest. I was in shock, didn't want to believe what was staring at me from between the lines. I skimmed through the passage again and again, tried to find another explanation. But with every rereading, it became clearer that the only possible explanation was the stark, disturbing one that had just occurred to me.

We're afraid of what truths might come out.

That's what Youssef had said about the disappeared, but I feel the very same fear now.

Why did Father do it? The question keeps going round and round in my head.

Next to the diary is the Rhino Nightclub card. It was still in my rucksack, crumpled and dirty in among my clothes. The only thing that survived the few days in the rubbish halfway intact was the photo, tucked away in the inside pocket. It's a little creased and wavy at the edges, but the colours are as bright as ever. I pick up the mobile Wissam got me and dial the number.

Just two rings, then laboured breathing on the other end.

"Sinan Aziz."

"I need to speak to Amir."

A pause.

"Who's this?"

"Samir el-Hourani."

"Samir? You're still in Lebanon?"

"Yes. Can you help me?"

Another pause and a sharp intake of breath.

"Didn't you meet him?" he asks.

"Yes, I did."

"Then you know where to find him."

"Yeah." I try to keep calm. "But I can't go all the way back to Brih. You managed to get hold of him quickly enough last time. Please, I need to speak to him."

Sinan Aziz falls silent. I picture him in his dark office, his huge belly brushing the edge of the desk. His enormous nostrils expanding as he breathes, his eyes narrowed to slits.

"I'm not making any promises."

"I realize that."

"Have you got a phone number I can give him?" He sounds irritated.

"Just a minute." Wissam stuck a note with my new number onto the charger. I read it out.

"What do you want me to tell him?"

I breathe in deeply, my hands shaking.

I spend the next few hours pacing, checking that the phone is fully charged. I call it from Wissam's landline to check I've given Aziz the right number. My chest feels like it's in a vice. Why did I have to examine that passage so closely? What I discovered won't help me. It just puts Father in a darker light.

When I was a kid, I had a trick. Before falling asleep, I'd try to think of Father so that I'd dream of him later. I'd replay my happiest moments with him: his weight on my mattress, his hand on my duvet, the dark brown irises around his pupils. I'd imagine us meeting again in the place where his stories were set. Sometimes it worked. I'd be close to him in my dreams, and the cold, desolate sense of loneliness would disappear until the next morning, when I'd wake up again without him.

My trick doesn't work here. I can no longer recall his warmth. So I turn to another childhood method of distraction: I try to find animals and patterns on the sunlit wall in the hall and in the kitchen sink, where the coffee grounds have left a grainy trail around the drain. This doesn't work either.

Hours go by. I walk around the apartment, running my finger along the books on the shelves, reading and instantly forgetting the blurbs on the backs of the DVDs. The slightest sound makes me jump: the squeak of the leather couch, the drip of the bathroom tap, the ticking of the kitchen clock. I wish Amir would just call me, even though I know he'll only confirm my suspicion. The phone vibrates, but it's just a message from Wissam saying where he's sitting in the canteen in case I decide to come. As the afternoon wears on, the furniture casts angular shadows across the floor and a chill creeps up my legs. I consider going outside to take my mind off things, but I don't want to risk losing coverage.

When the phone eventually rings, I rush from the hall into the kitchen, banging my shin and flopping into a chair with a curse. The display says it's an unknown number.

"Hello?"

"Hello Samir." His voice is thin and uncertain, and the noise in the background suggests he's holding the receiver away from his face. "Have you found your father?"

"No," I say breathlessly. "No, unfortunately not."

I look at the diary entry with my big question mark in the margin: 16 September 1982.

"But now I know what he did to you."

10

Beirut, 16 September 1982.

No one's there.
No use in calling.
No one's there.
Fairuz

9:00 a.m.
I went to see Abdallah. I said what had to be said.

6:50 p.m.
Now I know what to say if Hakim asks me to leave the country with him. I've no other choice.

11

There are moments in life when you experience something that makes you wonder. Then more of those moments follow. But it's only much later, when you barely remember those moments, that they acquire new meaning, because in the meantime you've learned more about someone or something, more than you knew before. All the inexplicable gestures, looks, movements, and behaviour suddenly make sense. Like finding a piece of a jigsaw and fitting it into the unfinished puzzle you've kept for years in case you'd one day manage to complete it.

Today I've found one of those puzzle pieces. Today changes everything.

Rassan is smoking in front of the old apartment building when Noura and I drive past, into the underground car park. The heat of the day has built up down here, fusing with the smell of oil and petrol. As my eyes are adjusting to the shade, I hear his footsteps echoing. He tosses his cigarette butt into the puddle beneath a leaking pipe, greets Noura, then me, and soon we're in a creaky lift on our way to the top floor.

"Is Youssef here too?" I ask quietly. Rassan shakes his head.

"No, he won't be here till tomorrow."

Noura's eyes meet mine in the mirror and she looks

down. I'd say she's in her mid-twenties. She has big green eyes, a small, straight nose, and pale skin sprinkled with freckles. Her hair falls in waves to her shoulders. In the car, she told me how she met Youssef. "The exhibition was called 'The Missing'. It was my own project—I'm studying art. I wanted to create a collage made from portraits of missing people, so I called on thousands of families to contribute photos of loved ones who had disappeared. Youssef brought a copy of his father's missing-person ad and said, 'You should get involved in something that's really going to make a difference.' I've been on board ever since." "What is it that drew you to him?" I asked. "His conviction." She checked the rear-view mirror as she wove through the heavy traffic. "He makes every one of us feel like we're part of something special, something import-ant." She gave a shy smile and said in a quiet voice, "Who doesn't dream of changing the course of history for the better?"

The lift pings and the door opens to a corridor. There are three padlocks on the door in front of us. None of them are locked.

"It's basically a flat, but we call it 'The Explosives Room'," Rassan says, knocking.

Explosives room? I want to ask, but already I hear foot-steps approaching. The door opens.

The flat is like a bunker crammed with painful memo-ries. Ring binders are stacked high against the walls. There's no furniture. Sheets of newspapers are spread out on the floor of one room; next to them, handwritten notes, and piles of documents in plastic sleeves. A pool of light spills onto the few tiles that aren't covered in paper. In another room, students are on their knees, sticking coloured notes onto folders. The floor is strewn with scissors, pens, and little paper circles that have escaped from hole punches.

We pass the kitchen, which has a roster stuck to the door. I'm amazed to see it contains twenty names; the archive appears to be staffed twenty-four hours a day.

"Watch your step," Rassan says, and I wonder why he's whispering all of a sudden. The walls of a third room are covered in missing-person ads along with photos of the missing husbands, wives, and children, some in colour, most of them black and white. There must be around a thousand of them.

Saad al-Deen Hussein al-Hajjar worked as a chauffeur in Tripoli.
On the morning of 8 July 1975, he had breakfast with his mother, who lives in Tarik el-Jdideh. He left his mother's apartment and never returned.
Anyone with information on his whereabouts is asked to contact Café Abou Hette; telephone: ...

All the ads are written in a similar tone. The missing people stare at me from the wall, and I have to avert my eyes. These ads tell more than the stories of disappearances. They're more than pleas for information. They offer glimpses of the everyday lives of families that were torn apart.

To whoever has my son, Adel Shamieh:
Please bring him back to me. I pray to God that your mothers' hearts never have to experience the pain I am suffering now.
He left my house on 4 May 1981 to repair his car in Sabra.
Please bring Adel back to me.

"How are you going to fit all this into one book?" I ask Rassan. I notice that I'm now whispering too.
"That's up to Youssef. We won't reproduce all of these

ads, of course, but they're helping us to work out just how many people went missing. The number's far higher than the government's official figure. Right now we're in the process of sorting everything. We keep the historical photos and microfilms over there." He points at a room where two young women are holding slides up to the light. Then he takes my arm and leads me to the door of a fourth room. "And here's where we keep the militias' flyers, posters, journals, and propaganda. Wissam said you were asking about that kind of thing. You're welcome to take a look."

Just as I'm about to enter the room, a guy calls Rassan over.

"Come on," Noura says. "I'll show you."

We step over boxes stuffed with flyers and newspapers. A young man is sitting cross-legged in front of one of them, filing magazines into a folder he's labelled "Amal, 1984." He briefly raises his head as we pass, then gets back to work straight away.

"Are they Amal militia magazines?"

Noura nods.

"These are all from 1984. We've already moved '81 to '83."

"Moved them?"

"We recently decided to split the archive up. It's safer not to keep all the material in one place. We're going to do the big move tomorrow, so it's good you came today."

"Where are you taking everything?"

"We've got our eye on a few locations around the city, but Youssef wants to take most of the documents to his village. He reckons that's the safest place for them."

Rassan comes into the room, scratching his head and looking grave.

"The silver car is outside," he says. "They followed you."

Noura makes a hissing noise and just about stops herself from cursing. "I'm sorry, I was really careful," she says.

"It's OK," Rassan says. "Everything will be gone from here tomorrow anyway. Samir, you should have a look around." He turns to Noura. "Don't worry. It'll be trickier for them once everything is divided up."

She stands there with her hands on her hips, her eyes downcast.

"Noura?" I ask. "Have you got any documents from the Forces Libanaises?"

"Forces Libanaises?" She looks at me as if I've just woken her from a deep sleep.

"Yes. Have you got anything? Or have you already moved it?"

"No, no." Scratching her forehead, she glances out the window. "We still have Forces Libanaises material. Medhi?"

The young man on the floor looks up at us and raises his eyebrows.

"Could you please show Samir everything we've gathered on the Forces Libanaises?" She turns to me. "Or are you looking for something in particular?"

"Yes, I am actually. A magazine."

"From what year?"

"1982. I'm not sure what month. Could you show me everything you have for January to June of that year?"

The boy nods and points to a box on the other side of the room.

The contours of my old apartment crawl out of the murky depths of my memory, the acrid smell of old paper, the awful emptiness that expanded as the walls became fuller. Having these magazines in front of me triggers the same oppressive anxiety that ruled my life for so many years. I leaf through them. Photos of young men celebrating as they drive through Beirut brandishing flags and guns, militiamen in heroic poses, FL insignia everywhere—the cedar in the red circle. Most of the articles insist on the necessity of the war and offer various justifications for the violence. A three-page essay on the history of the Middle East pays scant attention to historical facts in its depiction of Christians as the victims of the conflict.

In a May issue, I find the photo I've been dying to see since I visited Amir. It's so unfamiliar that I almost flip past it: two men in the centre facing the photographer, no one standing around watching them. It's much bigger than I imagined, taking up the whole page. The caption: "OUR LEADER, BASHIR GEMAYEL, WELCOMES SARKOUN YOUNAN, THE 25,000TH RECRUIT OF THE FORCES LIBA-NAISES." The contrast is sharper in black and white, though the chandelier above the two men loses some of its lustre. They're standing in front of the same velvet-carpeted staircase, of course, but it looks darker, and the banister looks grey rather than gold. It's nice to see Father as a young man. The uniform still looks weird on him from this perspective, the pistol out of place. But the dreamy expression that always puzzled me betrays the poet in him. The man who went out to the cedars to write, the romantic, the idealist. In showing him from the front rather than the side, this photo only accentuates his dreaminess.

I've never forgotten the low buzz of the Leitz Prado on our living room table. I can almost hear Yasmin's blue dress rustling, feel my sister's weight in my arms. And I'll never forget the click when the strange picture appeared on our wall.

I've replayed that scene so many times. Mother looking away, Father's eyes fixed on the picture of himself, a picture he appeared for a moment not to recognise, the silence that followed the click. I've always wondered why he kept the slide after promising Mother to get rid of it. I've also wondered why he never confronted me, though he knew I had it. And, of course, I've wondered what it is about that photo that caused him to change so drastically.

I reach into my rucksack, feel around for the zip of the inside pocket, pull out the photo, and place it beside the newspaper. The effect is astonishing. The newspaper shows the scene the way Bashir Gemayel had planned it: the lighting's right; the perspective is perfect, with the stairs leading up to a vanishing point; and the viewer's eye is immediately drawn to Bashir and Father. By comparison, my photo is clearly a snapshot taken by an amateur, perhaps one of the Carlton staff who wanted to capture the commotion caused by this celebrity's impromptu invasion of the hotel.

"So that's why he didn't just zoom in on Bashir and Father," I mutter. In my picture, the viewer's eye is drawn to the two men as well, but only because everyone else in the photo is looking in their direction.

"Holy shit!" Rassan shouts, making me jump. I was so engrossed in the photo that I didn't hear him coming. "Where did you get that?" he asks, picking up the photo. "It's the same scene, isn't it? Incredible. Where did you get it?"

"Please, Rassan, give it back."

He's standing over me, legs apart, mouth agape. His eyes keep darting between my photo and the picture in the newspaper.

"Don't tell me you know this guy!" he shouts.

"Shh, give it back, please."

"What's going on, Samir? You have to tell me where you got that picture!" His voice cracks with excitement. He looks like an archaeologist who has just discovered a sunken city.

I hear footsteps in the hall. I don't want the others to come in and see my photo.

"Hmm," says Rassan suddenly, and then he bursts out laughing.

"What's so funny?"

"Look at this." He kneels down beside me and lays the photo beside the newspaper.

"What?"

"I don't know who this Sarkoun Younan guy is, but he seems a bit distracted, don't you think?"

"What are you talking about, Rassan?"

I take a closer look at the photo in the newspaper. Bashir is looking directly at the camera. His eyes bore into me, as if he wants to drag me into the picture. Father has a far-away look on his face, as always. He seems to be looking slightly beyond the camera, focusing on something in the distance.

"He's smitten," Rassan says.

"What are you on about? Look, just give me a few more minutes with the picture and then I'll be on my way."

"Here," Rassan taps on the newspaper, right in the middle of Father's forehead. "Look at him. He's obviously smitten. Unbelievable! There he is, standing next to Bashir Gemayel, and he only has eyes for the girls."

"What girl?"

Rassan points to the photo beside the newspaper.

"That one," he says, pointing to a young woman standing among the onlookers. I recognise her. I recognise all the people in the picture, but I've never paid particular attention to her before.

"No, that can't be right," I say.

"Believe me, I know when someone's smitten, I can always tell, and he"—Rassan points to Father again—"is so smitten that he couldn't care less who's standing beside him. Follow his eyes. Take a good look."

The newspaper: Father is looking past the camera.

My photo: Father is looking towards the left edge of the picture, where the young woman is standing beside the magazine's photographer, among the other onlookers.

I feel I'm about to keel over.

"Not dreamy ..." My stomach muscles tense, my heart is pounding so hard it hurts. "In love. He's in love."

"Do you still need the photo?" Rassan asks. Tears fill my eyes, and I barely hear him. I study the young woman through a watery curtain. She's a little blurred, as the focus is on the centre of the picture, but her beauty is clear to see. A black dress falls over her delicate frame, and her hair ... her hair.

"Oh no. Please, no." I look in panic at Rassan, who stares back at me with a bewildered expression. "Please don't let this be true."

I feel utterly helpless, like a little child—and then I remember it, Father's story. Him sitting at the edge of my bed that last night.

He took off her veil and revealed a woman as beautiful as any legend. Her hair was jet black and held by a golden clasp, her eyes were Mediterranean blue, and her skin as pure and white as marble.

The clasp is holding the young woman's hair in the photo. She has a beautiful, elfin face, and she's looking right at my father.

I try to wipe away the tears with the back of my hand, but they keep dripping down onto the newspaper.

"My God, Samir," Rassan whispers.

I hear footsteps, lots of footsteps, and the room fills with people.

I close my eyes and see Amir on the terrace: *I do remember him saying something odd ...*

"What makes the photo special is what's going on around it," I whisper.

I hear the others murmuring, watching me sitting on the floor with Rassan beside me, but they seem very far away.

Only Amir is near. His voice is calm as he makes everything painfully clear:

He often went to see her, usually in the evenings after work. He'd be back in the hotel before his shift began in the morning.

I can't breathe, I press my wrist against my forehead.

I never met your mother.

Your father, madman that he was, climbed up the drainpipe to get to her balcony.

It feels like I'm being ripped apart.

It was lovely to see him like that.

The last time anyone saw me crying, I was a kid at a birthday party, on my knees in a garden. Now, once again, people are standing around, looking down at me incredulously. In a final excruciating flashback, I see Father before me, his eyes gleaming as he tells me what happened on the balcony:

"My son!" said Abu Youssef.

Fireworks transformed the street, the houses and the whole city into a dazzling spectacle ... Blazing rockets whooshed into the sky ... The night was full of shouts of joy.

12

Beirut, 17 September 1982

We were standing on the balcony when it happened. Israeli planes shot across the dark sky above us. They dropped flares, transforming the blackness into a sparkling sea of red and yellow, gilding the entire balcony. Screams and gunshots cut through the night. The flares descended in the south. They fell on Sabra and Chatila.

    Threw myself into bed. Thought it over. I'm done with it all.

    Nothing will ever be the same again.

    Nothing will ever be the same again.

13

"How should I label it?" Medhi asks, looking at the diary I've just handed him.

"I'm not sure," I say. "Maybe 'contemporary account'. Or 'eyewitness account'?"

"You're sure you don't need it anymore?"

I shake my head.

"I know you guys will take good care of it."

It's the next day, the day of the move. Students are dragging boxes out of the flat and piling up folders in the corridor. In the empty rooms, the sound of footsteps reverberates off the walls, which are bare apart from the dark outlines left behind by the missing-person ads. The students exude optimism as they form an assembly line and pass files and folders to each other. The last person in the line calls the lift to take the documents downstairs, where other students pick them up and load them into cars.

Medhi puts the diary into a box. Just as he's about to leave the room with it, I say, "Wait!"

He stops and turns around.

"You can have this too."

I pull the photo out of my trouser pocket and take one last look. In all these years of scrutinising it, how did I not notice that they were looking at each other? The reason for Father's sudden change of mood is now clear. When he saw the photo, a dam burst, and all the memories, all the feelings he'd been suppressing came flooding back. It reminded him that his marriage to Mother had taken place under duress, that he'd just come to terms with it. It showed him another life: a life in Lebanon, in Beirut—a life with this other woman.

Youssef is standing at the entrance to the underground car park. He sees me and waves.

"I'm glad you're coming with me," he says.

We've stacked boxes in the boot and on the back seat. Four cars leave the car park together and set out in different directions to bring the documents to safety.

I lean back as we drive out of the city. In the side mirror, I see dust clouds stirred up by the tyres. Eventually Beirut is little more than a cluster of bluish strokes.

"I told them I'm bringing a friend," Youssef says. "They're looking forward to seeing us."

Golden light spills over the mountains, and bellflowers bow their heads at the side of the road. When we set out, my legs felt numb. But they come back to life the farther we leave Beirut behind. First it feels like thousands of pinpricks, but the tingling stops as soon as I see the mountains rising ahead of us.

"You're very quiet. Everything ok?" Youssef gives me a concerned look.

"Yeah, I think so."

I wonder where the woman was from. Who her family was, how she met Father. What her name was. I wonder if Mother knew about her. If that's why she was furious with him for holding on to the picture. Or was it just because it was stupid and dangerous to keep a photo of himself standing beside a president who'd been assassinated not long after?

There's a rough beauty about the landscape here. Its empty vistas, well-trodden tracks, and extreme remoteness seem to capture how I'm feeling inside.

Youssef starts to sing. His voice is a little too high for the melancholy lyrics and melody; it's an incongruous song for someone beginning a new chapter in life. I get the impression he's singing it for me.

"*Ma fi ḥada, la tindahi, ma fi ḥada. shu qawlakun ṣaru ṣada? Ma fi ḥada.*"

No one's there. No use in calling. Have they turned into echoes? No one's there.

I close my eyes.

"Do you sing too?" he asks.

"Not really, not anymore."

"That's a shame. Why not?"

"I don't know any songs."

"Make them up. Make up a melody and then sing about whatever you're feeling." As the road winds its way southwards, mist comes down from the mountains and swallows up the foothills.

"That's what my father and I used to do," he says. "We used to make up songs and sing them together."

"That sounds like fun." Father and I used to sing our own songs too. What happened to the woman? Did he go back to her? Did they have their own songs?

After a steep descent, the road begins to climb again. Youssef switches off the engine and we come to a halt at the side of the road.

"We have to park here. There's no road into the village. Let's go and say hi first. They'll help us unload the car later."

Gravel crunches underfoot. Clumps of dry grass sprouting from the path become more frequent and eventually form a grassy track leading into a little wood. Twigs snap beneath our soles. It's cool in the shade. Through the canopy of pine needles, we catch the occasional glimpse of sky. The trees open out into a clearing, and a wide swathe of grass winds downwards, sheer cliffs on either side of it. A small stream flows down into the silent valley. Insects dance in the soft afternoon light cascading between the mountainsides. We look down from our vantage point like pioneers. It takes me a moment to realise that the grey patches on the side of the mountain are actually mud cabins. The grass on either side of the track is almost waist-high, the stalks swaying in the sunshine. It's a remote refuge, a well-kept secret.

"Are you going to show me where you used to live?" I ask Youssef.

I want to stand in the cabin where they embraced each other for the first time. Youssef and his father. I want to get a sense of the exact spot where they were reunited, because I can feel my passport in my pocket. I collected it this morning. I may not have found Father, but I've discovered his secret. Today I'm going to help Youssef lay the foundation for a project that will change his country forever. And then I must go back.

I make out the houses' square windows in the distance. A red ball is flying through the air in front of them. It looks as if the wind picked it up off the ground. Then I hear children laughing.

"Youssef!" they shout.

"Look, Youssef's here!"

Before we know it, a cluster of kids has gathered around us. They cling to his legs, giggling and asking, "Did you bring us anything?"

They peep at me shyly as we make our way towards the cabins. A couple of them run on ahead. "Mama, Papa, Youssef's here! He's got a friend with him!" they cry, and people start coming out of the houses.

Laughing, Youssef lifts up one of the kids and spins him

around. "Now me!" the others squeal, tugging at him and dragging him away. He looks at me, raises his hands apologetically and disappears behind a house.

As I watch him go, I feel a hand on my shoulder.

"Samir?" an old man asks.

"Yes?"

"Ahlan wa sahlan," he says, and smiles. A bristly beard lines his jaw, and there's a gap where his two front teeth should be. "I'm Abu Karim," he says, holding out his hand. "Youssef said you were coming along. We're delighted to have you. Come with me."

Everywhere I look, there are friendly faces welcoming me like I've just come home after a long absence. A village that time has forgotten. The mud walls are cracked, the roofs are covered in moss, old people sit fanning themselves in front of their cabins. There's a slight bend in the path as it leads past bright barberry shrubs and hens strutting through the grass.

The sun is low in the sky. Further ahead, people stand in a circle around an old man. I hear him speaking in a low voice and stop dead in my tracks.

"His house is a bit further ahead," Abu Karim says, waving me on.

I don't move. The wind carries the old man's voice over to me, and my muscles clench as the scales fall from my eyes.

"Abu Karim," I say in a low voice and point to the group. "When did he come back from Syria?"

The man knits his brows.

"Abu Youssef? 1992, al-hamdu lilhah." *Thank God.* "She was dying, his wife, when he came home. God knows what would have happened to the kid …"

I squint. The sun is blinding.

They all lead back to the beginning. And that's where you are. You and only you, the rustling bushes whisper.

"You were wrong, Amir," I murmur and walk on cautiously, holding my breath.

The circle opens as we approach, and the man turns to us. The sun is shining right into my eyes. I shield them with my hand, and all I can see is a silhouette coming towards me.

And everyone wondered what it could possibly be that Abu Youssef was hiding up there in his little house.

"Father?" I say, my voice trembling.

He steps out of the sunlight and stands in front of me. His beard is long and grey, and bags droop beneath his eyes, but I can see the little dimples on either side of his mouth. He meets my gaze and his eyes flicker.

14

I stamp my foot and twirl. My arm is on Youssef's shoulder, his on mine. The villagers have gathered around, clapping and singing while we dance. The young men quickly join us, and we line up opposite the women, who continue clapping. Shoulder to shoulder, we laugh and dance. Suddenly everyone's joining in. The children twirl, the women stamp their feet and throw us challenging looks, hands on their hips. We circle each other. An old TV on a windowsill provides the music—drums, tambourines, zithers, fiddles, and flutes. Even the older folk are on their feet, dancing. It's crazy. It's magical.

Through the twirling melee, I catch glimpses of Father making his way round the circle of dancers, his slight limp visible only to those who know.

A short time later, the aroma of barbecued meat wafts through the village. Steaming cups of coffee and platters of mezze appear on the tables. The flatbread is still soft and warm.

Beside me is Youssef, my brother.

"Please," Father said, "don't say anything to him." We were relaxing by the lake. The mountain range on the other side etched a restless cardiogram on the sky, spiking into the clouds. Behind us, the village lay bathed in afternoon sunlight, and children were laughing in the distance.

We sat there, hardly a word between us, as if the years had rendered us taciturn. There are moments in which silence is enough, when the bond between two people is so strong that not even the greatest strain can break it. Once everything had been explained, no more words were needed. It didn't take me long to fill him in. My voice caught at some parts of the story, and I felt my eyes light up at others. My hand was beside his on the grass, and our fingers touched from time to time.

He cried when I told him about Mother's death.

It didn't take long to tell his story either. He told it so quickly I find it hard to believe I spent so many years desperate to hear it. Her name was Layla. She was the daughter of the hotel's fruit supplier. When Father left her, she was pregnant. It must have seemed like the end of the world to him. I don't know if there was more to it than his naked fear of the consequences. Before he'd left her on the morning of 17 September, they'd stood on her balcony—he a Christian, she a Muslim—while Muslims were being massacred by Christians in the south of the city. The sky above them blazed with flares that were lighting up the camps. The militias were avenging Bashir's death. The war couldn't have made it any plainer—there was no future for their love.

Father must have realised in that moment that he'd have to leave the country, because the men behind the massacre were connected to the family of the woman he was due to marry. He must have been out of his mind with fear and worry. I find it deeply moving—because it's so typical of Father—that he refashioned reality in his stories to make it all more bearable. He invented a fairy-tale world in which he was a hero beloved by all, not a coward who vanished without trace.

"Without your mother, I'd never have had the courage to

leave," he said. "She was so much stronger than me."

He took her surname, though not as an act of revenge against his mother. "I wanted to be untraceable," he said. "I didn't want anyone to find me."

Anyone? That would have included Amir.

"He was the only one who could have linked me to Layla." Father looked out over the lake. A gentle breeze rippled the surface. Most of his face was hidden by his long beard, but the regret in his eyes shone all the more clearly.

"That's why you wanted him gone—you told Abdallah it was Amir who locked the cellar door."

A quiet "Yes."

And what about Youssef's surname?

Layla had put a missing-person notice in the paper, using the composite sketch. She didn't mention his name in the notice—I don't know whether she was trying to protect him or simply didn't know his surname. Needless to say, no one made contact. Layla's family disowned her because she was pregnant out of wedlock. Worse still, she was bearing the child of one of those hated Christians. Who knows what would have become of her and the baby if an old man who passed the corner where she begged every day hadn't taken pity on them? Before he died, a few years later, he married her and gave her his name.

"Hamoud," I said.

Father nodded without looking at me.

He cried again as we sat there. The sun was dipping behind the mountains, red like glowing embers, as he said, "I loved them both. I learned to love your mother. She was my rational love, the one with the brighter future, the woman with whom I wanted to start over." He clasped his fingers and looked into the cradle of his palms as if he saw his reflection there. "Layla was my irrational love, the young, impulsive one. I really did love both of them."

Of course, hearing all this pained me. I felt anger, disappointment and bitterness too, but also pride—pride that I'd actually succeeded in finding him. And even if it was disturbing to learn the real reason for his disappearance, it was comforting to know that there was a reason, and it wasn't me. I wished Nabil could see how all the little cogs were fitting together, how I'd solved the case. I'm sure he'd have been delighted that it all suddenly made sense—the secretive phone calls, the mysterious money transfers. After I was born, it seems Father could no longer ignore his guilty conscience. Seeing me must have been a daily reminder of that other child, the one he'd left behind. He told me he'd tracked Layla down and discovered that the child was a boy. She'd called him Youssef. He began to send her money, anonymously. But at some point she managed to trace the source of the money, and eventually discovered where we lived. On that awful winter's evening when Father had come home dripping wet and confused, he had just learned that his irrational love was dying, and he knew he had no choice but to leave us. He had decided to take responsibility, ten years too late. The country was attempting a new beginning and his first-born son was there, all alone.

What would I have done?

The logs are still burning when we return to the village with the boxes from the car. We stack them carefully in Father's living room. The young men who'd helped us with the boxes brush the dust off their clothes and bow politely as they leave the room. Youssef takes my arm and leads me outside. When I look back, I see our father take the faded newspaper out of the box and recognise himself in the photograph he used to have on his wall.

"This young man," says Abu Karim when we're all

gathered together that evening, "is going to bring us either a lot of trouble or honour and glory." He pinches Youssef's cheek. Youssef indulges him and everyone laughs.

"If anyone shows up and tries to take that stuff away, we'll put up a fight," another old man shouts.

"It's a pity you weren't collecting sports pages, young man." Abu Karim leans in and taps his chest. "You'd have found a photo of me for sure. I was a volley-ball player, a bloody good one."

"Maybe you'll get a whole chapter to yourself," someone says. Abu Karim waves a dismissive hand. More laughter.

The air is cooler up here in the mountains. The odd light is still on in the houses behind us, but we're shrouded in darkness. Only the glow from the shisha coals illuminates our faces each time someone takes a pull and passes the hose on. Father is sitting in a chair opposite me, stroking his beard with one hand. Our eyes meet. He smiles and I smile back. Then he looks beyond me into the distance.

"If he can pull off this project, he will change the country," Father said earlier, as we were making our way back to the village from the lake. We saw Youssef standing about a hundred metres away, waving at us. Father's voice sounded wistful. "Putting his idea into action is going to be difficult, but it could allow future generations to live a life that was unimaginable in my day."

I look over at Youssef. The others are still talking about the book, but he looks as if he's somewhere else, years ahead maybe, looking for a publisher, or up on a podium addressing a crowd of cheering young people. As he stares into the distance, he raises one hand to his chin, and in that instant he is our father all over.

We are both obsessed by the truth. We have both spent most of our lives searching for that truth. But while my journey ends here, his search will go on. I should be jumping up in outrage, I suppose, shouting at the top of my voice, because his ambitions are based on such false assumptions. But when I see them there together, I can't help but smile.

Perhaps it doesn't exist, the higher truth I'd always hoped for, the one eternal truth that answers all questions, that explains not just facts, causes, and effects, but also the deeper, unfathomable questions: What is it that connects us? Why do we feel drawn to each other? What is it that makes us feel like it was only yesterday that we met, when in fact it was years ago? If it does exist, that higher truth, then it may lie solely in the recognition that we cannot choose who we are. I see Father across from me, and I see Youssef, half-hidden in the shadows, his eyes fixed on a faraway place that promises a better future. And I think to myself, maybe that's what makes us brothers in the end: our father changed both our lives by telling us a story.

15

When Amir had to leave the Carlton, he and his parents could no longer afford to stay in Beirut. So they went back to Brih, where his parents were shot a year later because they refused to leave the Chouf. Amir was forced to watch. His punishment was to survive. He'd cursed Father for years, he told me on the phone.

I'm leaving the village after three days.

"Have you got the photo?" Father asked this morning. We were sitting in his living room, surrounded by boxes, like the day we'd moved into our new flat all those years ago.

I nodded and looked at the Polaroid. Abu Karim had taken the picture. Father's sitting very straight, looking directly at the camera. His beard is so long it's almost brushing his thighs. Youssef and I stand either side of him, each with a hand on his shoulder.

"Did you manage to get everything done?"

"Yes," I said. "Except for one last thing."

One day I'll tell my children about these days. They'll be waiting wide-eyed in their bedroom for the final chapter. Their eyes will light up when I tell them what it was like to meet Abu Youssef and his friend Amir. And I will describe the following scene in great detail:

The wind was whispering mysteriously as I looked up

the hill, which was bathed in a magical glow. Against this soft light, the two figures approaching each other on the slope looked like shadow puppets. One was bent, the other limping. I turned to leave just as Abu Youssef and Amir, after so many years, were reunited for one last adventure.

Epilogue

As the saying goes: If you think you understand Lebanon, it's because someone has not explained it to you properly. The same could be said of my father. Like Lebanon, he remains a mystery to everyone who loved him. A master of the art of survival. An opportunist. A storyteller. He embodied Lebanon like no one else I ever knew—a love of poetry and a love of a party were as much a part of him as melancholy moods and an ability to turn a blind eye to reality. Is he a bad man because of the things he did? Or is it the things he did that make him so human, because they show how he always followed his heart? Did he find what he was looking for? I don't know. I didn't ask. The last time I saw him up close, I studied him for a long time so that I'll still be able to remember his face when the colours of the Polaroid have faded. I think of the little dimples at the corners of his dry lips; the wrinkles, especially on his forehead; the way his beard curls; the deep brown of his now tired eyes.

The sky is cross-hatched in green, the sunshine filters through the needle-canopy of the cedar I'm sitting under. A lizard darts across a stone. The air is full of the trees' resiny smell. Beirut sparkles far below, and the mountains to the north disappear in the haze. I am always deeply moved when I think of Lebanon: its undying beauty no scars can destroy, its tragedy, its blessing to be a home to so many—though this has also been partly its undoing. And I'm always deeply impressed by how it perseveres, how it resists this undoing and finds a way to rise up with all its modest strength. Up here you don't see the lines that divide the country. Up here, you don't hear the seething. You don't feel any of the tension in the air down there. This is what Lebanon looked like once. This is the country as Father knew it, the country he learned to love.

One of my favourite characters in a childhood story once said, "There are two kinds of feelings associated with the word 'farewell'. A farewell can be sad because what you are leaving behind is so precious and important that you are loath to leave it. But a farewell can also be happy, because the power of what lies ahead does not stir sadness but joyful anticipation."

I know how the story ends now, I text Yasmin. My screen lights up moments later: *Can't wait to hear it.*

The cedar I'm leaning against is still young and much smaller than the others. But it's old enough to have seen this country change, and it will undoubtedly live through many more changes. Will they be for the better, as my brother believes? I don't know. Perhaps it is essential that we disappear one day, so that future generations can write about us. We won't feature in the history books we leave behind, so others will be forced to look for clues, to ask who we were, what we did to each other, and why. But many waves will lap at the shore between this and then. Many aeons will go by. And in the end? In the end, the cedars will be there, standing close together, looking down on Lebanon. And if the wind comes from the right direction, blowing up from the sea, you will hear them. You'll hear the cedars whispering to each other that I once sat in their shade. That I came this way to find my father.

Short history of the Lebanese civil war to 1992

1970: PLO militants are driven out of Jordan in the Black September conflict. They regroup in Lebanon. Many Palestinians had already taken refuge there in 1948, fleeing from Israeli troops.

13 April 1975: In retaliation for an attack on a Christian church, Maronite Phalangists kill twenty-seven Palestinian passengers on a bus in Beirut. This marks the start of the civil war. The country is rapidly divided and subdivided into territories controlled solely by whichever military organisation has claimed them. The Green Line, the invisible border separating Muslims and Christians, runs right through Beirut.

Two broad coalitions oppose each other in the civil war: The Lebanese Front on one side, comprising right-wing and predominantly Christian parties, headed by the Phalange (also known as Kata'ib); and the Lebanese National Movement on the other, comprising Palestinian guerrillas, Nasserists, Baathists, Druze, Muslims, and leftists. These coalitions go through various permutations and combinations throughout the war.

June 1976: The Lebanese National Movement has taken control of large areas of Lebanon. Syria sends 30,000 soldiers to keep the Christian government in power in neighbouring Lebanon.

1977: Bashir Gemayel, son of Phalange leader Pierre Gemayel, sets up the Forces Libanaises (FL) militia to support the Lebanese Front coalition. In the following years, the FL absorbs several other Christian militias, sometimes forcibly.

March 1978: Palestinian militants kill thirty-nine Israelis near Tel Aviv. Three days later, the Israeli Army invades southern Lebanon. "Operation Litani" is intended to drive the PLO out. The Israeli occupation of southern Lebanon lasts a few months, after which the Army of Free Lebanon takes over the region. It fights the PLO and its allies, as well as, after 1982, the new Shia force, Hezbollah.

6 June 1982: The second invasion of Lebanon, "Operation Peace for Galilee," under defence minister Ariel Sharon, begins. Two months later, Israeli troops surround west Beirut in order to force the PLO to withdraw.

21 August 1982: A multinational force of US, French, Italian, and British soldiers arrives in Beirut to oversee the PLO withdrawal.

23 August 1982: The multinational force maintains order during the elections. Bashir Gemayel is elected president of Lebanon.

30 August 1982: Led by Yassir Arafat, around 6,500 PLO fighters leave Beirut. Israel claims there are still terrorists in the refugee camps.

14 September 1982: Bashir Gemayel is killed in an attack on the Phalange headquarters.

15 September 1982: Israeli troops invade west Beirut again and surround the refugee camps.

16–18 September 1982: Israeli forces allow the Phalangist militia to raid the Palestinian refugee camps Sabra and Chatila in Beirut. Since the PLO's withdrawal, the camps' residents have been predominantly civilian. The massacre claims between 20,000 and 35,000 lives.

1983–1985: One failed reconciliation conference after another leads to a series of abductions and political murders.

July 1985: Israeli forces withdraw to a "security zone" in southern Lebanon, a border strip between 10 and 20 kilometres wide. Hezbollah begins its campaign of guerrilla attacks.

November 1989: The Lebanese parliament and members of the Arab League agree on a peace plan. The Taif accord slightly redistributes the seats in the Lebanese parliament, granting Muslims additional seats because they now account for the majority of the population.

August–October 1992: The first parliamentary elections in twenty years are held in Lebanon. Billionaire Rafiq Hariri is appointed prime minister. Solidere, his development company, plays a major role in the country's reconstruction. Hariri's assassination in 2005 sparks the Cedar Revolution, after which Syria withdraws all of its troops from Lebanon.

The following works were a source of help and
inspiration while I was writing this novel:

Bernhardt, Karl-Heinz. *Der alte Libanon*. Koehler &
    Amelang, 1976.
Chidiac, May. *Ich werde nicht schweigen!* Blanvalet, 2009.
Fisk, Robert. *Pity the Nation: The Abduction of Lebanon*.
    Nation Books, 2002.
Fisk, Robert. *Sabra und Shatila*. Promedia, 2011.
Knudsen, Are, and Michael Kerr, editors. *Lebanon:
    After the Cedar Revolution*. Hurst, 2012.
Konzelmann, Gerhard. *Der unheilige Krieg: Krisenherde
    im Nahen Osten*. DTV, 1988.
Pott, Marcel, and Renate Schimkoreit-Pott. *Beirut:
    Zwischen Kreuz und Koran*. Westermann, 1985.
Von Broich, Sigrid. *Libanon: warum es geschah*. BOD, 2004.
Vorländer, Dorothea, editor. *Libanon: Land der Gegensätze*.
    Verlag der Ev.-Luth. Mission, 1980.

I wish to thank

my wife, Kathleen, for her patience, support and under-standing, without which I could never have written this novel. Thanks too to my parents, who have always encour-aged me to tell stories. I am very grateful to my agent, Markus Michalek, for his dedication to and belief in this story, to the entire team at AVA International, to my edi-tor, Andreas Paschedag, for his passion and commitment, and to the team at Berlin Verlag for their faith in me. I also greatly appreciate the support provided by the City of Munich in the form of a literary grant. My special thanks go to Kamil el-Hourani, who spent many hours sharing his harrowing experiences of the Lebanese civil war and the details of his escape. Several other people provided valuable support and advice: Professor Georges Tamer from the University of Erlangen-Nuremberg; Klaus Schmid, chairperson of the Evangelical Association for Schneller Schools in Lebanon; Houda Jaber, who transcribed Arabic passages; Paul Khauli of the American University of Bei-rut, who introduced me to Beirut's nightlife and student scene; the employees of UMAM Documentation and Re-search in Beirut, who allowed me to view their archives; and the Deutsche Evangelische Gemeinde Beirut, which showed me great hospitality.